Thomas Siddell

Gunnerkrigg Court™

Orientation

Published by
ARCHAIA™

Written & Illustrated by

Thomas Siddell

Designer
Scott Newman

Editor
Dafna Pleban

Group Editor
Rebecca Taylor

Ross Richie *CEO & Founder*
Mark Smylie *Founder of Archaia*
Matt Gagnon *Editor-in-Chief*
Filip Sablik *President of Publishing & Marketing*
Stephen Christy *President of Development*
Lance Kreiter *VP of Licensing & Merchandising*
Phil Barbaro *VP of Finance*
Bryce Carlson *Managing Editor*
Mel Caylo *Marketing Manager*
Scott Newman *Production Design Manager*
Irene Bradish *Operations Manager*
Christine Dinh *Brand Communications Manager*
Dafna Pleban *Editor*
Shannon Watters *Editor*
Eric Harburn *Editor*
Rebecca Taylor *Editor*
Ian Brill *Editor*

Chris Rosa *Assistant Editor*
Alex Galer *Assistant Editor*
Whitney Leopard *Assistant Editor*
Jasmine Amiri *Assistant Editor*
Cameron Chittock *Assistant Editor*
Kelsey Dieterich *Production Designer*
Jillian Crab *Production Designer*
Kara Leopard *Production Designer*
Devin Funches *E-Commerce & Inventory Coordinator*
Andy Liegl *Event Coordinator*
Brianna Hart *Executive Assistant*
Aaron Ferrara *Operations Assistant*
José Meza *Sales Assistant*
Michelle Ankley *Sales Assistant*
Elizabeth Loughridge *Accounting Assistant*
Stephanie Hocutt *PR Assistant*

ARCHAIA™

BOOM! Studios, 5670 Wilshire Boulevard, Suite 450, Los Angeles, CA 90036-5679. Printed in China.

Softcover Edition
ISBN: 978-1-60886-703-5
eISBN: 978-1-61398-374-4
First Edition, First Printing.

Hardcover Edition
ISBN: 978-1-60886-749-3
eISBN: 978-1-61398-420-8
Second Edition, First Printing.

Table of Contents

my name is antimony carver.
I would like to share with
you the strange events that
took place while I attended
school at...

Gunnerkrigg Court

Chapter 1:

The Shadow and The Robot

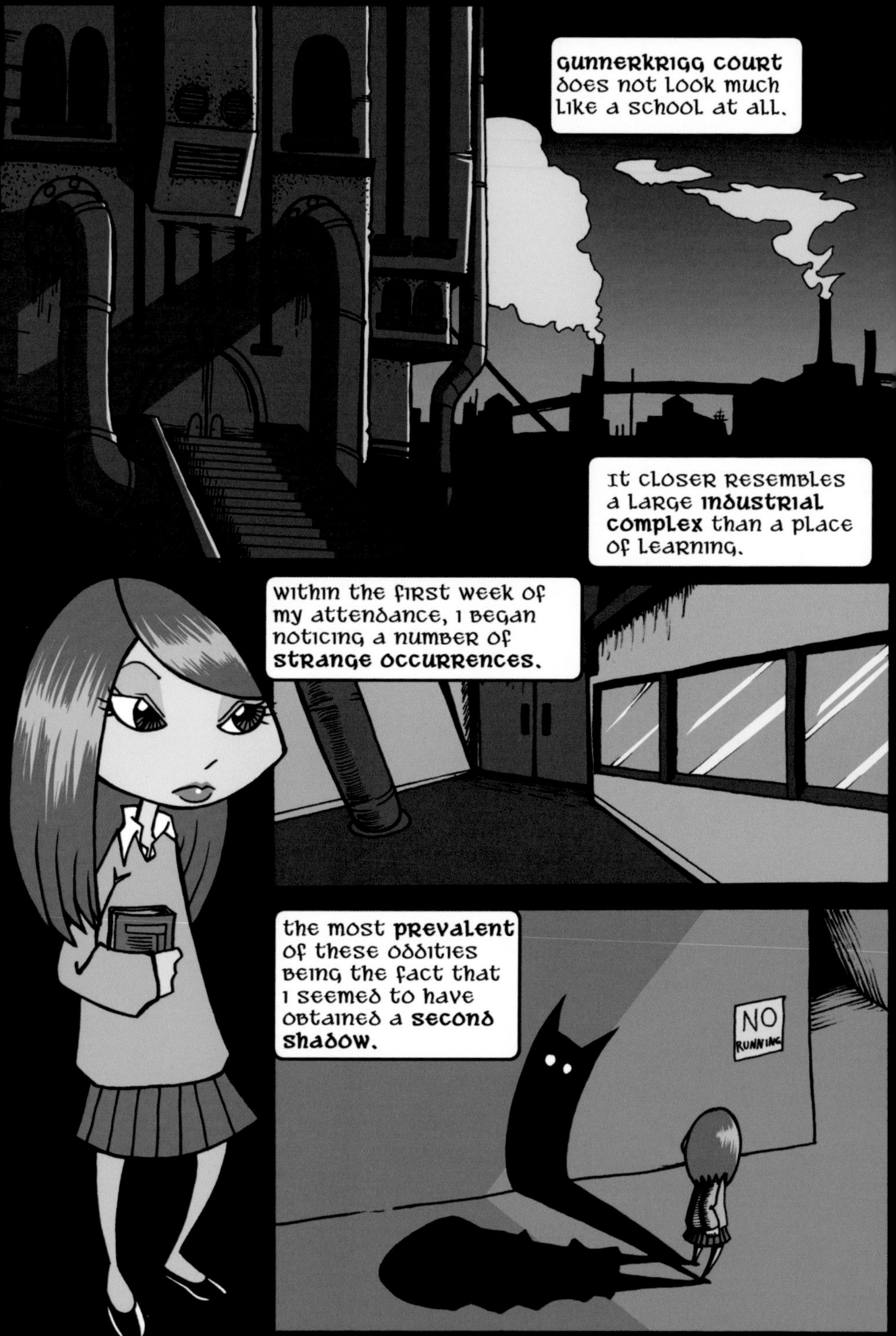
Gunnerkrigg Court does not look much like a school at all.
It closer resembles a large industrial complex than a place of learning.
Within the first week of my attendance, I began noticing a number of strange occurrences.
The most prevalent of these oddities being the fact that I seemed to have obtained a second shadow.
NO RUNNING

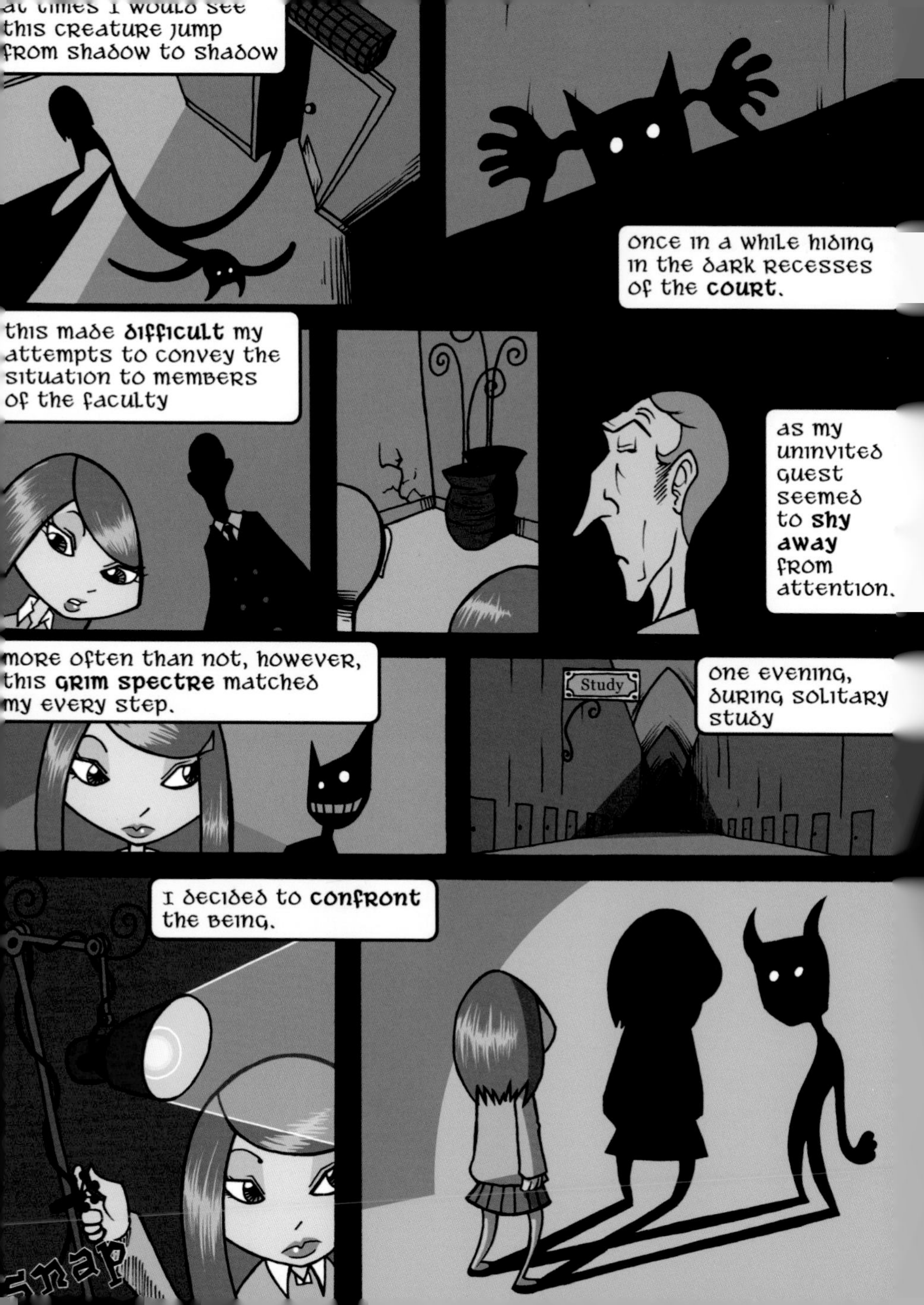
at times I would see this creature jump from shadow to shadow
once in a while hiding in the dark recesses of the court.
this made difficult my attempts to convey the situation to members of the faculty
as my uninvited guest seemed to shy away from attention.
more often than not, however, this grim spectre matched my every step.
Study
one evening, during solitary study
I decided to confront the being.
snap

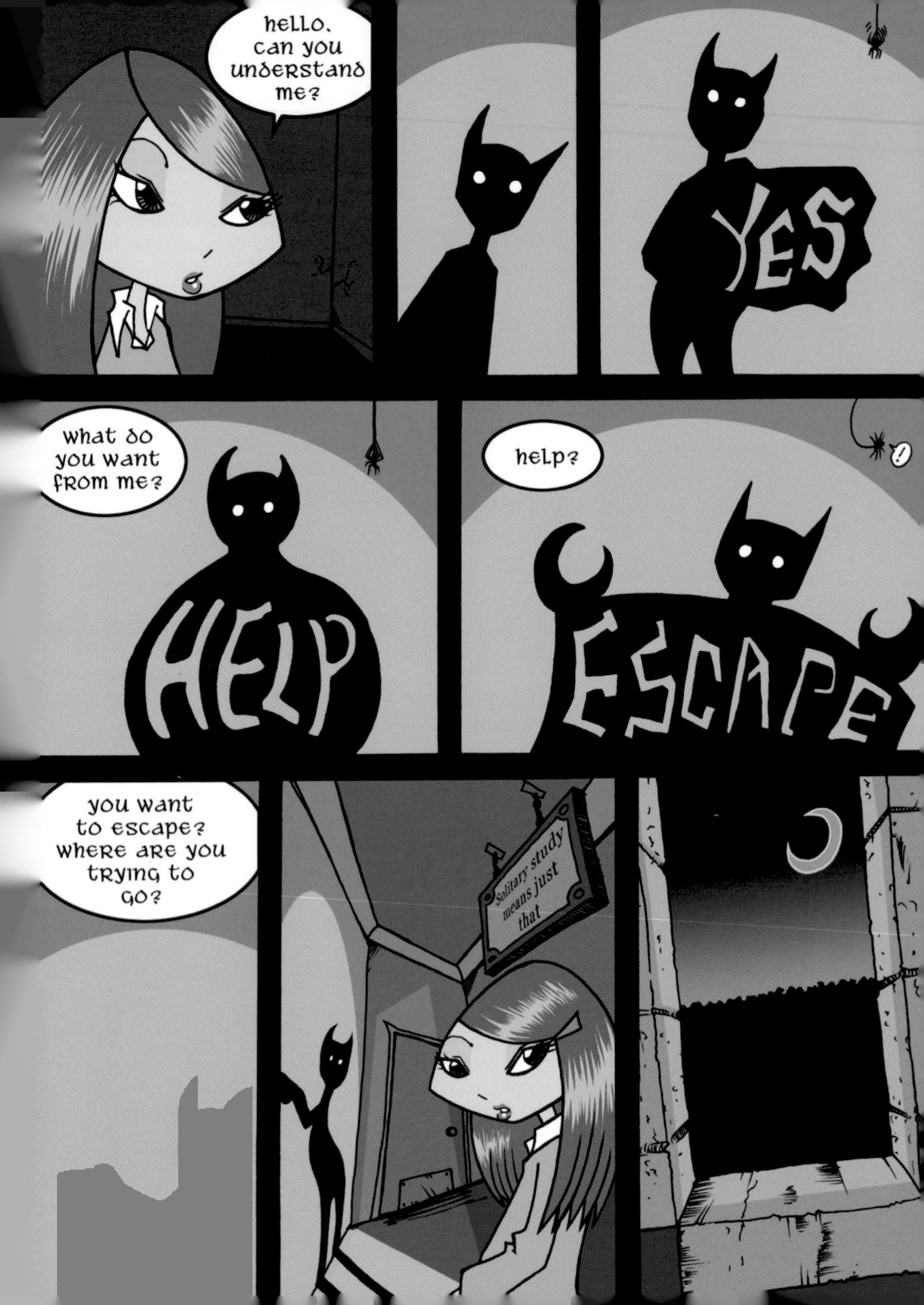
hello, can you understand me?
YES
what do you want from me?
HELP
help?
!
ESCAPE
you want to escape? where are you trying to go?
Solitary study means just that

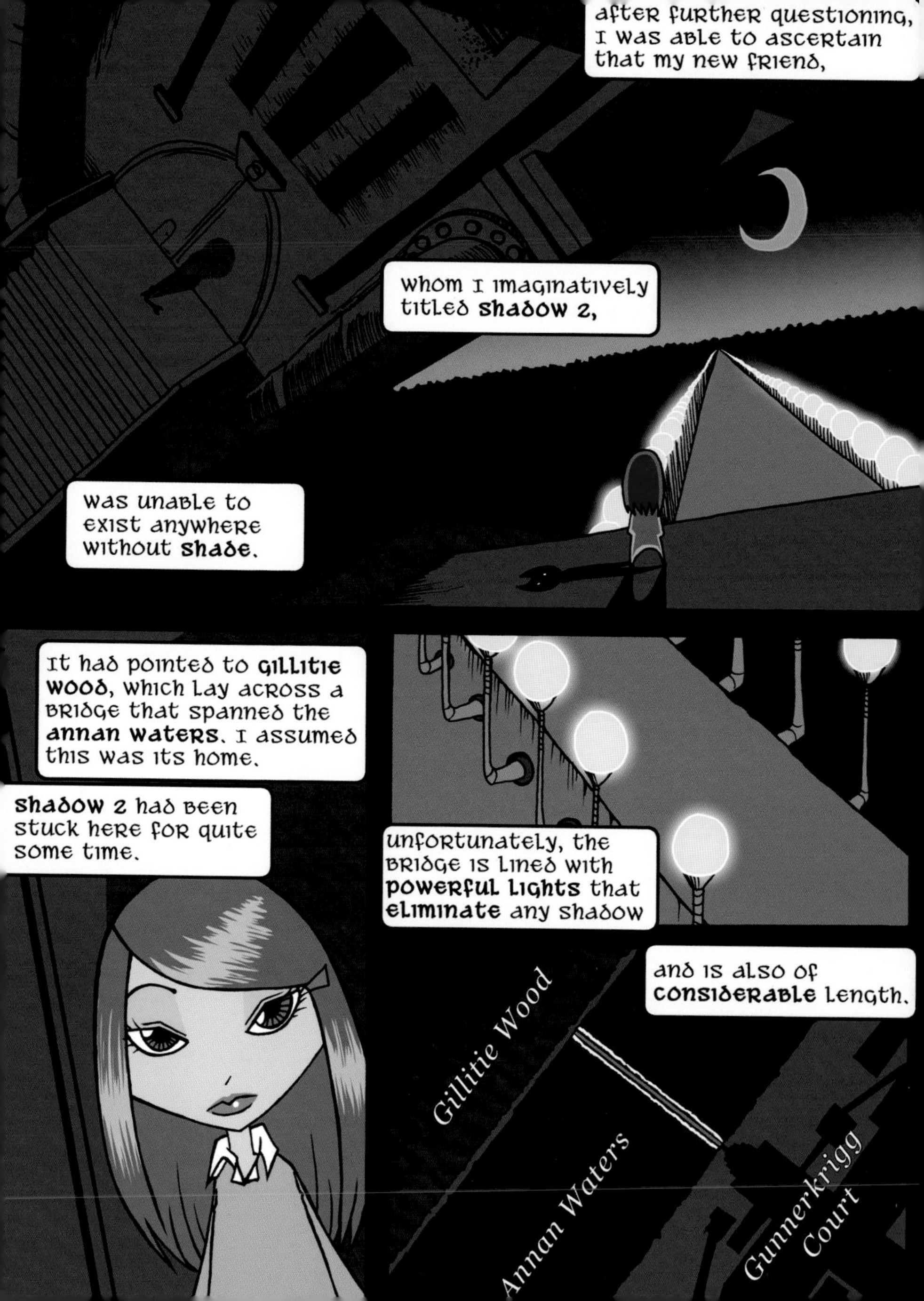
after further questioning, I was able to ascertain that my new friend,
whom I imaginatively titled shadow 2,
was unable to exist anywhere without shade.
It had pointed to gillitie wood, which lay across a bridge that spanned the annan waters. I assumed this was its home.
shadow 2 had been stuck here for quite some time.
unfortunately, the bridge is lined with powerful lights that eliminate any shadow
and is also of considerable length.
Gillitie Wood
Annan Waters
Gunnerkrigg Court

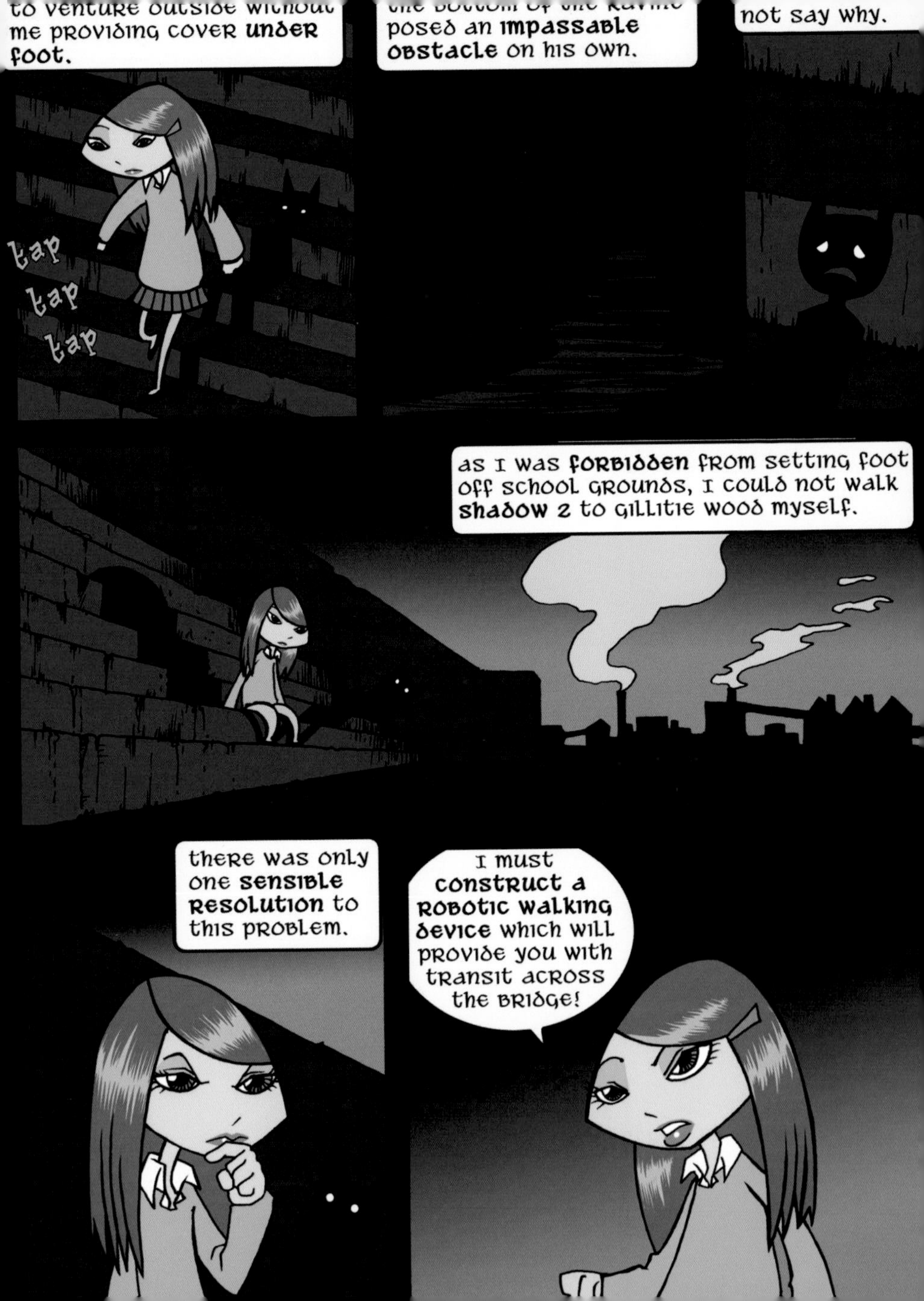
me providing cover under foot.
posed an impassable obstacle on his own.
not say why.
tap tap tap
as I was forbidden from setting foot off school grounds, I could not walk shadow 2 to gillitie wood myself.
there was only one sensible resolution to this problem.
I must construct a robotic walking device which will provide you with transit across the bridge!

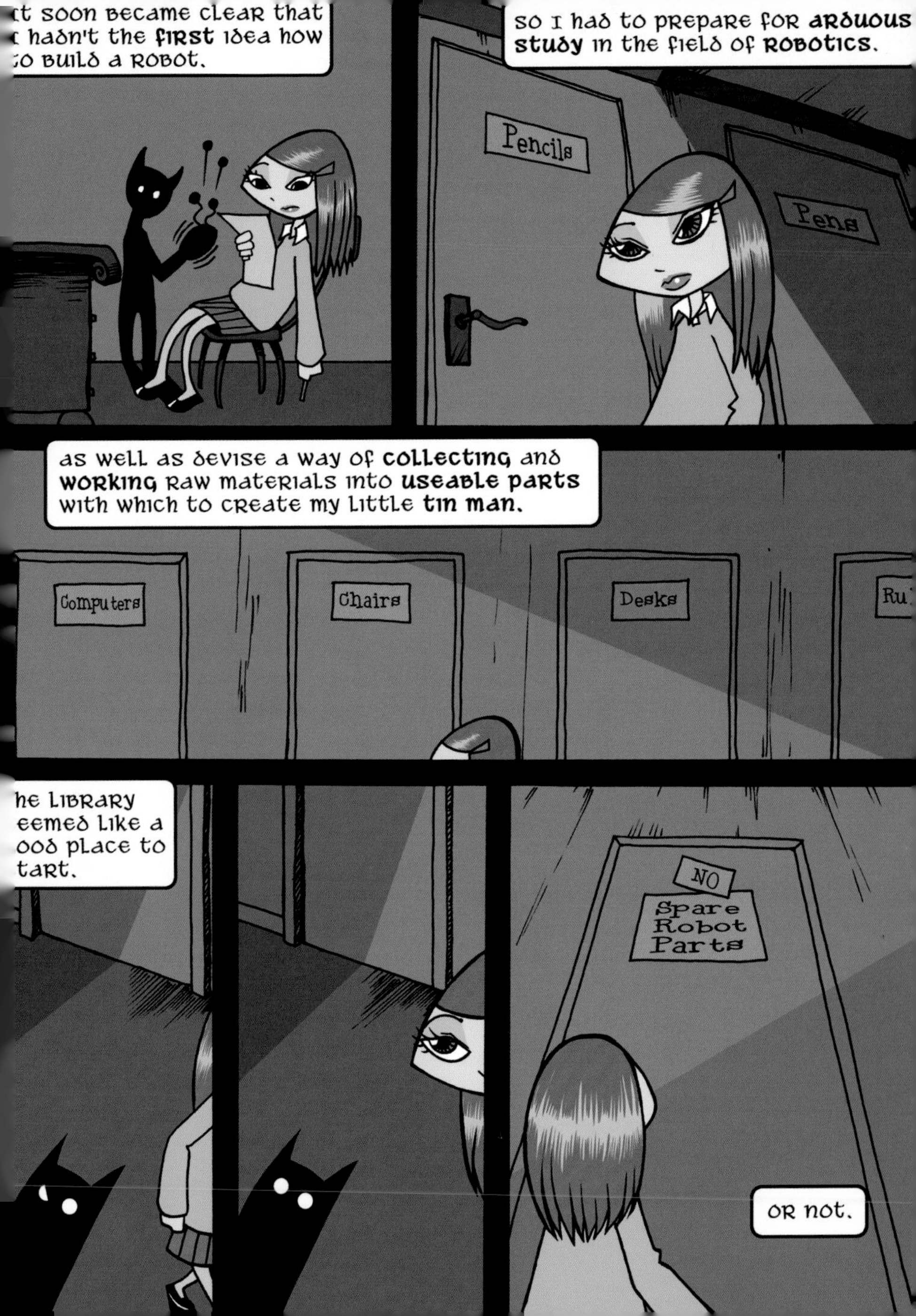
t soon became clear that hadn't the first idea how o build a robot.
so I had to prepare for arduous study in the field of robotics.
Pencils
Pens
as well as devise a way of collecting and working raw materials into useable parts with which to create my little tin man.
Computers
Chairs
Desks
Ru
he library eemed like a ood place to tart.
NO
Spare Robot Parts
or not.

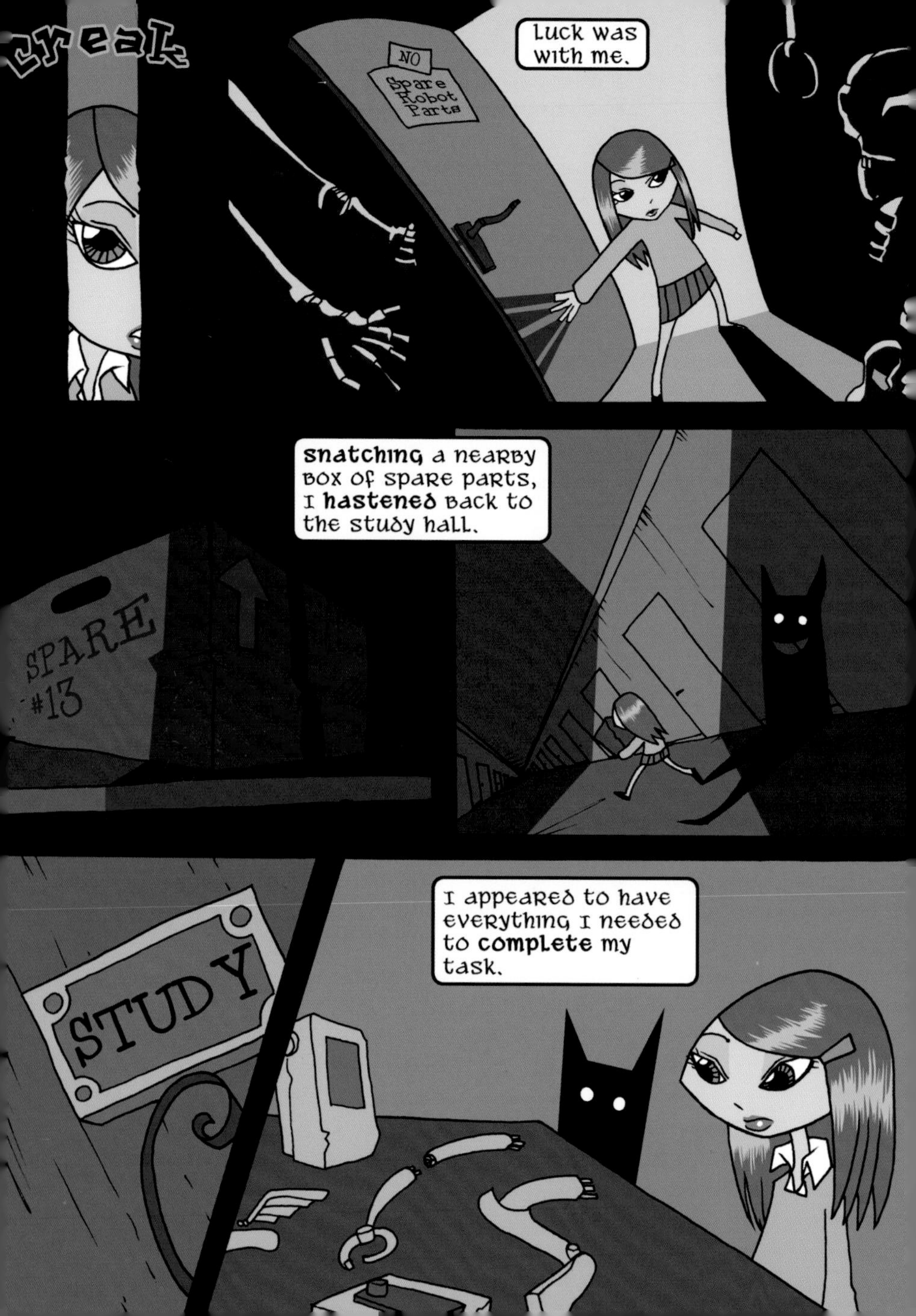
creak
NO
Spare Robot Parts
Luck was with me.
snatching a nearby box of spare parts, I hastened back to the study hall.
SPARE #13
STUDY
I appeared to have everything I needed to complete my task.

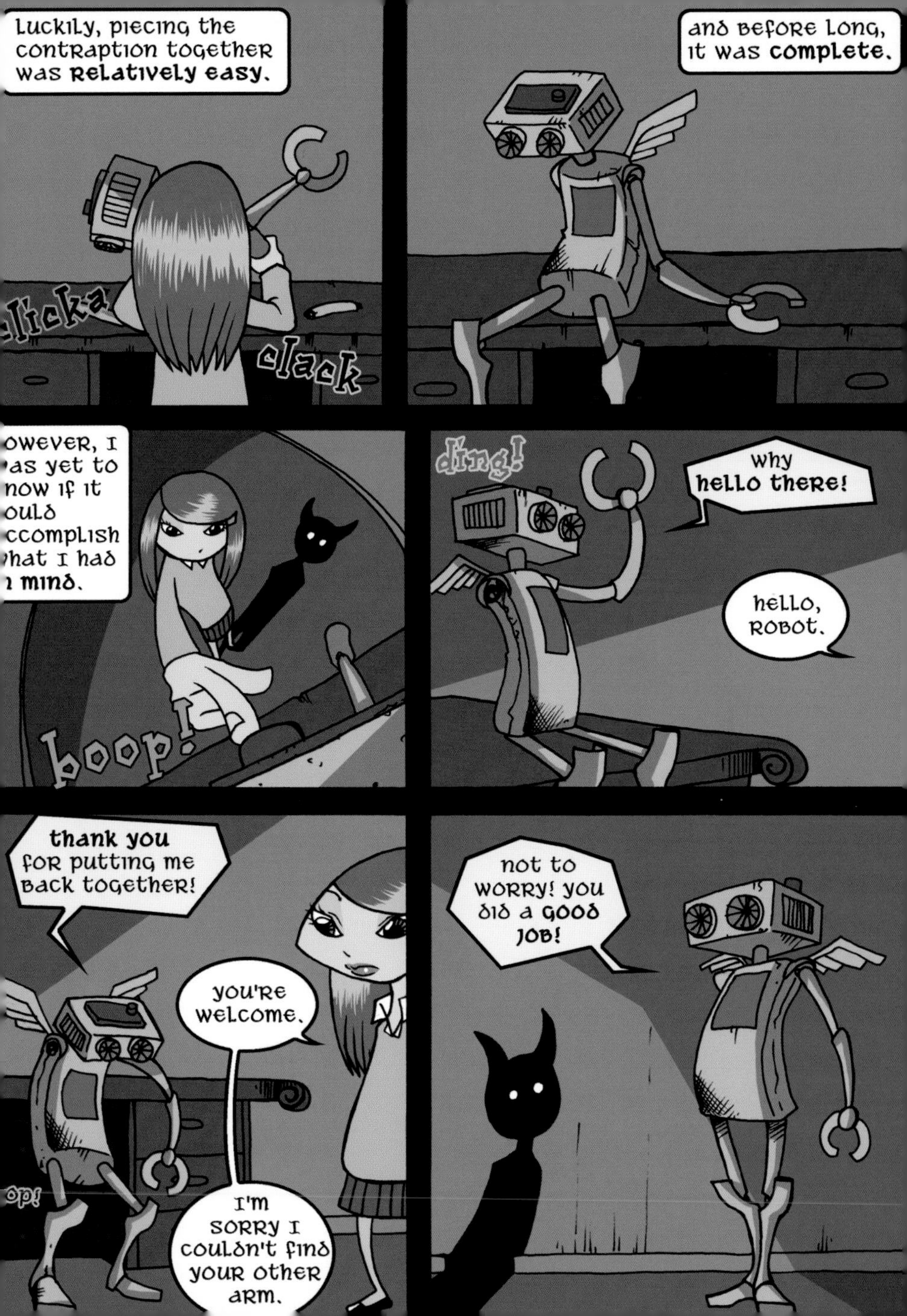
LUCKILY, PIECING THE CONTRAPTION TOGETHER WAS RELATIVELY EASY.
clicka
clack
AND BEFORE LONG, IT WAS COMPLETE.
OWEVER, I 'AS YET TO NOW IF IT OULD CCOMPLISH 'HAT I HAD MIND.
boop!
ding!
WHY HELLO THERE!
HELLO, ROBOT.
THANK YOU FOR PUTTING ME BACK TOGETHER!
YOU'RE WELCOME.
I'M SORRY I COULDN'T FIND YOUR OTHER ARM.
op!
NOT TO WORRY! YOU DID A GOOD JOB!

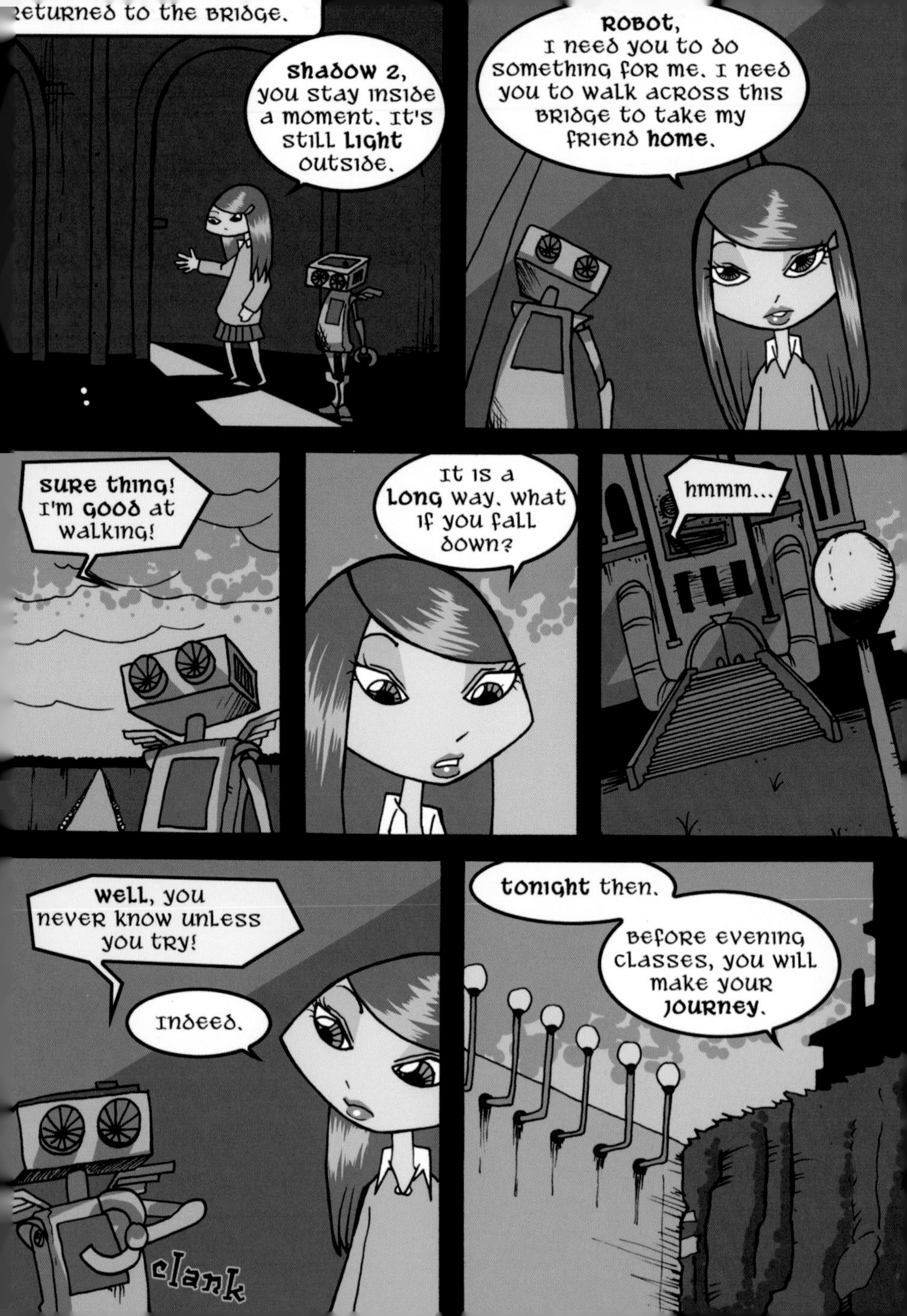
returned to the BRIDGE.
SHADOW 2, you stay inside a moment. It's still light outside.
ROBOT, I need you to do something for me. I need you to walk across this BRIDGE to take my friend home.
SURE THING! I'M GOOD at walking!
It is a LONG way. What if you fall down?
hmmm...
WELL, you never know unless you try!
Indeed.
tonight then.
Before evening classes, you will make your journey.
clank

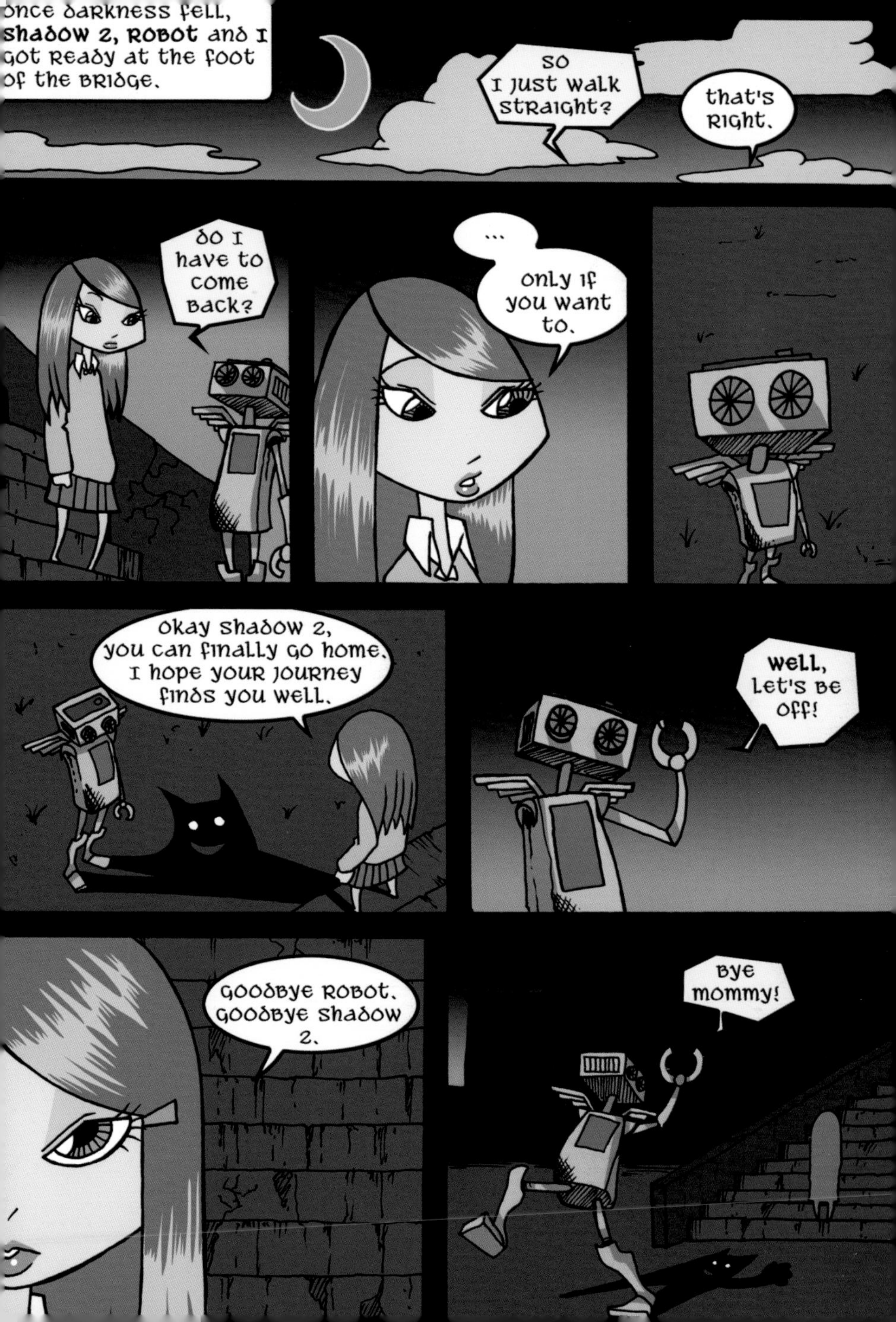

once darkness fell, shadow 2, robot and I got ready at the foot of the bridge.
so I just walk straight?
that's right.
do I have to come back?
...
only if you want to.
okay shadow 2, you can finally go home. I hope your journey finds you well.
well, let's be off!
goodbye robot. goodbye shadow 2.
bye mommy!

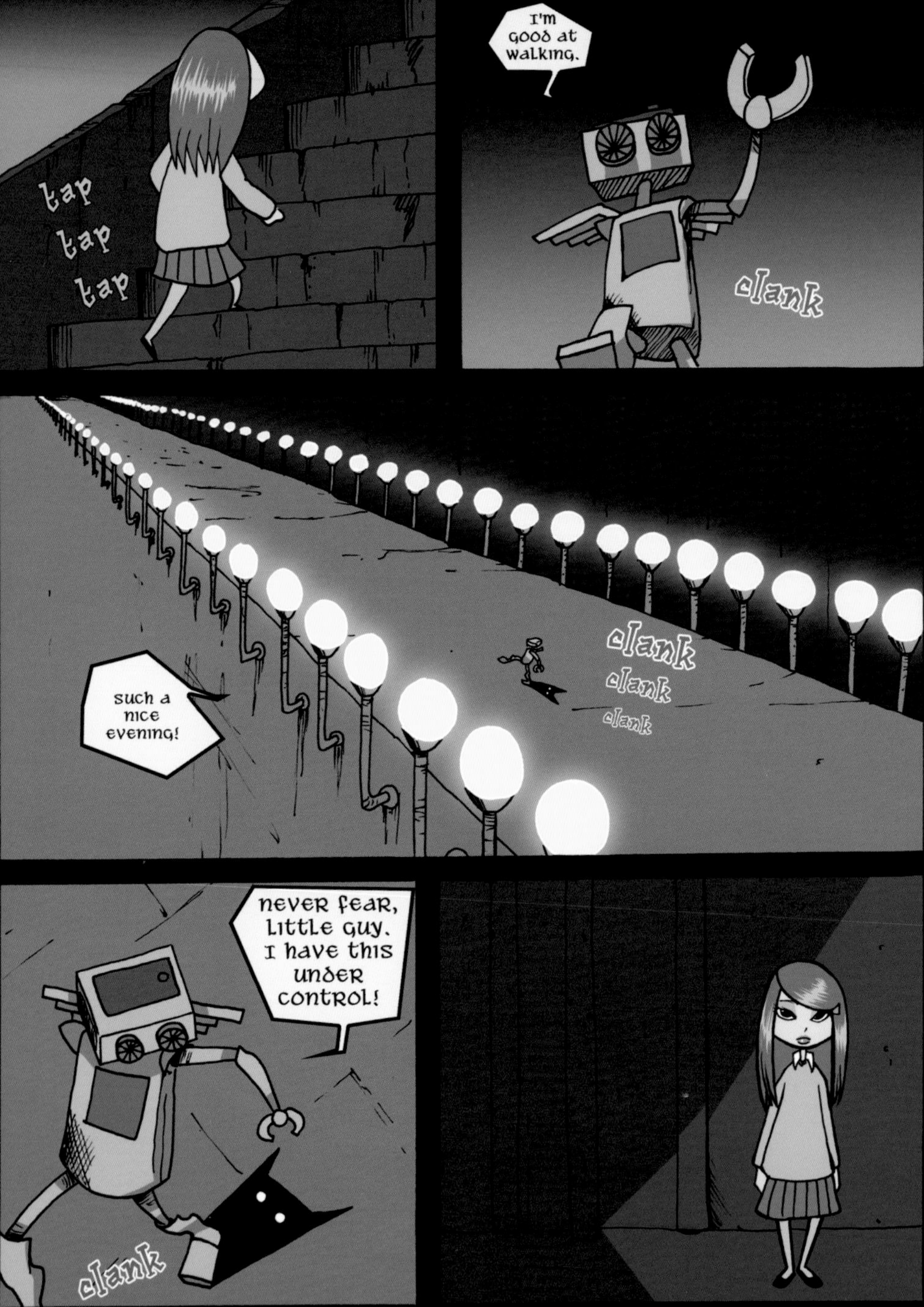
tap
tap
tap
I'm good at walking.
clank
such a nice evening!
clank
clank
clank
never fear, little guy. I have this under control!
clank

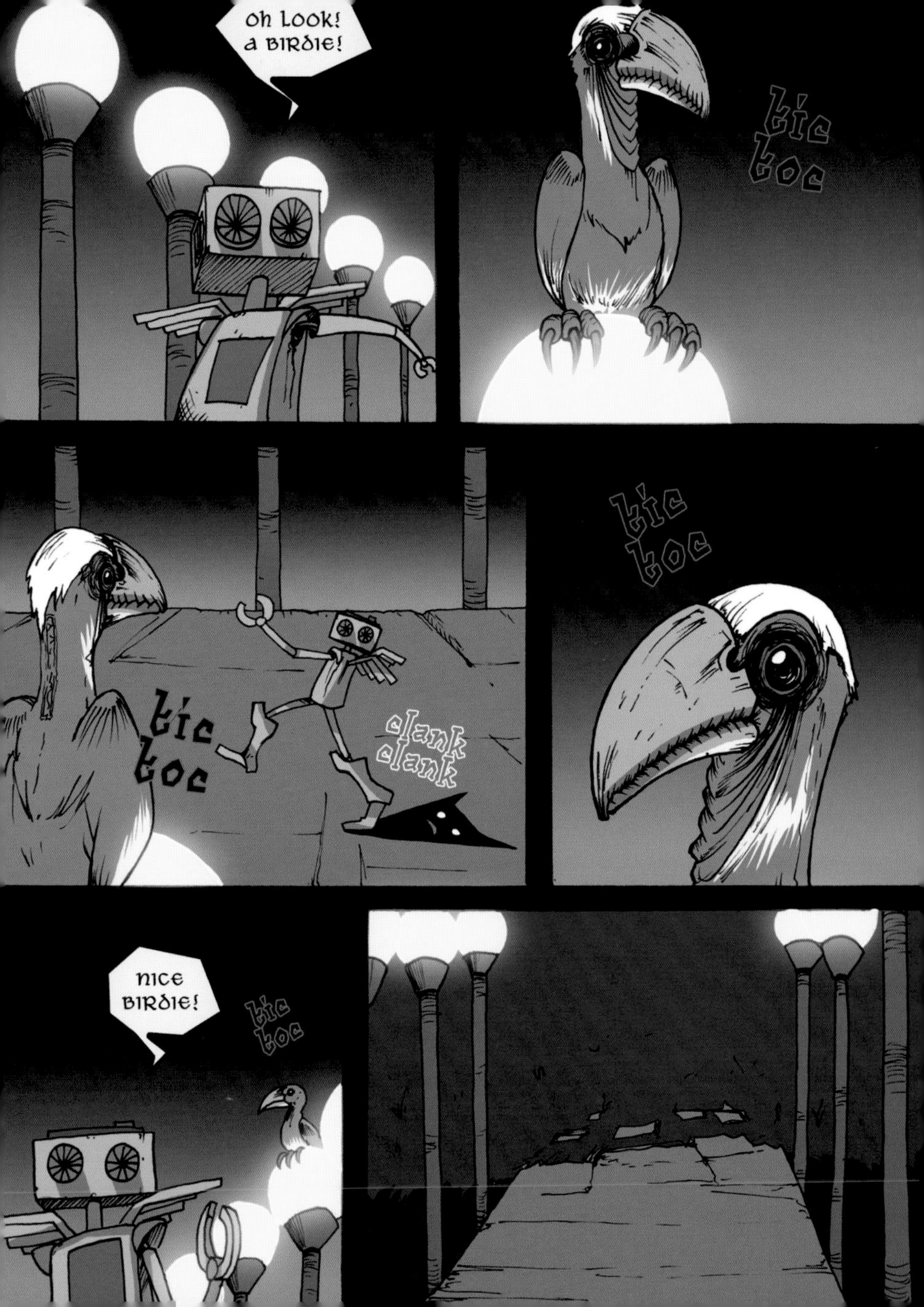
OH LOOK! A BIRDIE!
tic toc
tic toc
tic toc
clank clank
tic toc
NICE BIRDIE!
tic toc

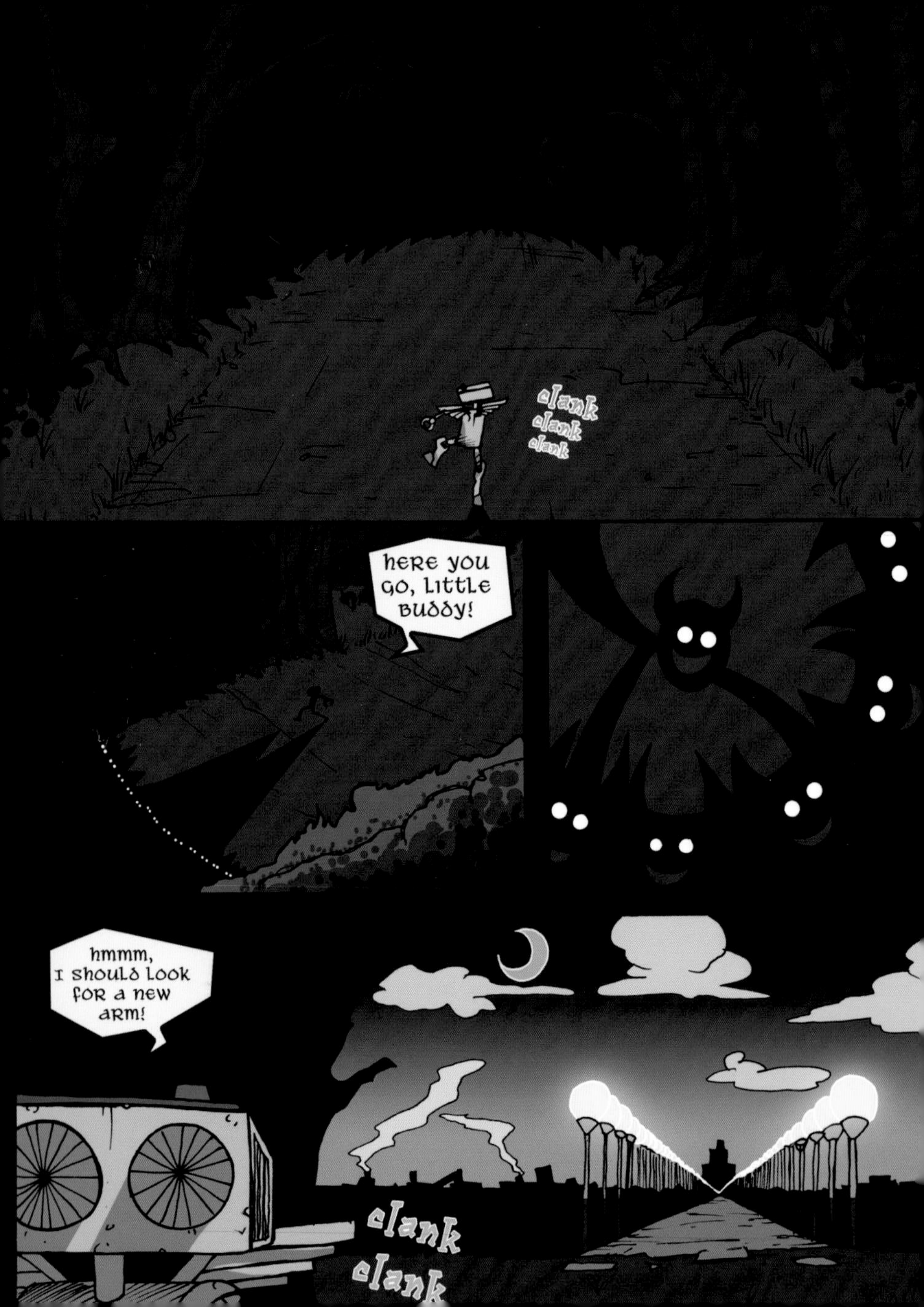
clank
clank
clank
here you go, little buddy!
hmmm, I should look for a new arm!
clank
clank

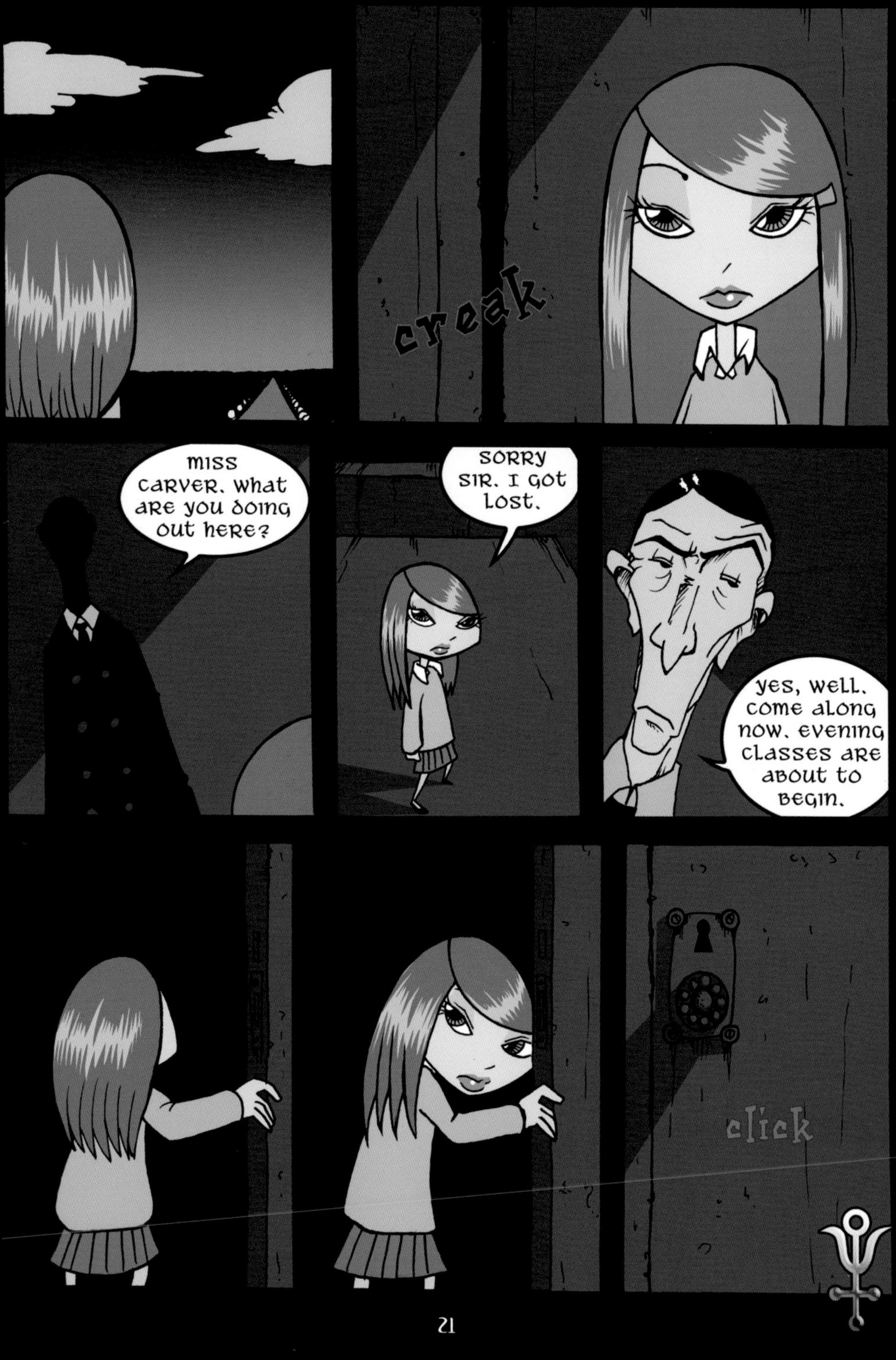
creak
MISS CARVER. WHAT ARE YOU DOING OUT HERE?
SORRY SIR. I GOT LOST.
YES, WELL. COME ALONG NOW. EVENING CLASSES ARE ABOUT TO BEGIN.
click

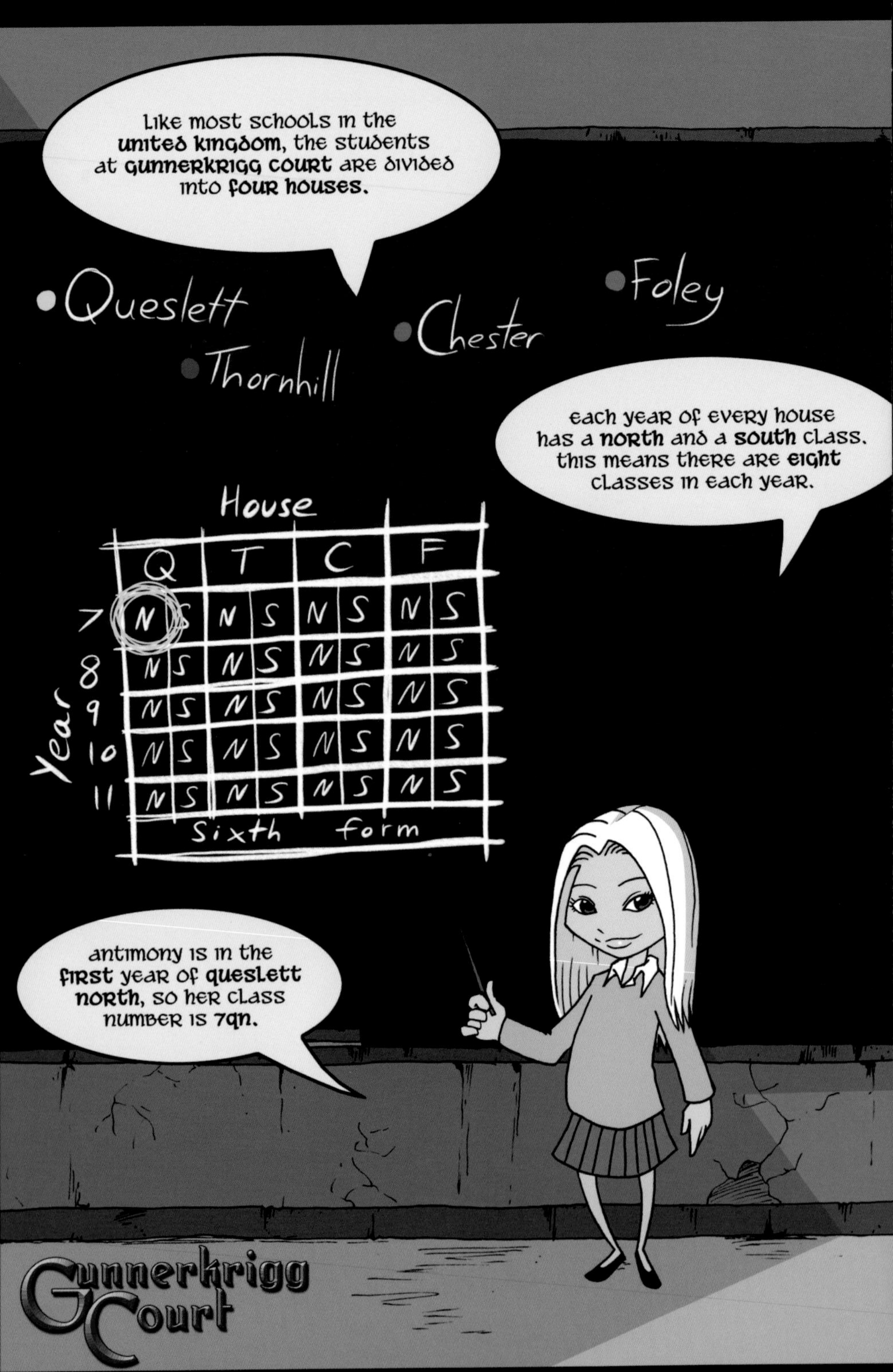
Like most schools in the united kingdom, the students at gunnerkrigg court are divided into four houses.
•Queslett
•Thornhill
•Chester
•Foley
Each year of every house has a north and a south class. This means there are eight classes in each year.
House
Q T C F
Year
7 N S N S N S N S
8 N S N S N S N S
9 N S N S N S N S
10 N S N S N S N S
11 N S N S N S N S
Sixth form
Antimony is in the first year of queslett north, so her class number is 7qn.
Gunnerkrigg Court

Gunnerkrigg Court

Chapter 2:

Schoolyard Myths

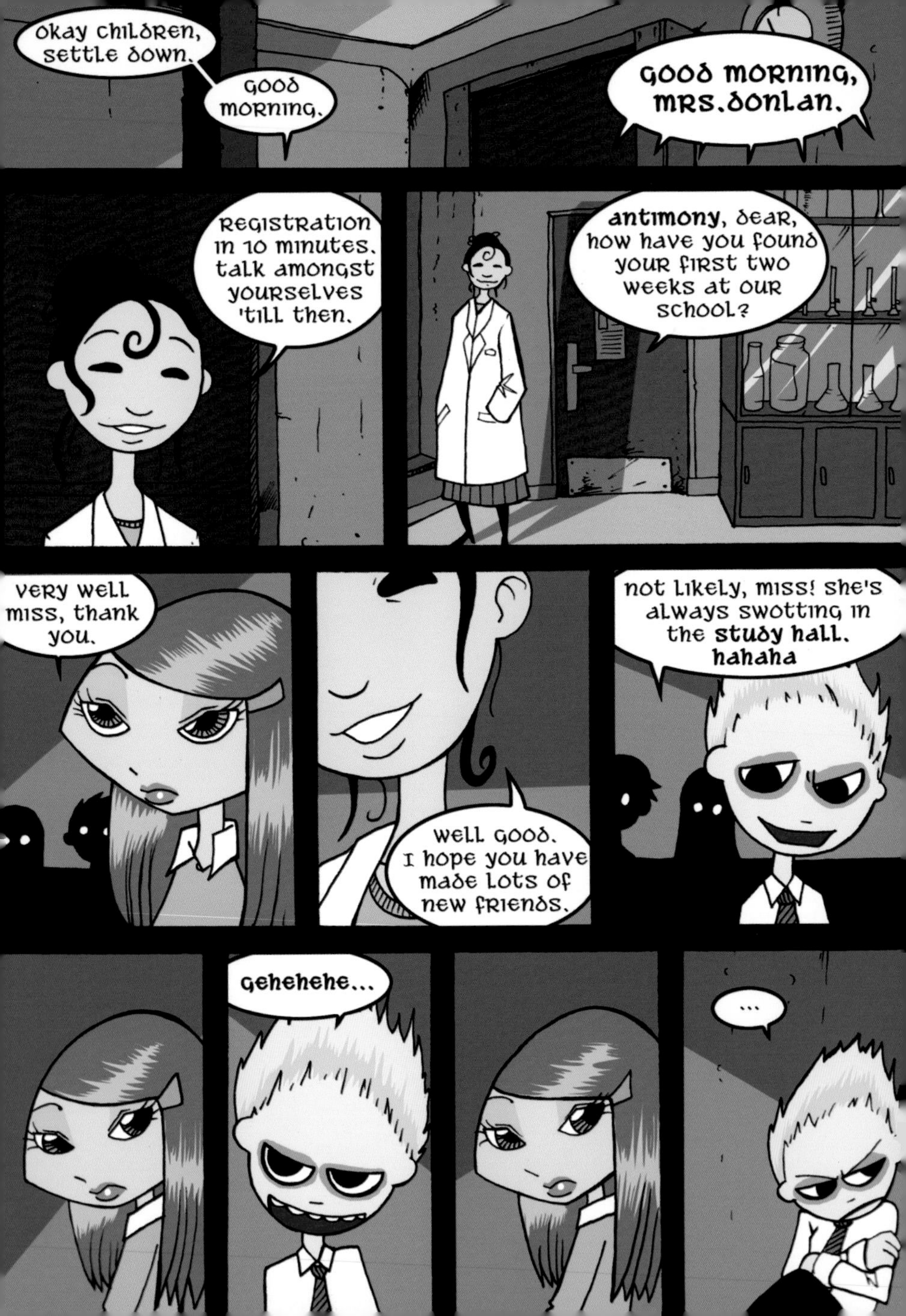
okay children, settle down.
good morning.
GOOD MORNING, MRS.DONLAN.
Registration in 10 minutes. talk amongst yourselves 'till then.
antimony, dear, how have you found your first two weeks at our school?
very well miss, thank you.
well good. I hope you have made lots of new friends.
not likely, miss! she's always swotting in the study hall. hahaha
gehehehe...
...

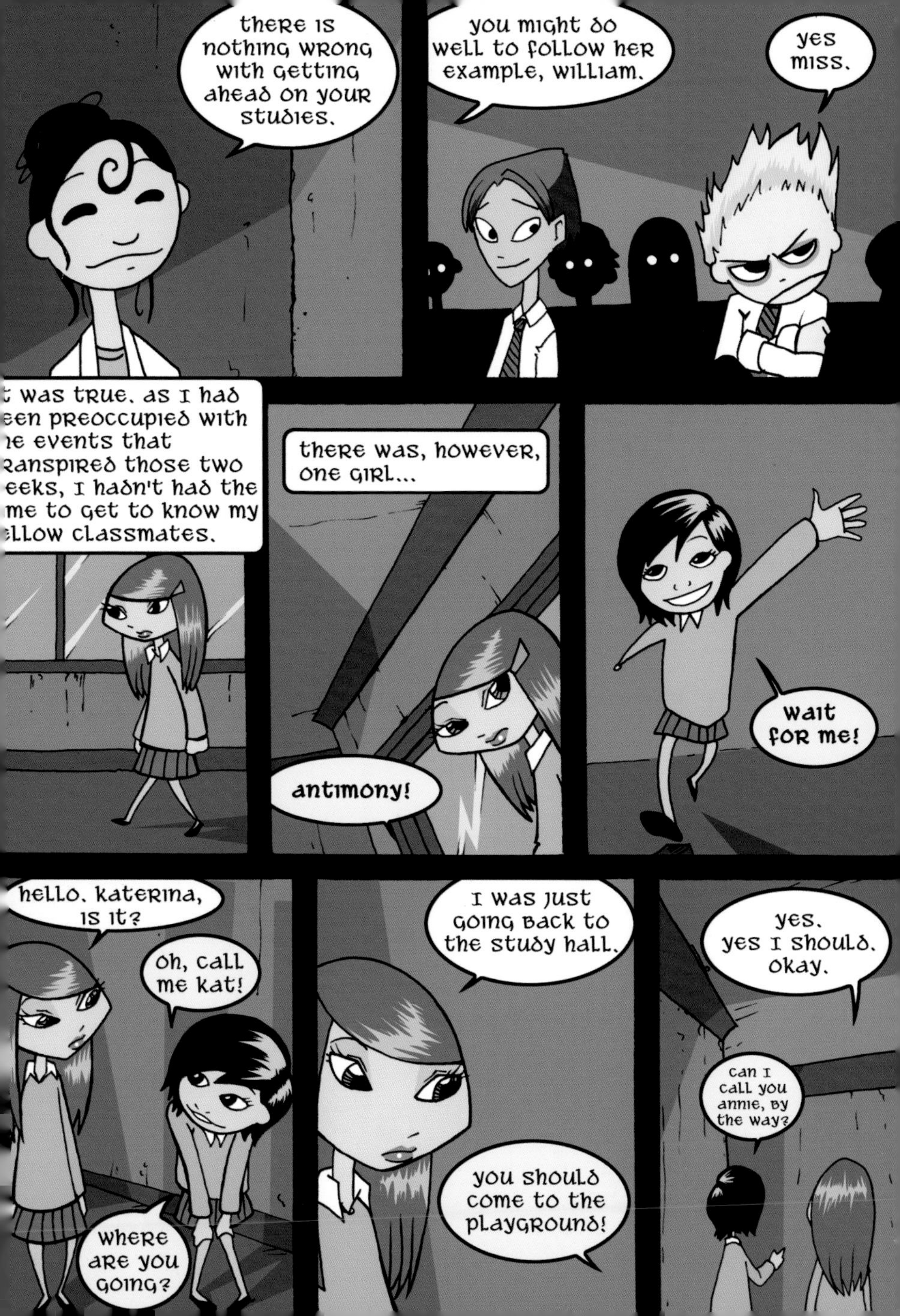
there is nothing wrong with getting ahead on your studies.
you might do well to follow her example, william.
yes miss.
t was true. as I had een preoccupied with ie events that ranspired those two eeks, I hadn't had the me to get to know my ellow classmates.
there was, however, one girl...
antimony!
wait for me!
hello. katerina, is it?
oh, call me kat!
where are you going?
I was just going back to the study hall.
you should come to the playground!
yes. yes I should. okay.
can I call you annie, by the way?

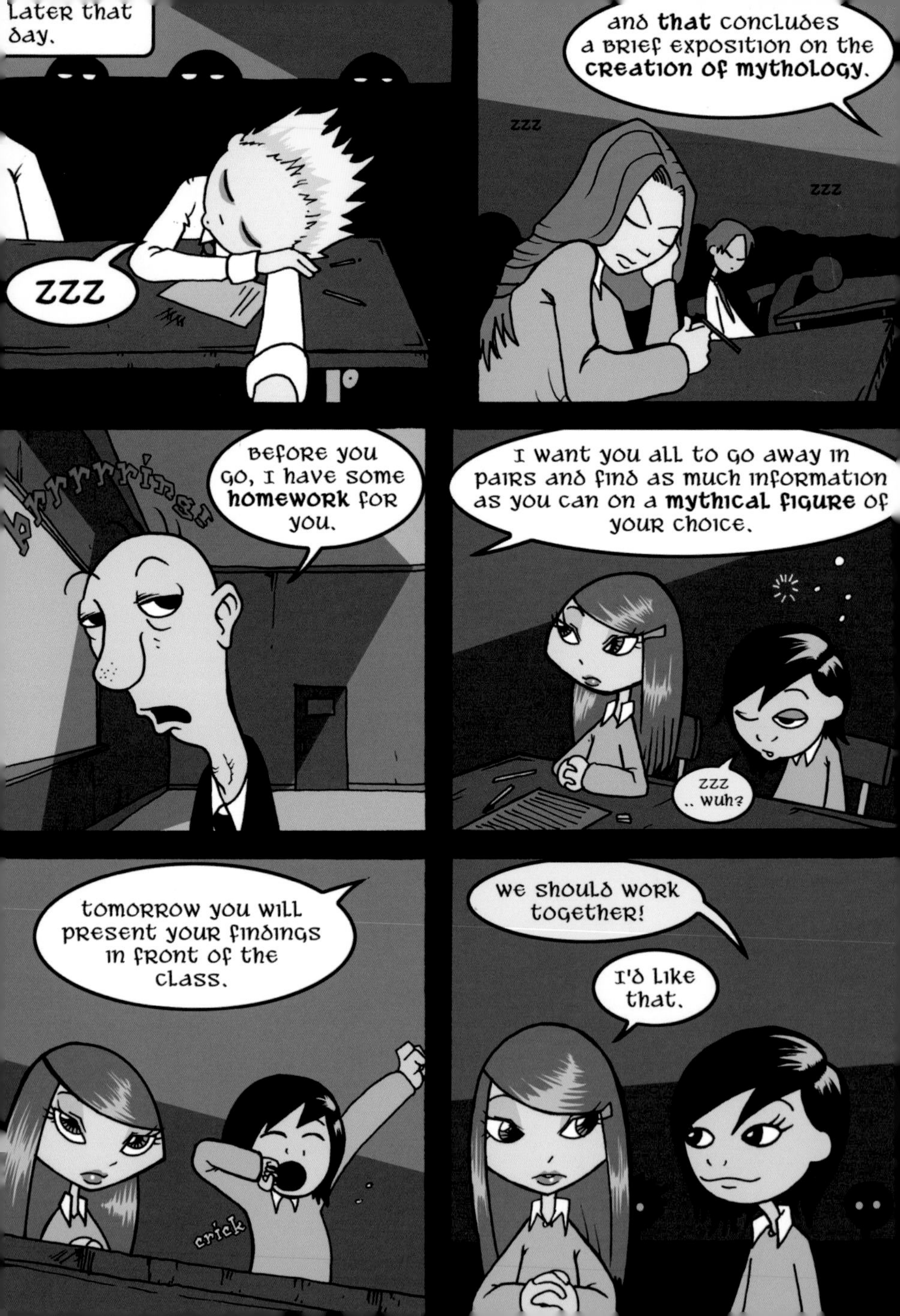
Later that day.
ZZZ
and **that** concludes a brief exposition on the **creation of mythology**.
ZZZ
ZZZ
Brrrrring!
Before you go, I have some **homework** for you.
I want you all to go away in pairs and find as much information as you can on a **mythical figure** of your choice.
ZZZ .. wuh?
tomorrow you will present your findings in front of the class.
crick
we should work together!
I'd like that.

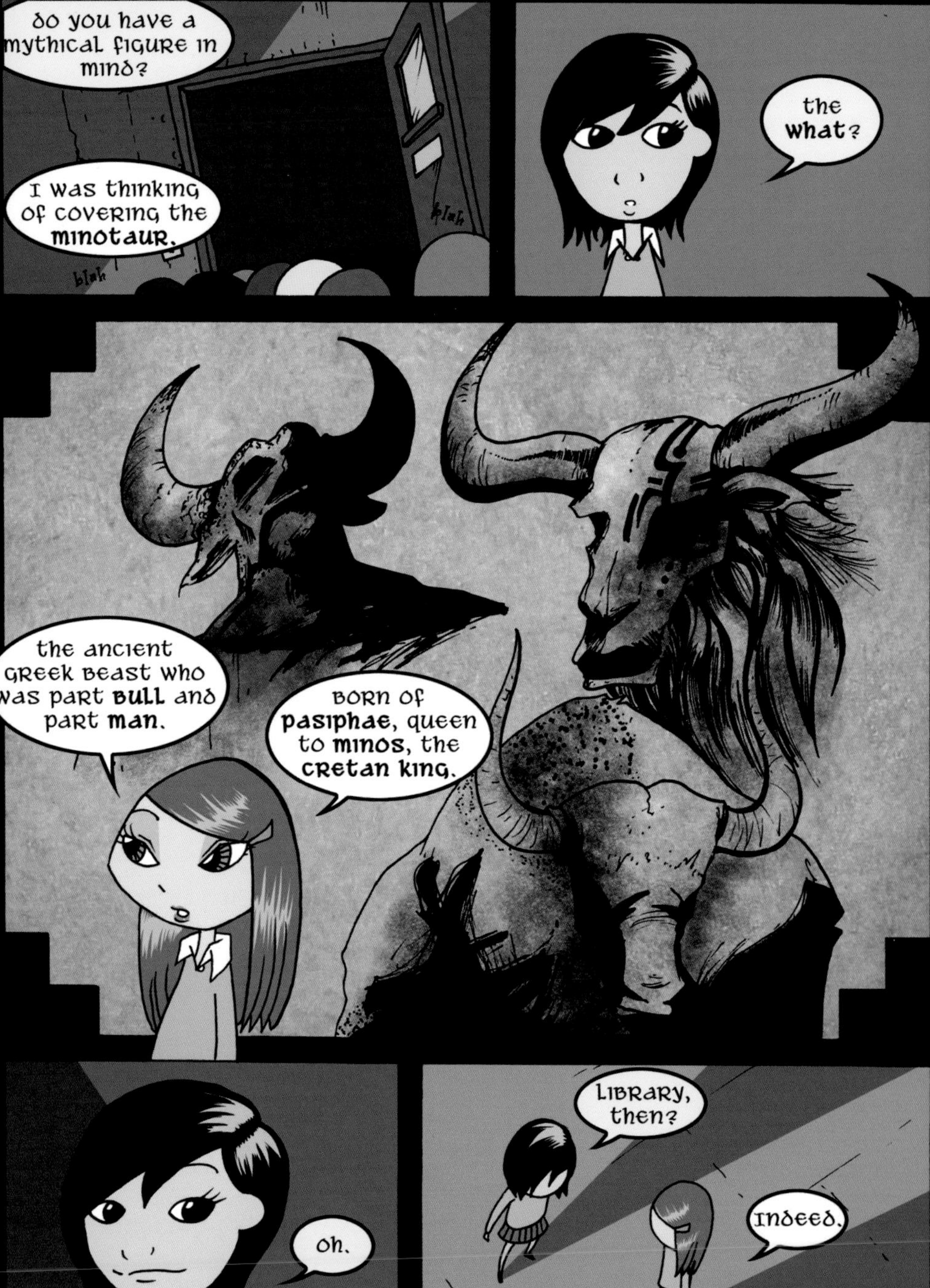
do you have a mythical figure in mind?
I was thinking of covering the minotaur.
blah
blah
the what?
the ancient greek beast who was part bull and part man.
born of pasiphae, queen to minos, the cretan king.
oh.
library, then?
indeed.

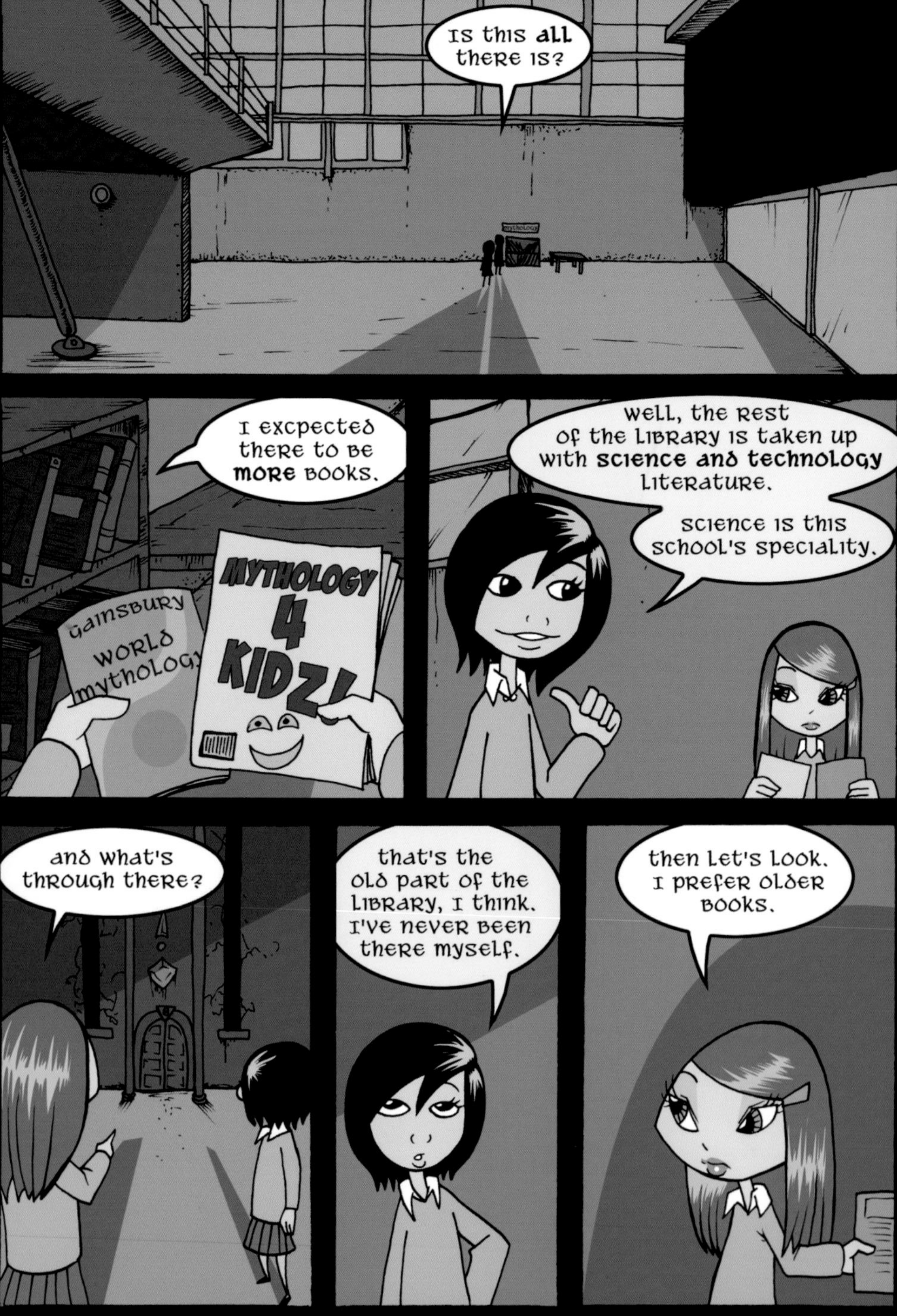
Is this all there is?
mythology
I excpected there to be more books.
Gainsbury World mythology
MYTHOLOGY 4 KIDZ!
Well, the rest of the library is taken up with science and technology literature.
Science is this school's speciality.
And what's through there?
That's the old part of the library, I think. I've never been there myself.
Then let's look. I prefer older books.

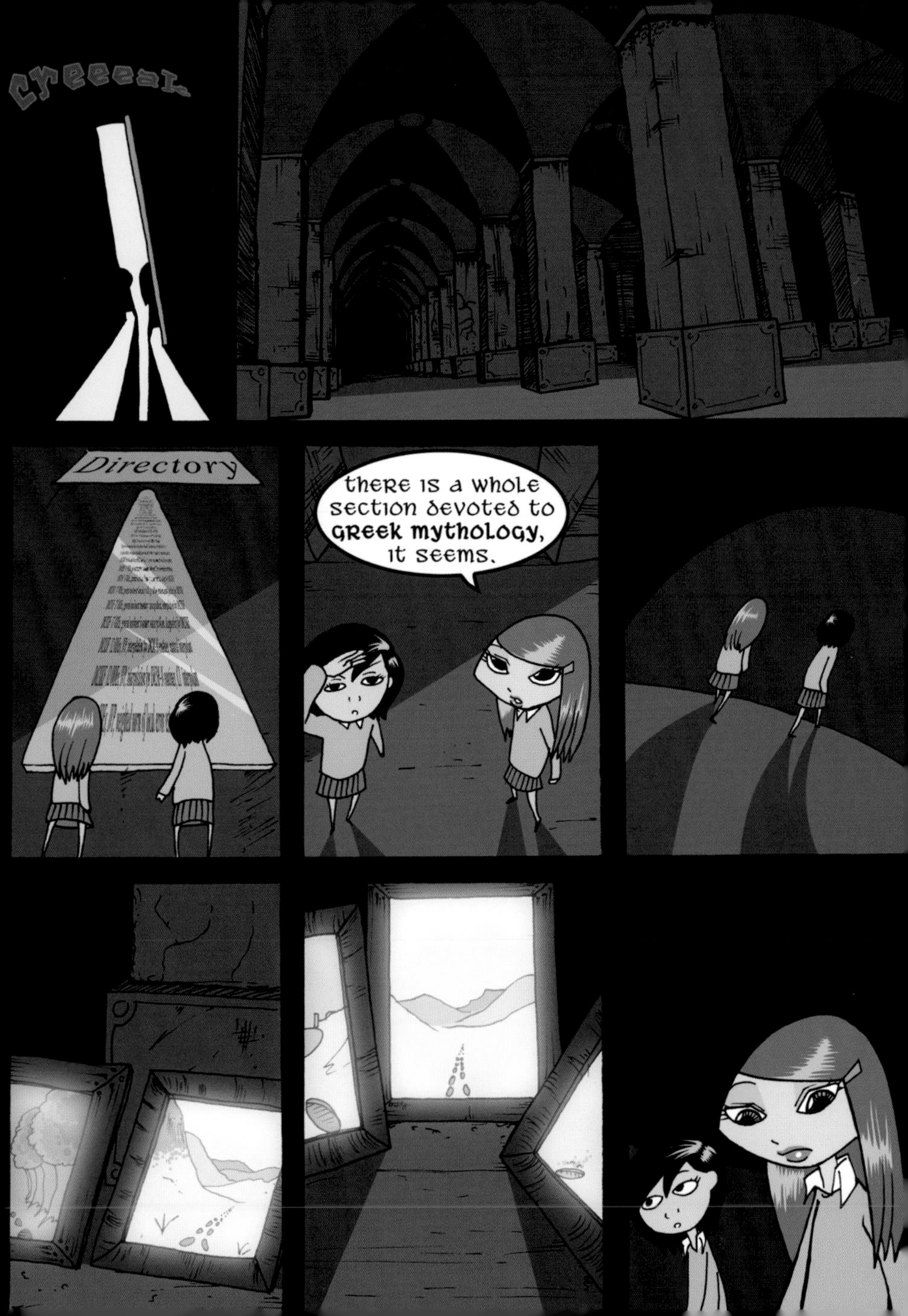
creeeak
Directory
there is a whole section devoted to GREEK mythology, it seems.

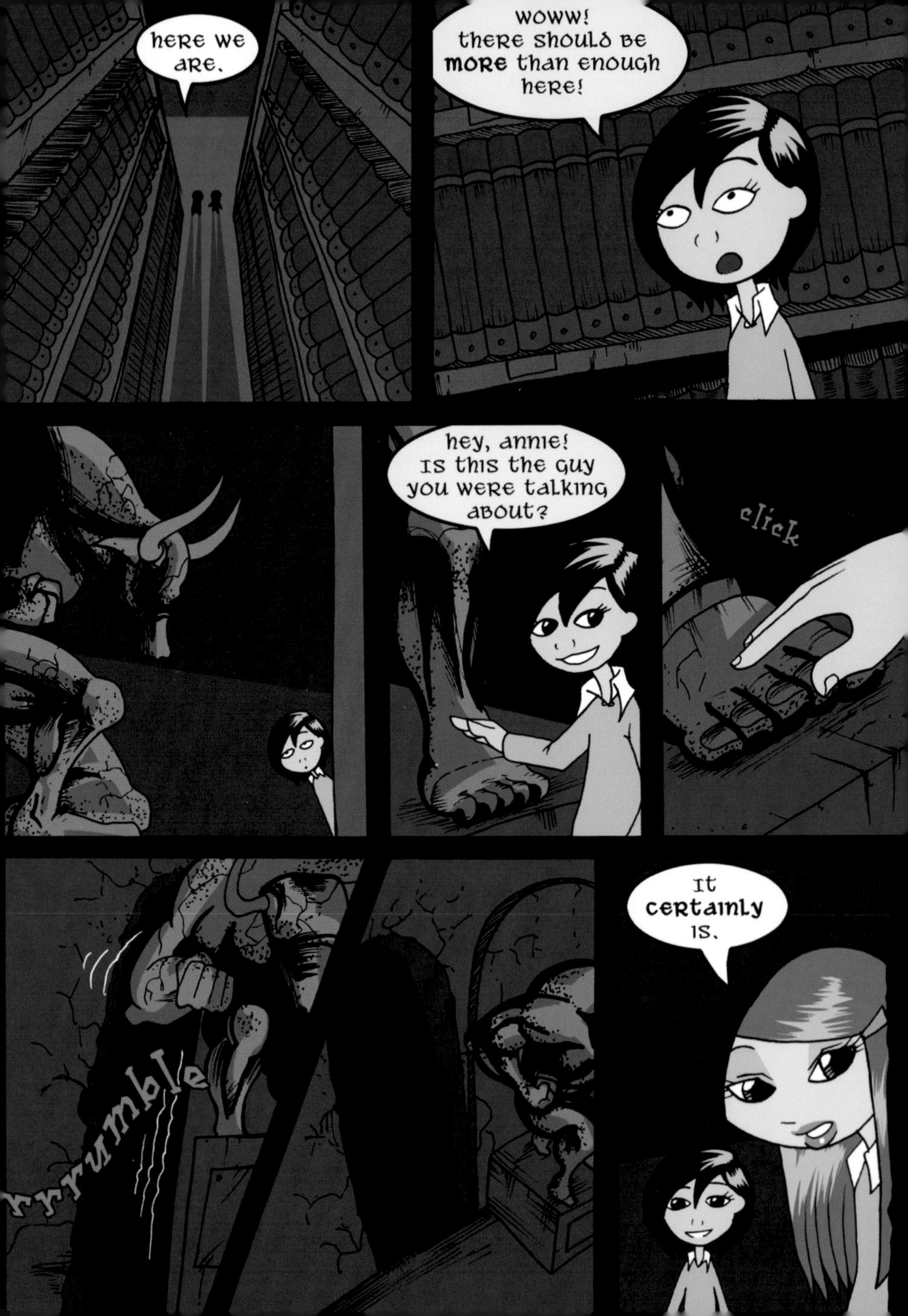
here we are.
woww! there should be **more** than enough here!
hey, annie! is this the guy you were talking about?
click
rrrumble
it **certainly** is.

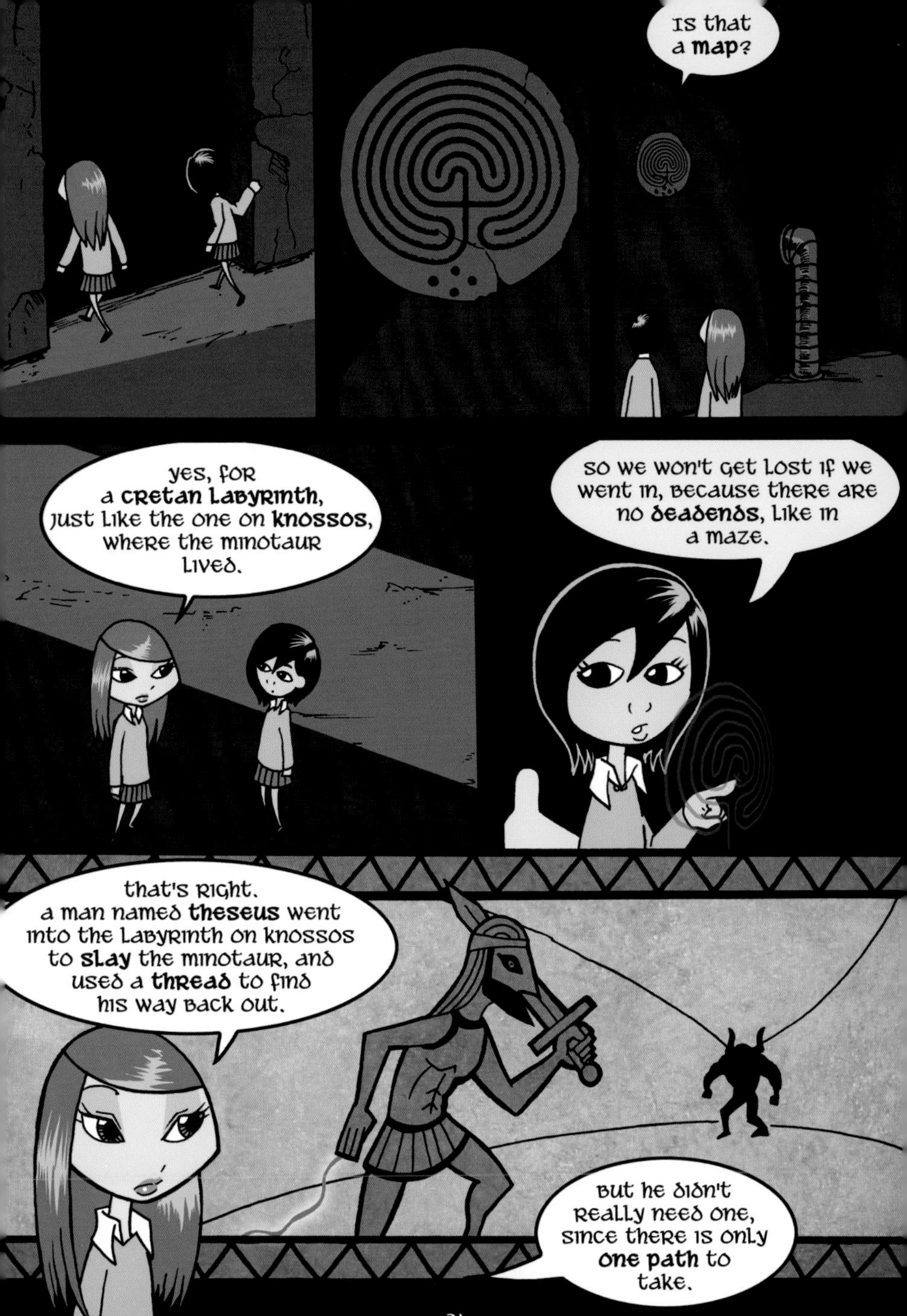
Is that a map?
yes, for a cretan Labyrinth, just like the one on knossos, where the minotaur lived.
so we won't get lost if we went in, because there are no deadends, like in a maze.
that's right. a man named theseus went into the Labyrinth on knossos to slay the minotaur, and used a thread to find his way back out.
But he didn't really need one, since there is only one path to take.

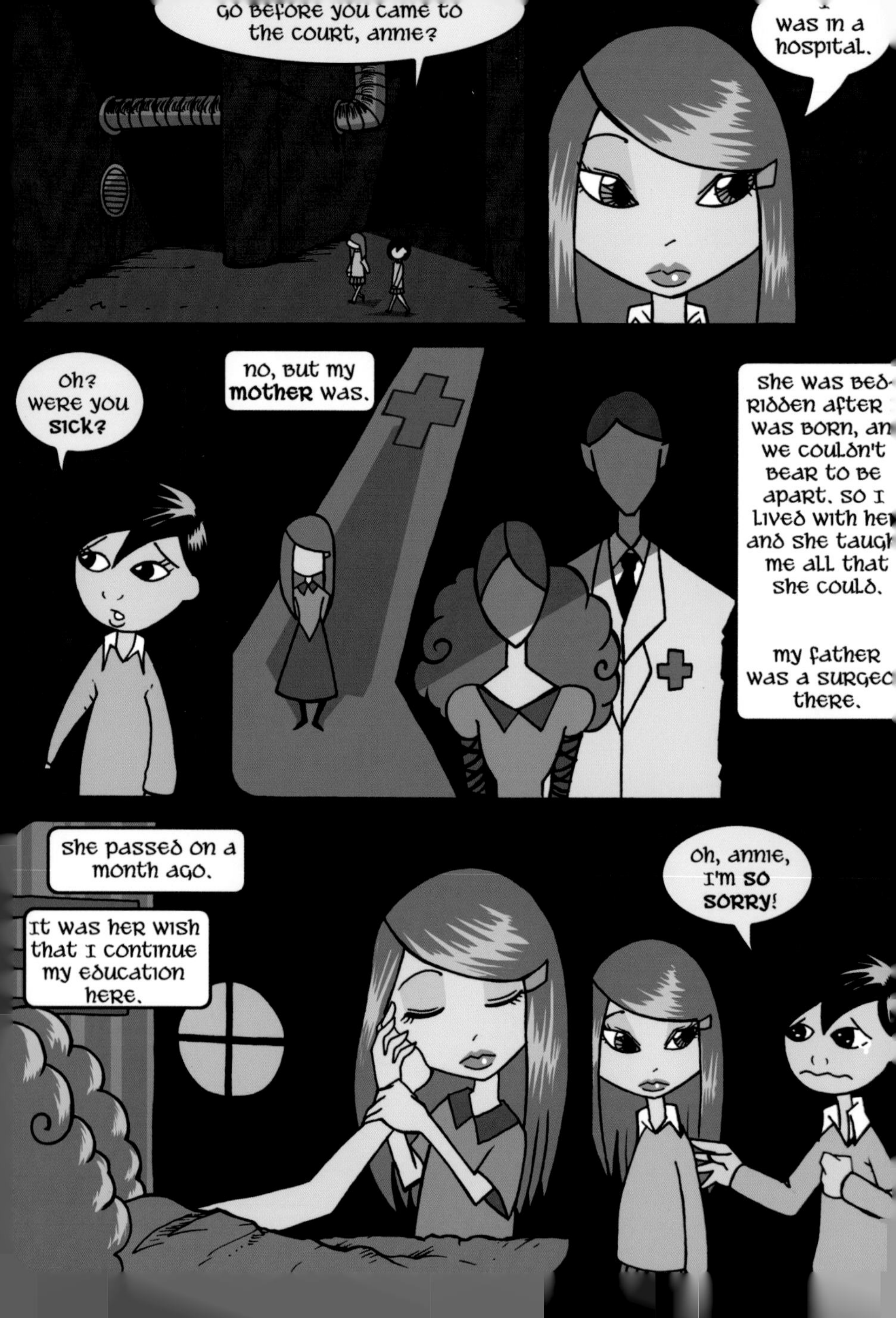
go before you came to
the court, annie?
was in a
hospital.
oh?
were you
sick?
no, but my
mother was.
she was bed-
ridden after
was born, an
we couldn't
bear to be
apart. so I
lived with he
and she taugh
me all that
she could.
my father
was a surgec
there.
she passed on a
month ago.
it was her wish
that I continue
my education
here.
oh, annie,
I'm so
sorry!

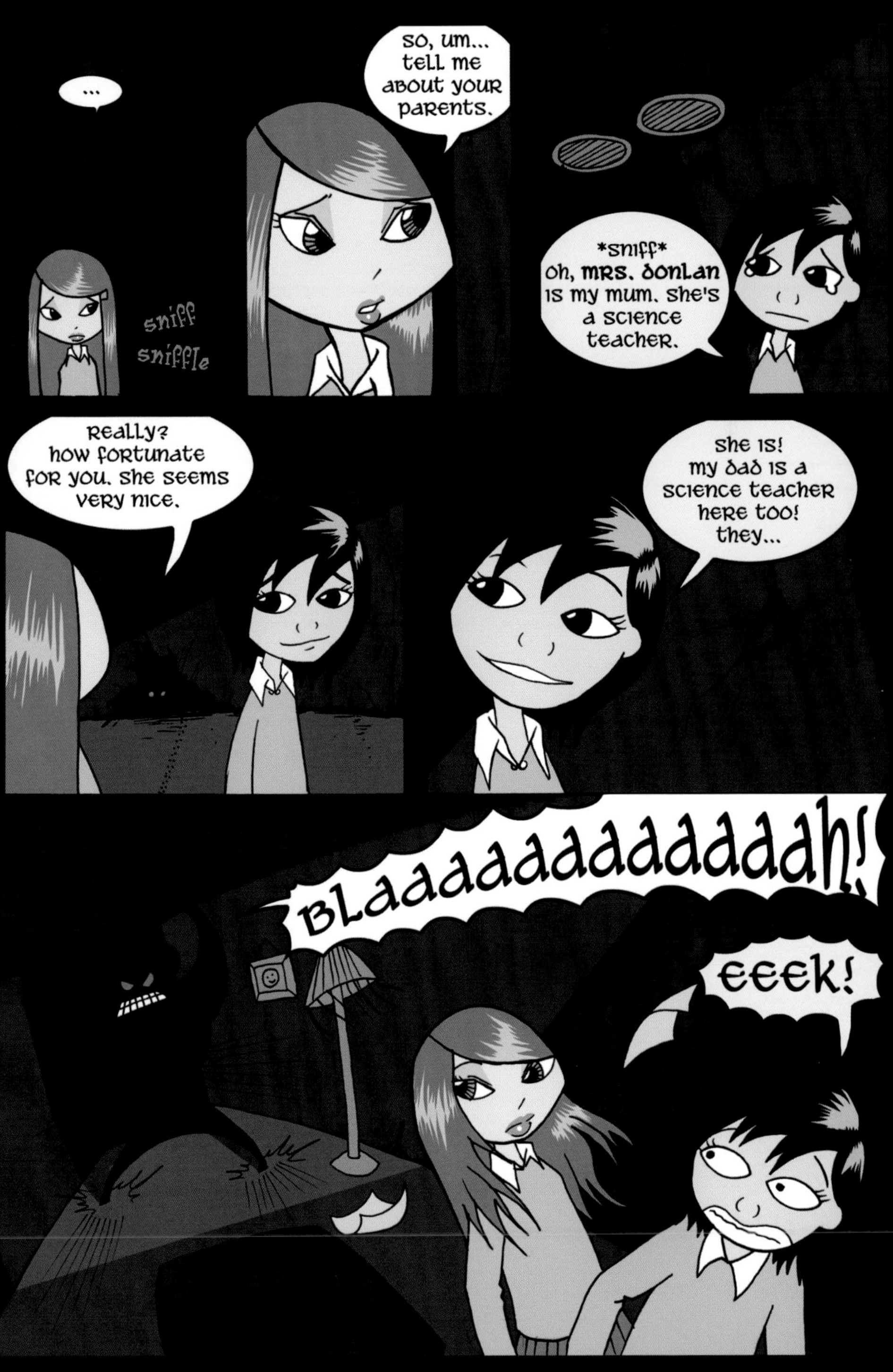
...
So, um... tell me about your parents.
sniff
sniffle
sniff
Oh, Mrs. Donlan is my mum. She's a science teacher.
Really? How fortunate for you. She seems very nice.
She is! My dad is a science teacher here too! They...
BLAAAAAAAAAAAAAH!
EEEK!

HELLO, SIR. MY NAME IS ANTIMONY.

WHO DARES **INTRUDE** ON THE MINOTAUR'S LAIR?!

GOOD DAY.

PHEW, YOU GIRLS GAVE ME A FRIGHT, SNEAKING AROUND LIKE THAT.

Floomph

IT WOULD APPEAR THAT WE HAVE JUST COMPLETED OUR HOMEWORK.

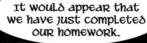

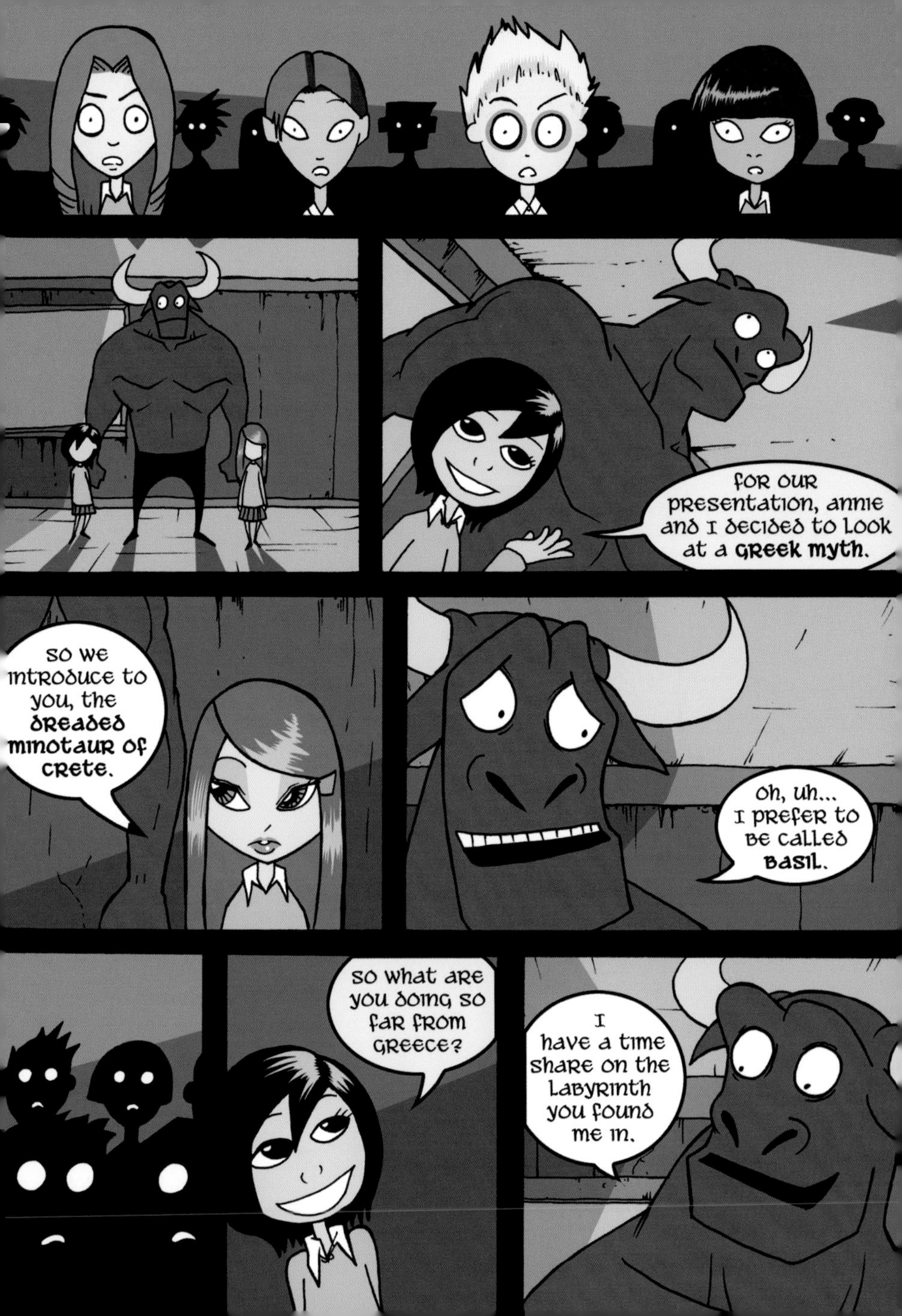
FOR OUR PRESENTATION, ANNIE AND I DECIDED TO LOOK AT A GREEK MYTH.
SO WE INTRODUCE TO YOU, THE DREADED MINOTAUR OF CRETE.
OH, UH... I PREFER TO BE CALLED BASIL.
SO WHAT ARE YOU DOING SO FAR FROM GREECE?
I HAVE A TIME SHARE ON THE LABYRINTH YOU FOUND ME IN.

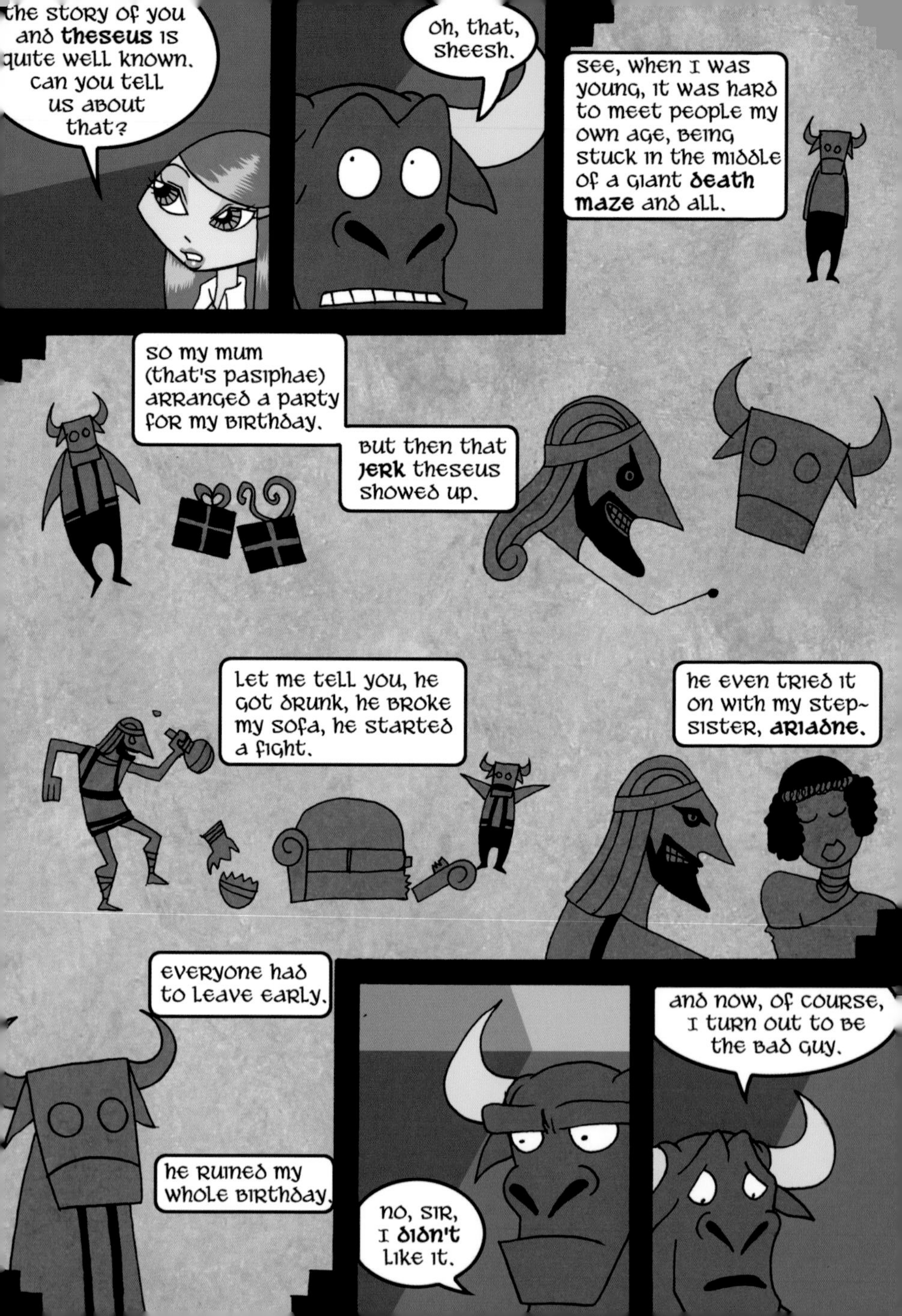
the story of you and theseus is quite well known. can you tell us about that?
oh, that, sheesh.
see, when I was young, it was hard to meet people my own age, being stuck in the middle of a giant death maze and all.
so my mum (that's pasiphae) arranged a party for my birthday.
but then that jerk theseus showed up.
let me tell you, he got drunk, he broke my sofa, he started a fight.
he even tried it on with my step-sister, ariadne.
everyone had to leave early.
he ruined my whole birthday.
and now, of course, I turn out to be the bad guy.
no, sir, I didn't like it.

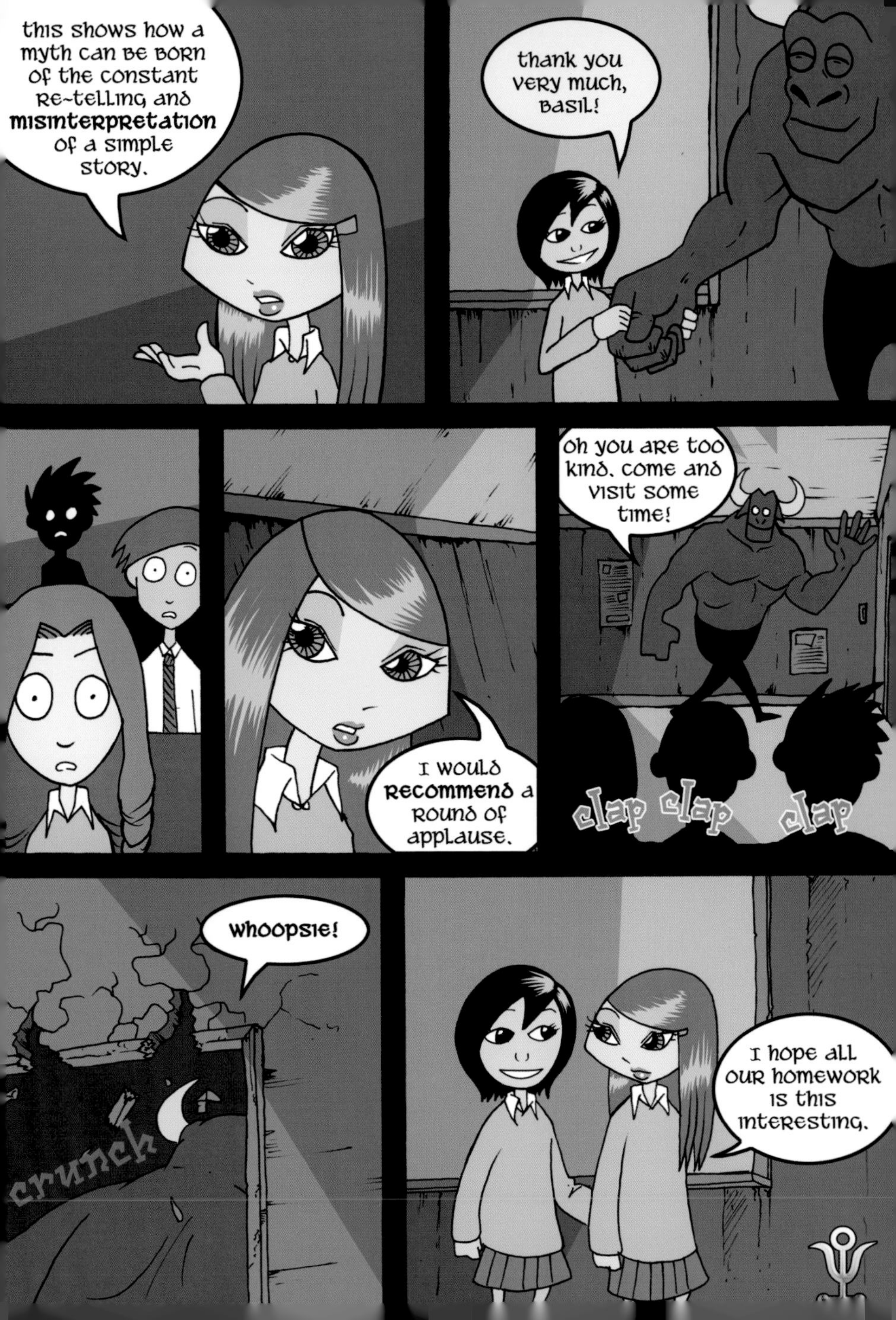
this shows how a myth can be born of the constant re-telling and **misinterpretation** of a simple story.
thank you very much, Basil!
I would **recommend** a round of applause.
oh you are too kind. come and visit some time!
clap clap clap
whoopsie!
crunch
I hope all our homework is this interesting.

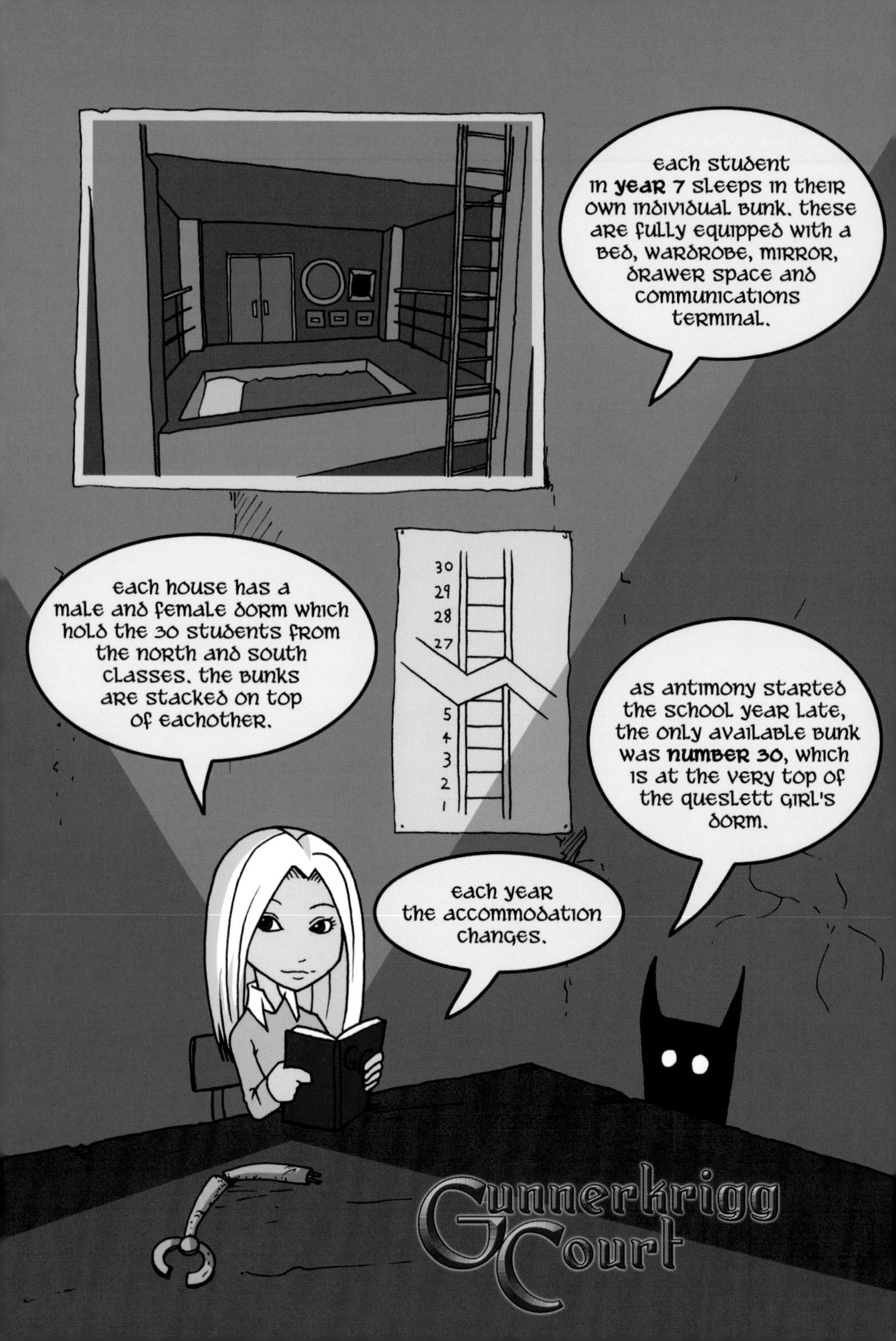
each student in **year 7** sleeps in their own individual bunk. these are fully equipped with a bed, wardrobe, mirror, drawer space and communications terminal.
each house has a male and female dorm which hold the 30 students from the north and south classes. the bunks are stacked on top of eachother.
30
29
28
27
5
4
3
2
1
as antimony started the school year late, the only available bunk was **number 30**, which is at the very top of the queslett girl's dorm.
each year the accommodation changes.
Gunnerkrigg Court

Gunnerkrigg Court

Chapter 3:

Reynardine

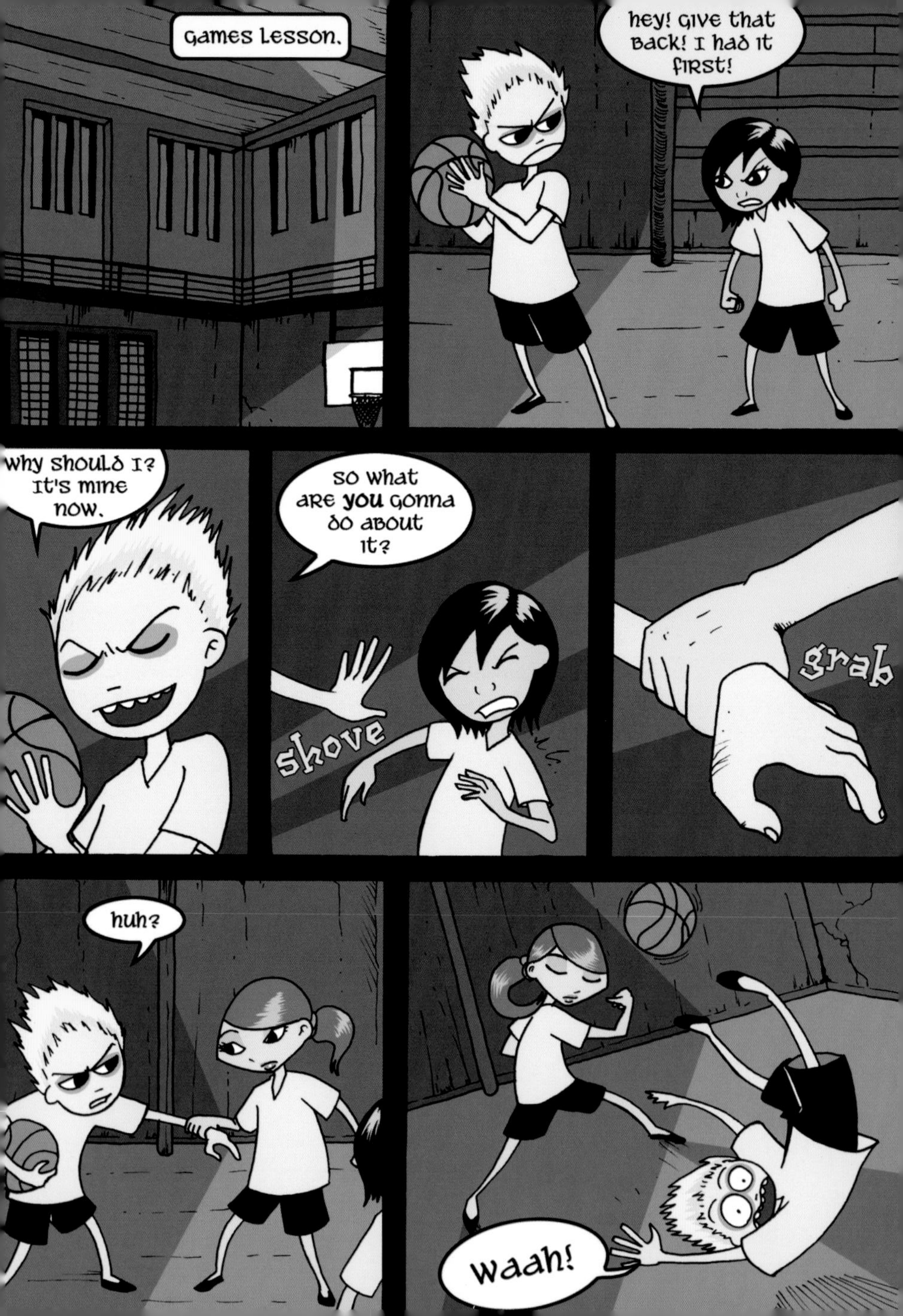
Games Lesson.
hey! Give that Back! I had it first!
why should I? It's mine now.
so what are **you** gonna do about it?
shove
grab
huh?
Waah!

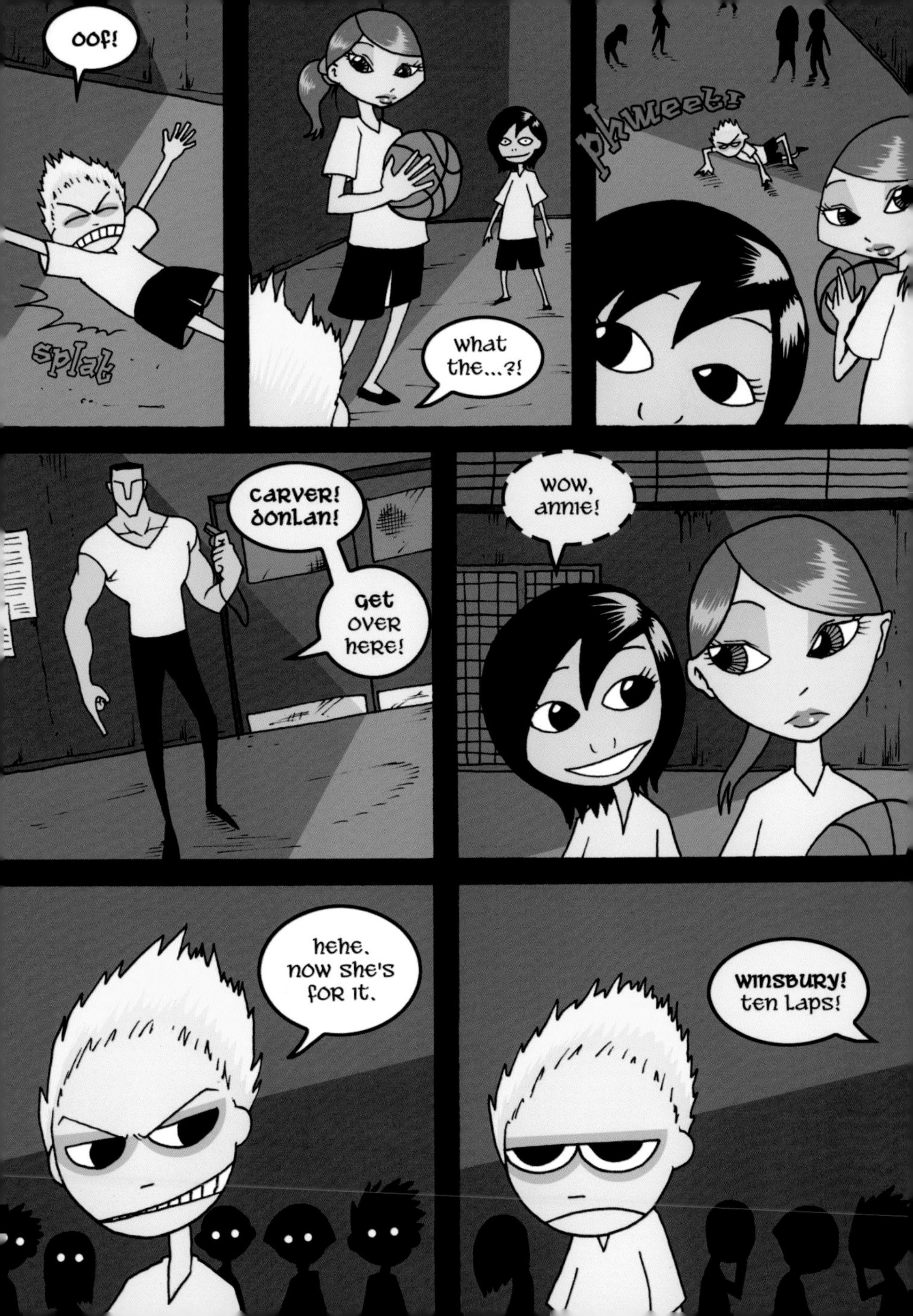
oof!
splat
what the...?!
phweet!
carver! donlan!
get over here!
wow, annie!
hehe. now she's for it.
winsbury! ten laps!

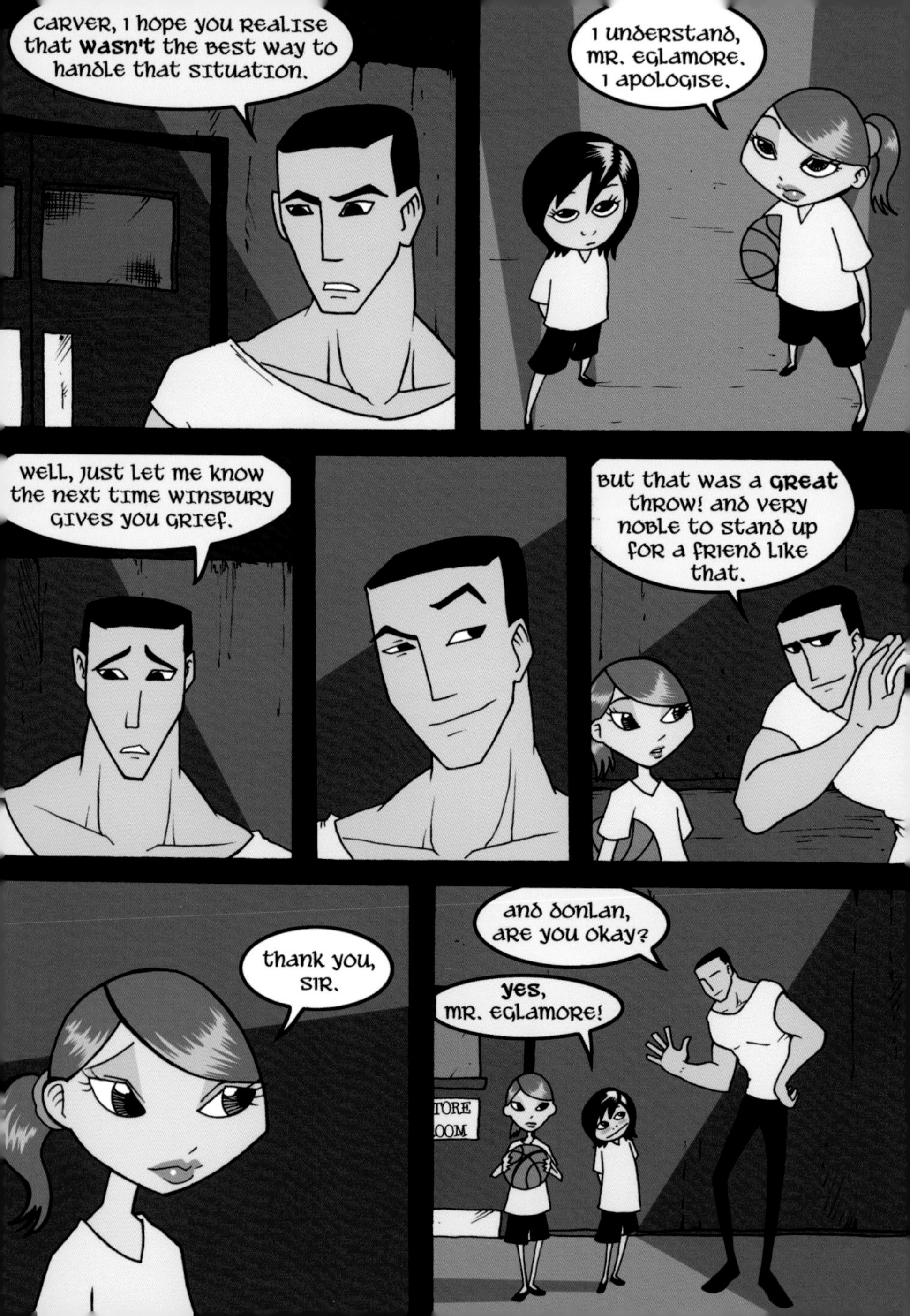
CARVER, I HOPE YOU REALISE THAT **WASN'T** THE BEST WAY TO HANDLE THAT SITUATION.
I UNDERSTAND, MR. EGLAMORE. I APOLOGISE.
WELL, JUST LET ME KNOW THE NEXT TIME WINSBURY GIVES YOU GRIEF.
BUT THAT WAS A **GREAT** THROW! AND VERY NOBLE TO STAND UP FOR A FRIEND LIKE THAT.
THANK YOU, SIR.
AND DONLAN, ARE YOU OKAY?
YES, MR. EGLAMORE!

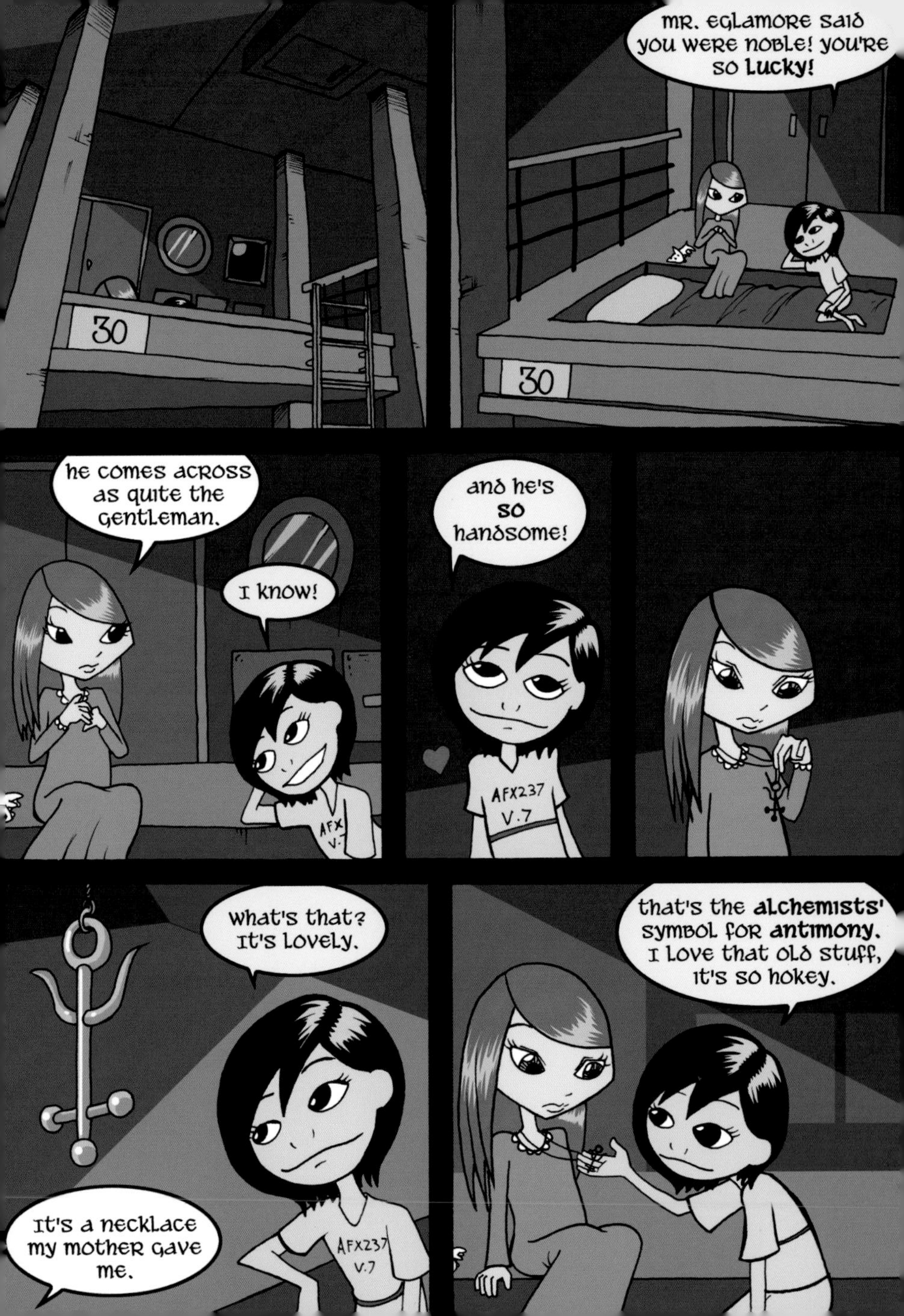
mr. eglamore said you were noble! you're so lucky!
he comes across as quite the gentleman.
I know!
and he's so handsome!
what's that? It's lovely.
It's a necklace my mother gave me.
that's the alchemists' symbol for antimony. I love that old stuff, it's so hokey.
30
30
AFX237 V.7
AFX V.7
AFX237 V.7

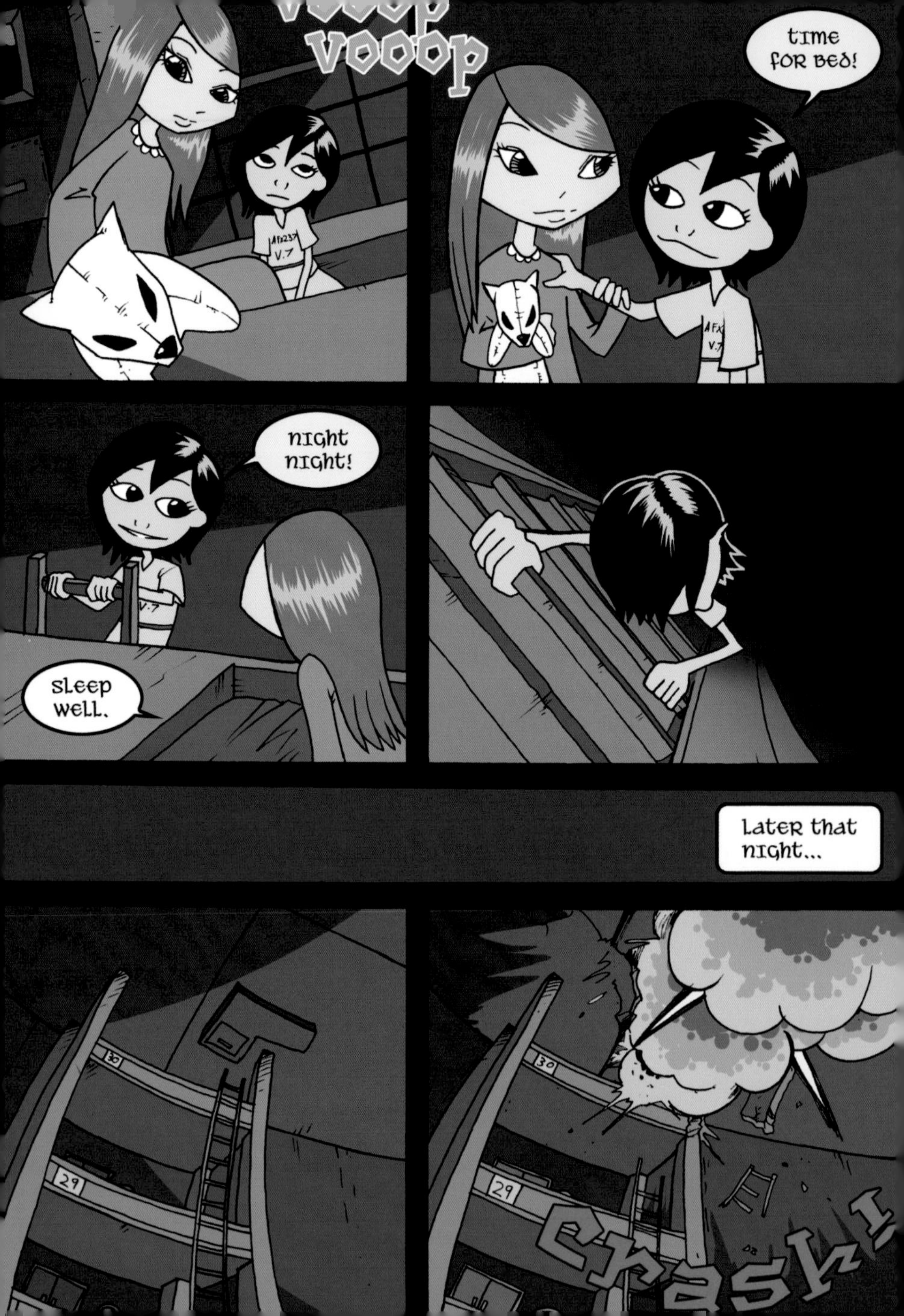
vooop
time for bed!
night night!
sleep well.
later that night...
crash!

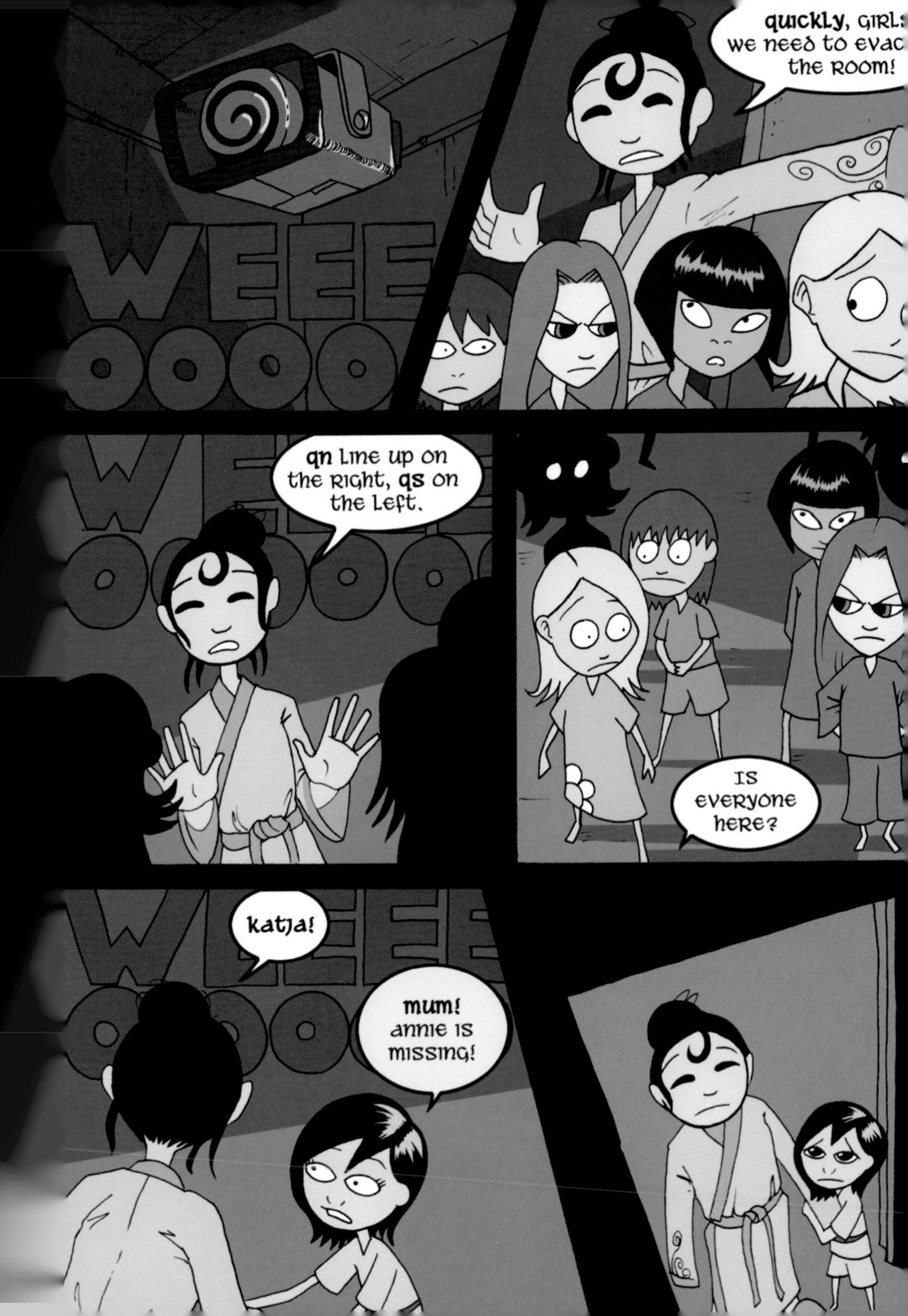
WEEE
OOOO
quickly, GIRL
we need to evac
the ROOM!
qn Line up on the Right, qs on the Left.
IS everyone here?
katja!
mum! annie is missing!

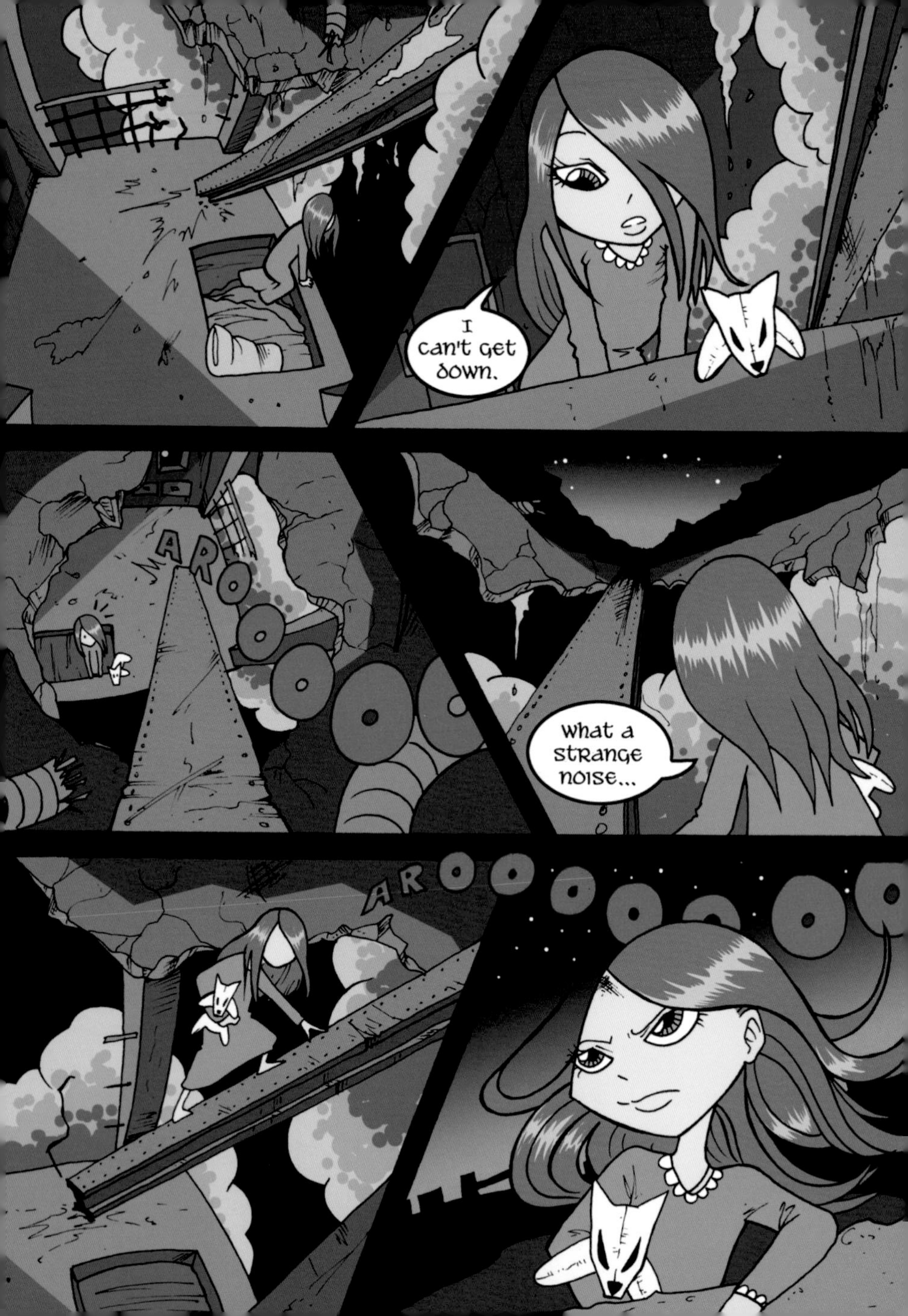
I can't get down.
AROOOOOO
What a strange noise...
AROOOOOOOO

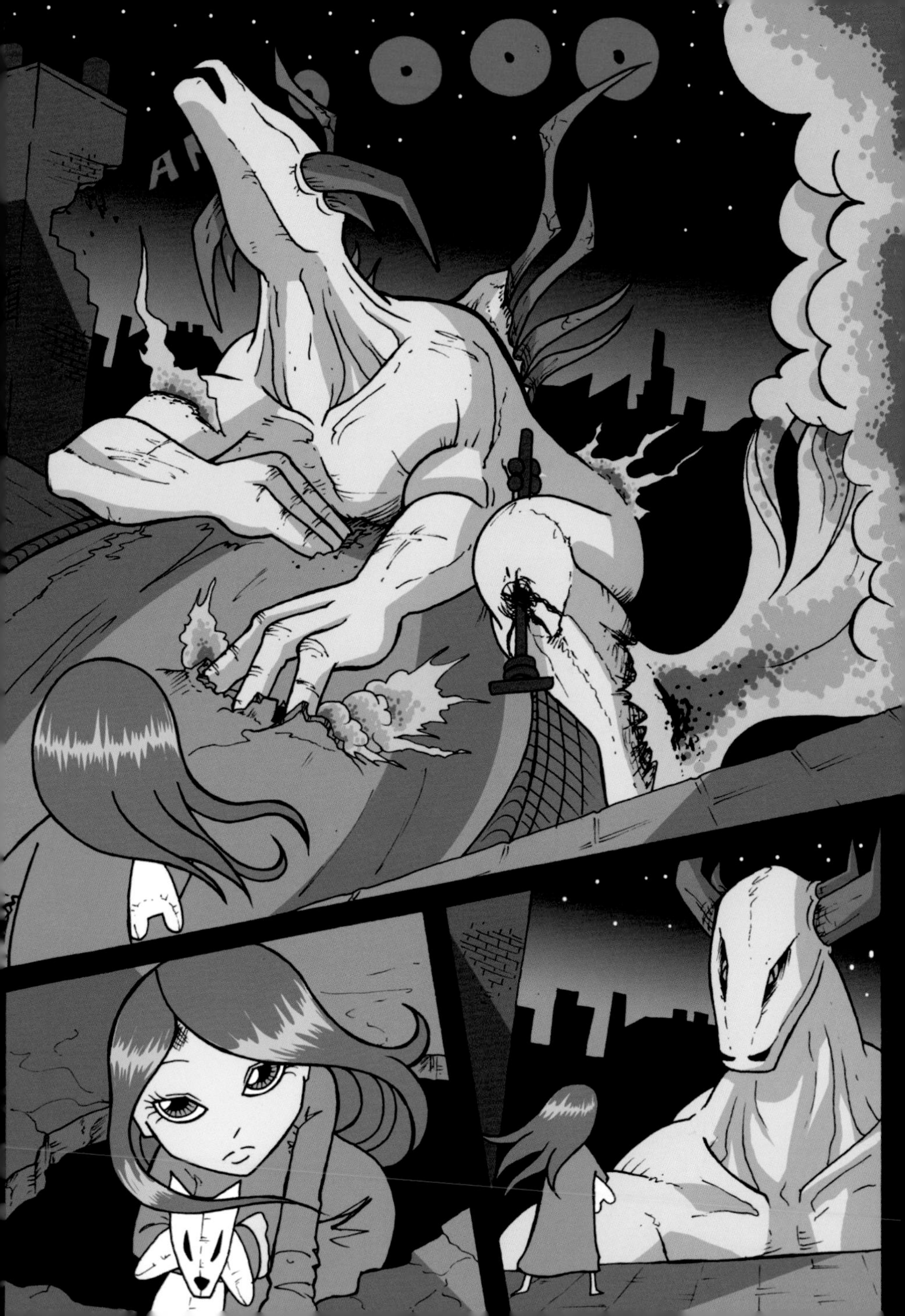
AN

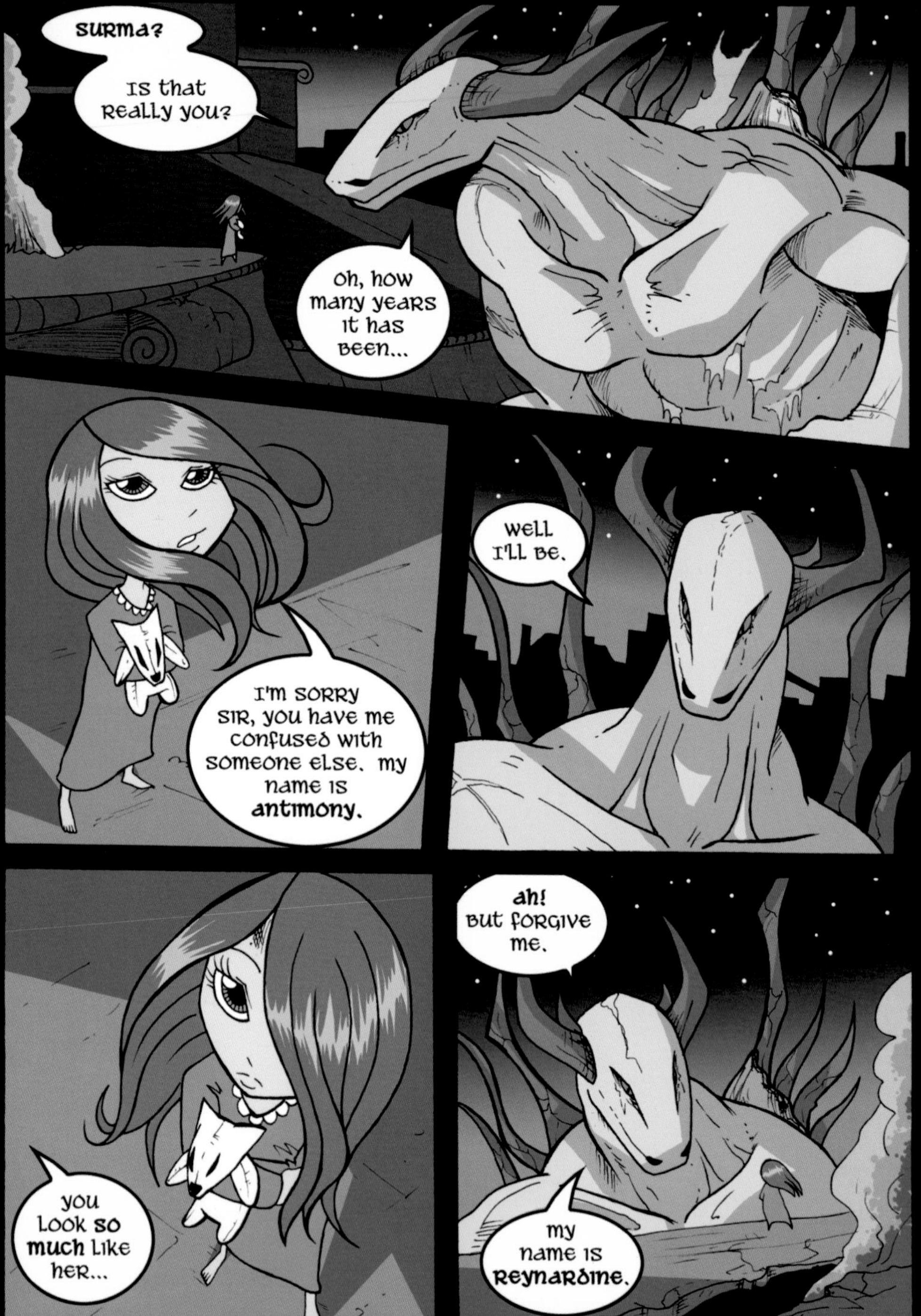
surma?
Is that Really you?
oh, how many years it has been...
I'm sorry sir, you have me confused with someone else. my name is **antimony.**
well I'll be.
you look **so much** like her...
ah! But forgive me.
my name is **Reynardine.**

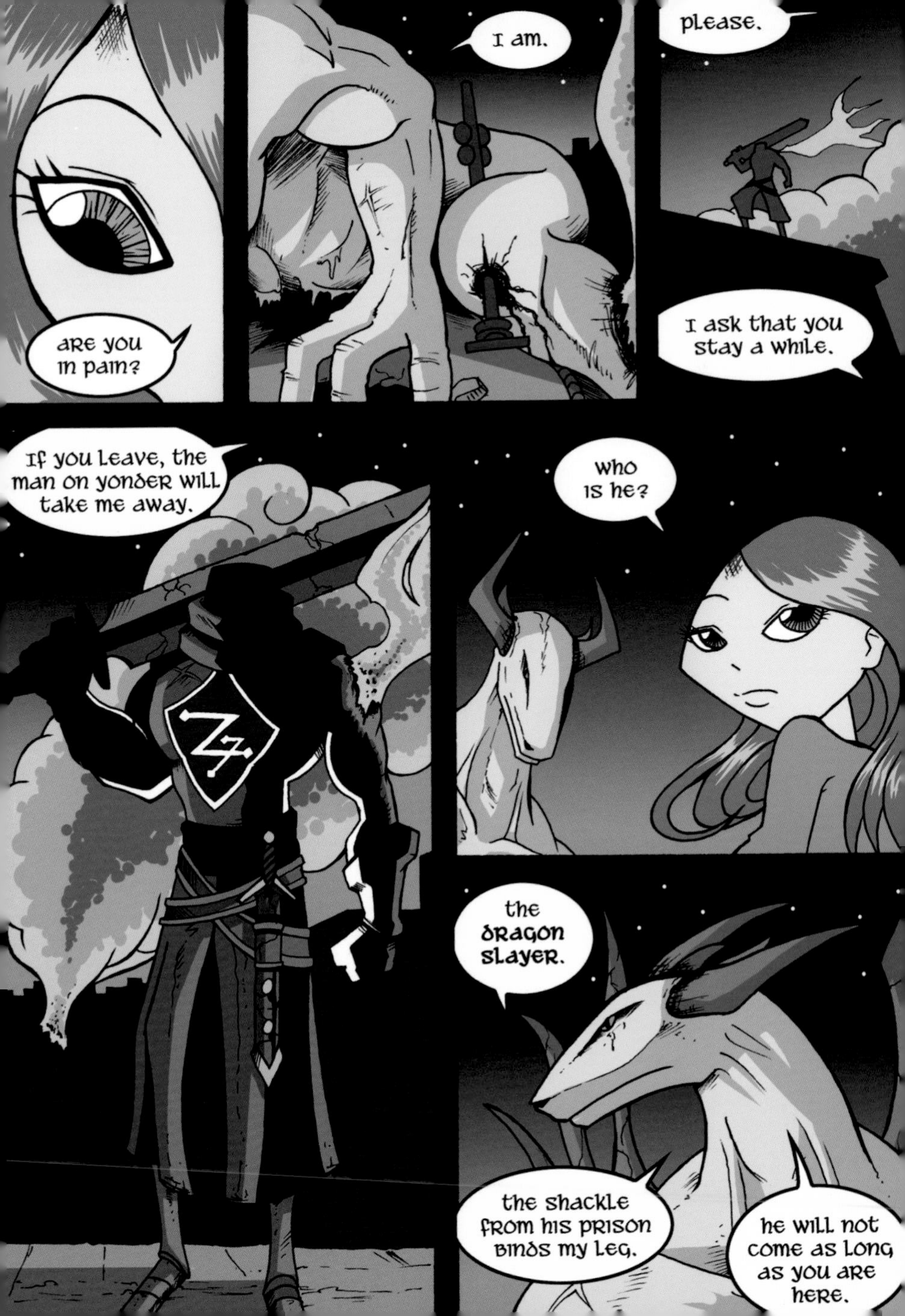
are you in pain?
I am.
please.
I ask that you stay a while.
If you leave, the man on yonder will take me away.
who is he?
the dragon slayer.
the shackle from his prison binds my leg.
he will not come as long as you are here.

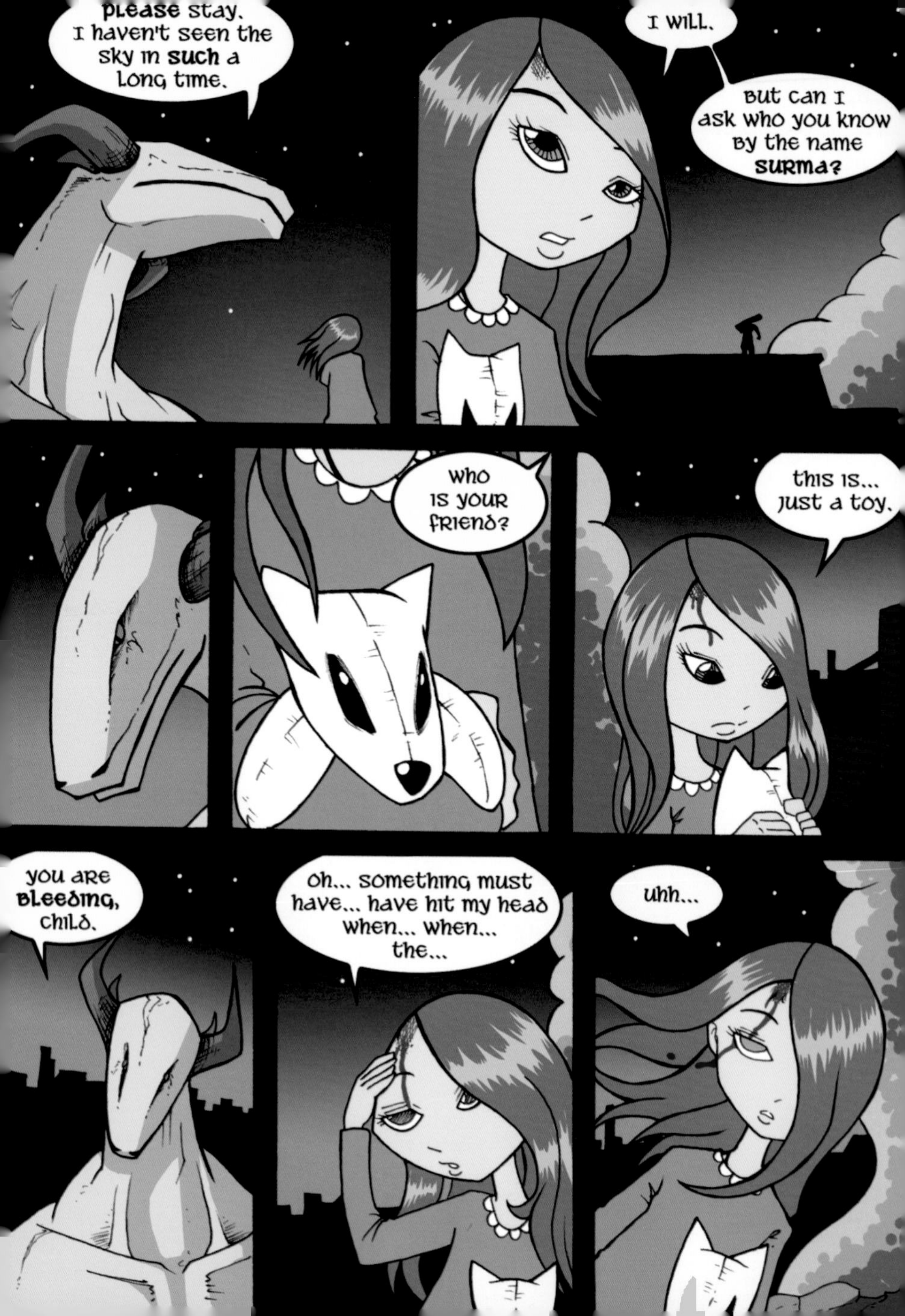
please stay. I haven't seen the sky in such a long time.
I will.
But can I ask who you know by the name SURMA?
who is your friend?
this is... just a toy.
you are bleeding, child.
oh... something must have... have hit my head when... when... the...
uhh...

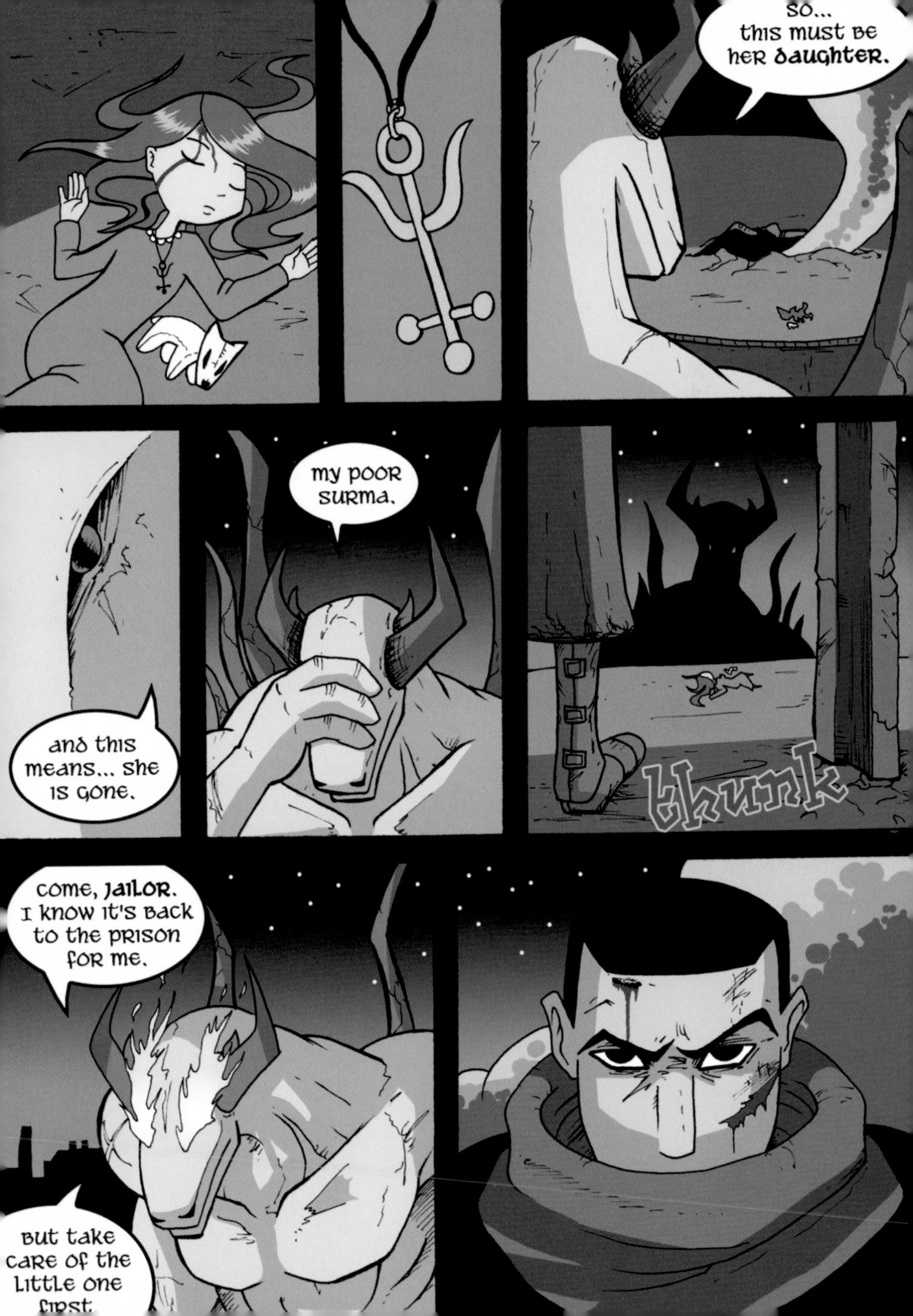
so...
this must be
her daughter.
my poor
surma.
and this
means... she
is gone.
thunk
come, jailor.
I know it's back
to the prison
for me.
but take
care of the
little one
first.

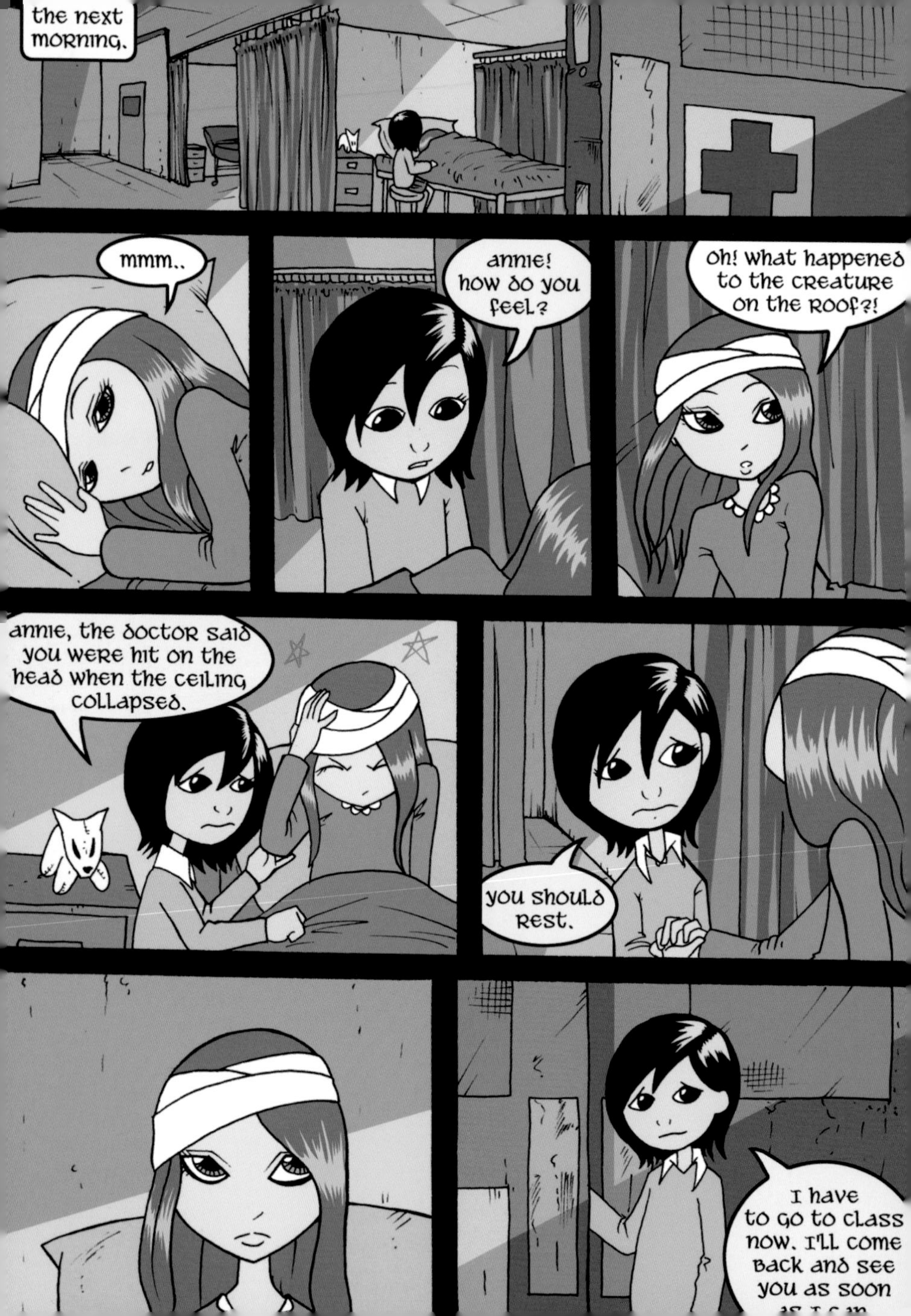
the next morning.
mmm..
annie! how do you feel?
oh! what happened to the creature on the roof?!
annie, the doctor said you were hit on the head when the ceiling collapsed.
you should rest.
I have to go to class now. I'll come back and see you as soon

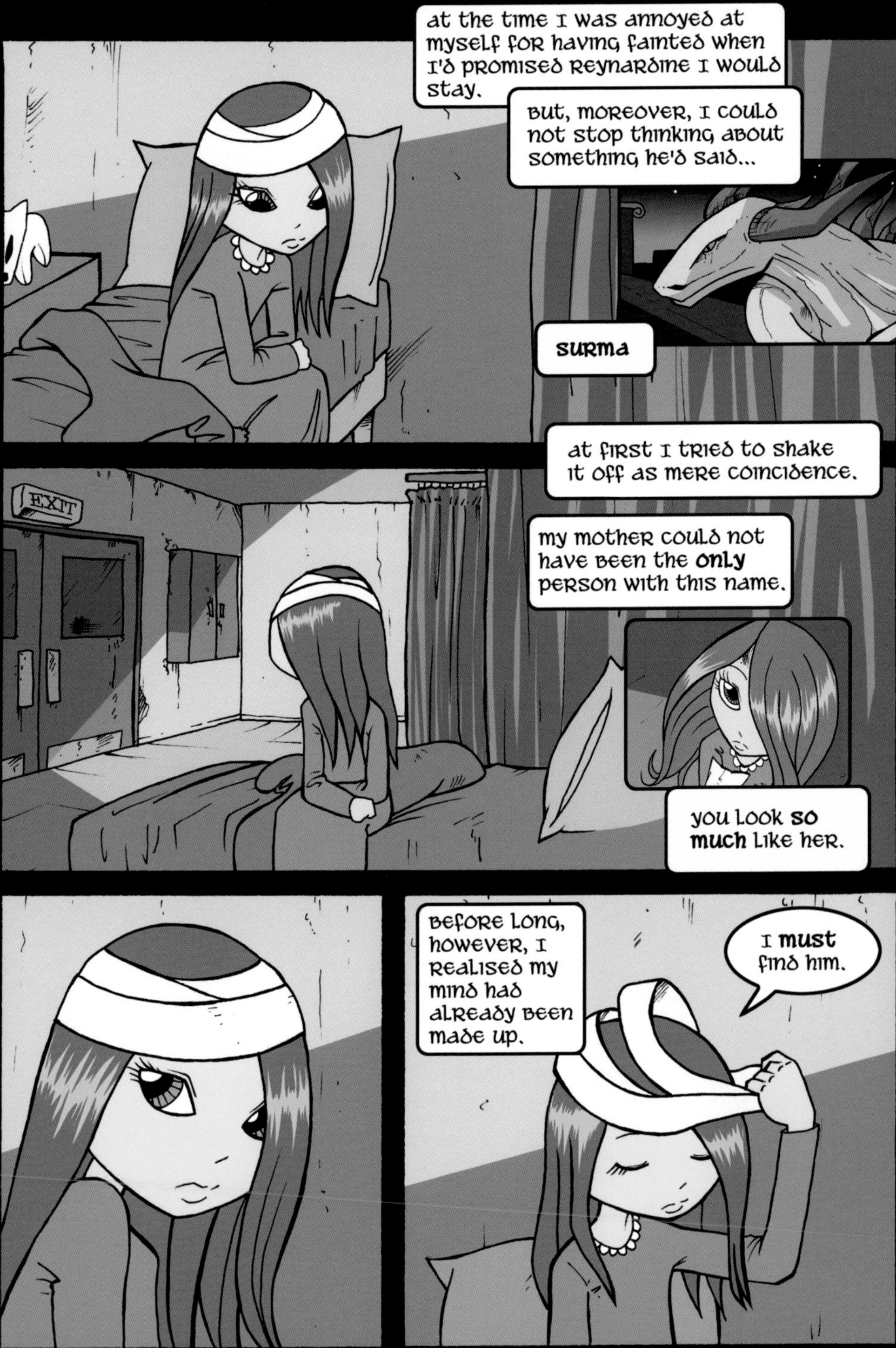
at the time I was annoyed at myself for having fainted when I'd promised Reynardine I would stay.
But, moreover, I could not stop thinking about something he'd said...
Surma
at first I tried to shake it off as mere coincidence.
EXIT
my mother could not have been the **only** person with this name.
you look **so much** like her.
Before long, however, I realised my mind had already been made up.
I **must** find him.

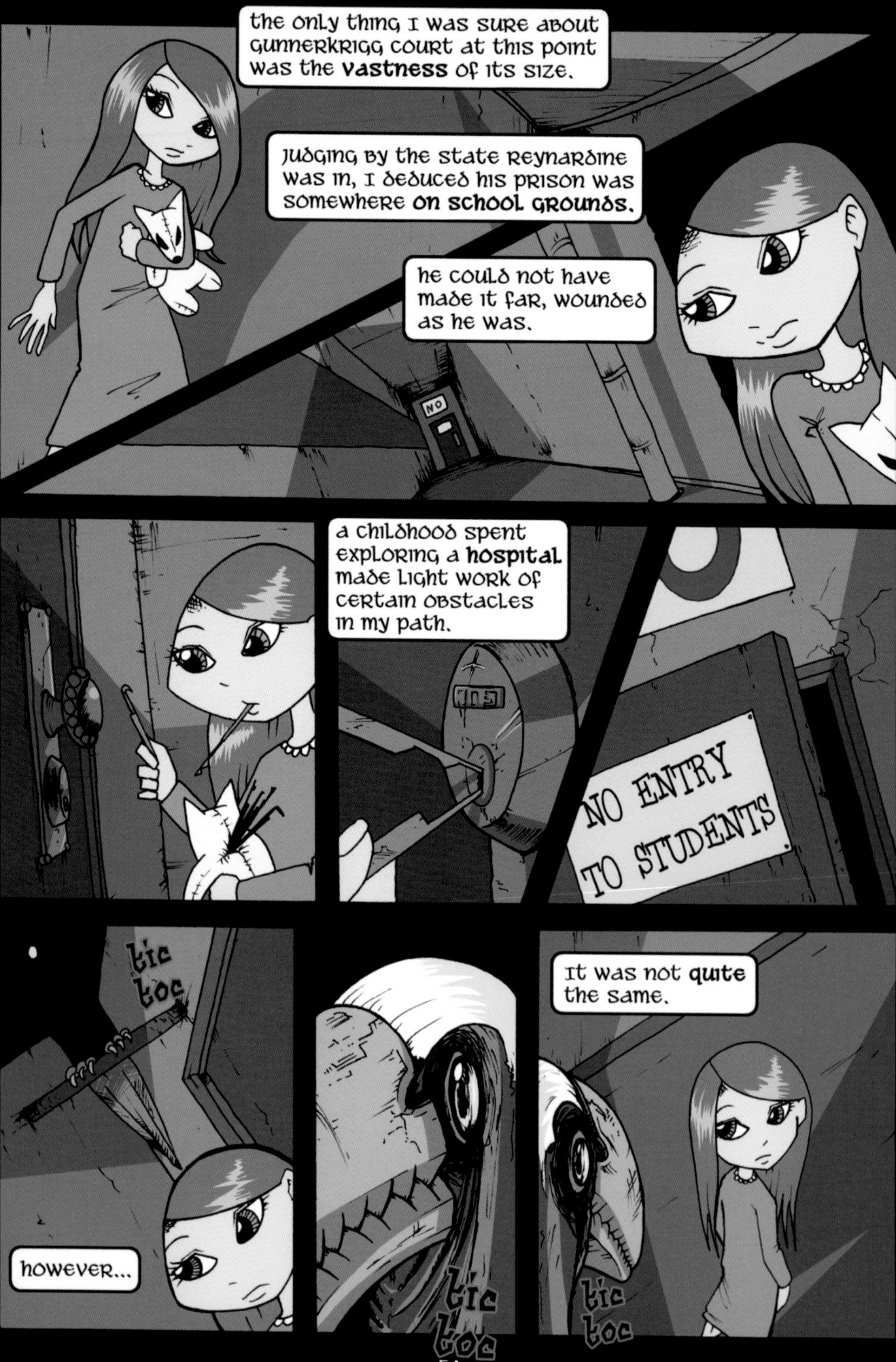
the only thing I was sure about Gunnerkrigg Court at this point was the **vastness** of its size.
Judging by the state Reynardine was in, I deduced his prison was somewhere **on school grounds.**
he could not have made it far, wounded as he was.
NO
a childhood spent exploring a **hospital** made light work of certain obstacles in my path.
NO ENTRY TO STUDENTS
tic toc
however...
tic toc
It was not **quite** the same.
tic toc

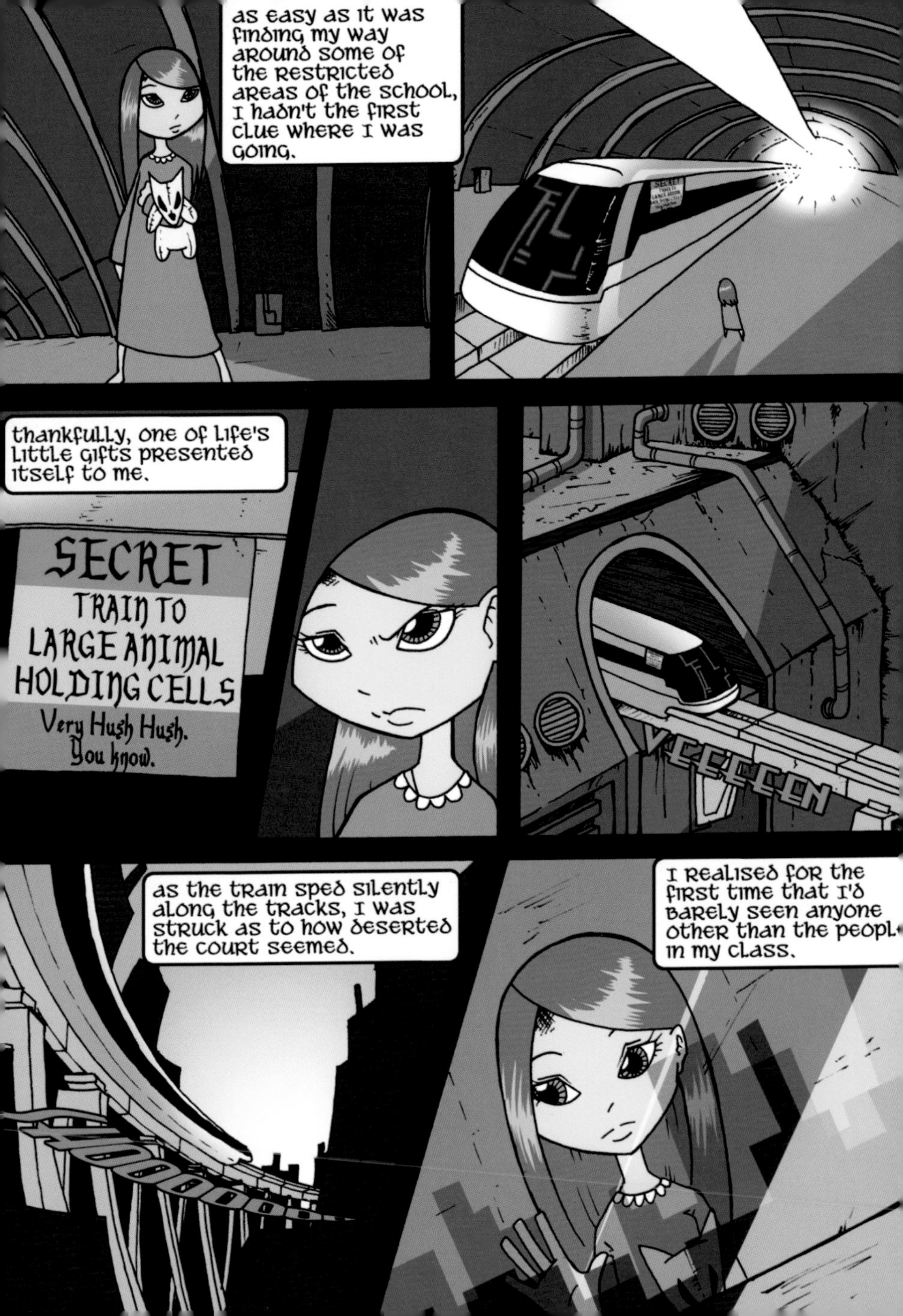
as easy as it was finding my way around some of the restricted areas of the school, I hadn't the first clue where I was going.
thankfully, one of life's little gifts presented itself to me.
SECRET
TRAIN TO LARGE ANIMAL HOLDING CELLS
Very Hush Hush. You know.
as the train sped silently along the tracks, I was struck as to how deserted the court seemed.
I realised for the first time that I'd barely seen anyone other than the peopl
in my class.

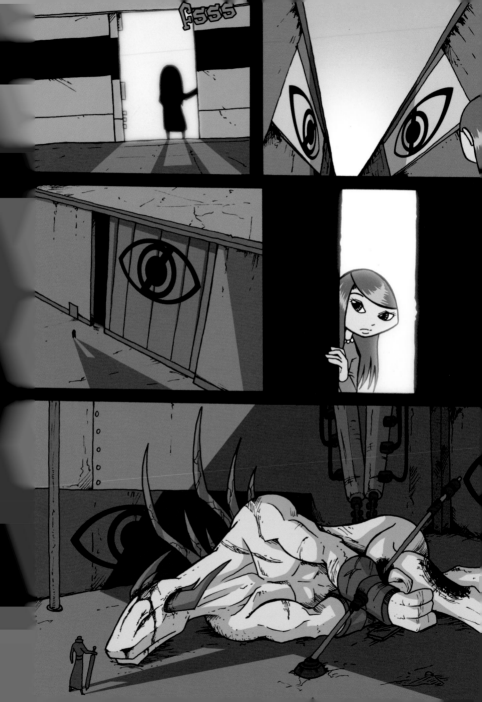

FSSS

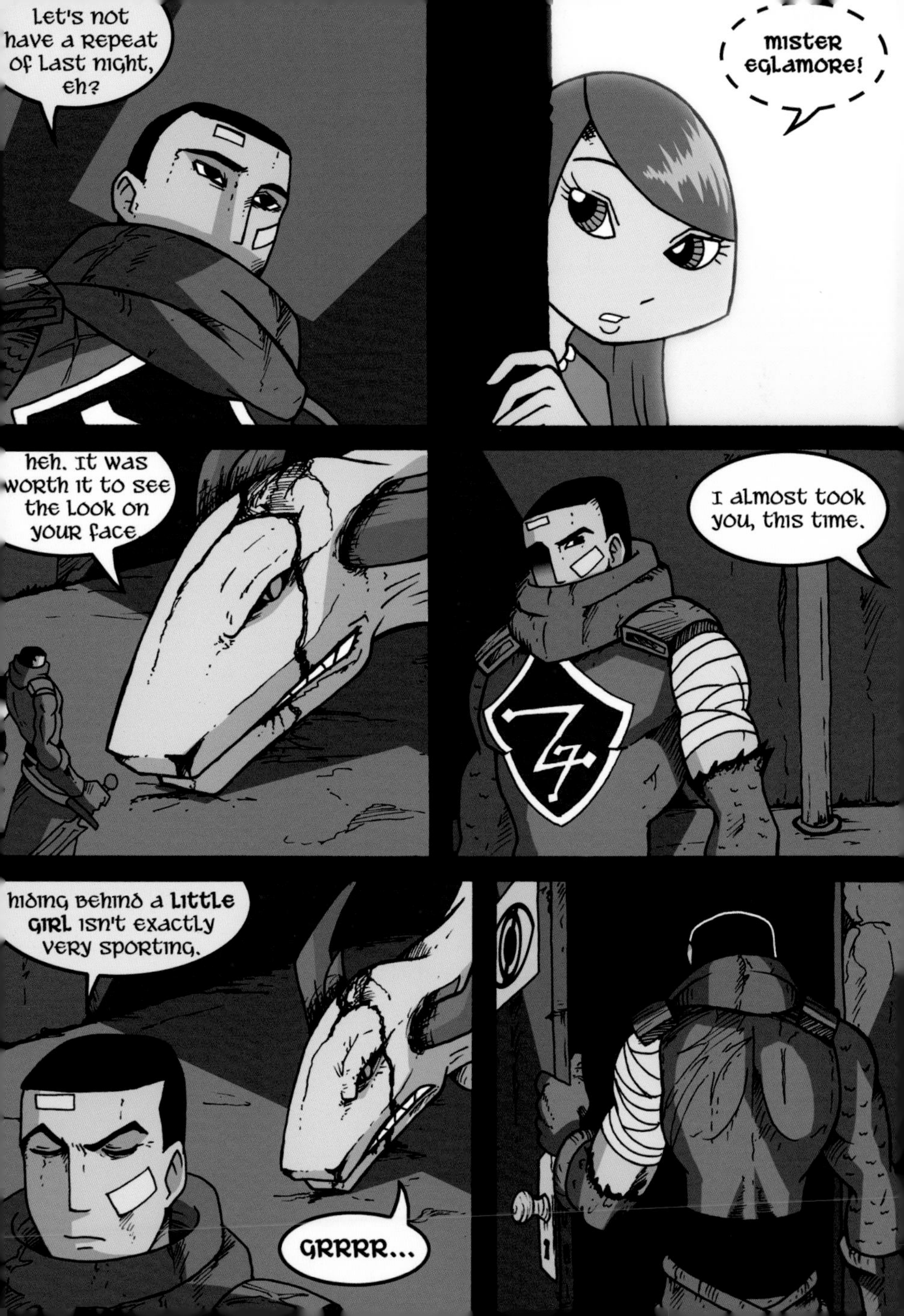
Let's not have a repeat of last night, eh?
mister eglamore!
heh. It was worth it to see the look on your face
I almost took you, this time.
hiding behind a little girl isn't exactly very sporting.
GRRRR...

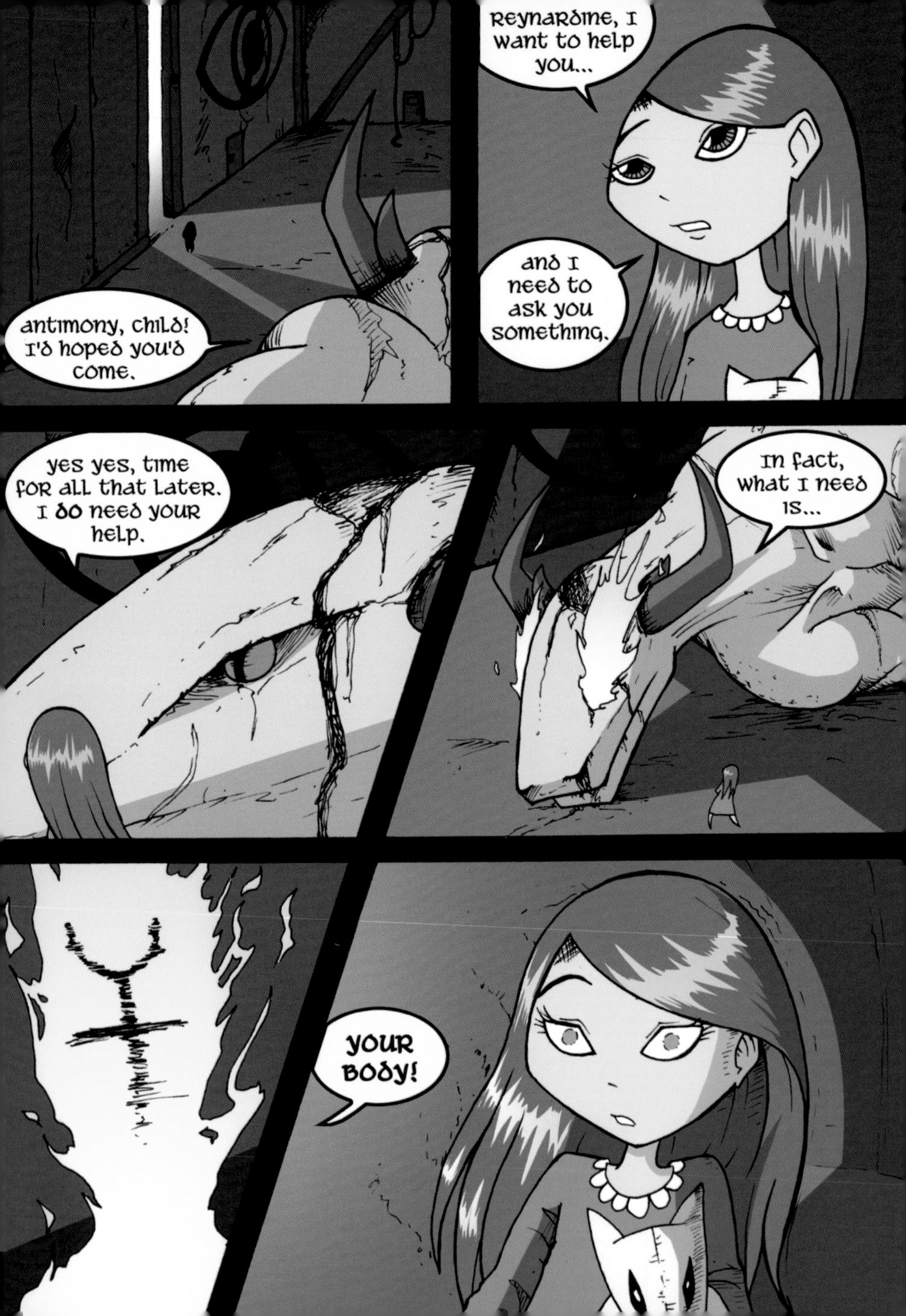
antimony, child! I'd hoped you'd come.
Reynardine, I want to help you...
and I need to ask you something.
yes yes, time for all that later. I do need your help.
In fact, what I need is...
YOUR BODY!

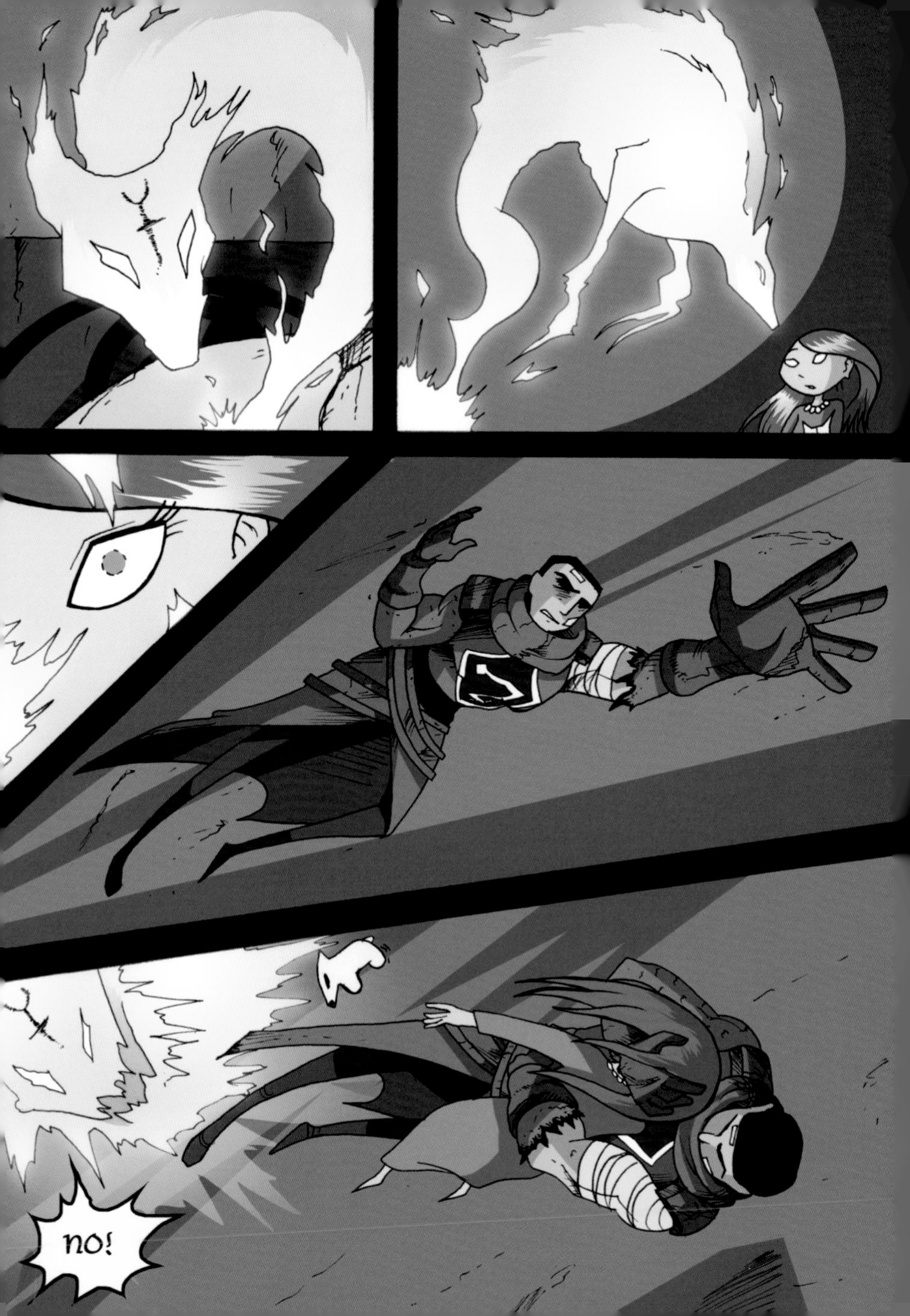
no!

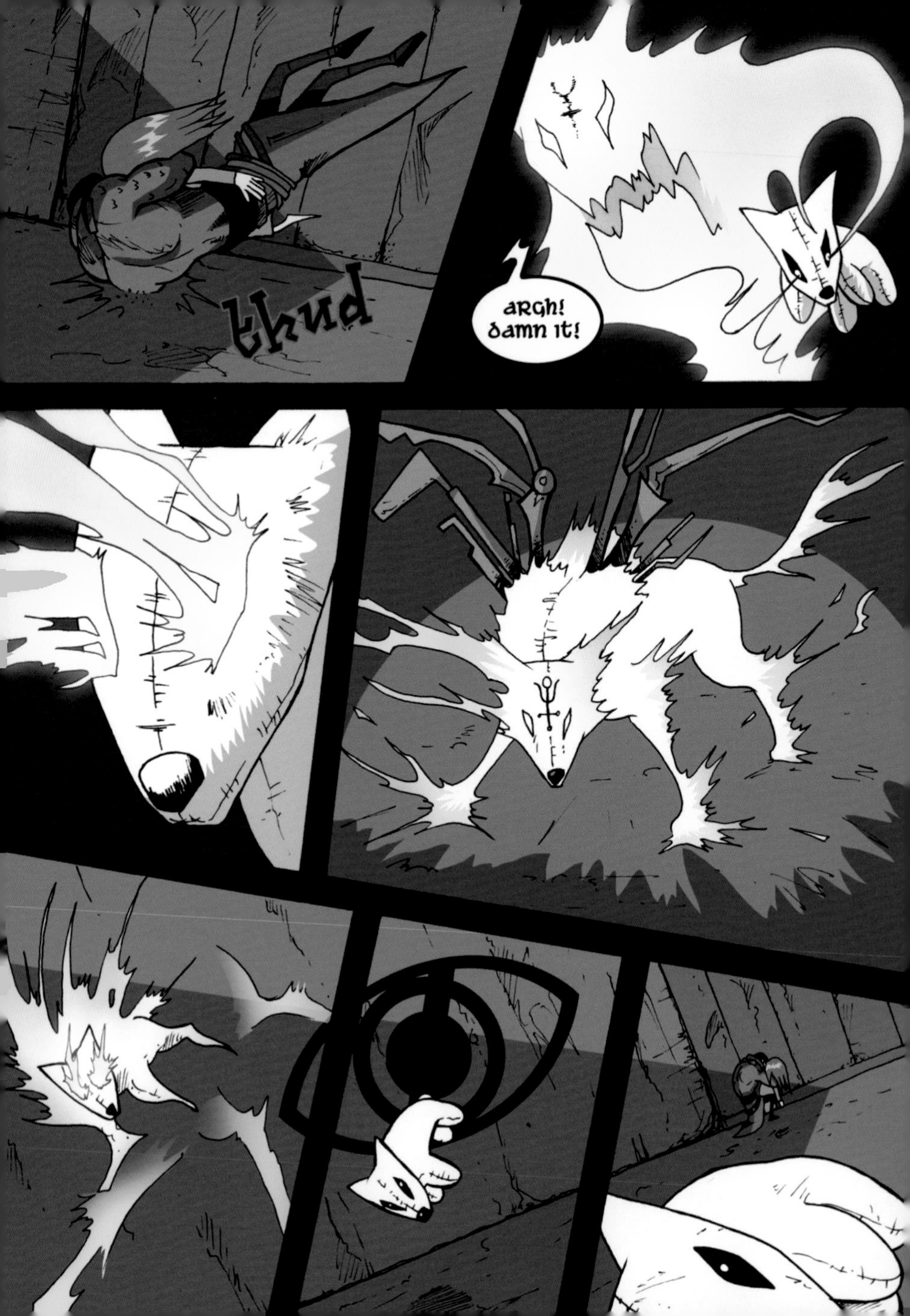
thud
argh! damn it!

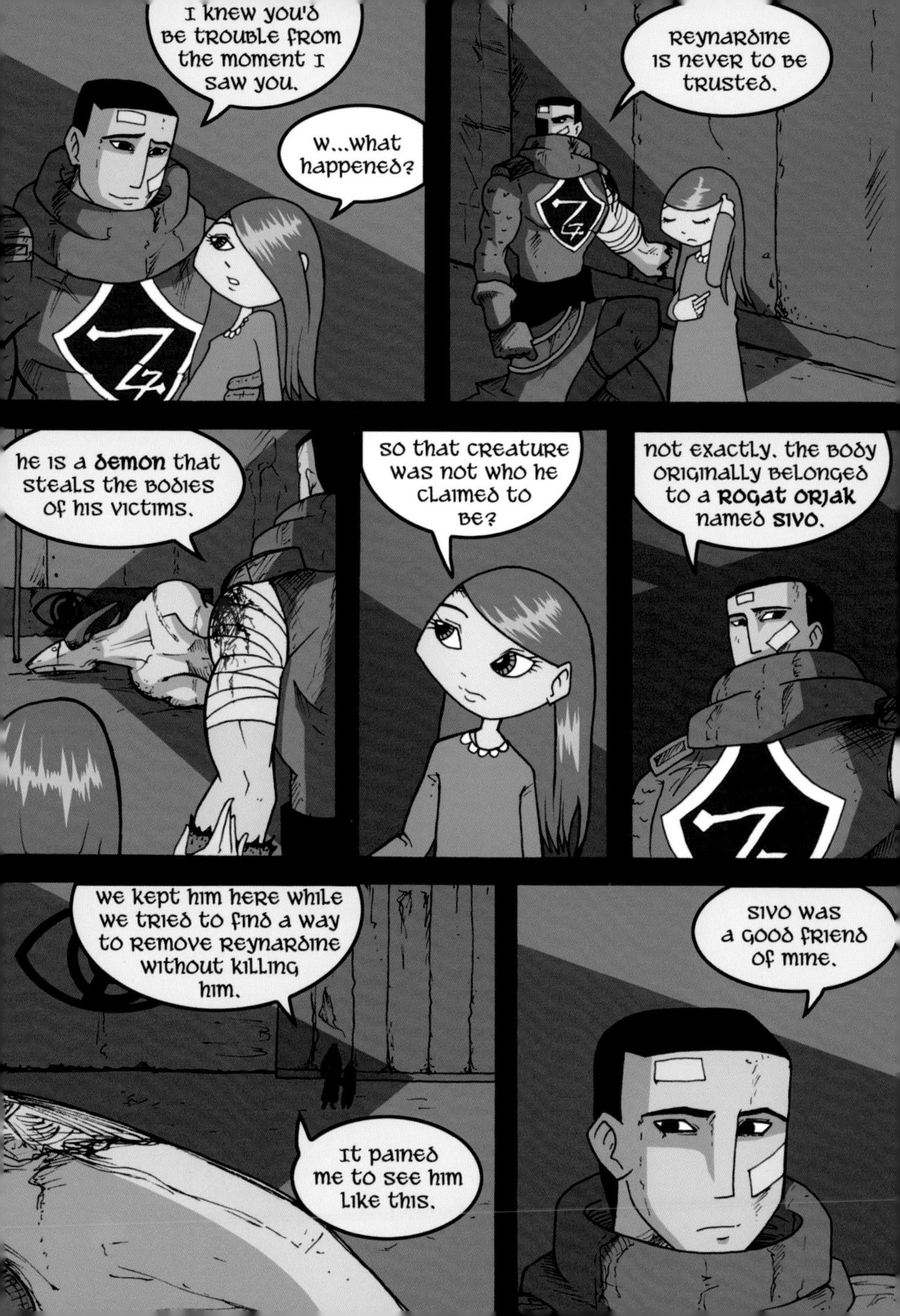
I knew you'd be trouble from the moment I saw you.
w...what happened?
Reynardine is never to be trusted.
he is a demon that steals the bodies of his victims.
so that creature was not who he claimed to be?
not exactly. the body originally belonged to a ROGAT ORJAK named SIVO.
we kept him here while we tried to find a way to remove Reynardine without killing him.
It pained me to see him like this.
SIVO was a good friend of mine.

IT'S BETTER FOR HIM THIS WAY. HE CAN FINALLY REST IN PEACE.

WHAT HAPPENED TO REYNARDINE?

WITHOUT ANOTHER BODY TO JUMP IN TO, HE MUST HAVE DIED AS WELL. I CAN'T SAY I'M SORRY.

WHEN HE LEAVES A BODY, IT DIES. WE HOPED TO FIND A WAY TO STOP THIS... BUT IT'S BEEN OVER 5 YEARS.

THEN... YOU **SAVED** MY LIFE.

DON'T WORRY ABOUT IT.

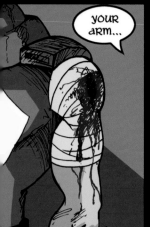

YOUR ARM...

IT'S FINE. WE SHOULD GET YOU BACK.

ZBOGOM, STARI PRIJATELJ.

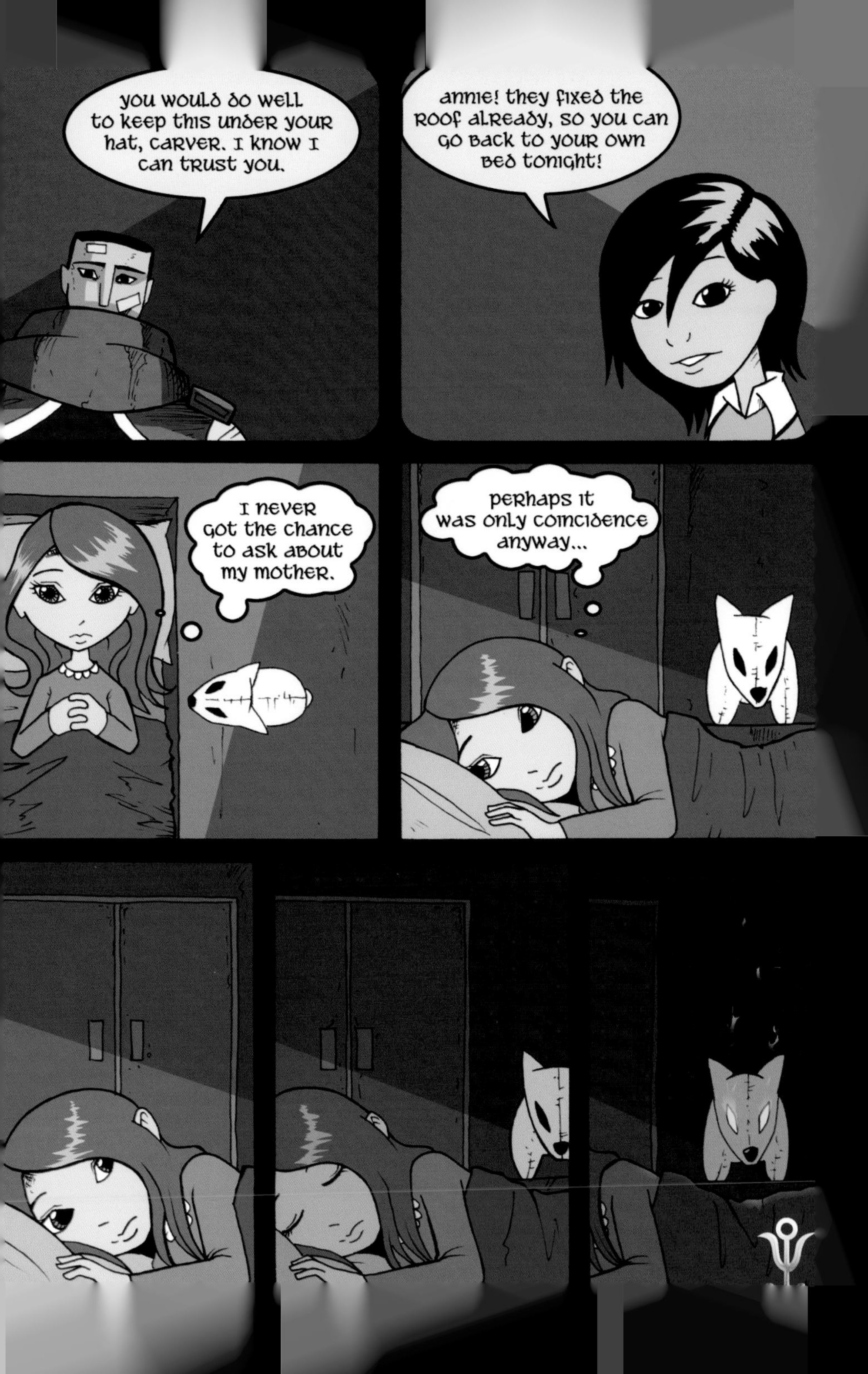
you would do well to keep this under your hat, carver. I know I can trust you.
annie! they fixed the roof already, so you can go back to your own bed tonight!
I never got the chance to ask about my mother.
perhaps it was only coincidence anyway...

Rogat Orjak
(Horned Giant)

Originally discovered in the Bovec mountains on the Slovenian/Italian border, the **Rogat Orjak** is native to most European regions. Rarely seen, these retiring creatures feed mainly on sheep and mountain goats. Sir Eugene Gould is credited with first human contact.

Possible depiction of an Orjak found, amongst others, near a cave in Trabzon, Turkey.

'I came upon [the creature] and he looked me square in the eyes, blood from a Bighorn dripping from its mouth. I was surprised, and relieved, when he offered me a leg.' - E. Gould.

Possessing a high level of intelligence and the ability to speak, the Orjak is generally found to be mild tempered and non-confrontational despite their large size. Upper torso musculature is surprisingly similar to human physique.

First reports of the Orjak date back to early 11th century while images of similar creatures predate these by many centuries.

A tooth currently on display at the Palaeontological Institute, Russian Academy of Science, Moscow. Originally procured by E.Gould. Later lost in a Poker match in Kursk.

'We like to keep a low profile. Best not to draw attention to ourselves, unlike those [common dragons]. And where are they now, eh?' - Kos, Orjak.

Sketch from E.Gould's field notebook.

Sketch from E.Gould's field notebook.

Possible depiction of an Orjak in a 16th Century manuscript.

Gunnerkrigg Court

Chapter 4:

Not Very Scary

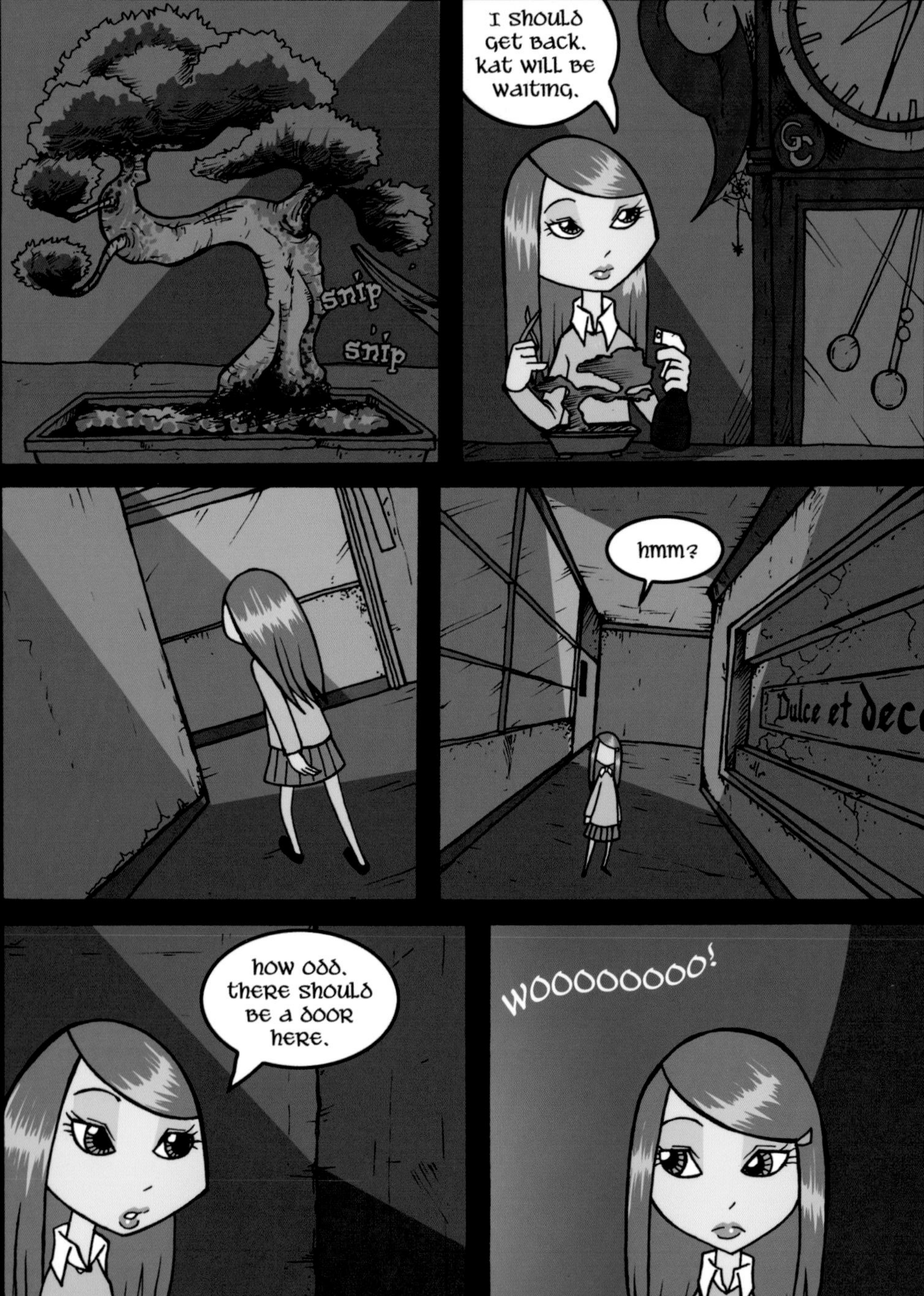
snip
snip
I should get back. kat will be waiting.
hmm?
Dulce et dec
how odd. there should be a door here.
WOOOOOOOO!

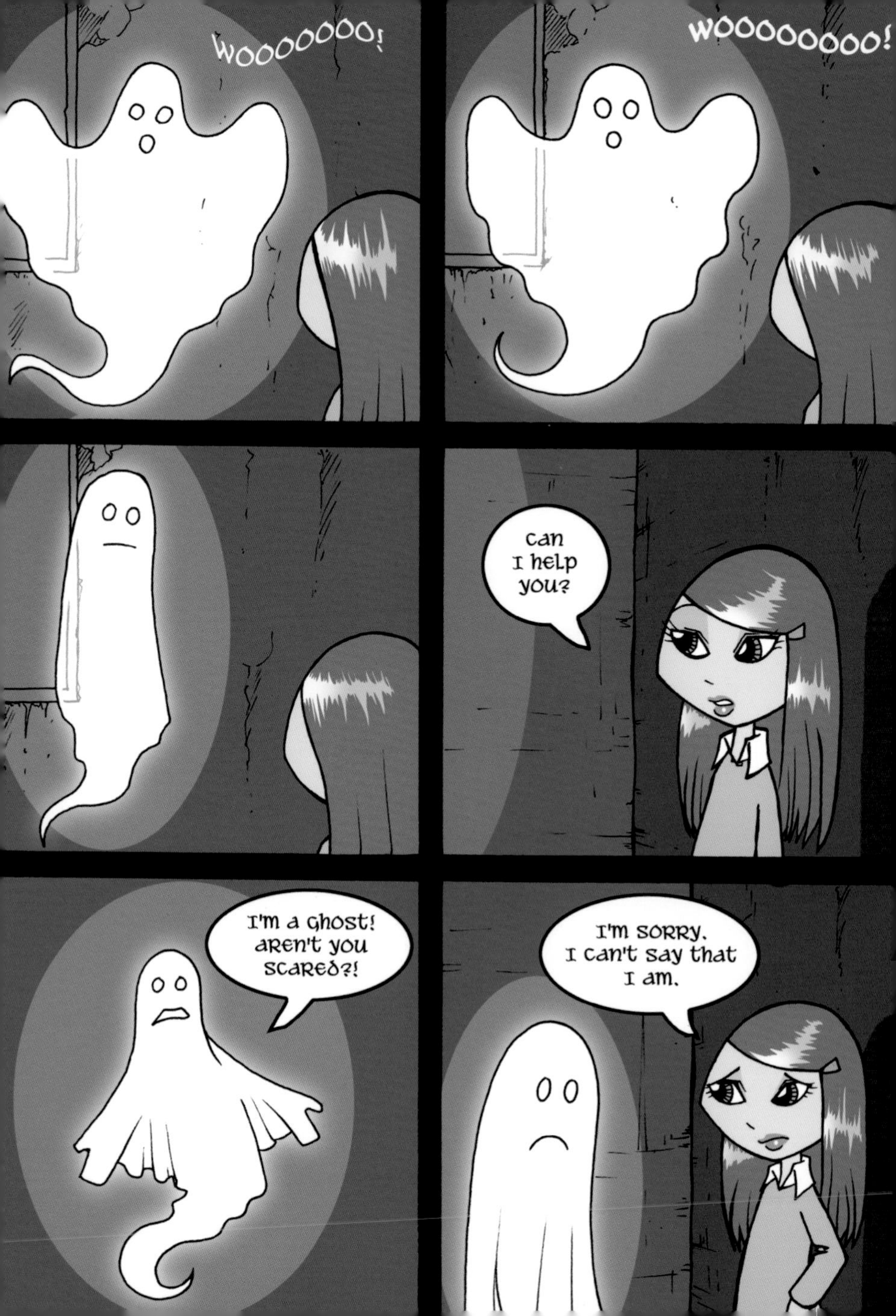
WOOOOOOO!
WOOOOOOOOO!
CAN I HELP YOU?
I'M A GHOST! AREN'T YOU SCARED?!
I'M SORRY. I CAN'T SAY THAT I AM.

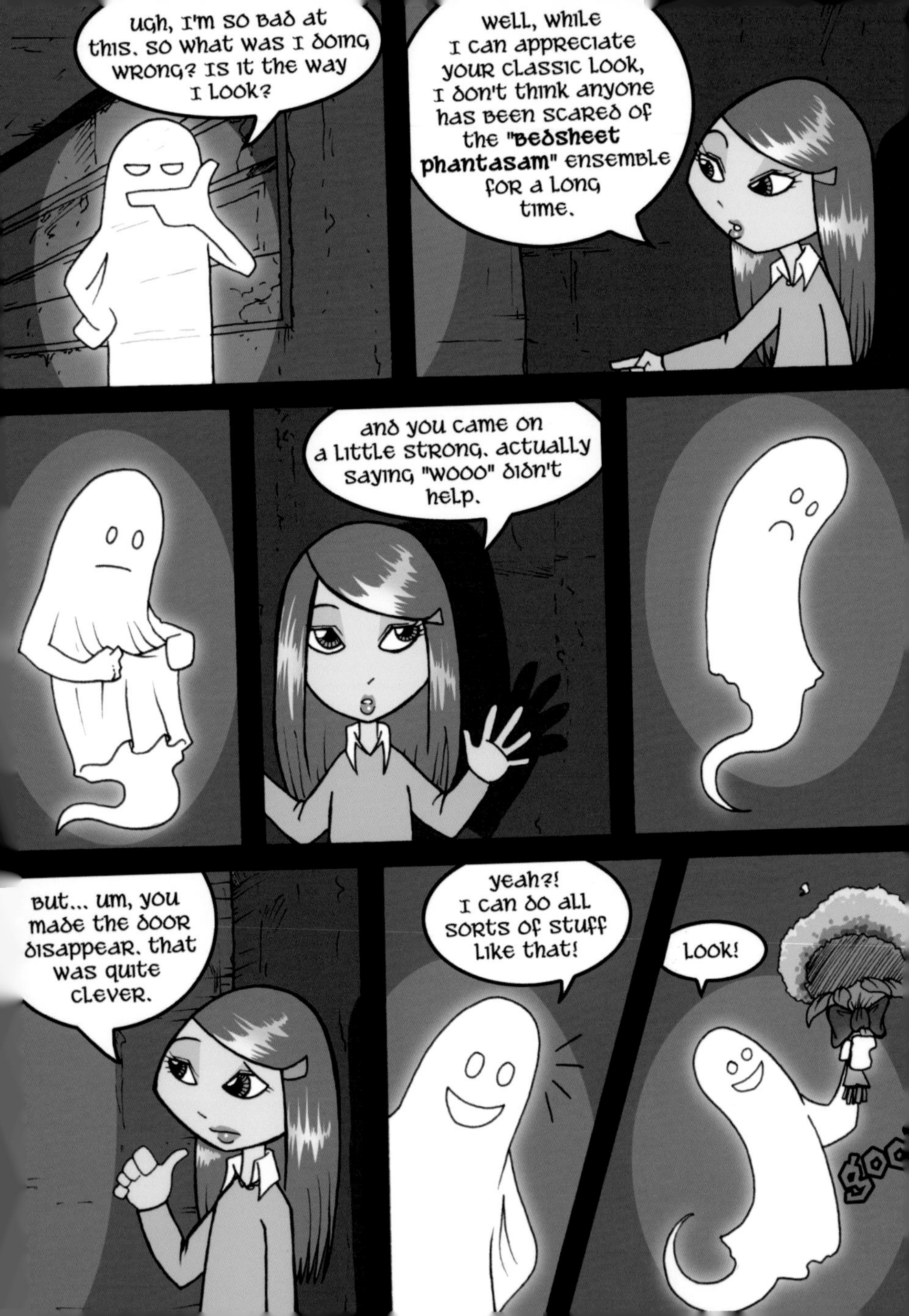
ugh, I'm so bad at this. so what was I doing wrong? is it the way I look?
well, while I can appreciate your classic look, I don't think anyone has been scared of the "bedsheet phantasam" ensemble for a long time.
and you came on a little strong. actually saying "WOOO" didn't help.
but... um, you made the door disappear. that was quite clever.
yeah?! I can do all sorts of stuff like that!
LOOK!

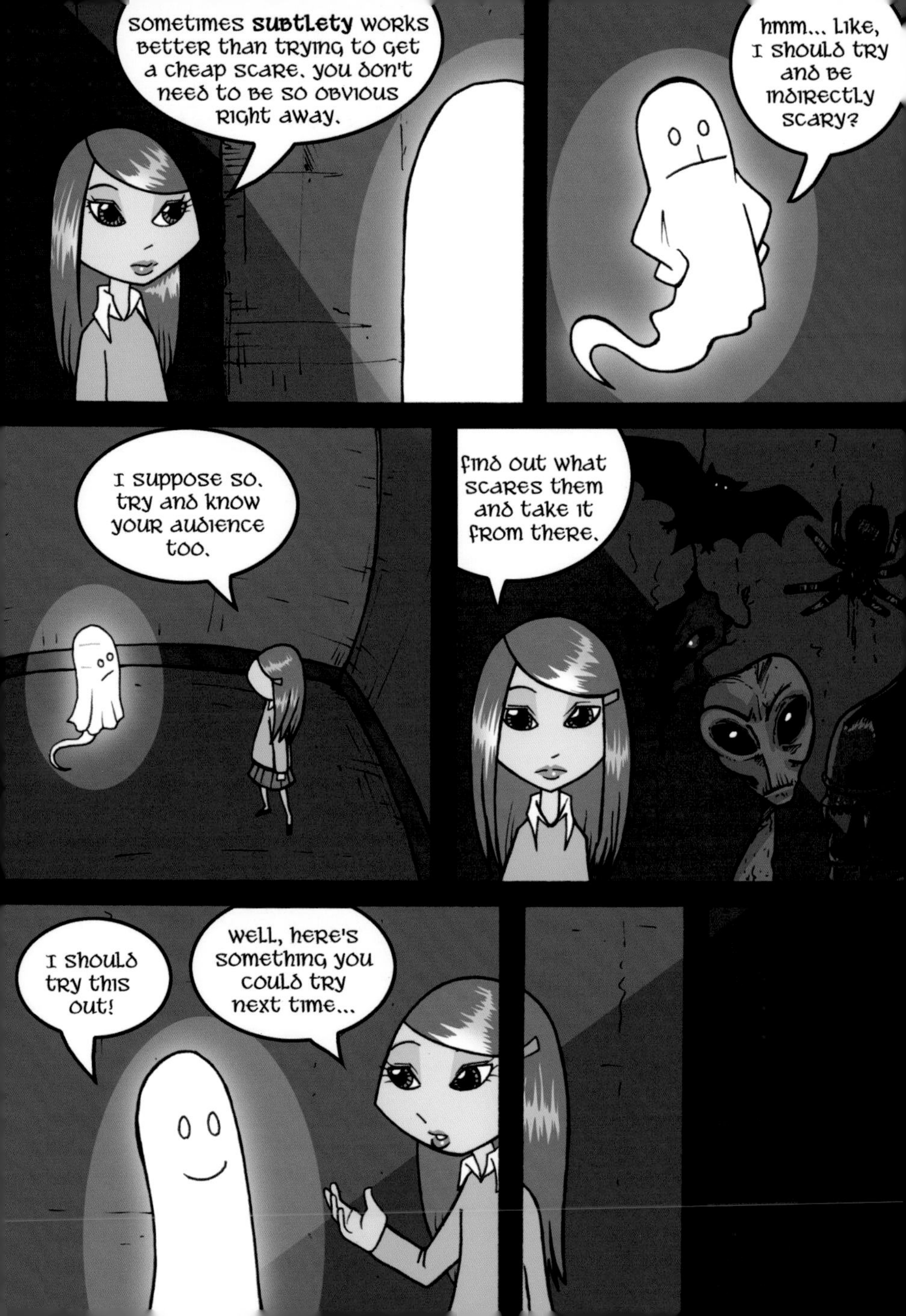
sometimes **subtlety** works better than trying to get a cheap scare. you don't need to be so obvious right away.
hmm... like, I should try and be indirectly scary?
I suppose so. try and know your audience too.
find out what scares them and take it from there.
I should try this out!
well, here's something you could try next time...

¡Oh!

¿PERO, ∂onde está la puerta?

¿eh?

¡je je! un GLOBO.

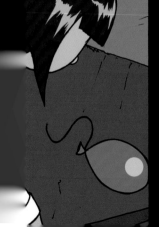

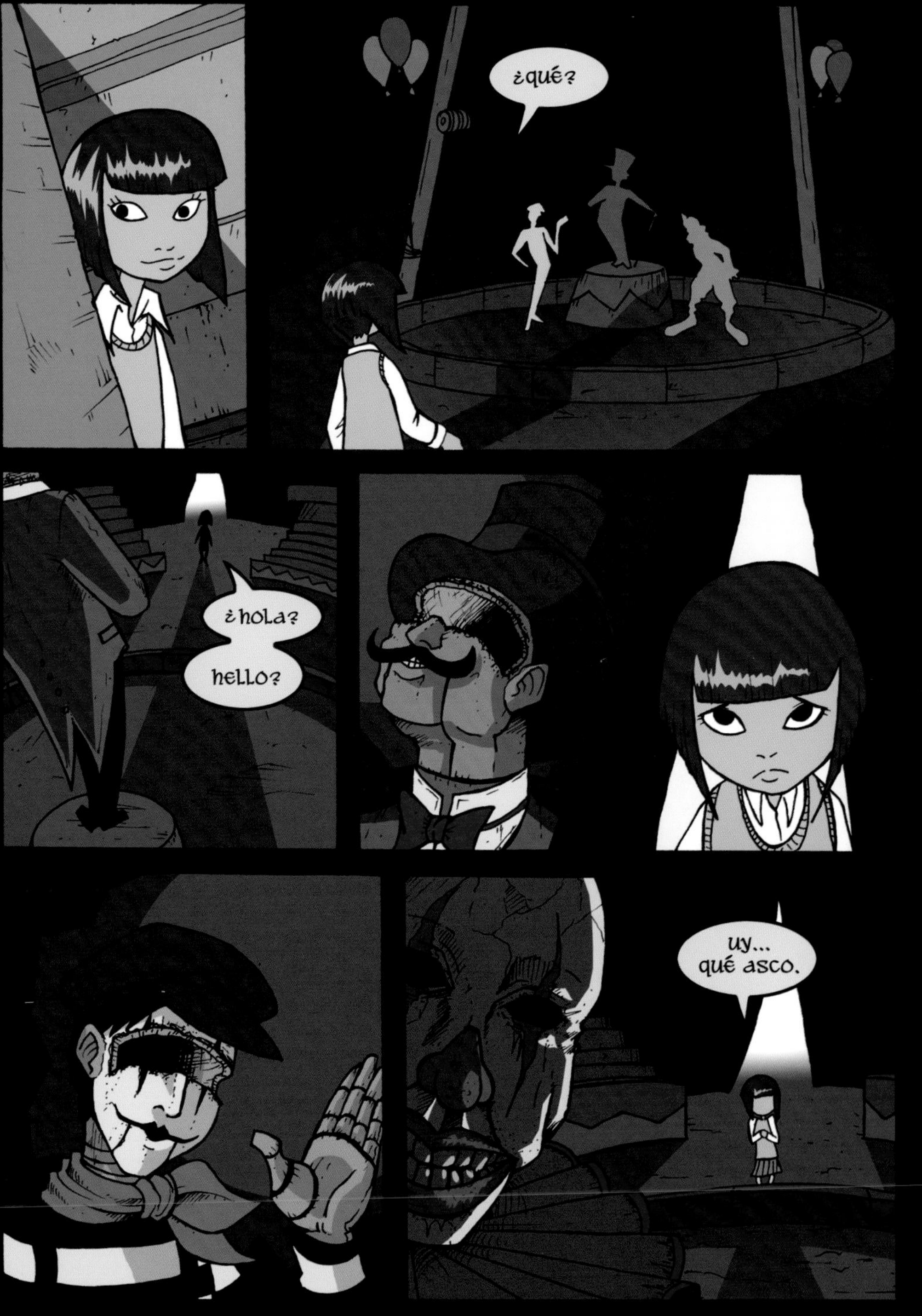
¿qué?
¿hola?
hello?
uy...
qué asco.

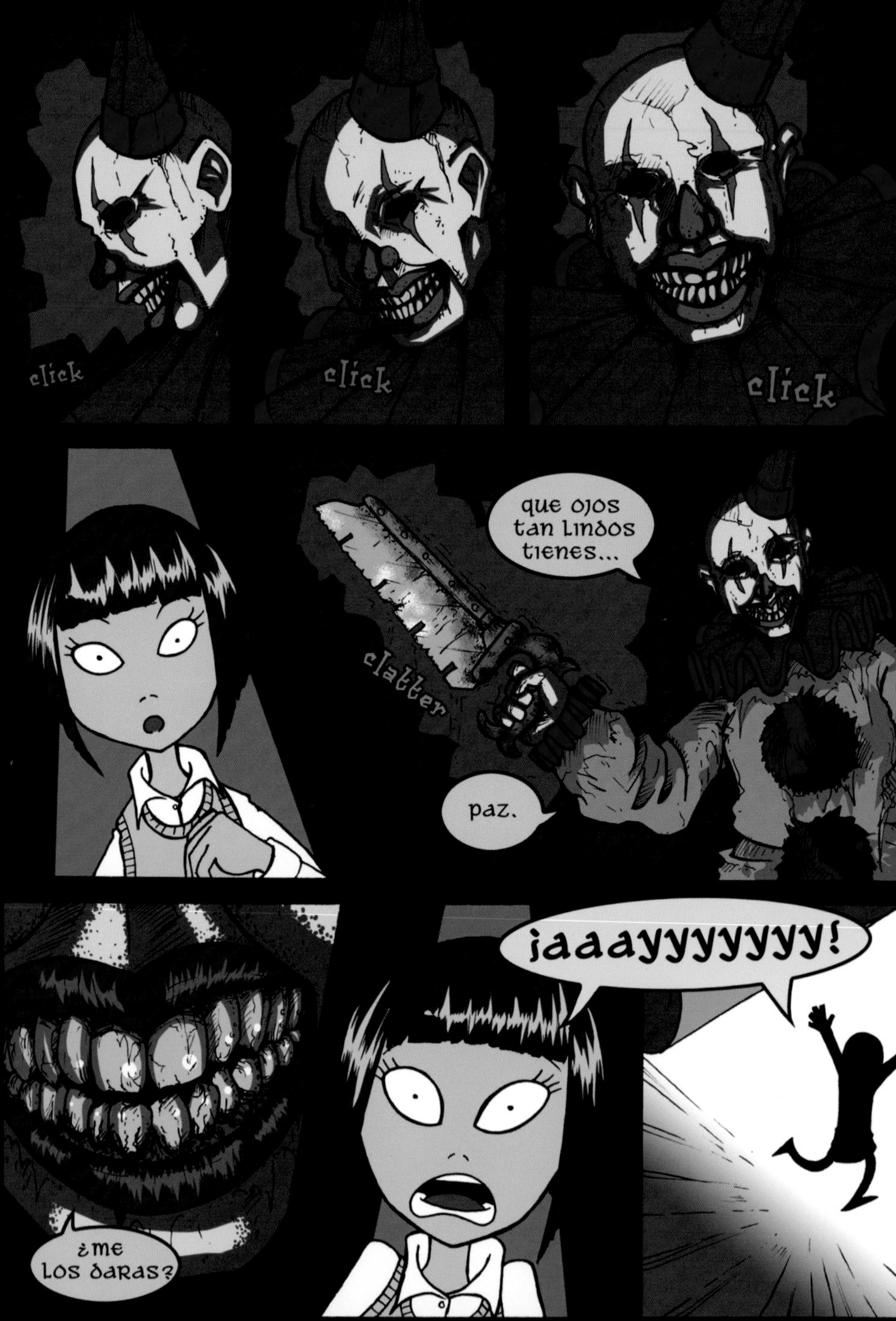
click
click
click
que ojos tan lindos tienes...
clatter
paz.
¿me los daras?
¡aaayyyyyyy!

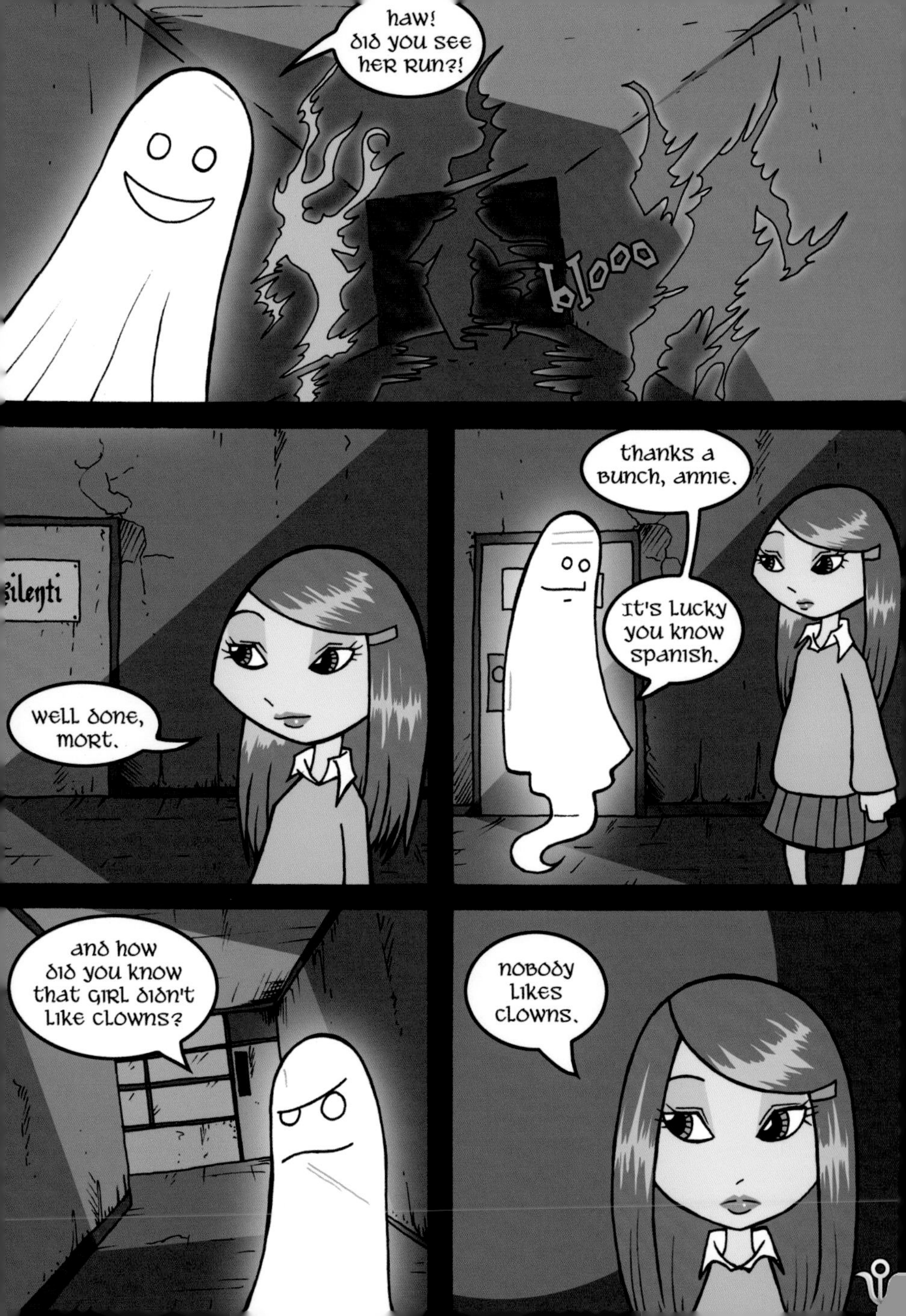
haw! did you see her run?!
blooo
silenti
well done, mort.
thanks a bunch, annie.
it's lucky you know spanish.
and how did you know that girl didn't like clowns?
nobody likes clowns.

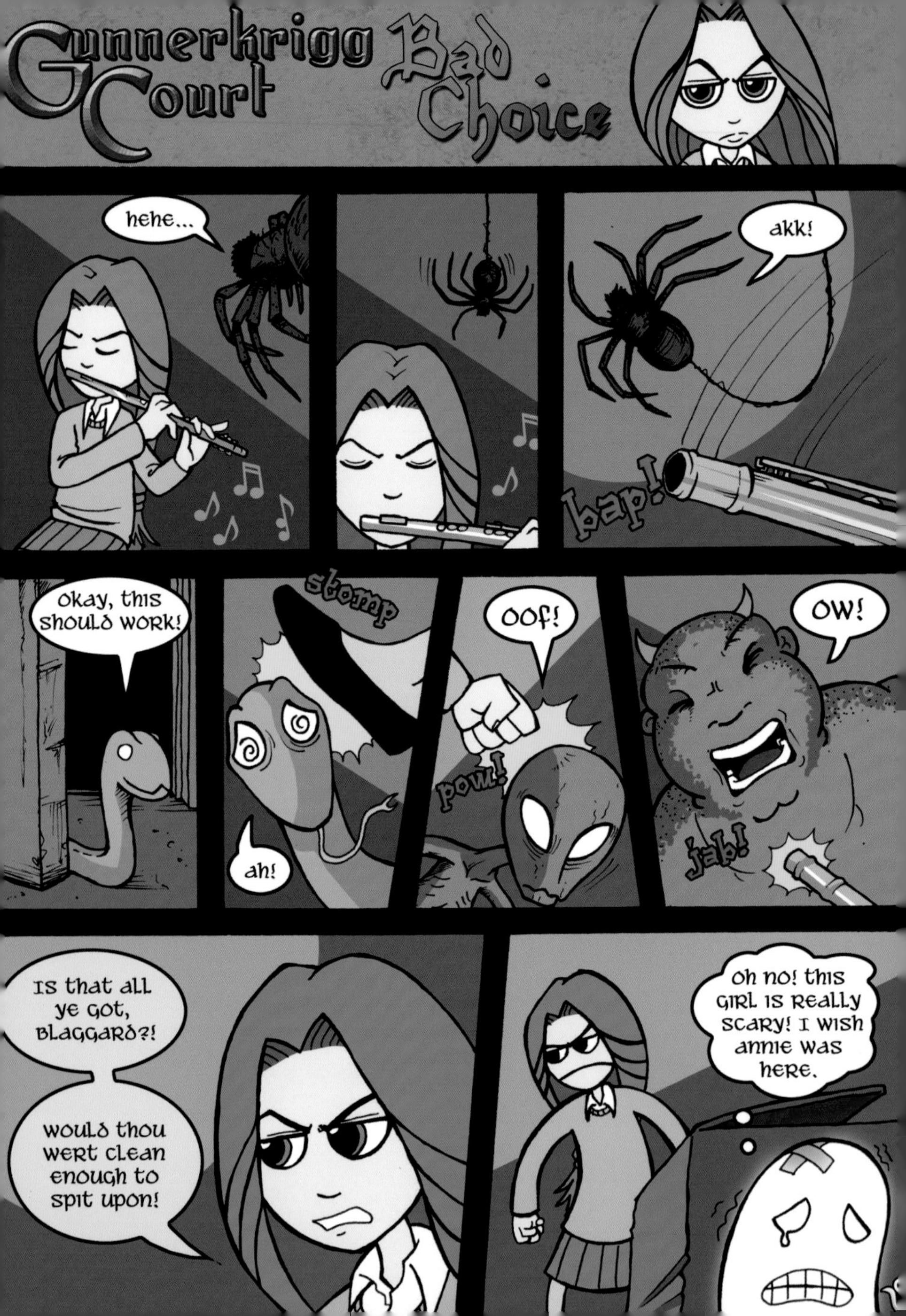
Gunnerkrigg Court
Bad Choice
hehe...
akk!
bap!
Okay, this should work!
stomp
ah!
OOF!
pow!
OW!
jab!
Is that all ye got, blaggard?!
Would thou wert clean enough to spit upon!
Oh no! this girl is really scary! I wish annie was here.

Gunnerkrigg Court

Chapter 5:

Two Strange Girls

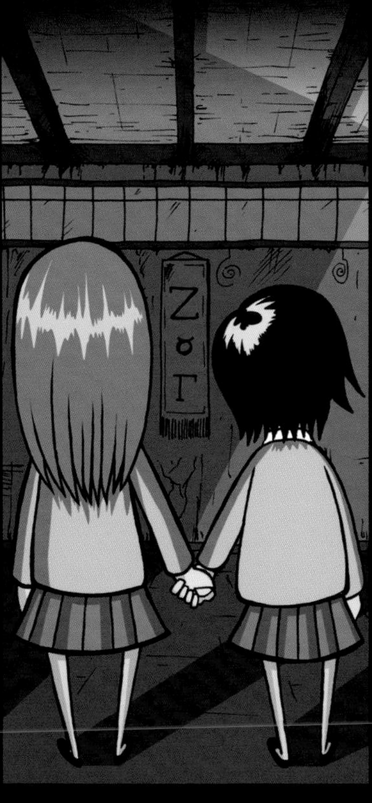

Z
ŏ
Γ

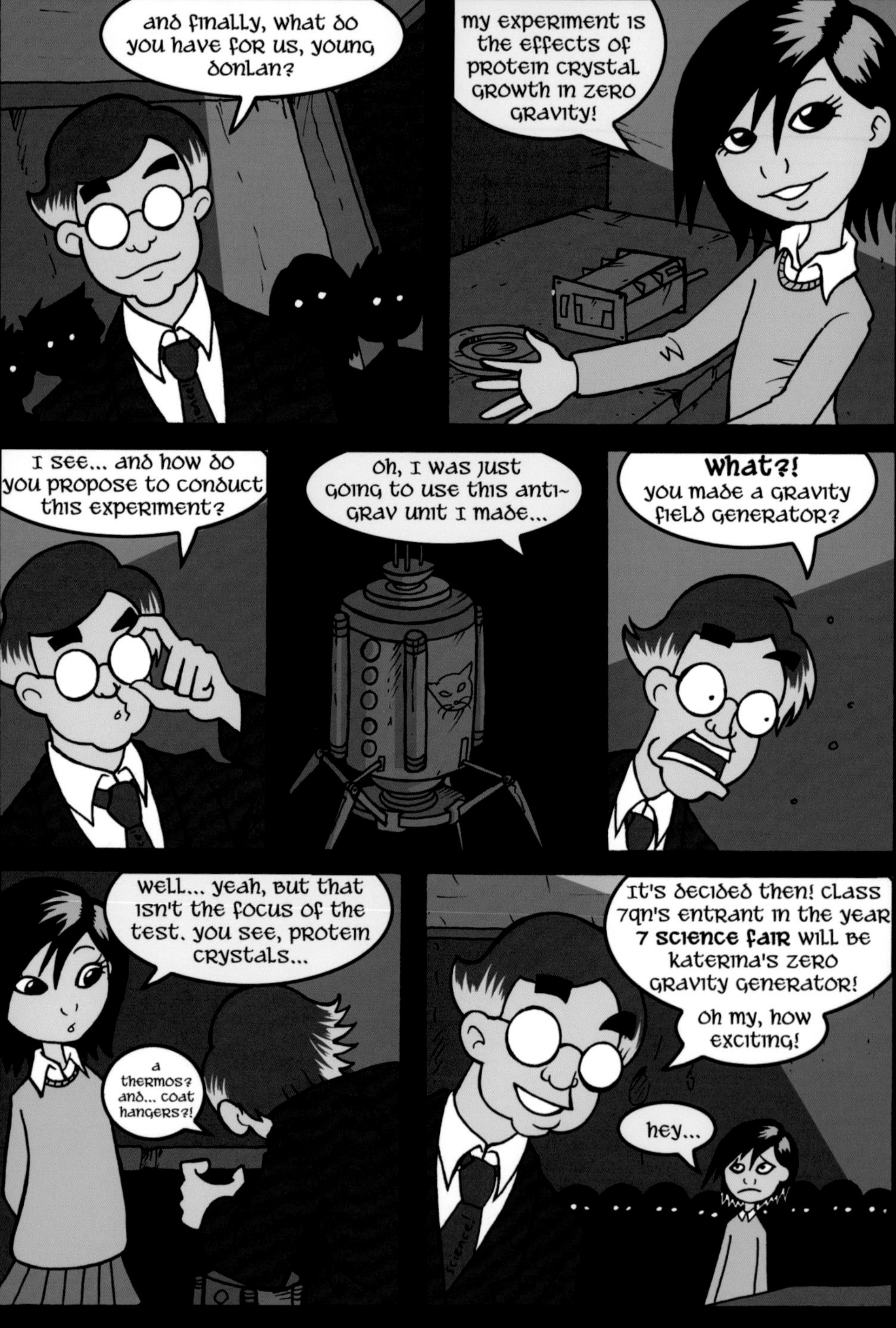
and finally, what do you have for us, young donlan?
my experiment is the effects of protein crystal growth in zero gravity!
I see... and how do you propose to conduct this experiment?
oh, I was just going to use this anti-grav unit I made...
what?! you made a gravity field generator?
well... yeah, but that isn't the focus of the test. you see, protein crystals...
a thermos? and... coat hangers?!
It's decided then! class 7qn's entrant in the year 7 science fair will be katerina's zero gravity generator!
oh my, how exciting!
hey...

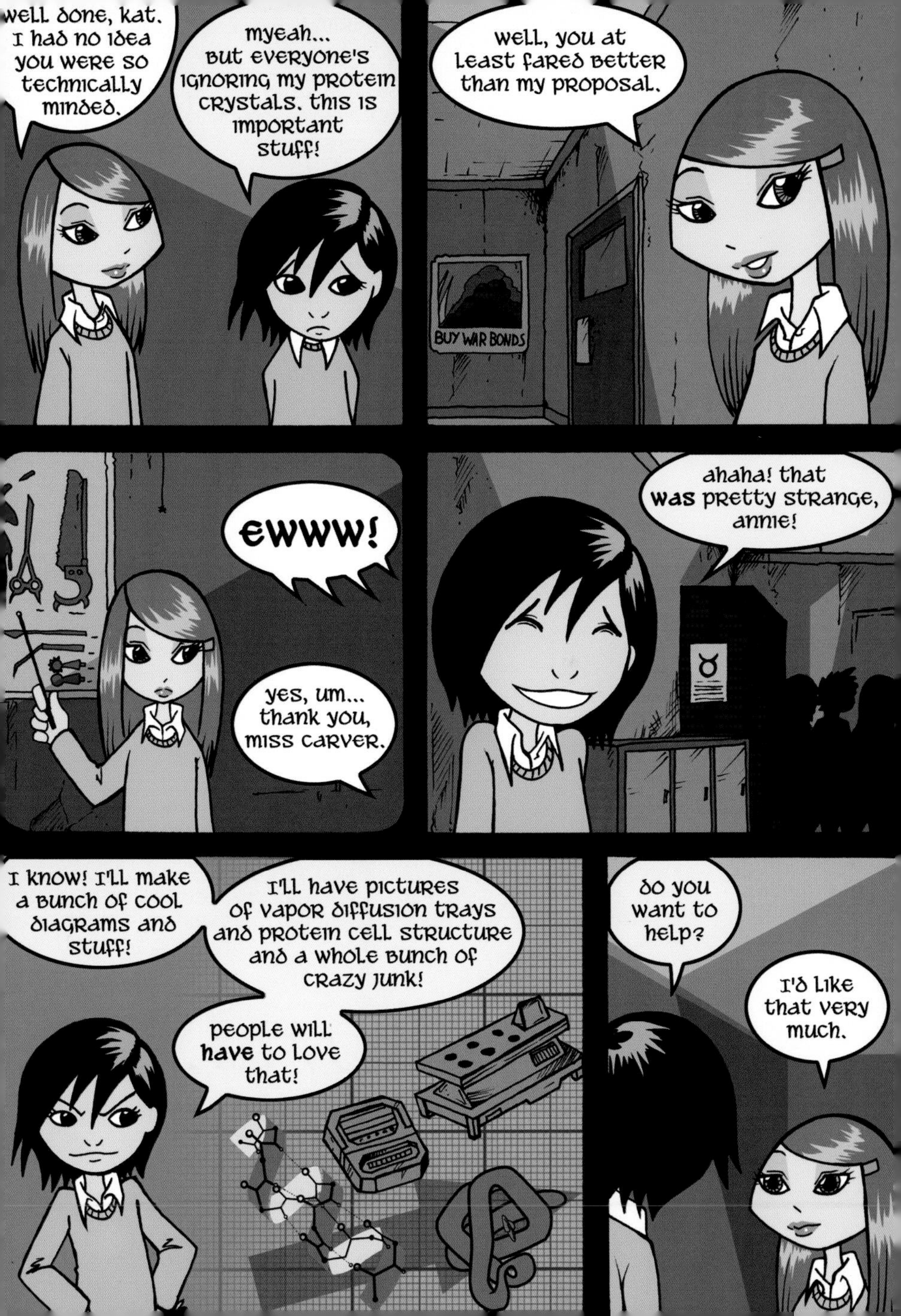
well done, kat. I had no idea you were so technically minded.
myeah... but everyone's ignoring my protein crystals. this is important stuff!
well, you at least fared better than my proposal.
BUY WAR BONDS
EWWW!
yes, um... thank you, miss carver.
ahaha! that was pretty strange, annie!
I know! I'll make a bunch of cool diagrams and stuff!
I'll have pictures of vapor diffusion trays and protein cell structure and a whole bunch of crazy junk!
people will have to love that!
do you want to help?
I'd like that very much.

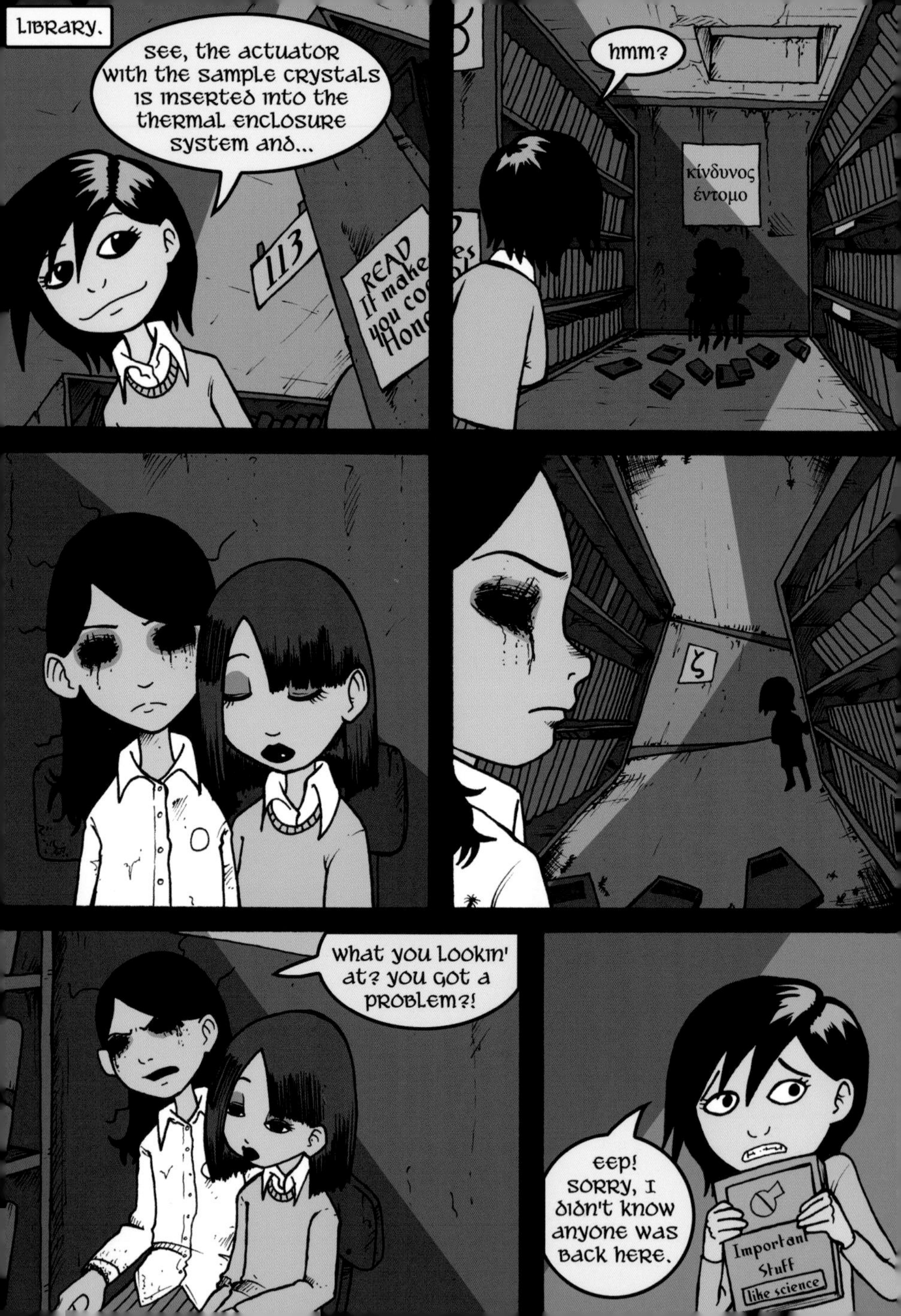
LIBRARY.
see, the actuator with the sample crystals is inserted into the thermal enclosure system and...
113
READ
hmm?
κίνδυνος έντομο
ζ
what you lookin' at? you got a problem?!
eep! sorry, I didn't know anyone was back here.
Important Stuff
like science

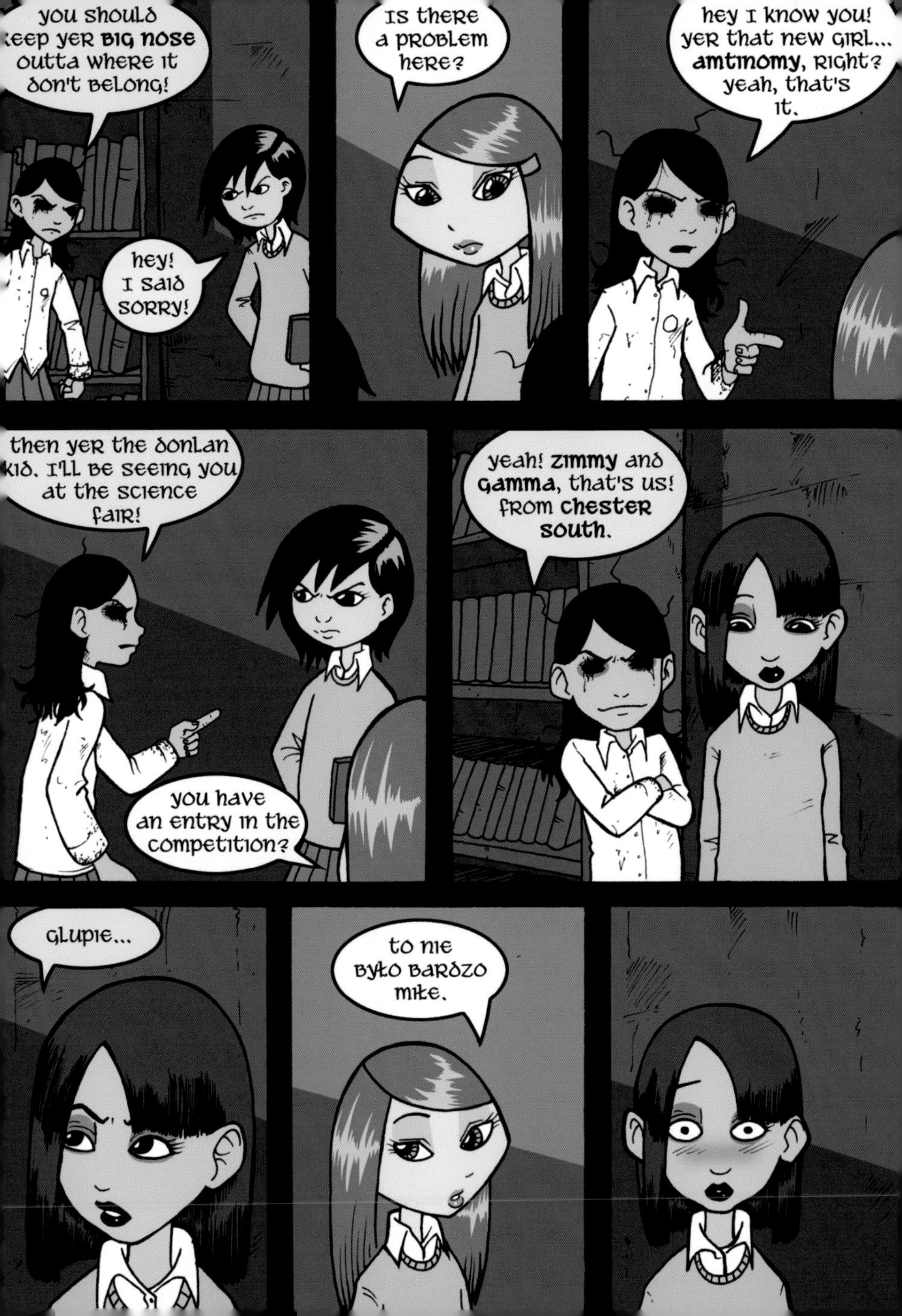
you should keep yer BIG NOSE outta where it don't belong!
hey! I said sorry!
Is there a problem here?
hey I know you! yer that new girl... amtinomy, right? yeah, that's it.
then yer the donlan kid. I'll be seeing you at the science fair!
you have an entry in the competition?
yeah! zimmy and gamma, that's us! from chester south.
glupie...
to nie było bardzo miłe.

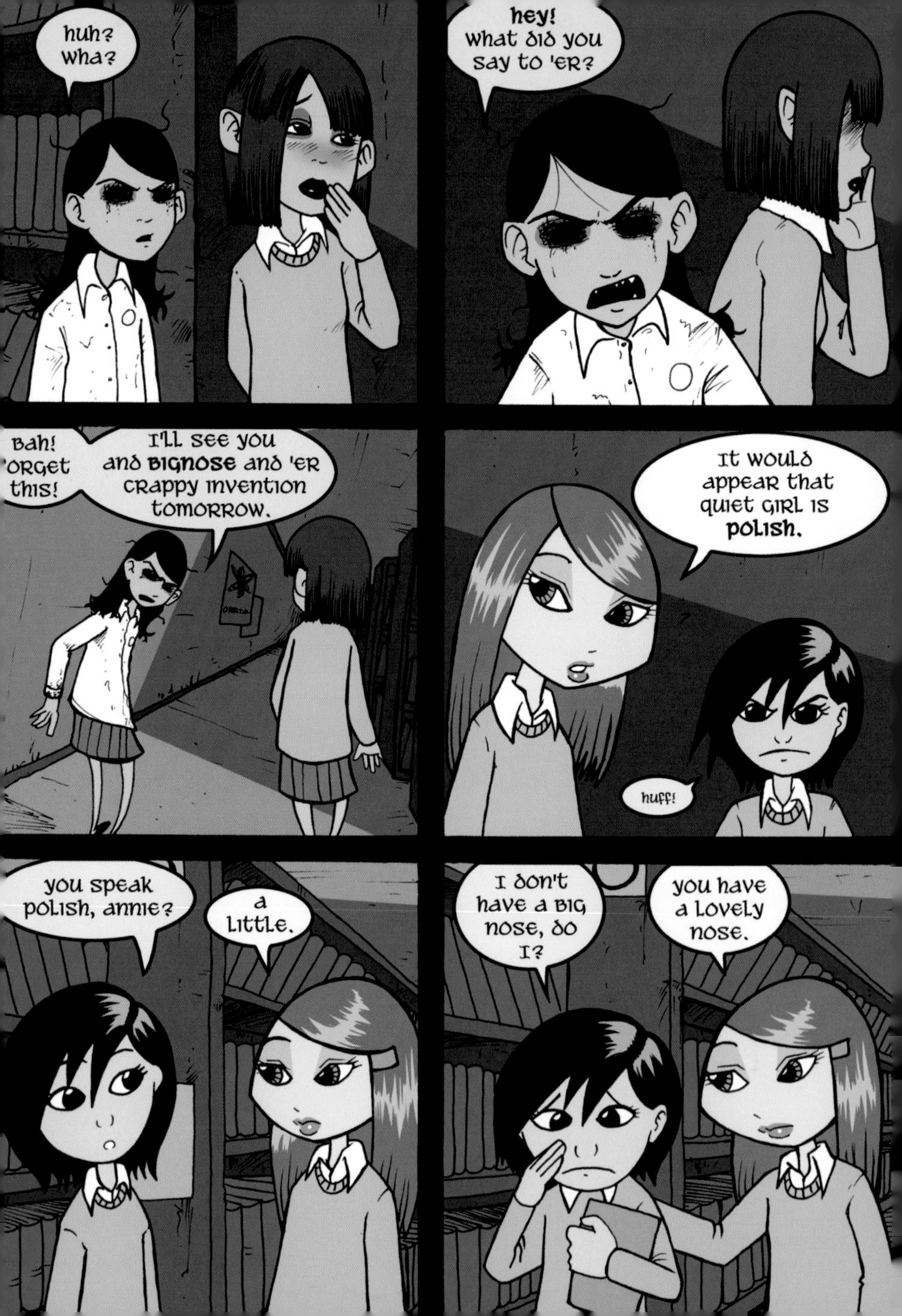
huh? wha?
hey! what did you say to 'er?
Bah! 'orget this!
I'll see you and BIGNOSE and 'er crappy invention tomorrow.
It would appear that quiet girl is polish.
huff!
you speak polish, annie?
a little.
I don't have a big nose, do I?
you have a lovely nose.

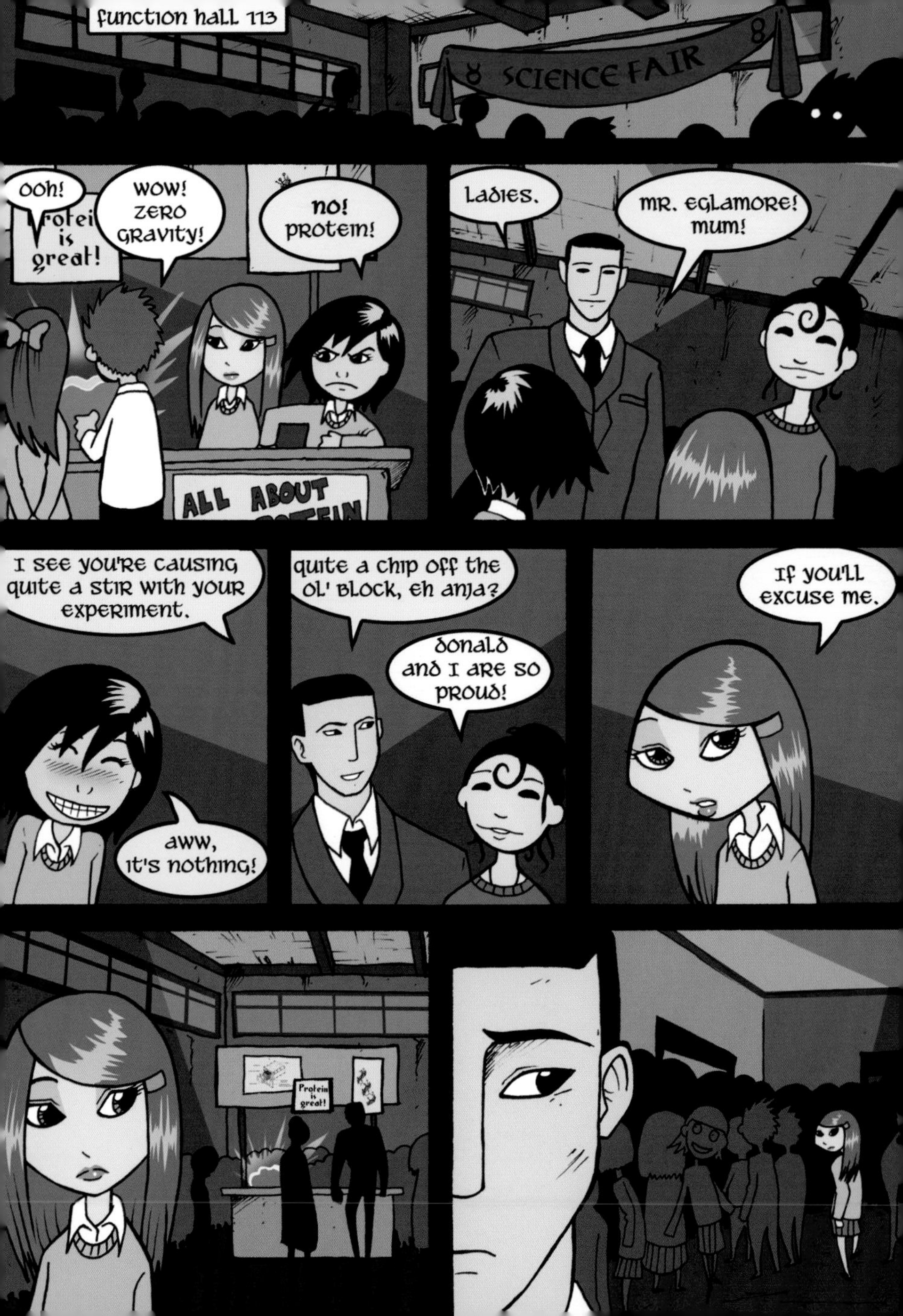
function hall 113
SCIENCE FAIR
OOh!
WOW! ZERO GRAVITY!
no! PROTEIN!
ALL ABOUT
Ladies.
MR. EGLAMORE! MUM!
I SEE YOU'RE CAUSING quite A STIR WITH YOUR EXPERIMENT.
aww, it's nothing!
quite a chip off the OL' BLOCK, eh anja?
donald and I ARE SO PROUD!
If you'll excuse me.
Protein is great!

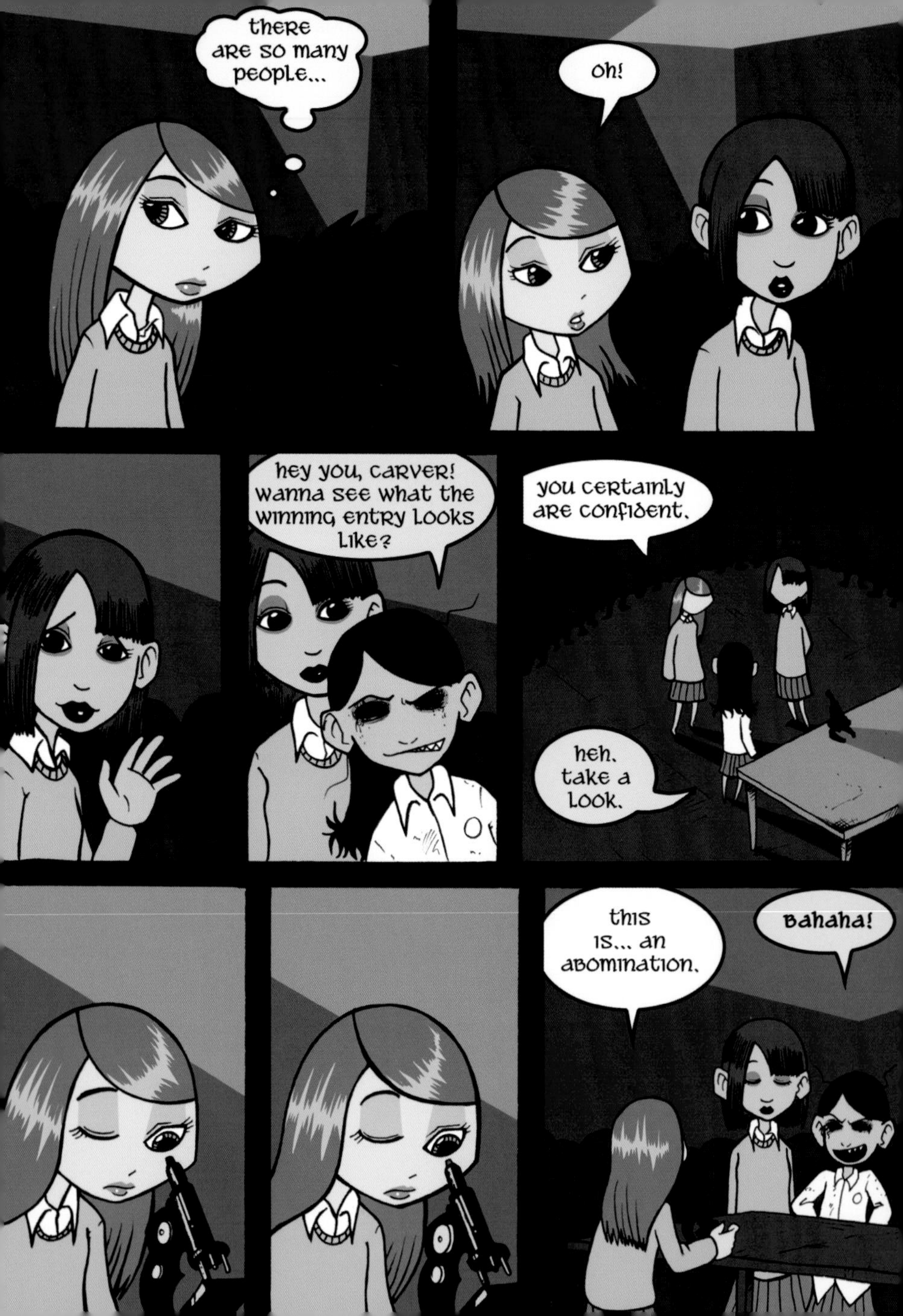
there are so many people...
oh!
hey you, carver! wanna see what the winning entry looks like?
you certainly are confident.
heh. take a look.
this is... an abomination.
Bahaha!

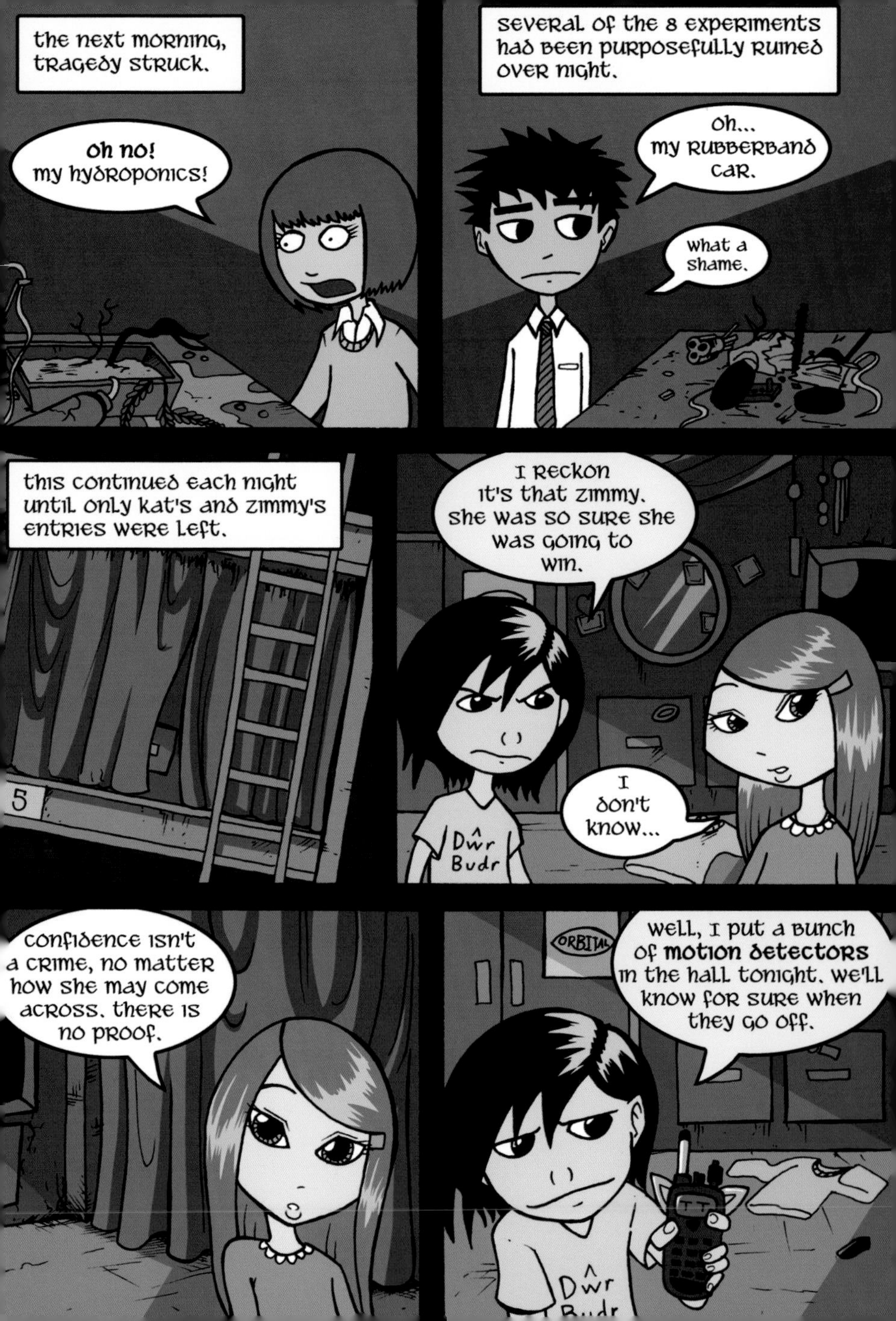
the next morning, tragedy struck.
oh no! my hydroponics!
several of the 8 experiments had been purposefully ruined over night.
oh... my rubberband car.
what a shame.
this continued each night until only kat's and zimmy's entries were left.
5
I reckon it's that zimmy. she was so sure she was going to win.
Dŵr Budr
I don't know...
confidence isn't a crime, no matter how she may come across. there is no proof.
ORBITAL
well, I put a bunch of **motion detectors** in the hall tonight. we'll know for sure when they go off.

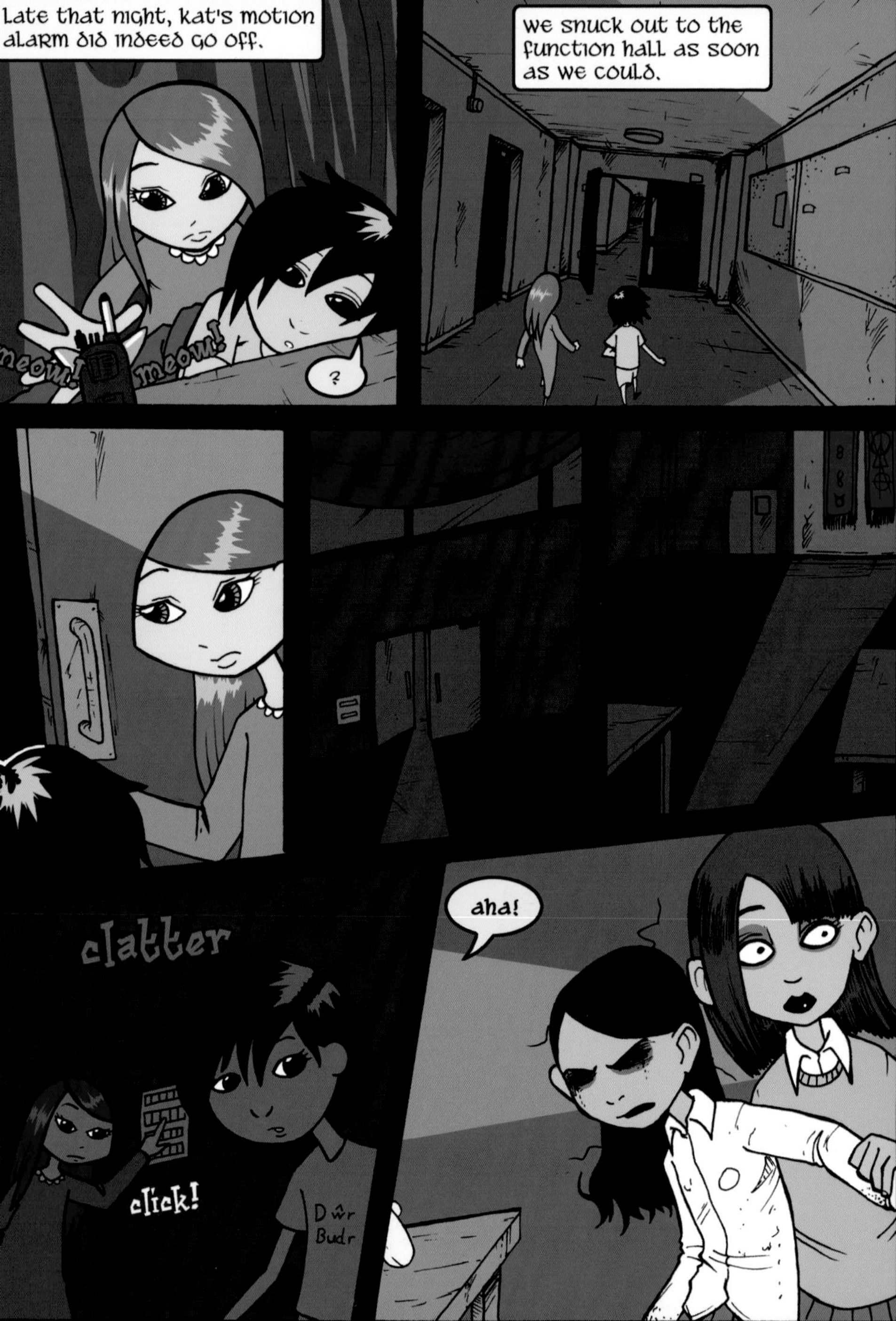
Late that night, kat's motion alarm did indeed go off.
meow! meow!
?
we snuck out to the function hall as soon as we could.
clatter
click!
Dŵr Budr
aha!

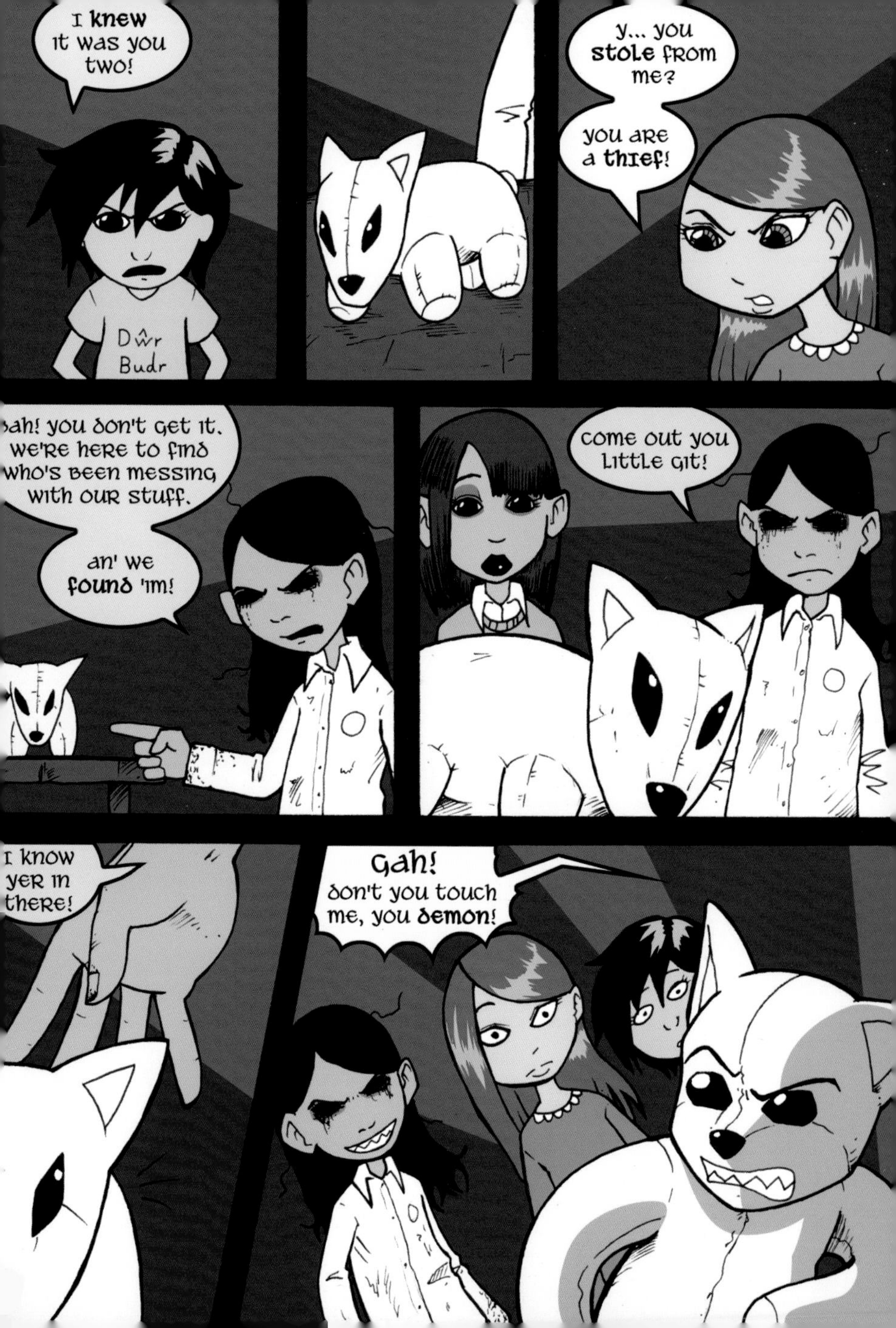
I knew it was you two!
Dŵr Budr
y... you stole from me?
you are a thief!
bah! you don't get it. we're here to find who's been messing with our stuff.
an' we found 'im!
come out you little git!
I know yer in there!
Gah! don't you touch me, you demon!

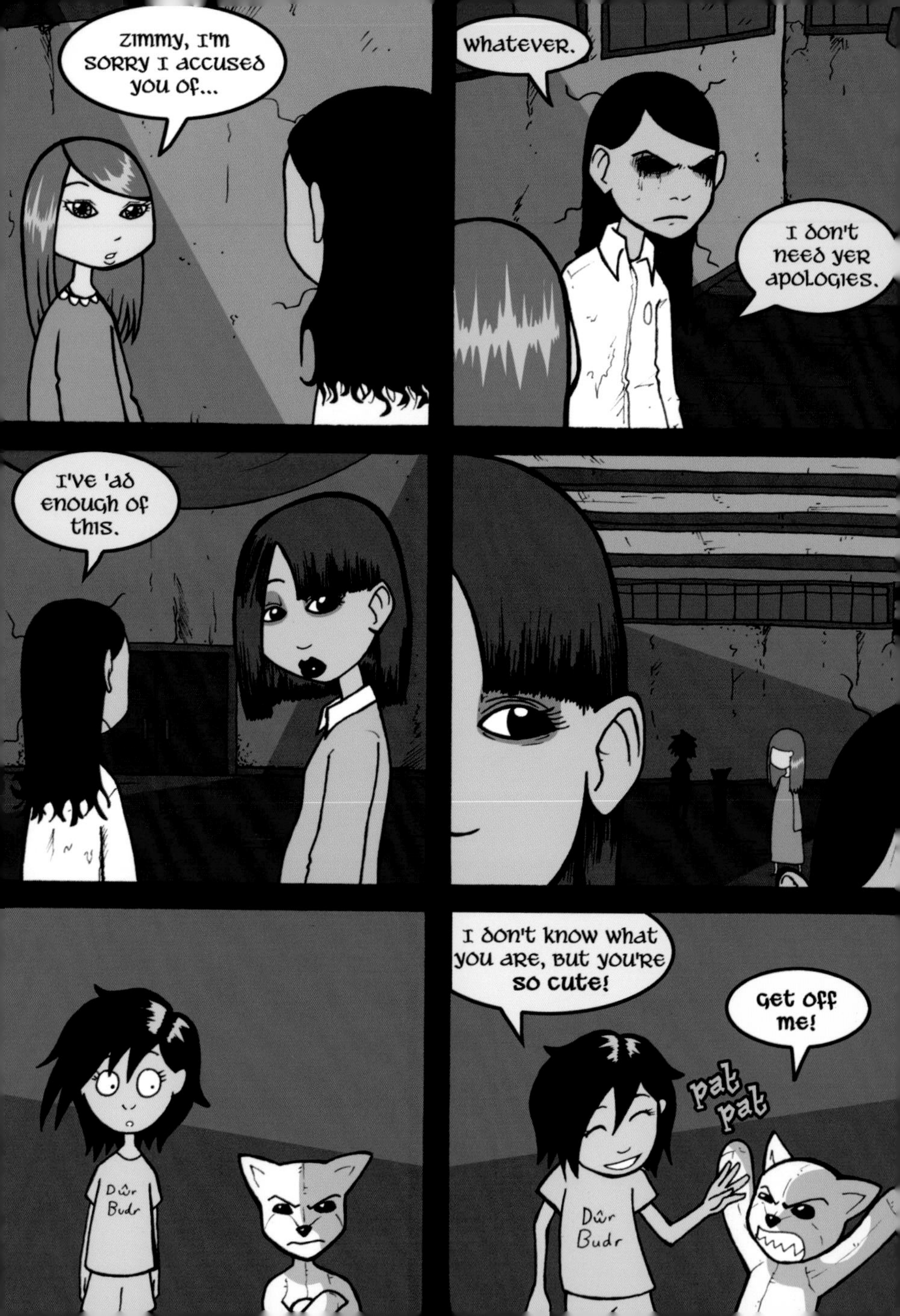
ZIMMY, I'M SORRY I ACCUSED YOU OF...
WHATEVER.
I DON'T NEED YER APOLOGIES.
I'VE 'AD ENOUGH OF THIS.
I DON'T KNOW WHAT YOU ARE, BUT YOU'RE SO CUTE!
GET OFF ME!
PAT PAT
DŴR BUDR
DŴR BUDR

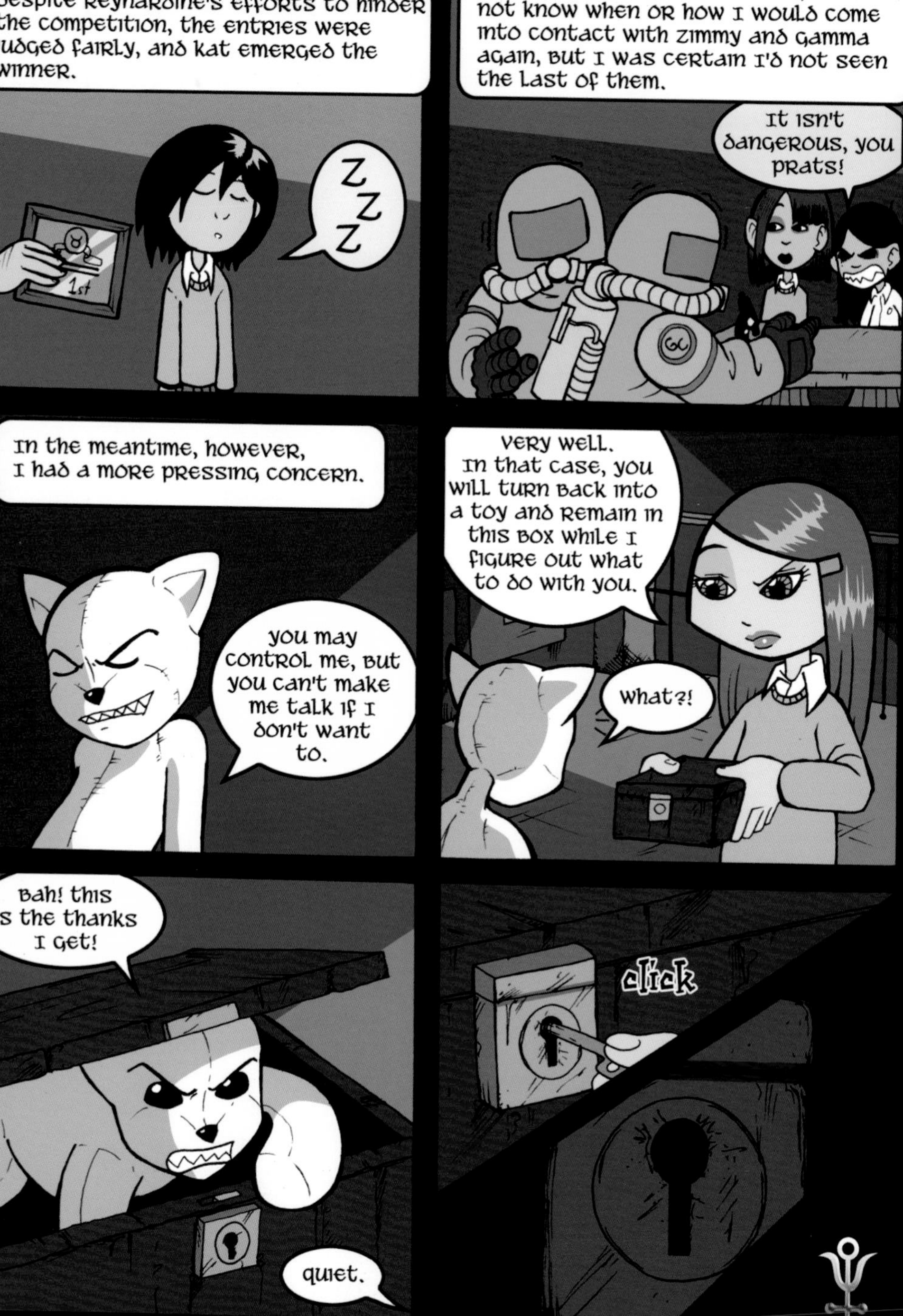
espite Reynardine's efforts to hinder the competition, the entries were udged fairly, and kat emerged the winner.
Z Z Z
1st
not know when or how I would come into contact with zimmy and gamma again, but I was certain I'd not seen the last of them.
It isn't dangerous, you prats!
In the meantime, however, I had a more pressing concern.
you may control me, but you can't make me talk if I don't want to.
Very well. In that case, you will turn back into a toy and remain in this box while I figure out what to do with you.
What?!
Bah! this s the thanks I get!
quiet.
click

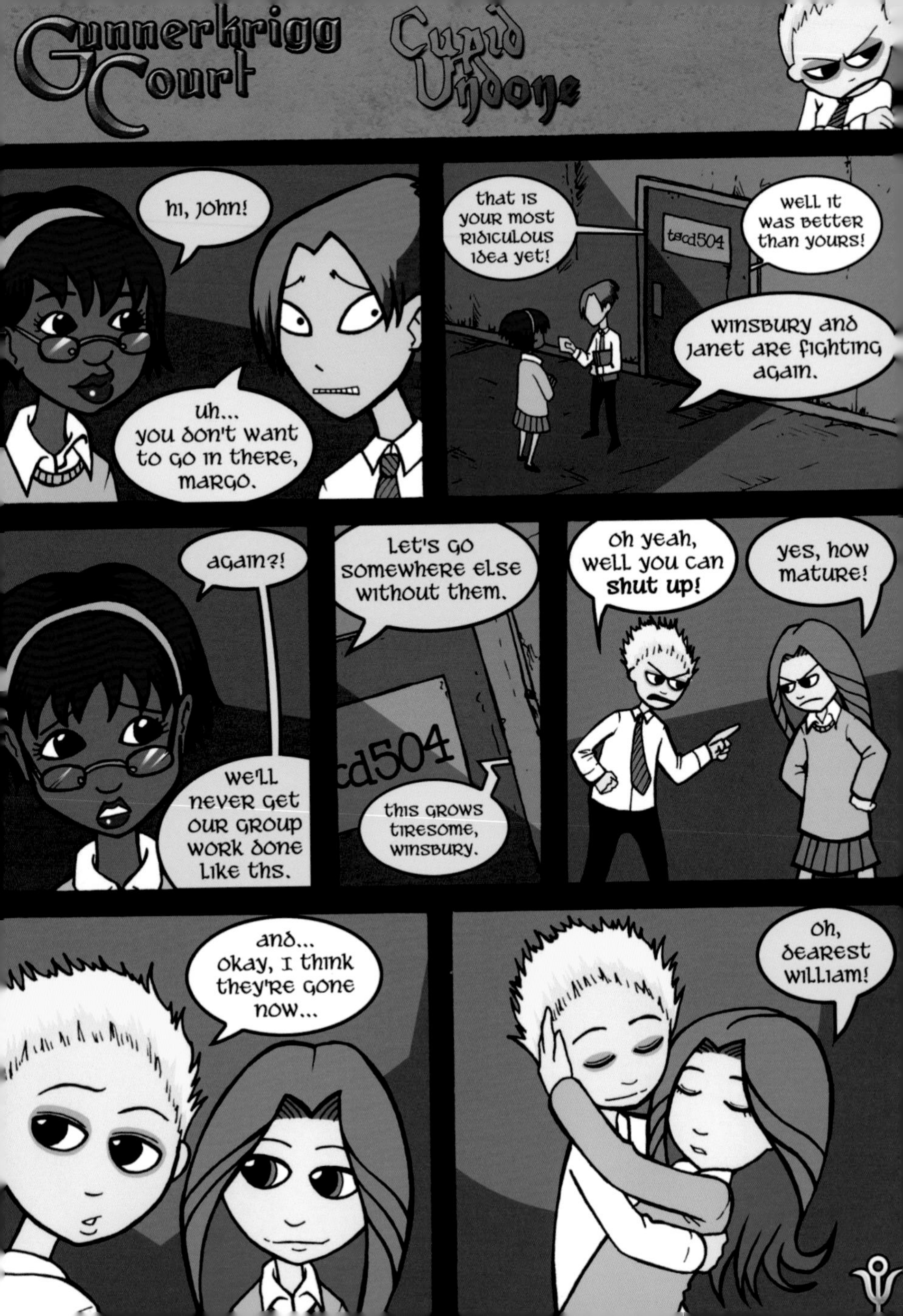
Gunnerkrigg Court
Cupid Undone
hi, John!
uh... you don't want to go in there, margo.
that is your most ridiculous idea yet!
tscd504
well it was better than yours!
winsbury and janet are fighting again.
again?!
we'll never get our group work done like ths.
let's go somewhere else without them.
cd504
this grows tiresome, winsbury.
oh yeah, well you can **shut up!**
yes, how mature!
and... okay, I think they're gone now...
oh, dearest william!

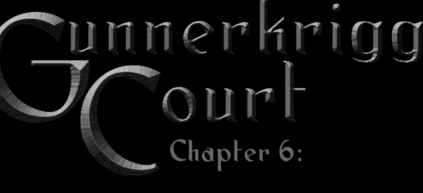

Gunnerkrigg Court

Chapter 6:

A Handful of Dirt

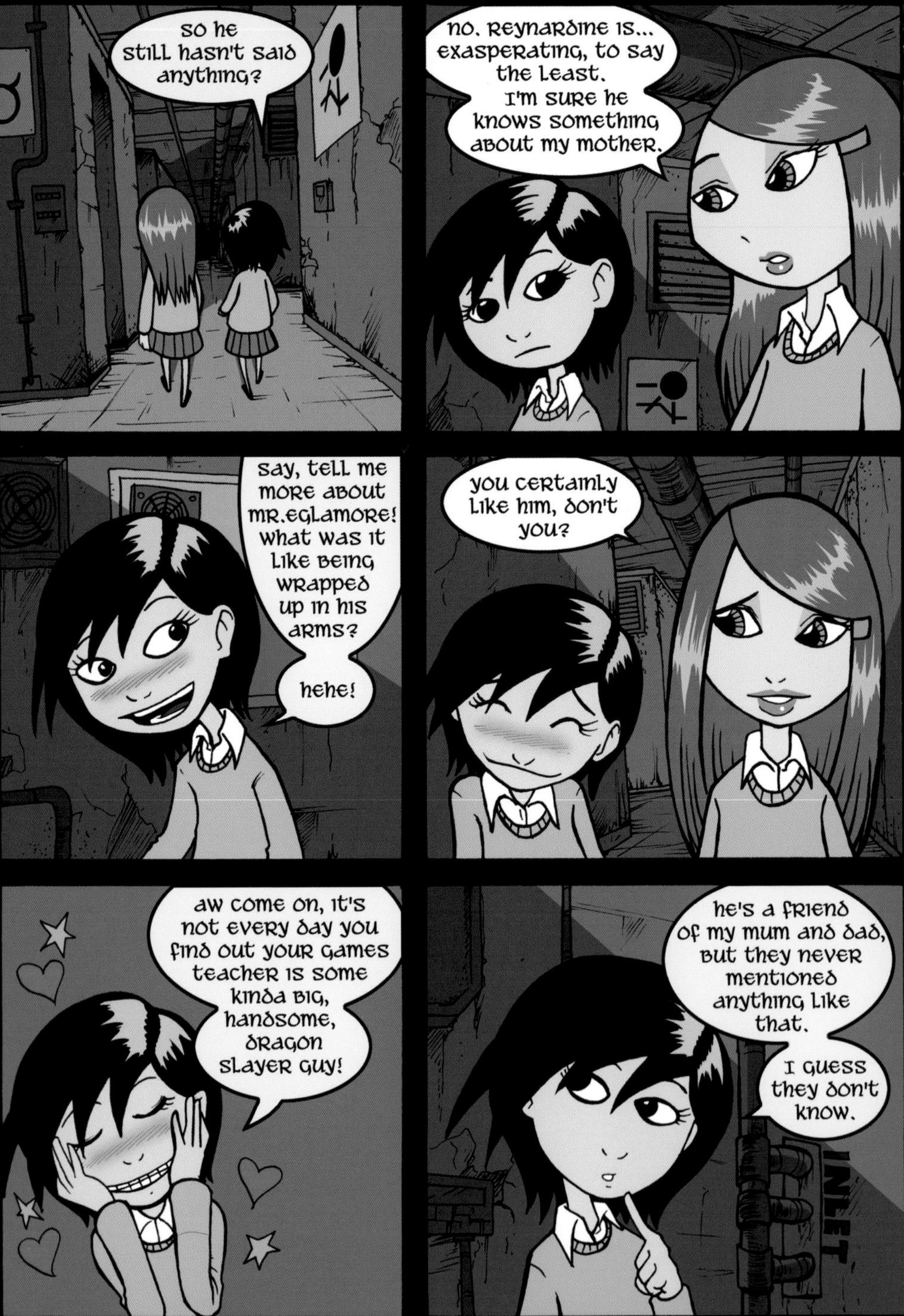
so he still hasn't said anything?
no. Reynardine is... exasperating, to say the least.
I'm sure he knows something about my mother.
say, tell me more about mr.eglamore! what was it like being wrapped up in his arms?
hehe!
you certainly like him, don't you?
aw come on, it's not every day you find out your games teacher is some kinda big, handsome, dragon slayer guy!
he's a friend of my mum and dad, but they never mentioned anything like that.
I guess they don't know.
INLET

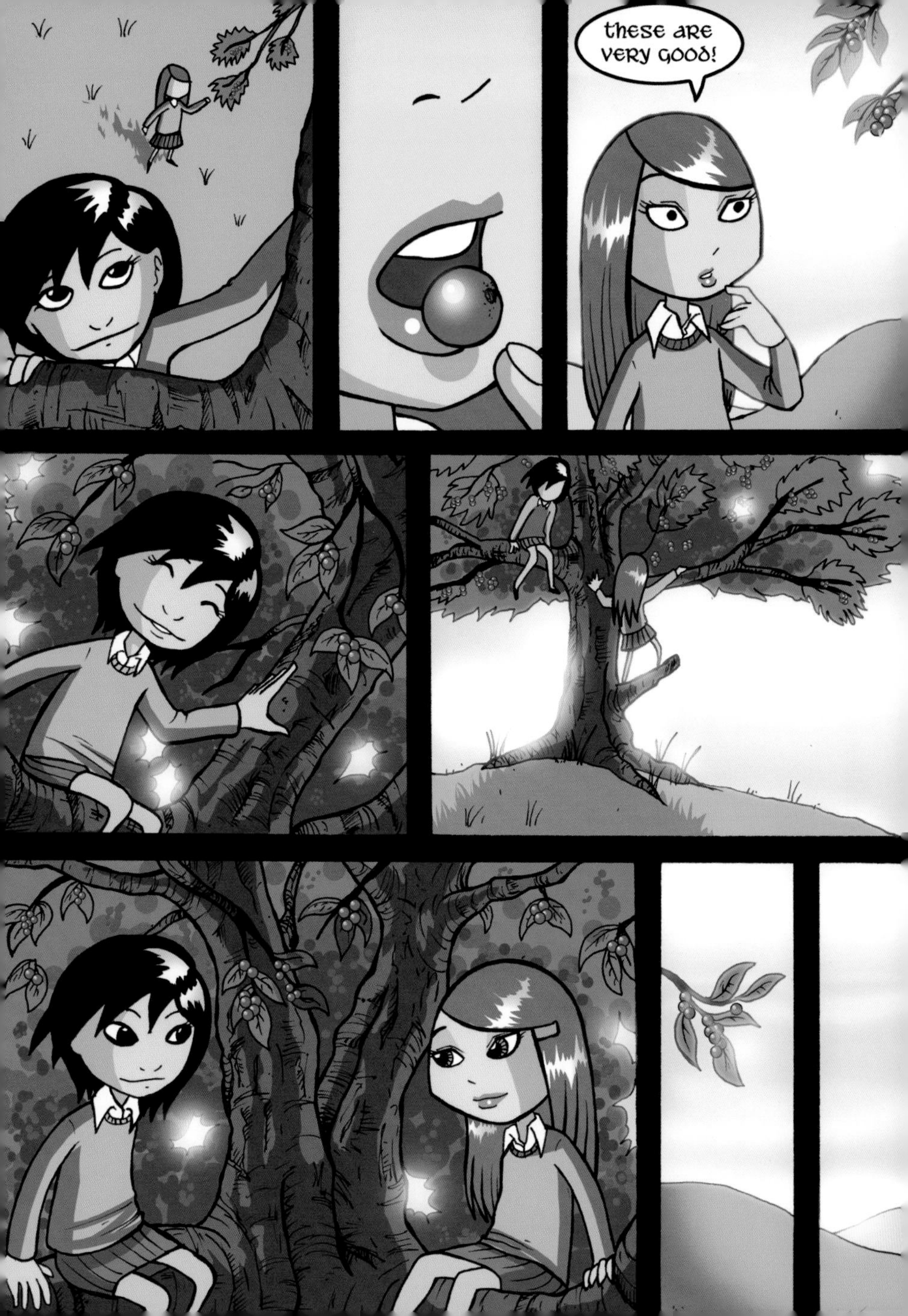
these are
very good!

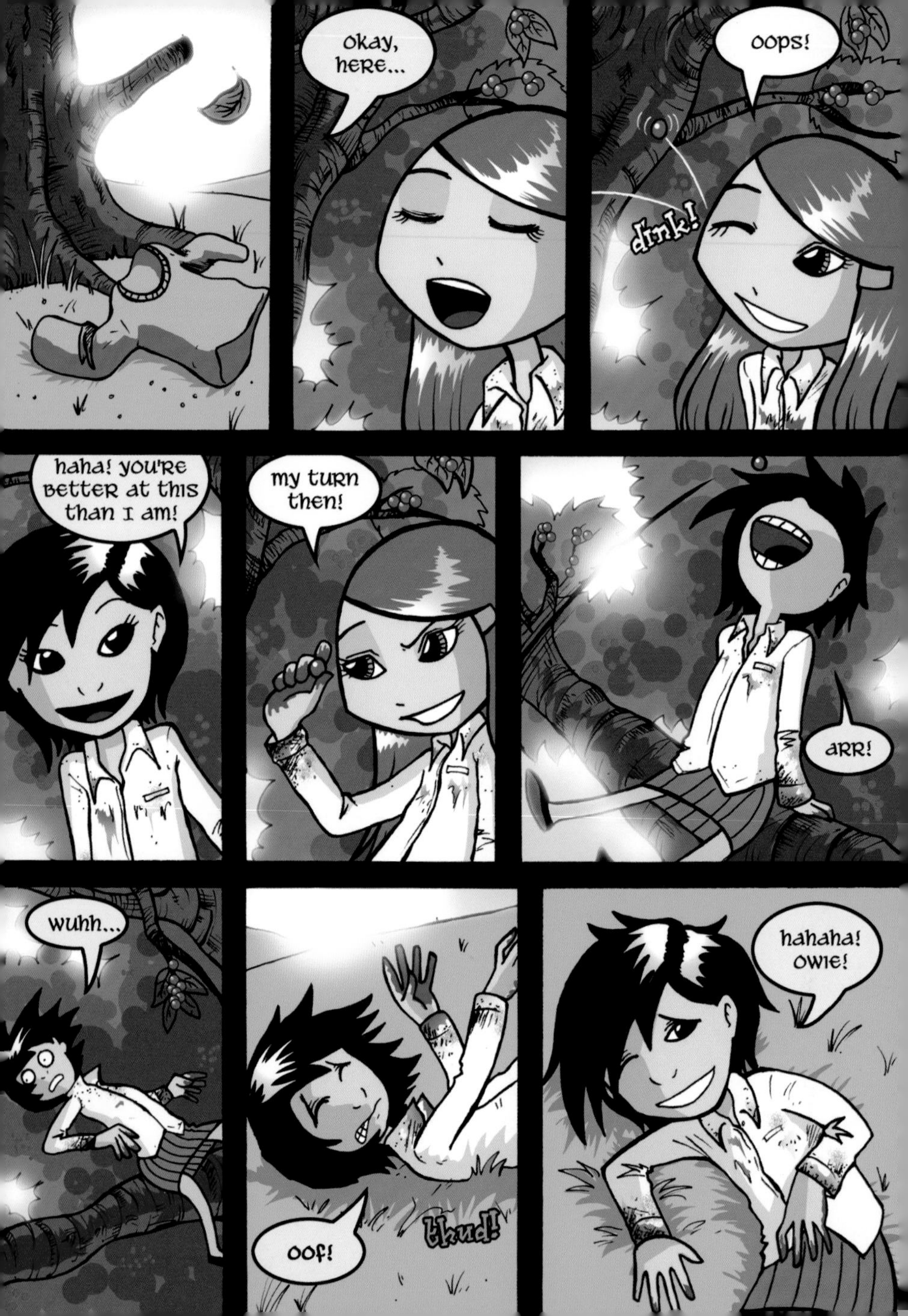
okay, here...
oops!
dink!
haha! you're better at this than I am!
my turn then!
arr!
wuhh...
oof!
thud!
hahaha! owie!

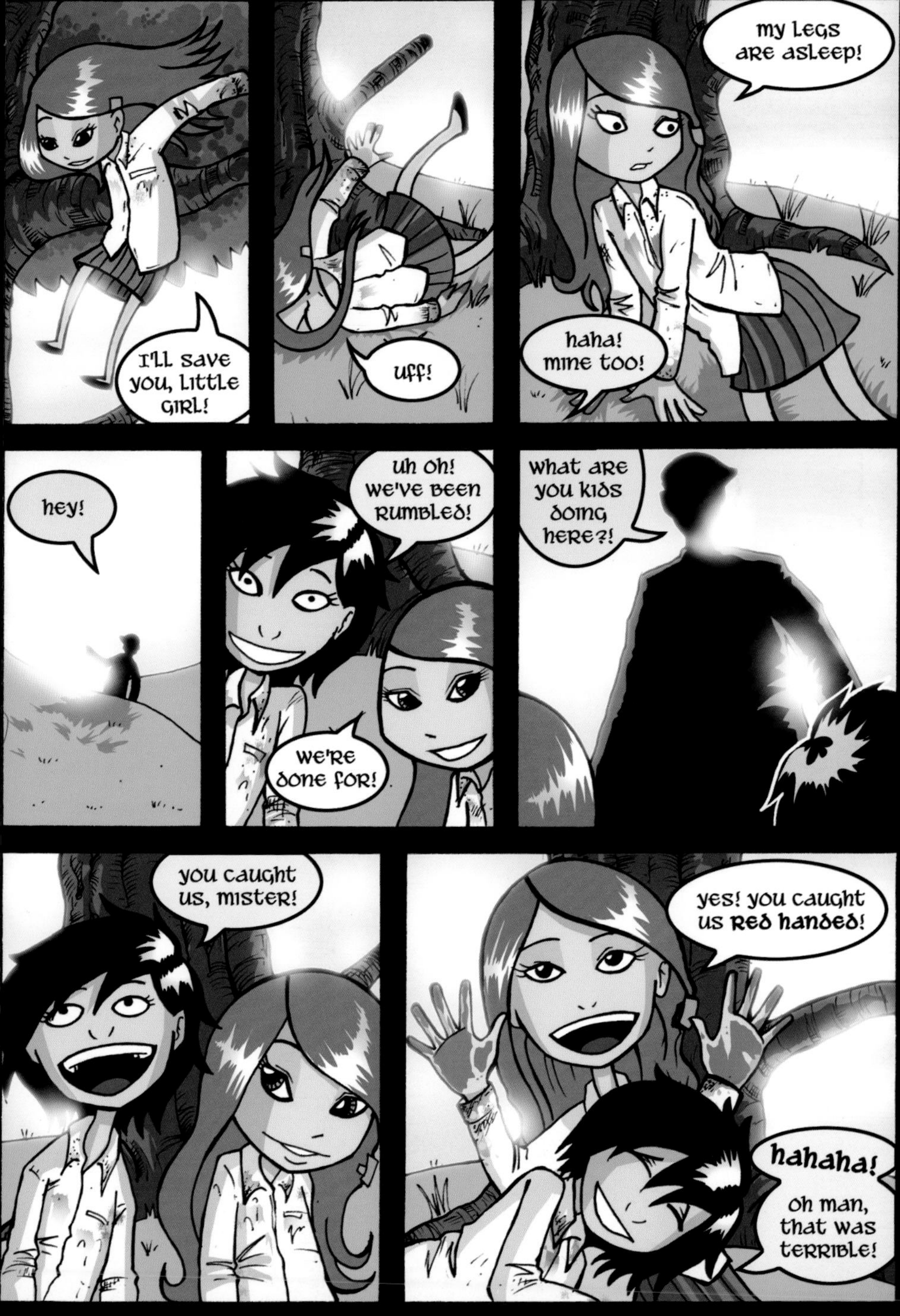
I'LL SAVE YOU, LITTLE GIRL!
UFF!
MY LEGS ARE ASLEEP!
HAHA! MINE TOO!
HEY!
UH OH! WE'VE BEEN RUMBLED!
WE'RE DONE FOR!
WHAT ARE YOU KIDS DOING HERE?!
YOU CAUGHT US, MISTER!
YES! YOU CAUGHT US RED HANDED!
HAHAHA!
OH MAN, THAT WAS TERRIBLE!

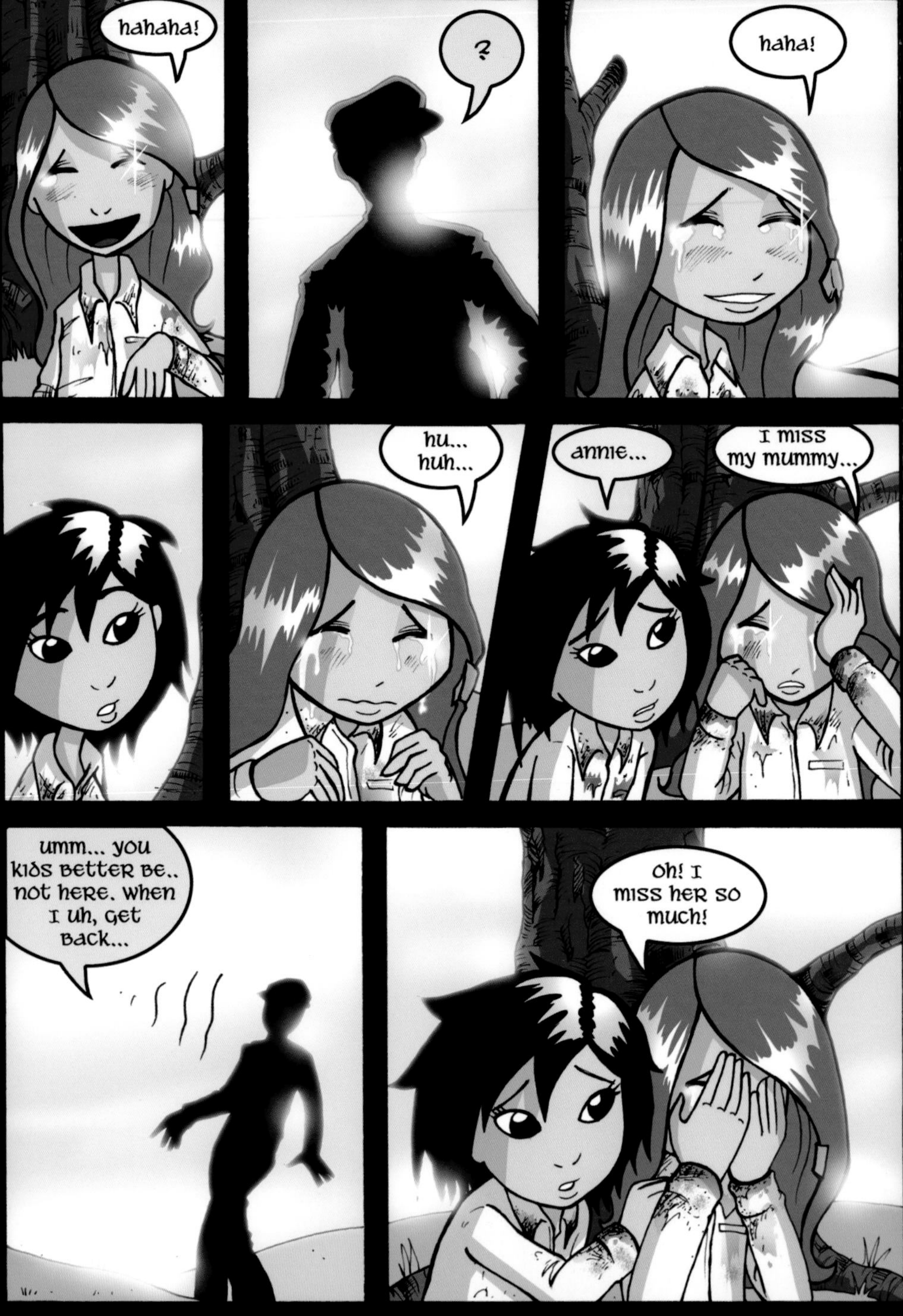

hahaha!
?
haha!
hu... huh...
annie...
I miss my mummy...
umm... you kids better be.. not here. when I uh, get back...
Oh! I miss her so much!

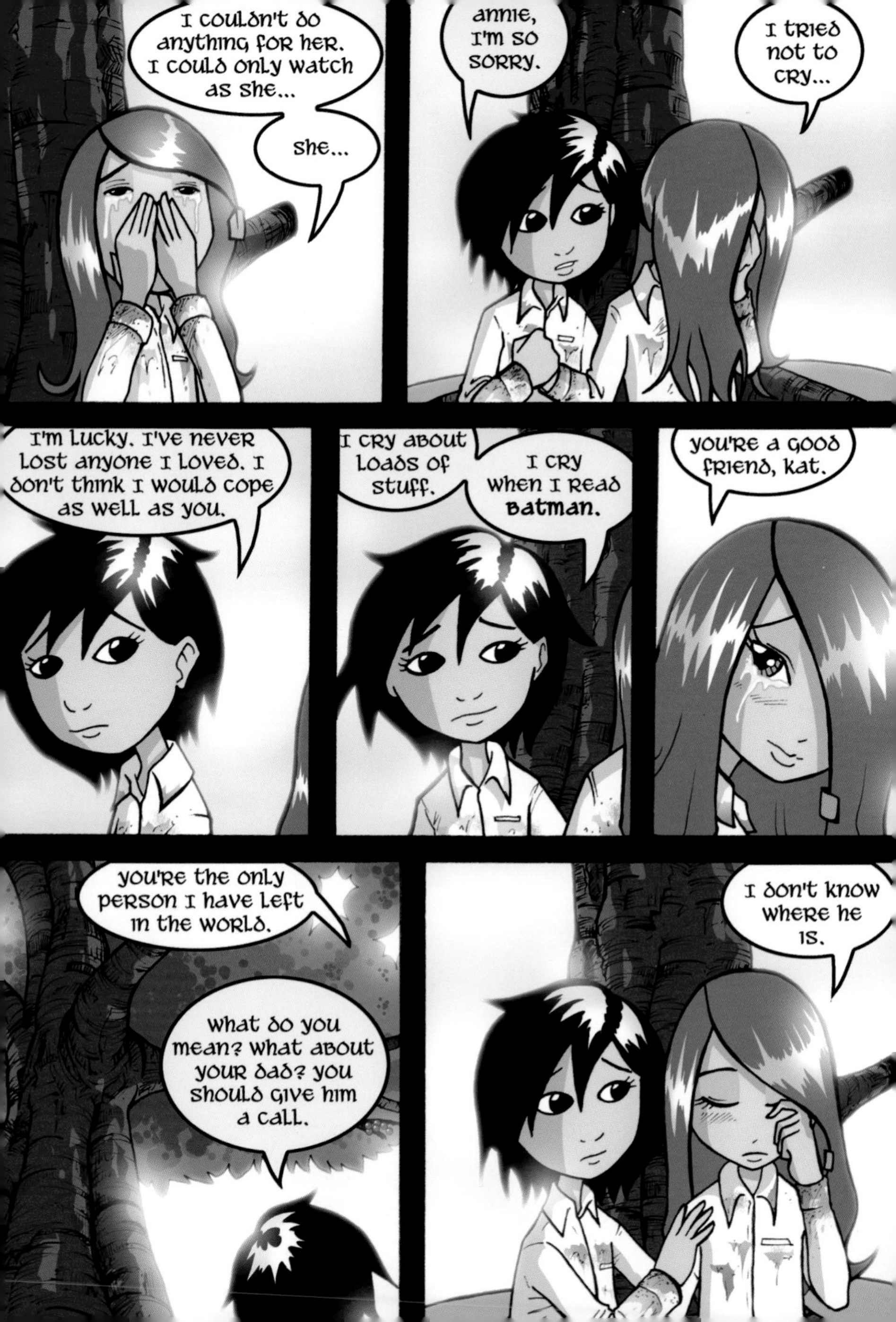
I couldn't do anything for her. I could only watch as she...
she...
annie, I'm so sorry.
I tried not to cry...
I'm lucky. I've never lost anyone I loved. I don't think I would cope as well as you.
I cry about loads of stuff.
I cry when I read **Batman**.
you're a good friend, kat.
you're the only person I have left in the world.
what do you mean? what about your dad? you should give him a call.
I don't know where he is.

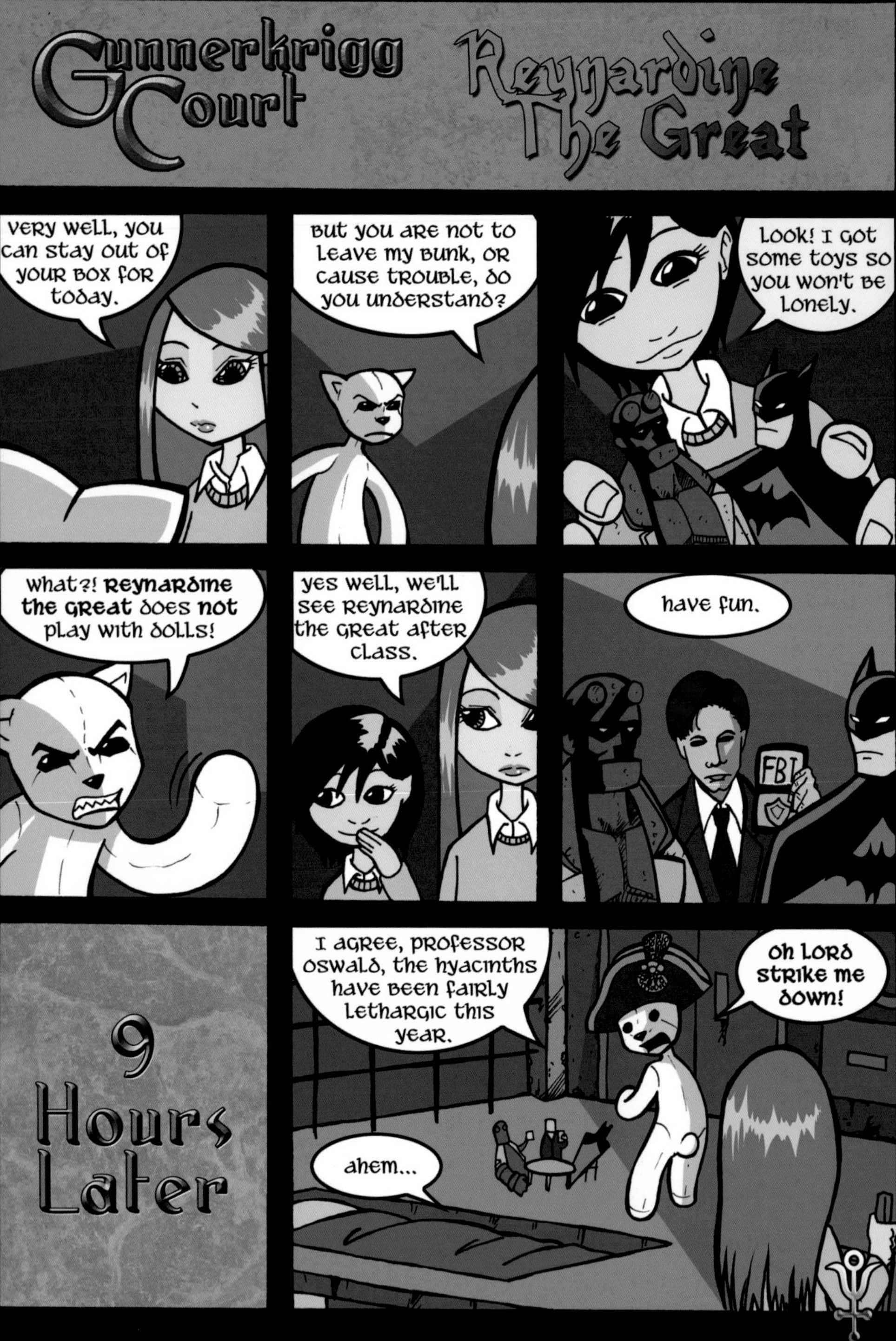
Gunnerkrigg Court
Reynardine The Great
very well, you can stay out of your box for today.
but you are not to leave my bunk, or cause trouble, do you understand?
look! I got some toys so you won't be lonely.
what?! Reynardine the great does not play with dolls!
yes well, we'll see Reynardine the great after class.
have fun.
FBI
9 Hours Later
I agree, professor oswald, the hyacinths have been fairly lethargic this year.
oh lord strike me down!
ahem...

Gunnerkrigg Court

Chapter 7:

Of New And Old

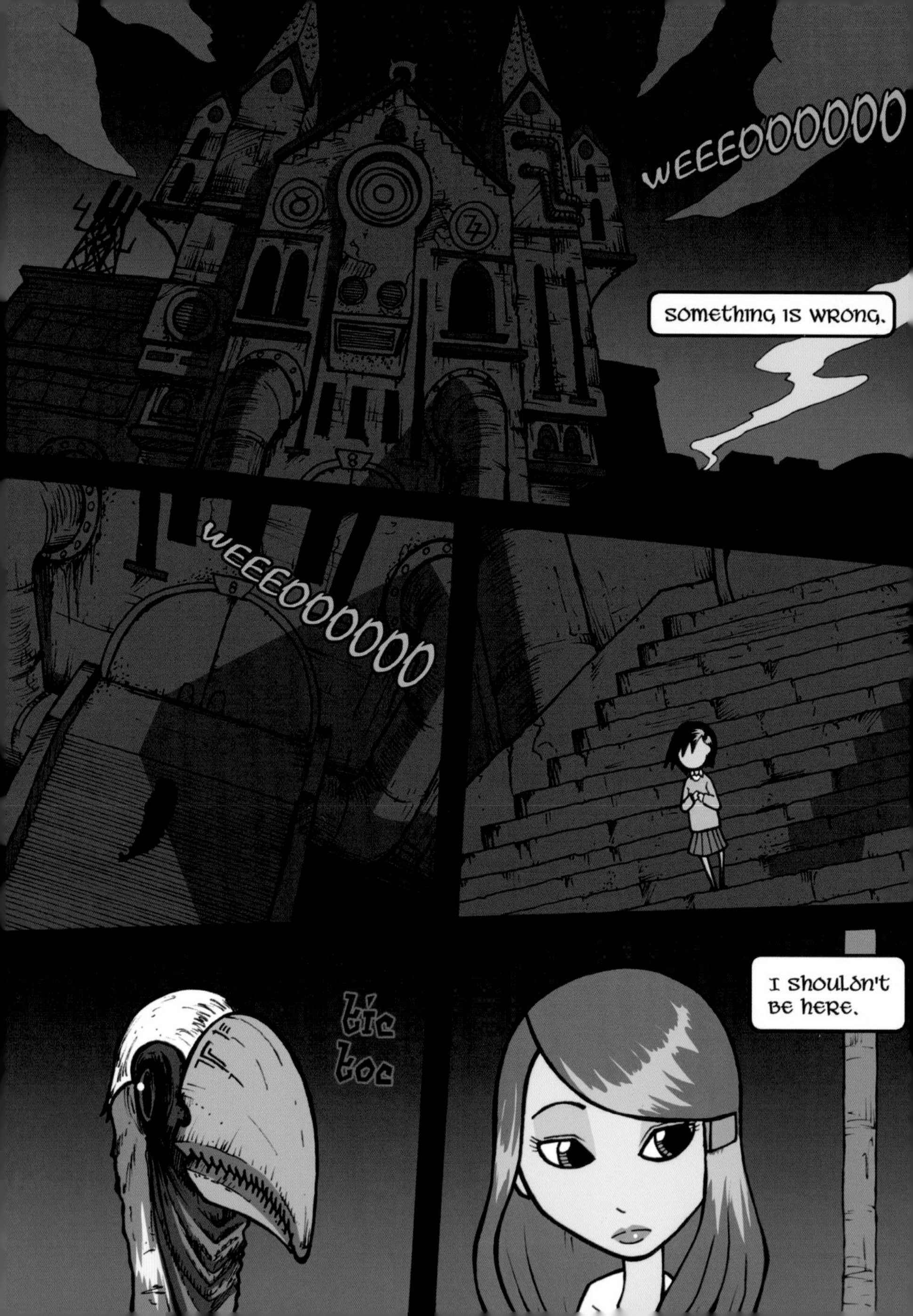
WEEEOOOOOOO
something is wrong.
WEEEOOOOOO
tic toc
I shouldn't be here.

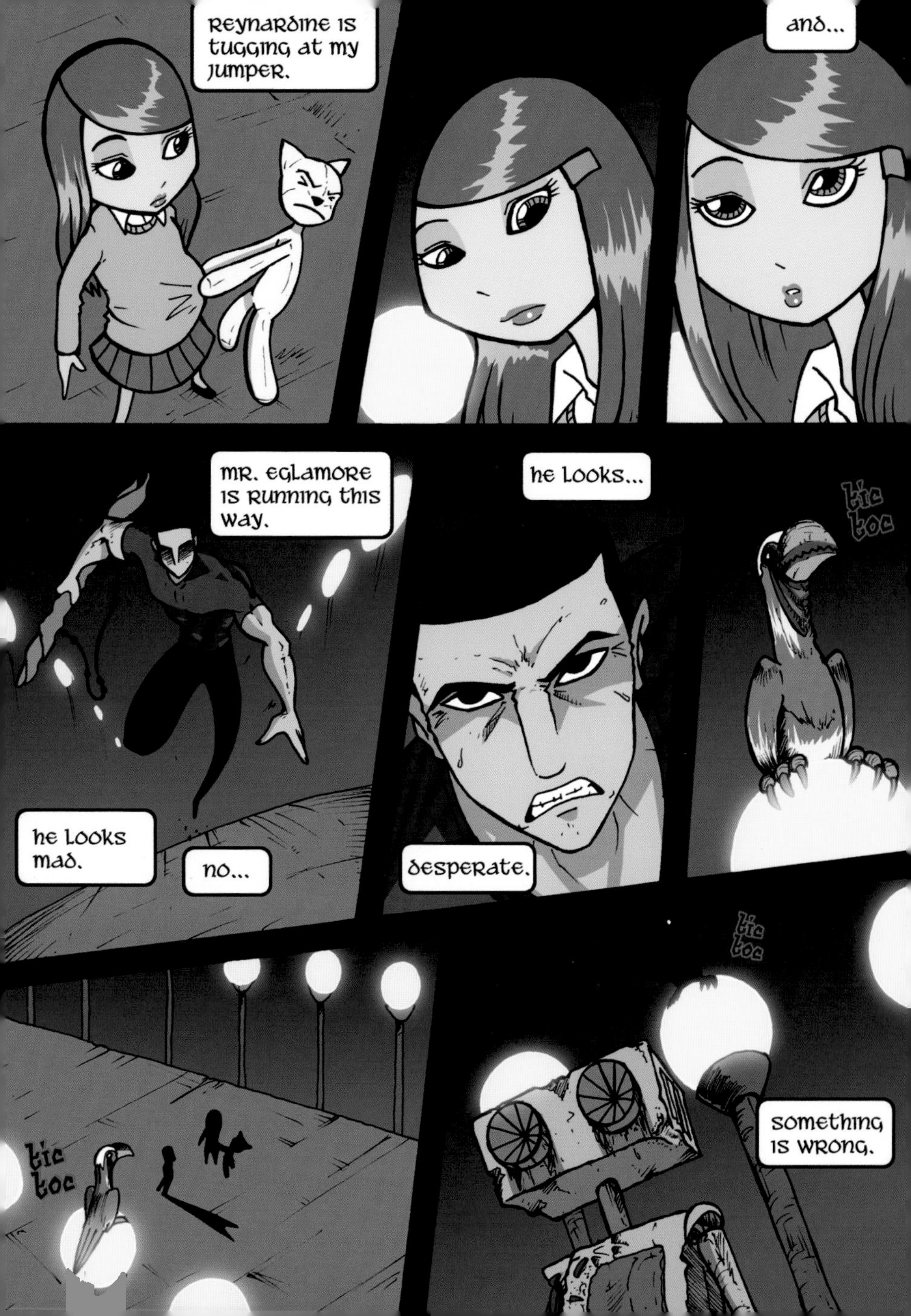

Reynardine is tugging at my jumper.
and...
Mr. Eglamore is running this way.
he looks...
tic toc
he looks mad.
no...
desperate.
tic toc
tic toc
something is wrong.

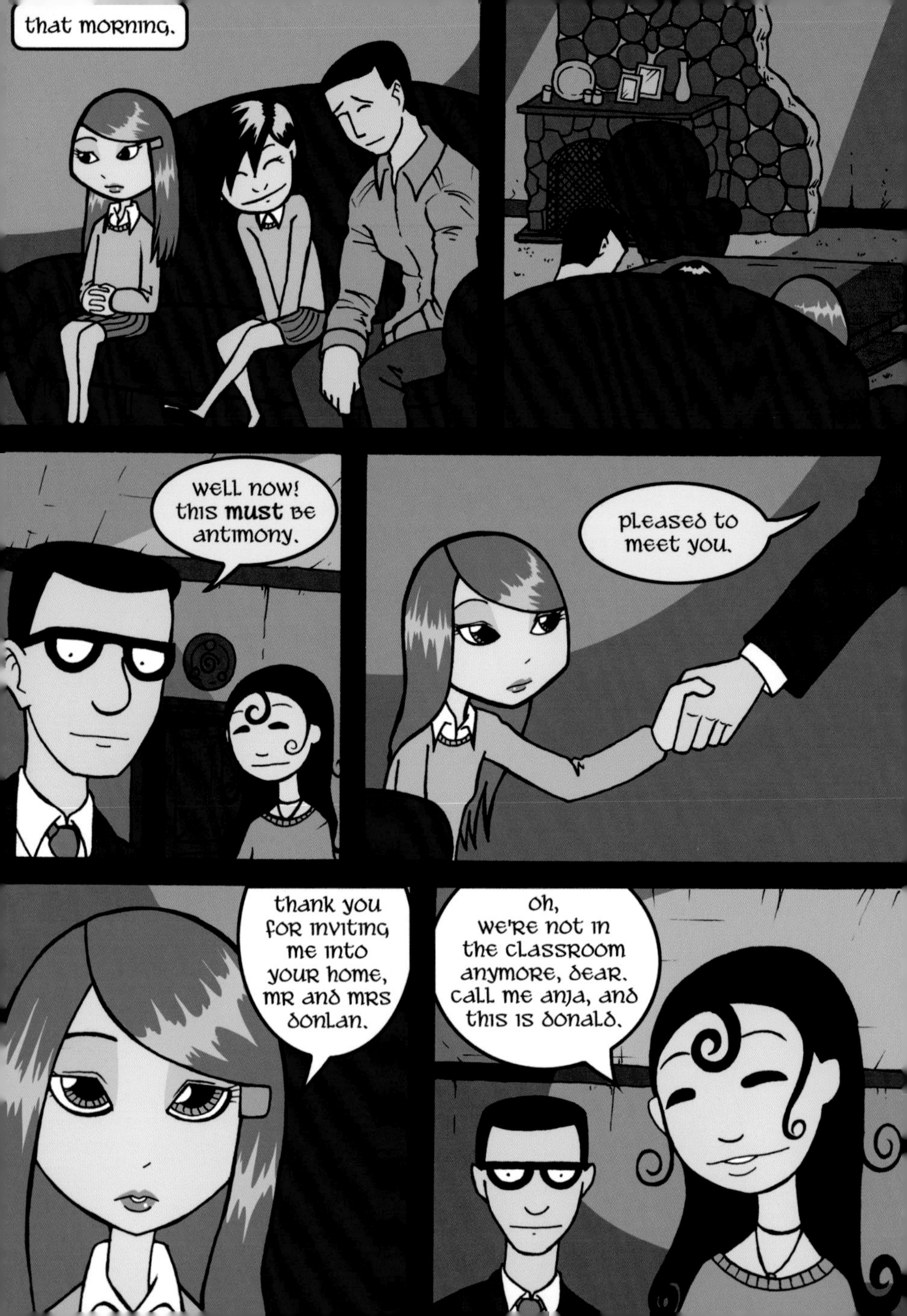
that morning.
well now! this **must** be antimony.
pleased to meet you.
thank you for inviting me into your home, mr and mrs donlan.
oh, we're not in the classroom anymore, dear. call me anja, and this is donald.

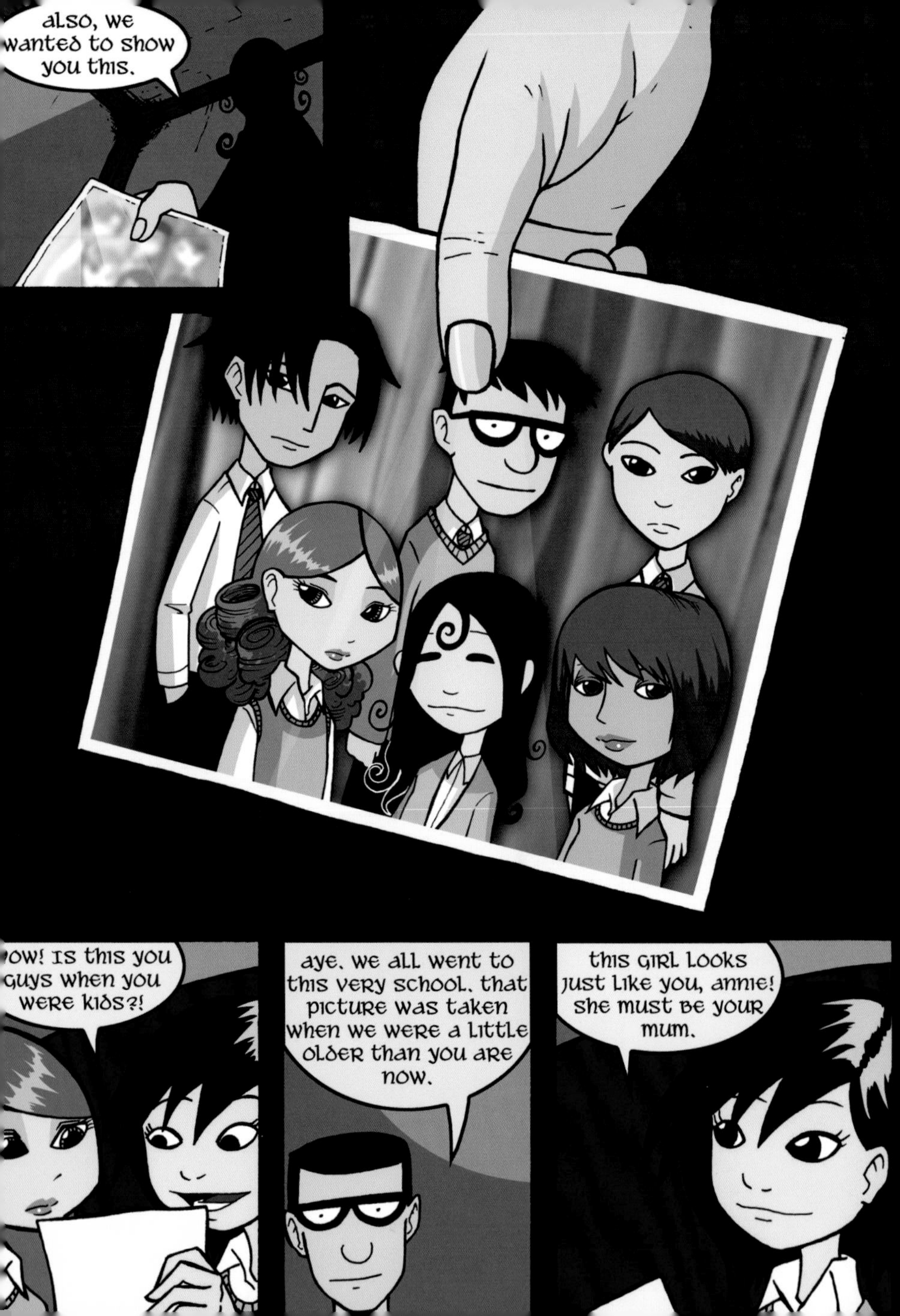
also, we wanted to show you this.
OW! IS this you guys when you were kids?!
aye. we all went to this very school. that picture was taken when we were a little older than you are now.
this girl looks just like you, annie! she must be your mum.

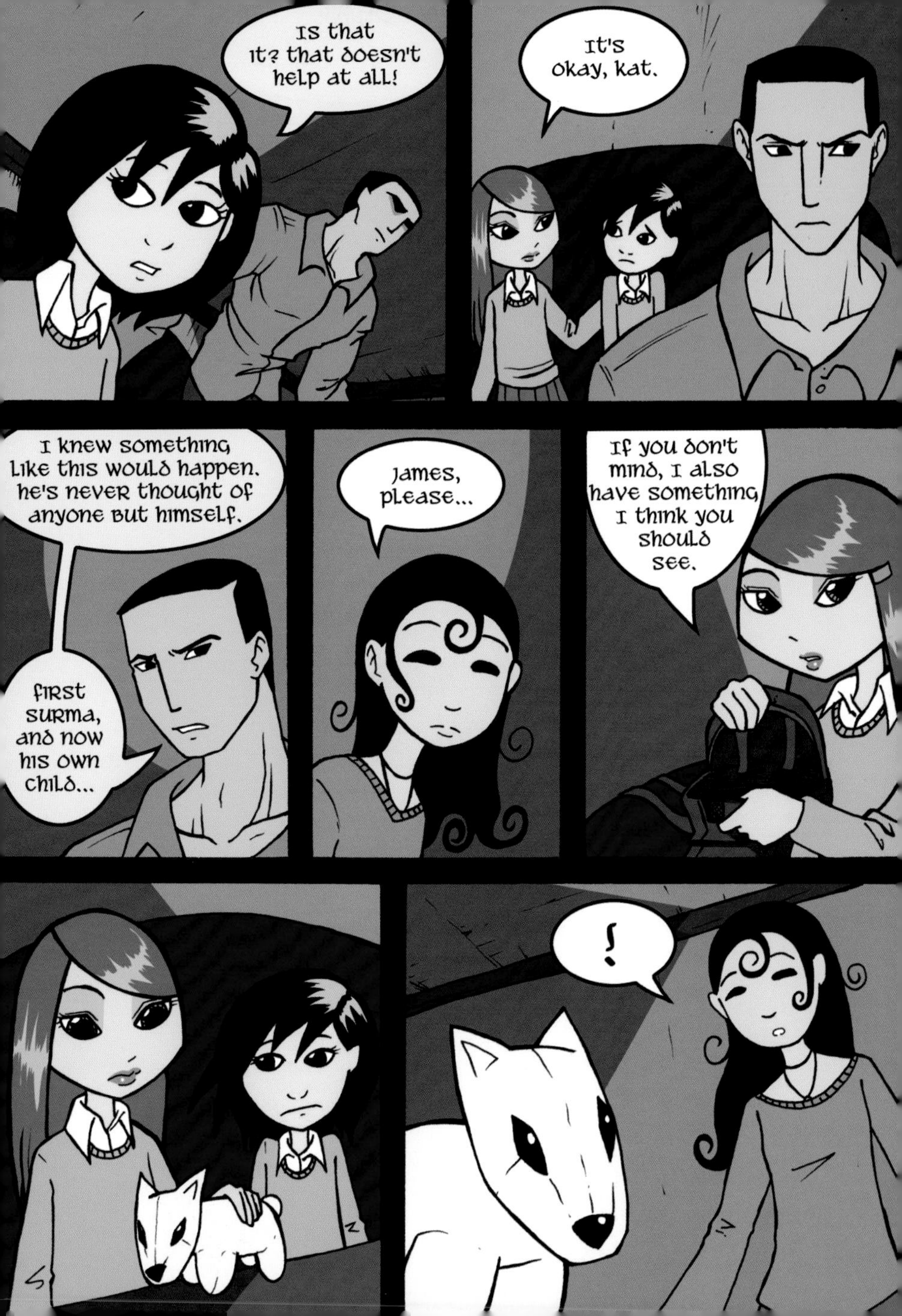
Is that it? that doesn't help at all!
It's okay, kat.
I knew something like this would happen. he's never thought of anyone but himself.
first surma, and now his own child...
james, please...
If you don't mind, I also have something I think you should see.
!

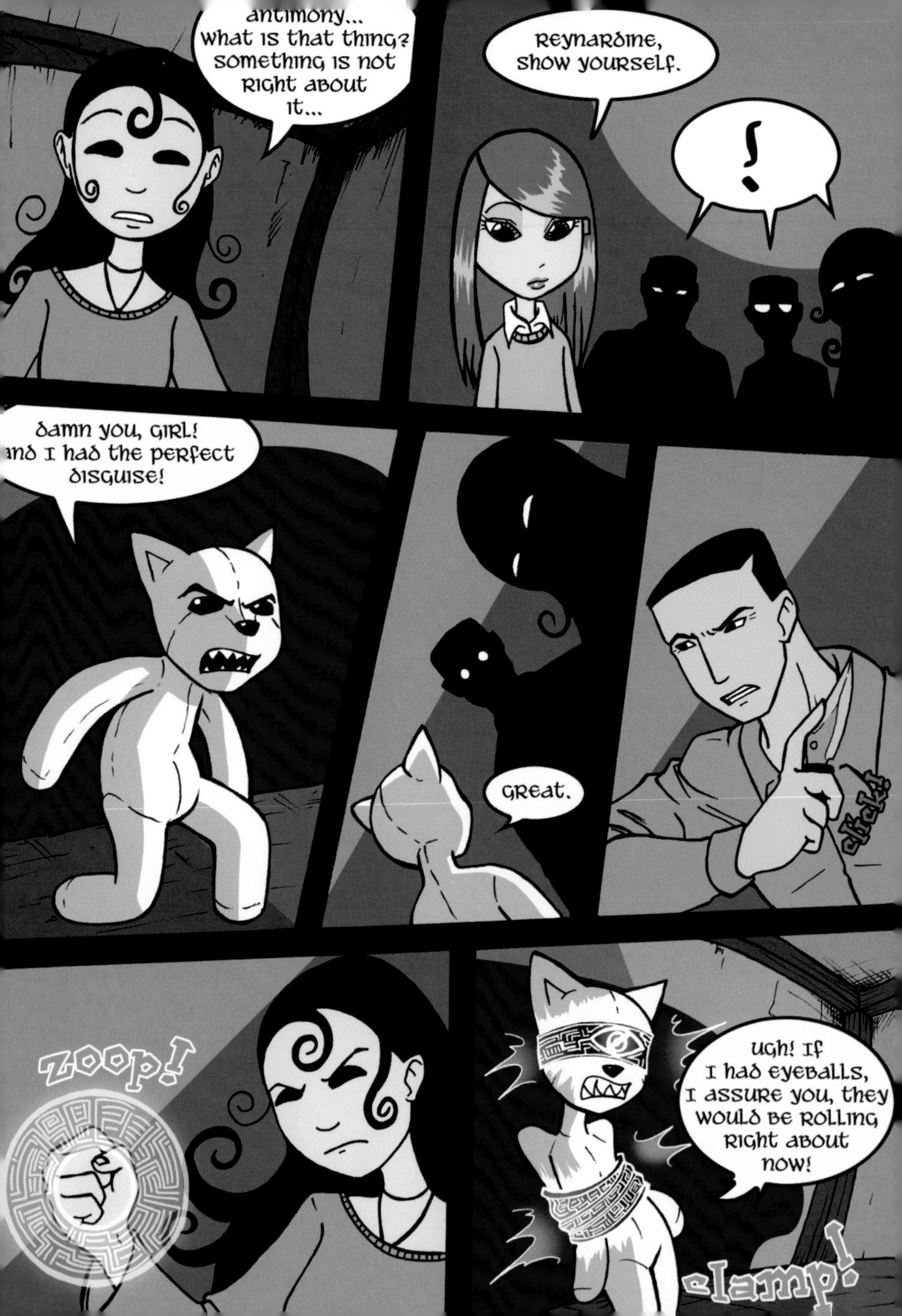

antimony... what is that thing? something is not right about it...
reynardine, show yourself.
!
damn you, girl! and I had the perfect disguise!
great.
click!
zoop!
ugh! if I had eyeballs, I assure you, they would be rolling right about now!
clamp!

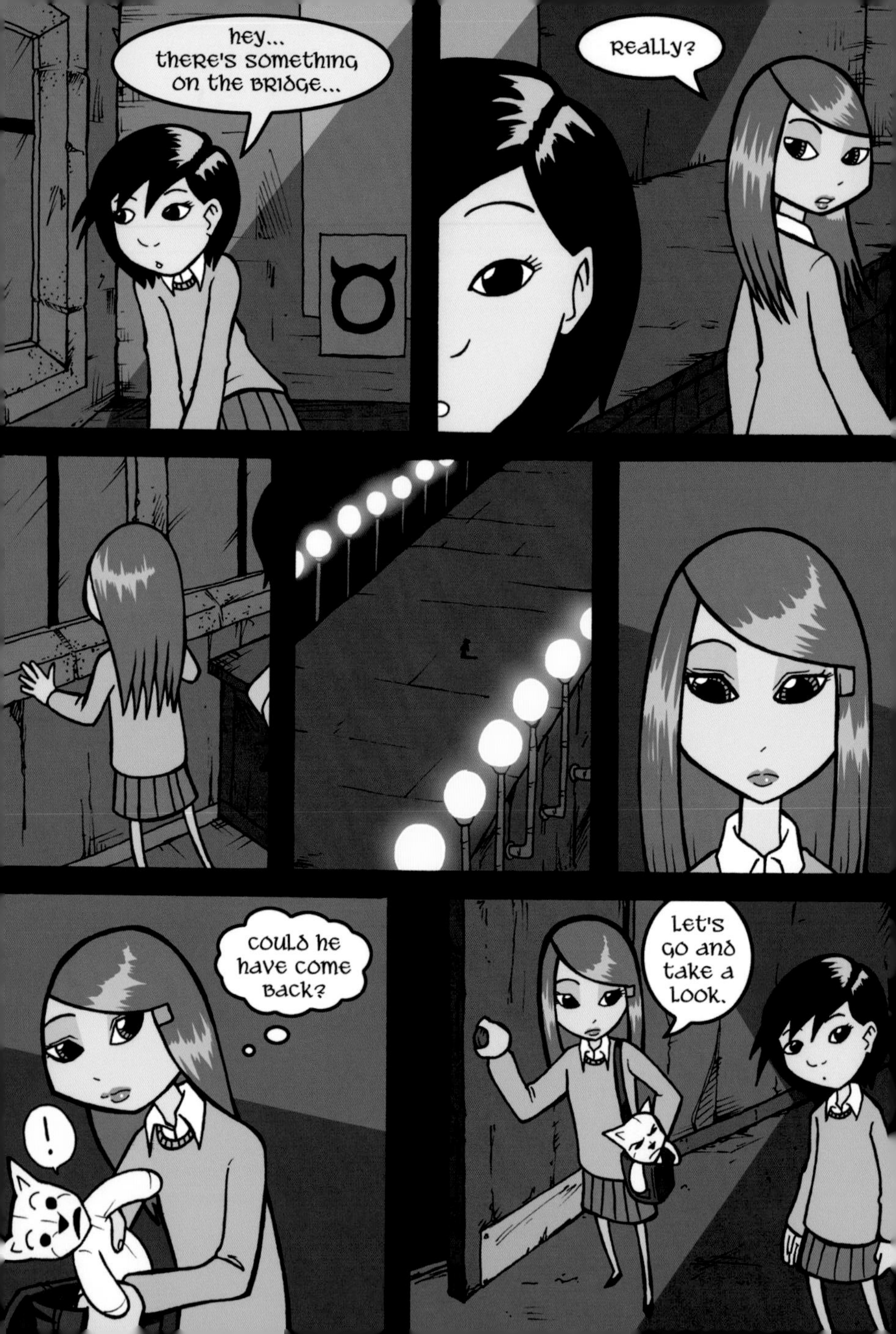
hey...
there's something on the bridge...
Really?
could he have come back?
!
Let's go and take a look.

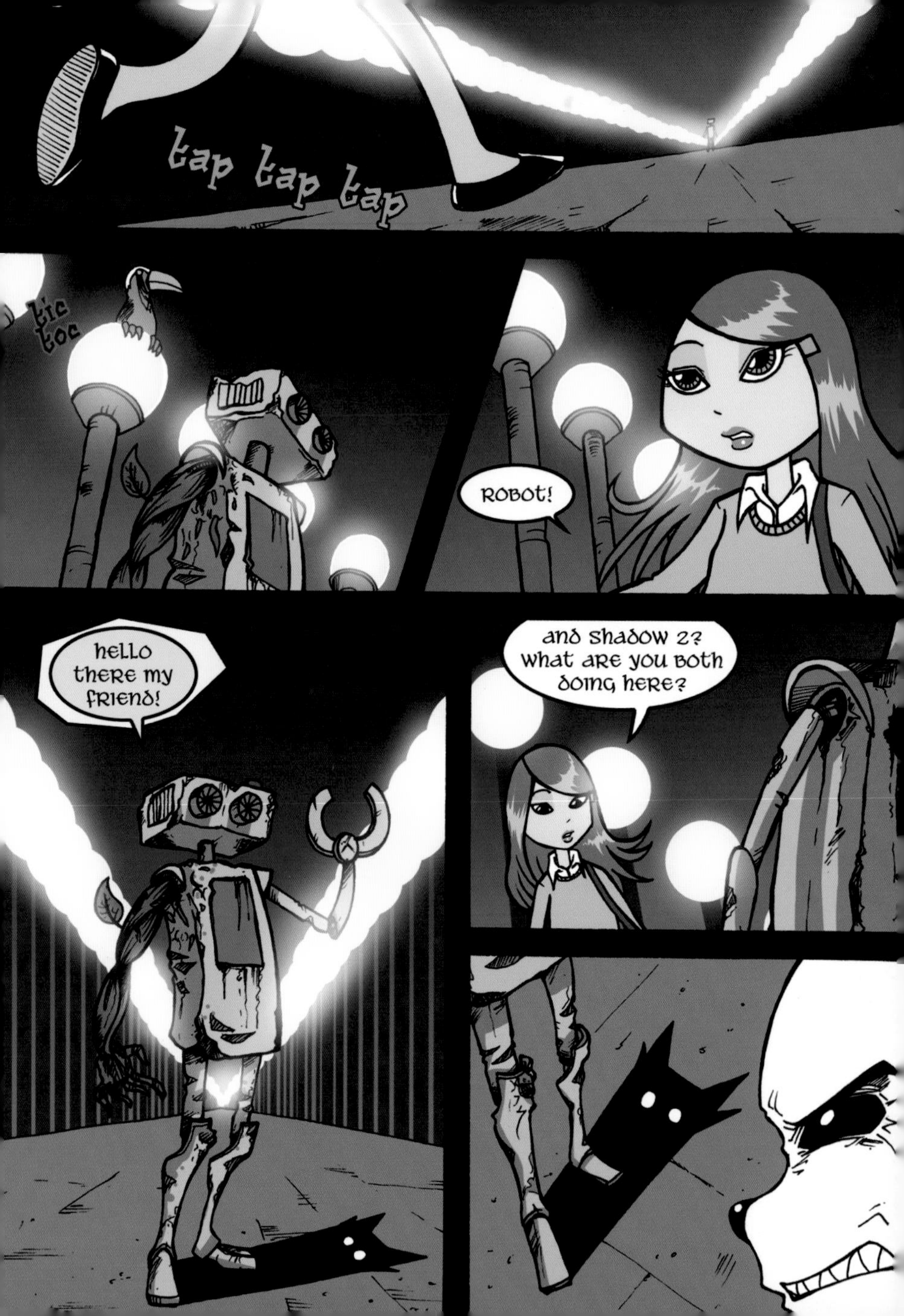
tap tap tap
tic toc
ROBOT!
hello there my friend!
and shadow 2? what are you both doing here?

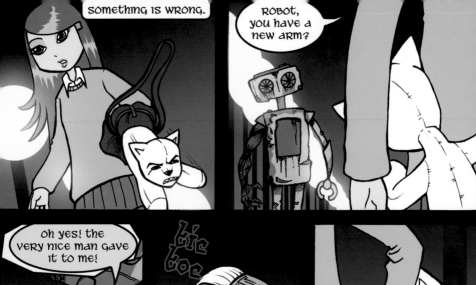

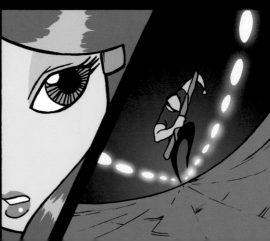

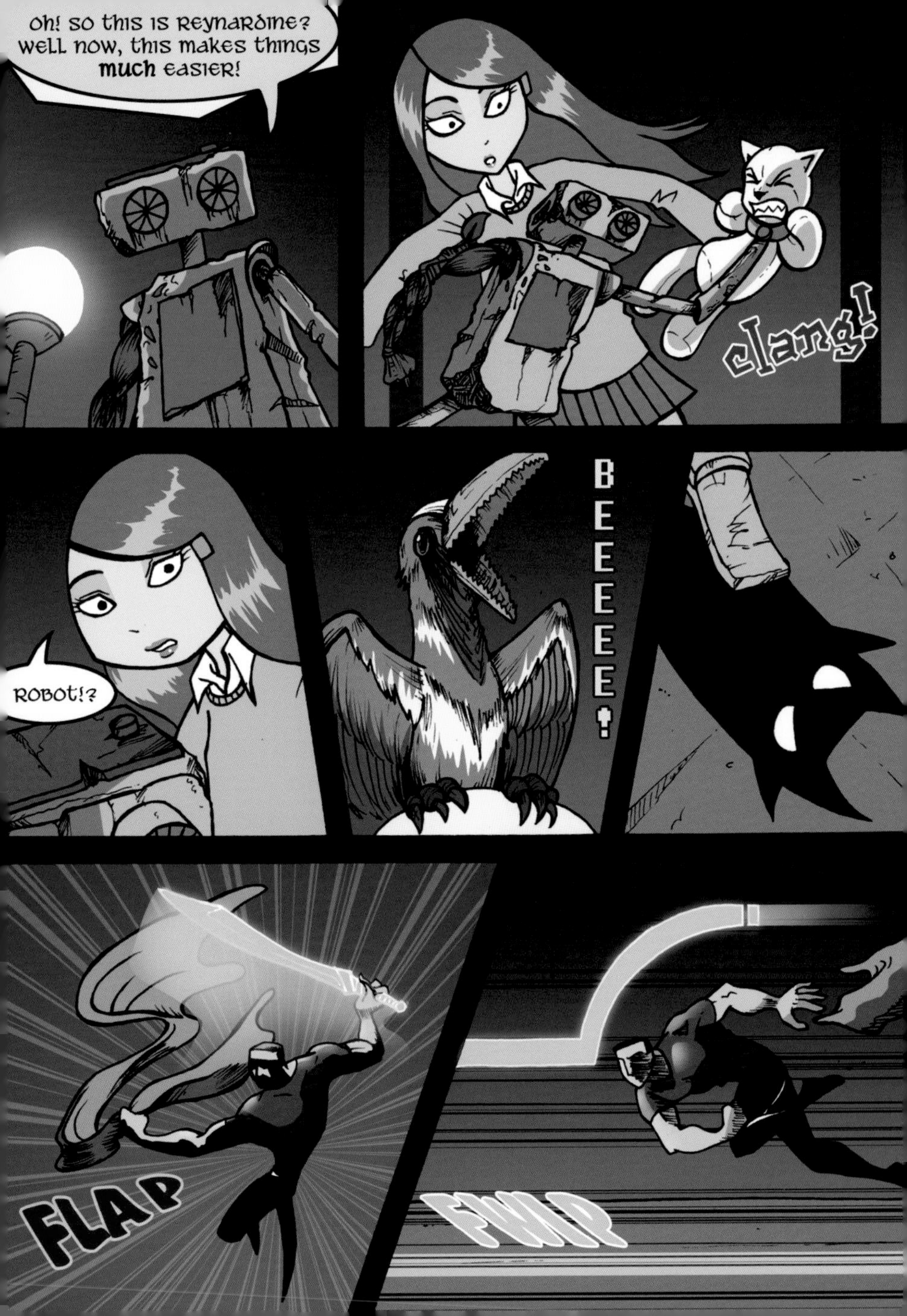

Oh! so this is Reynardine? well now, this makes things much easier!
clang!
ROBOT!?
BEEEEEE!
FLAP
FWIP

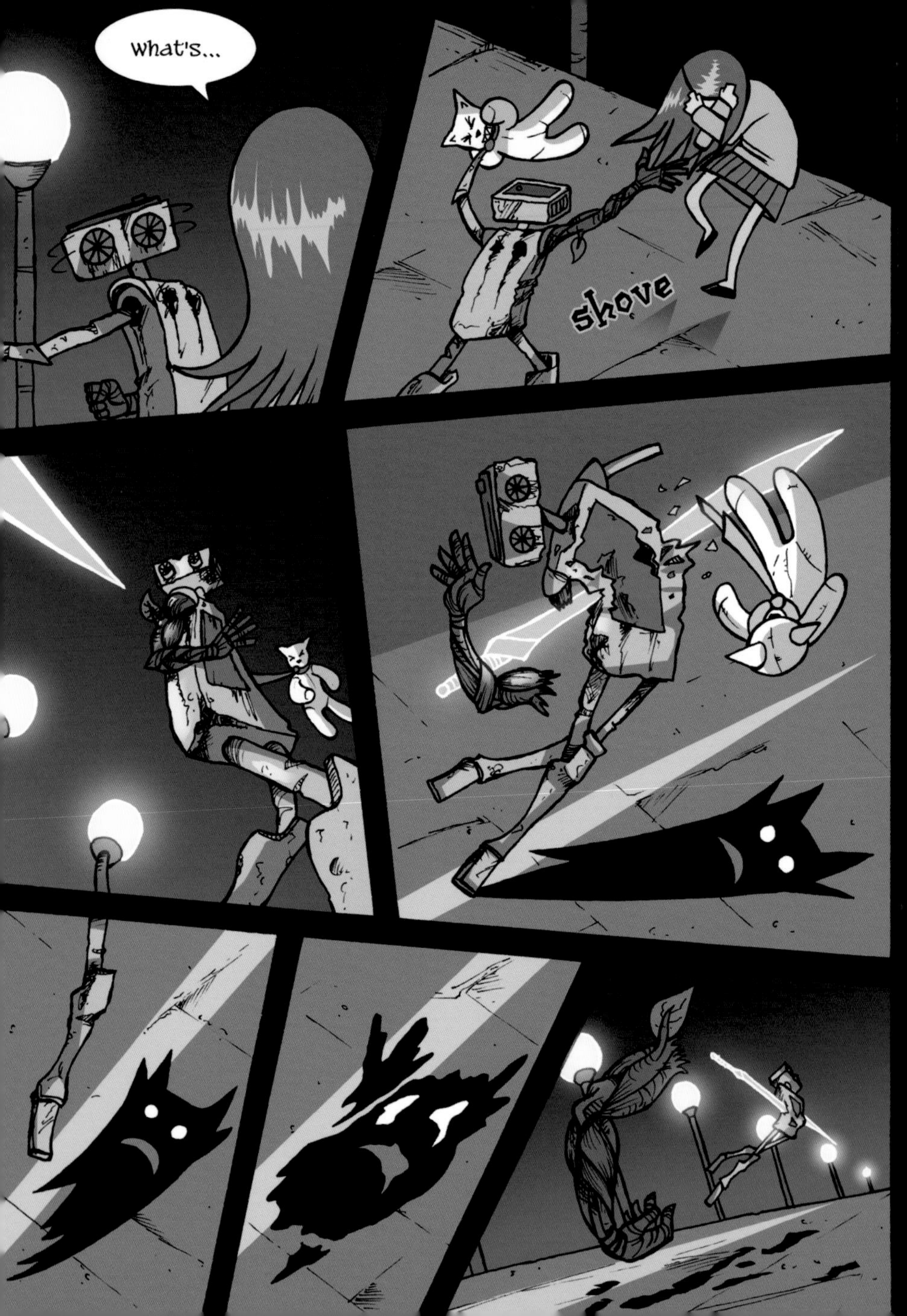
what's...
shove

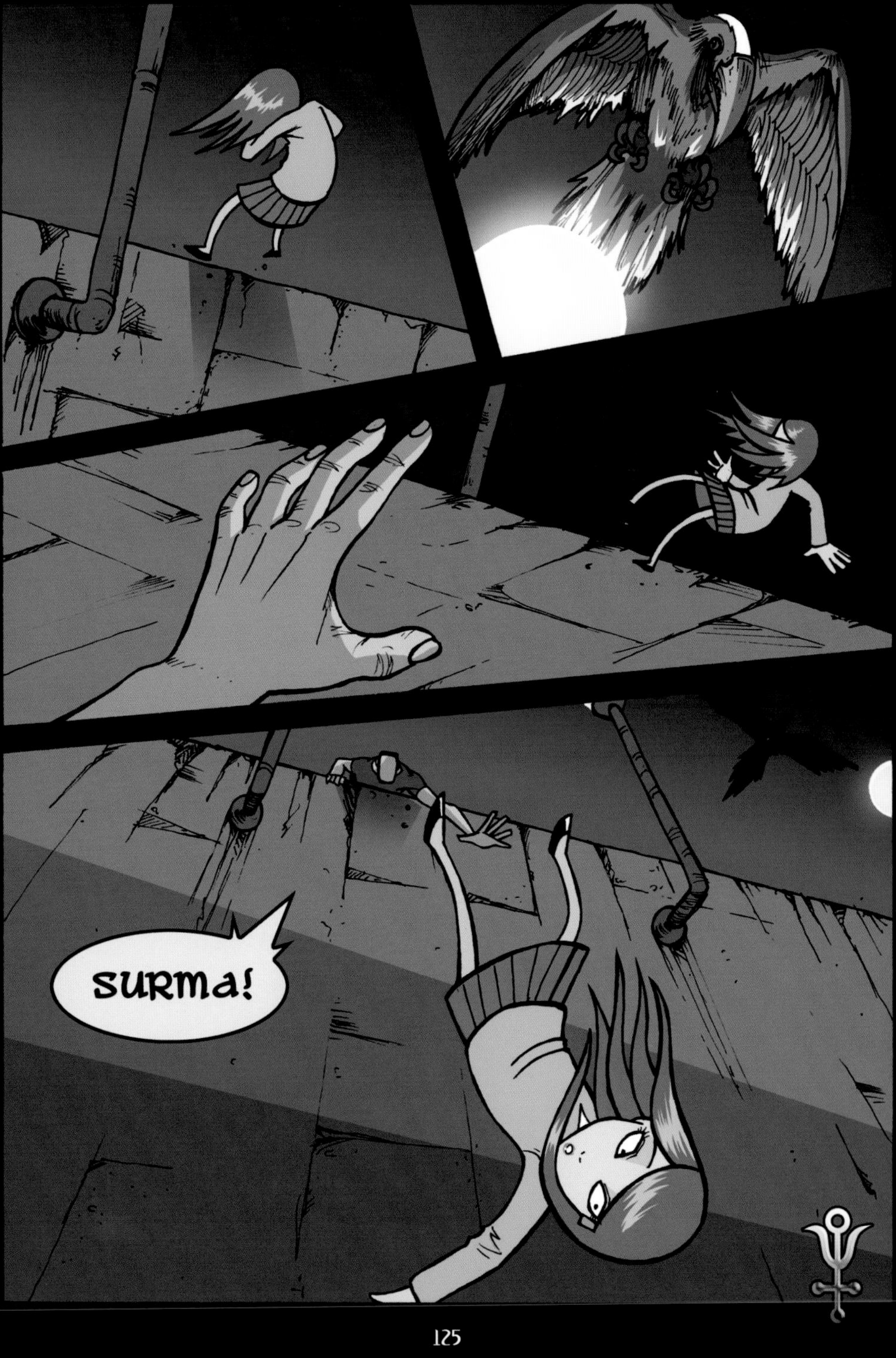
SURMA!

Ora Lege Relege Labora Et Invenies VII

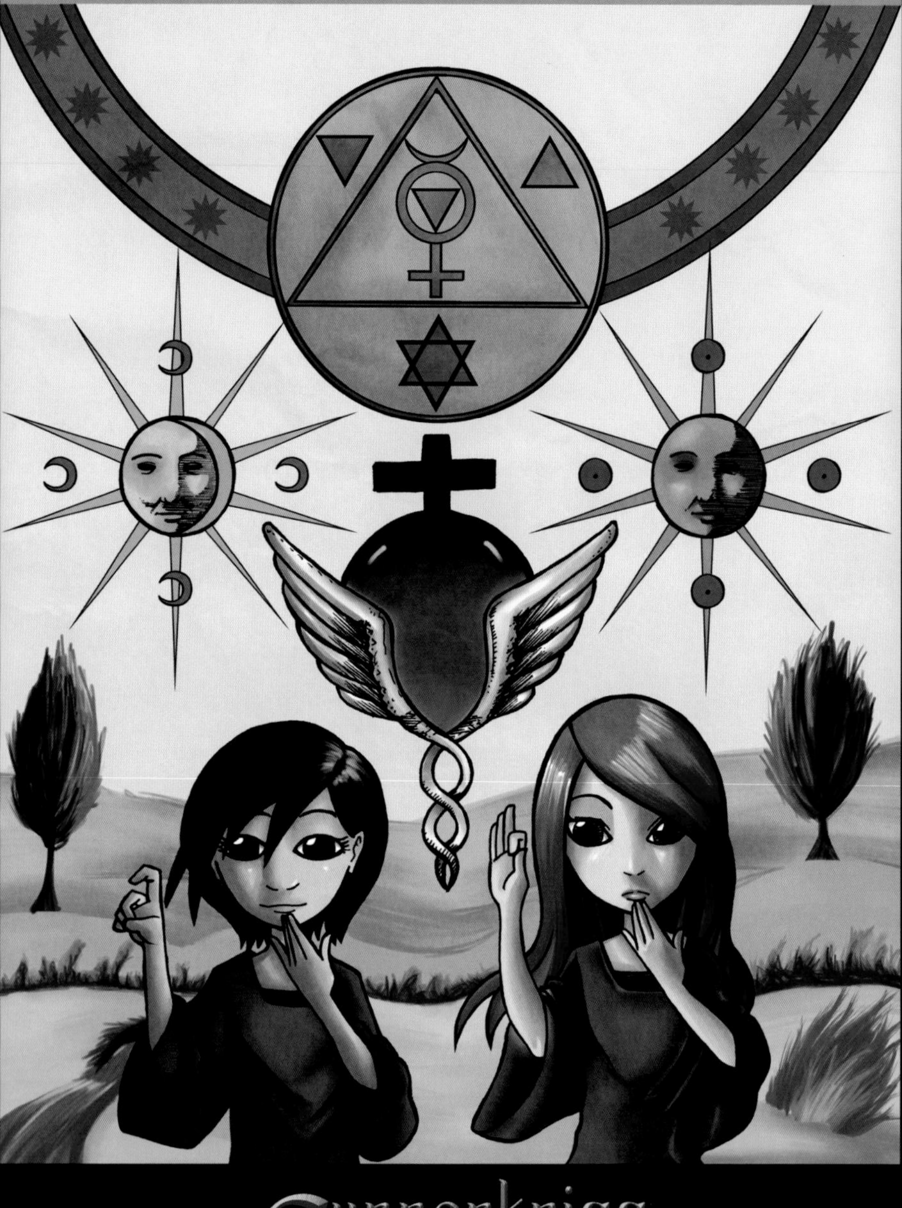

Gunnerkrigg Court

Gunnerkrigg Court

Chapter 8:

Broken Glass And Other Things

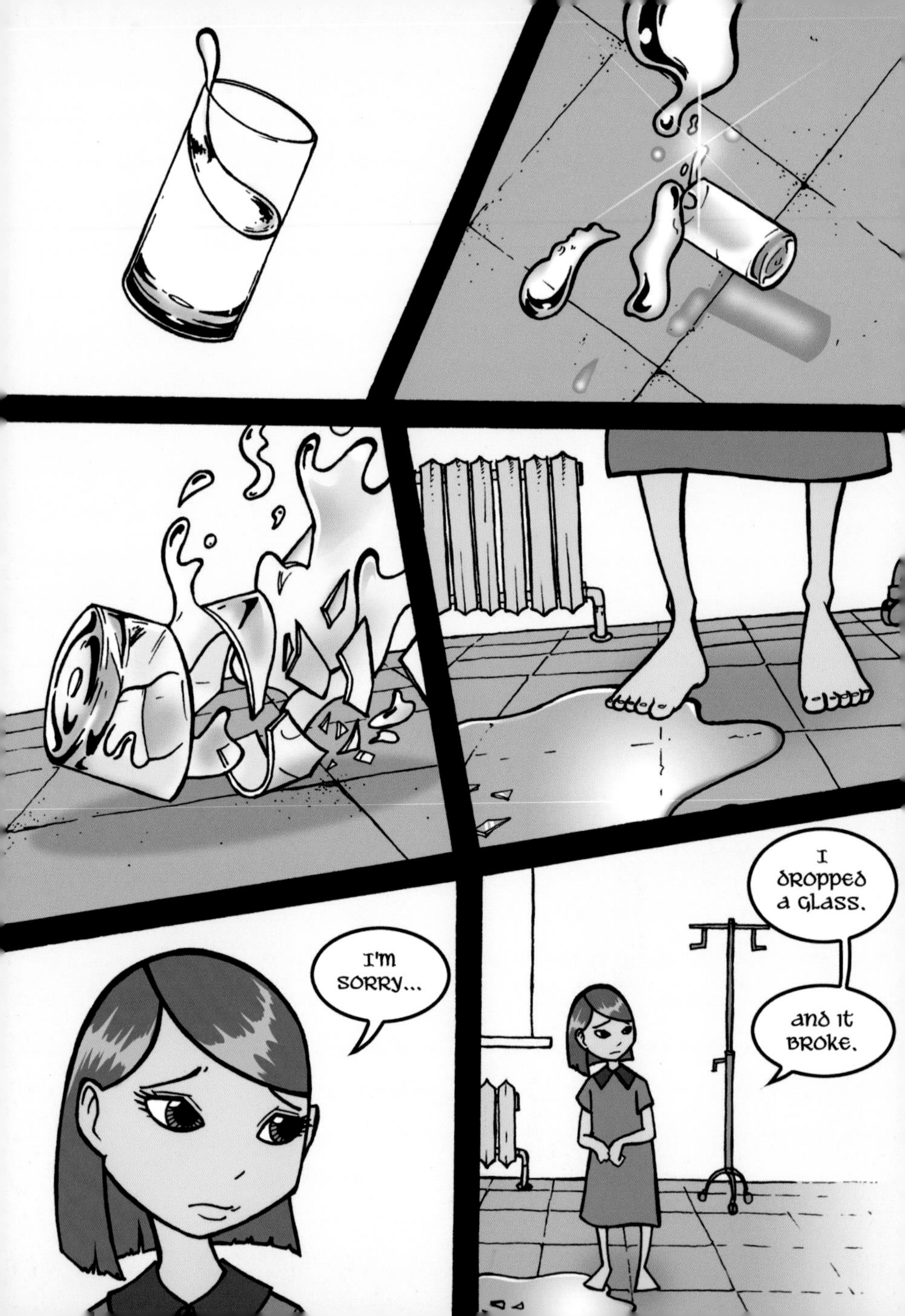
I'M SORRY...
I DROPPED A GLASS.
AND IT BROKE.

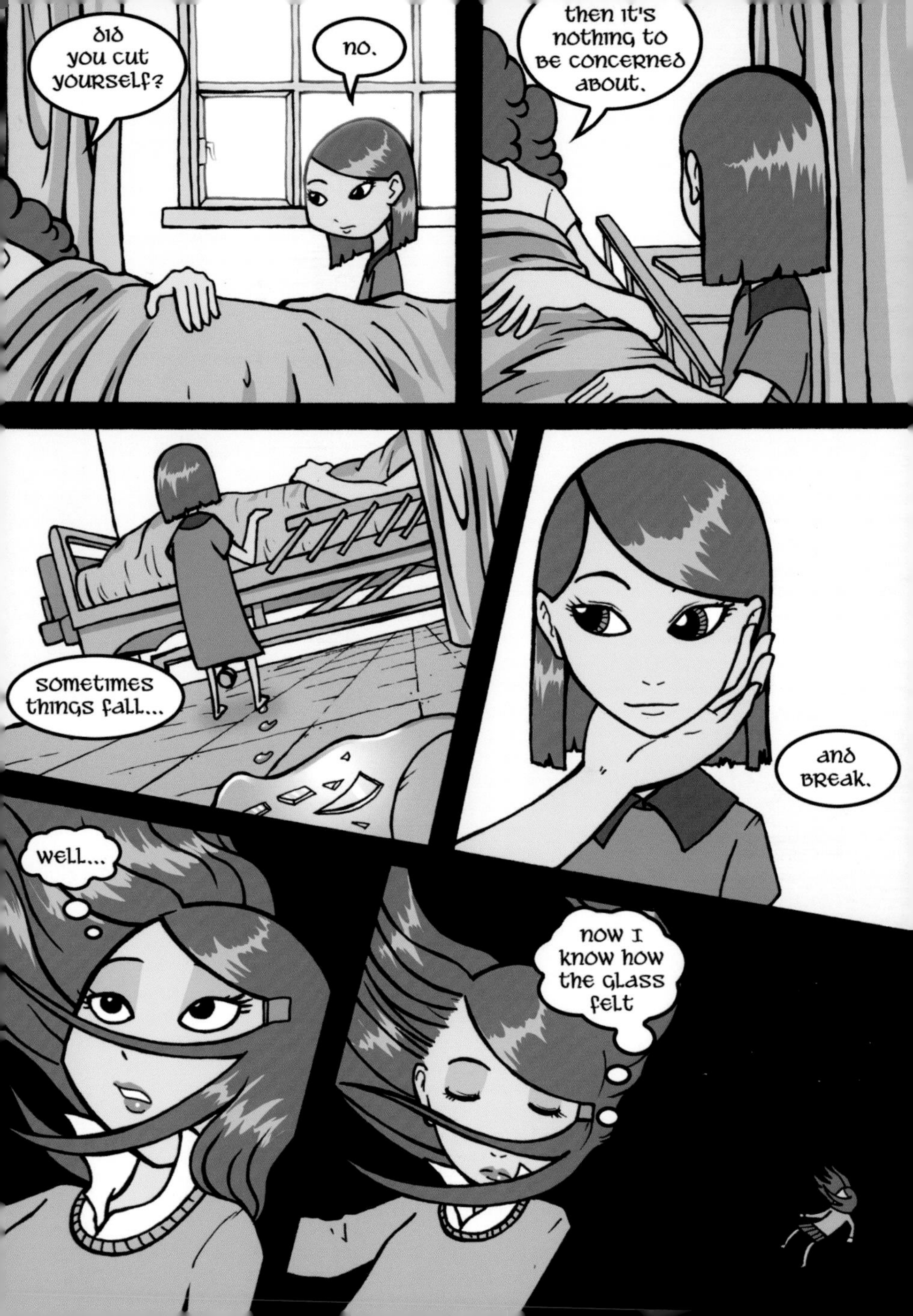
did you cut yourself?
no.
then it's nothing to be concerned about.
sometimes things fall...
and break.
well...
now I know how the glass felt

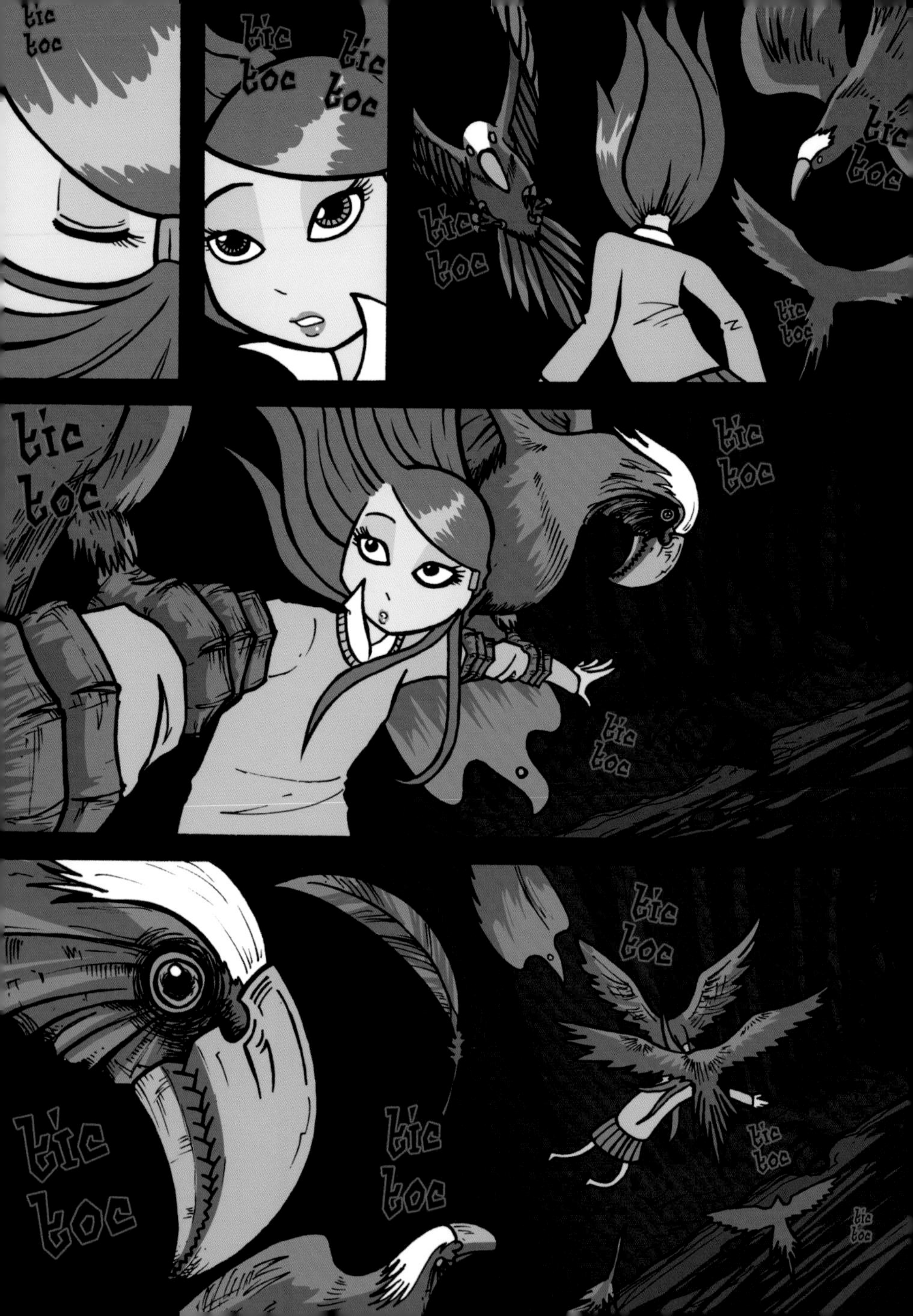
tic toc
tic toc
tic toc
tic toc
tic toc
tic toc
tic toc
tic toc
tic toc
tic toc
tic toc
tic toc
tic toc
tic toc
tic toc

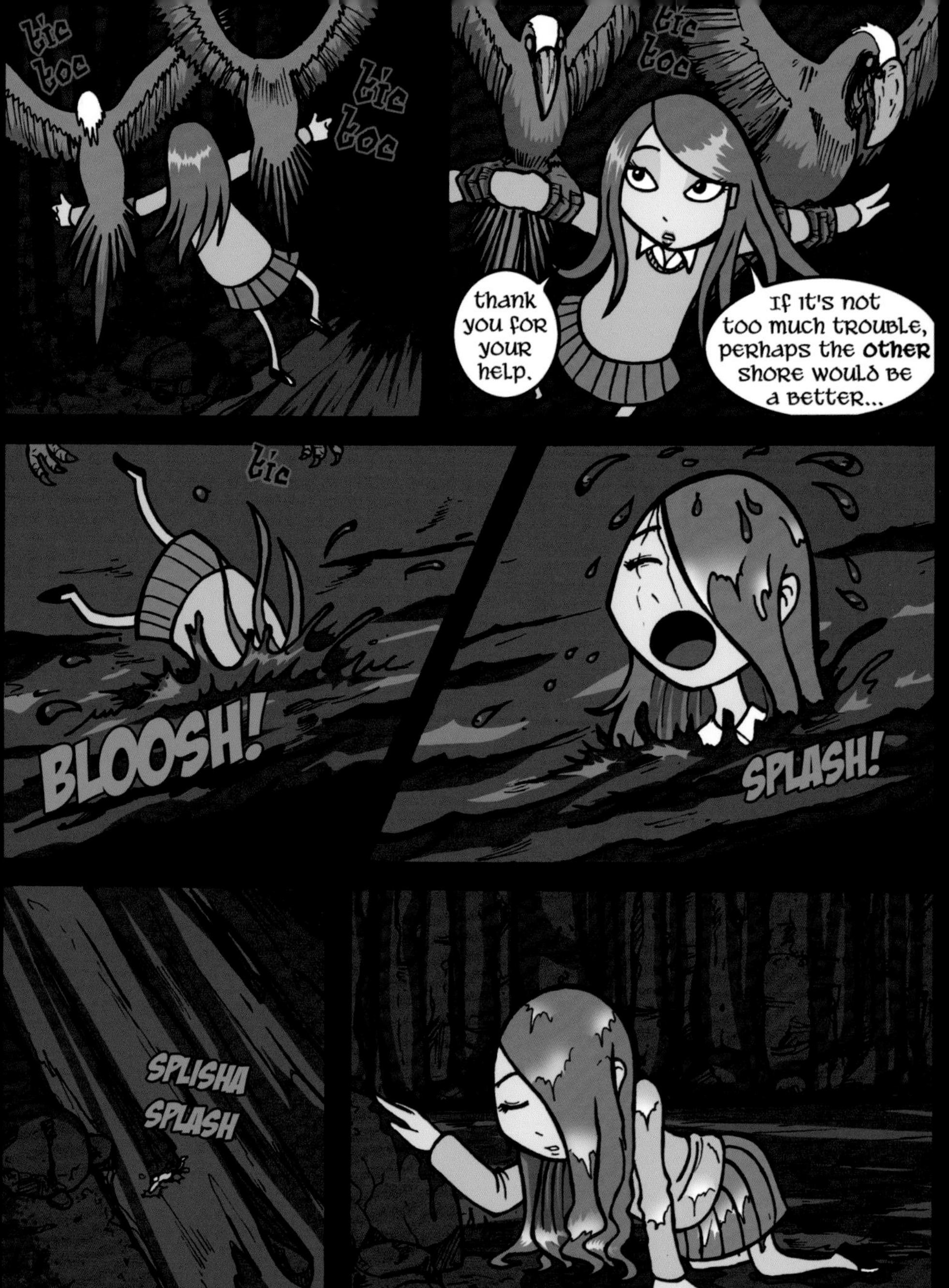
tic toc
tic toc
tic toc
thank you for your help.
If it's not too much trouble, perhaps the **other** shore would be a better...
tic
BLOOSH!
SPLASH!
SPLISHA SPLASH

my eyes soon became accustomed to the darkness.

though there was not much to see.

In the distance there was a light, shining dimly from the opposite shore.

despite the river being far too large to cross on my own, I decided to investigate further.

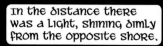

I found something.

But then...

132

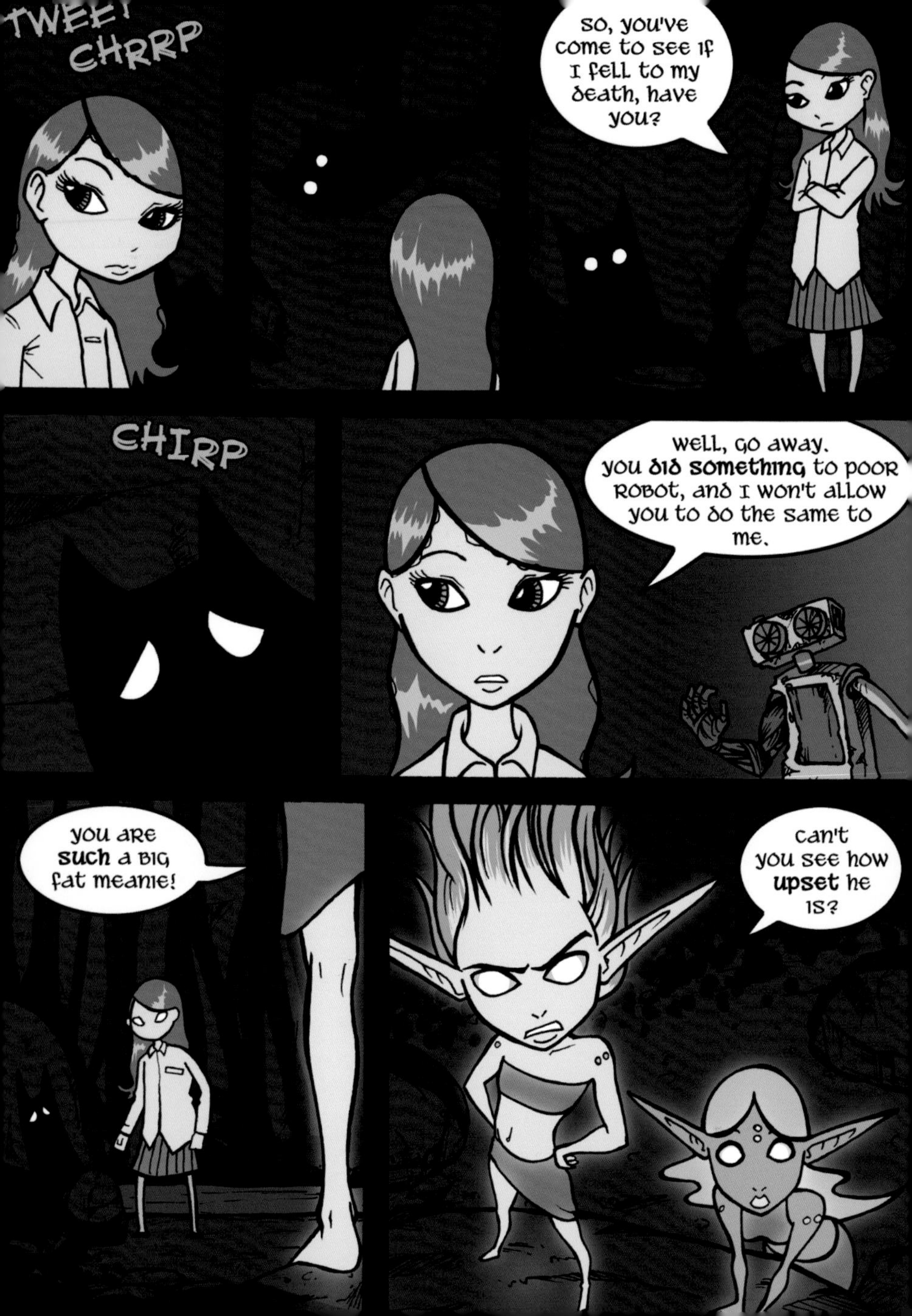
TWEET
CHRRP
SO, YOU'VE COME TO SEE IF I FELL TO MY DEATH, HAVE YOU?
CHIRP
WELL, GO AWAY. YOU **DID SOMETHING** TO POOR ROBOT, AND I WON'T ALLOW YOU TO DO THE SAME TO ME.
YOU ARE **SUCH** A BIG FAT MEANIE!
CAN'T YOU SEE HOW **UPSET** HE IS?

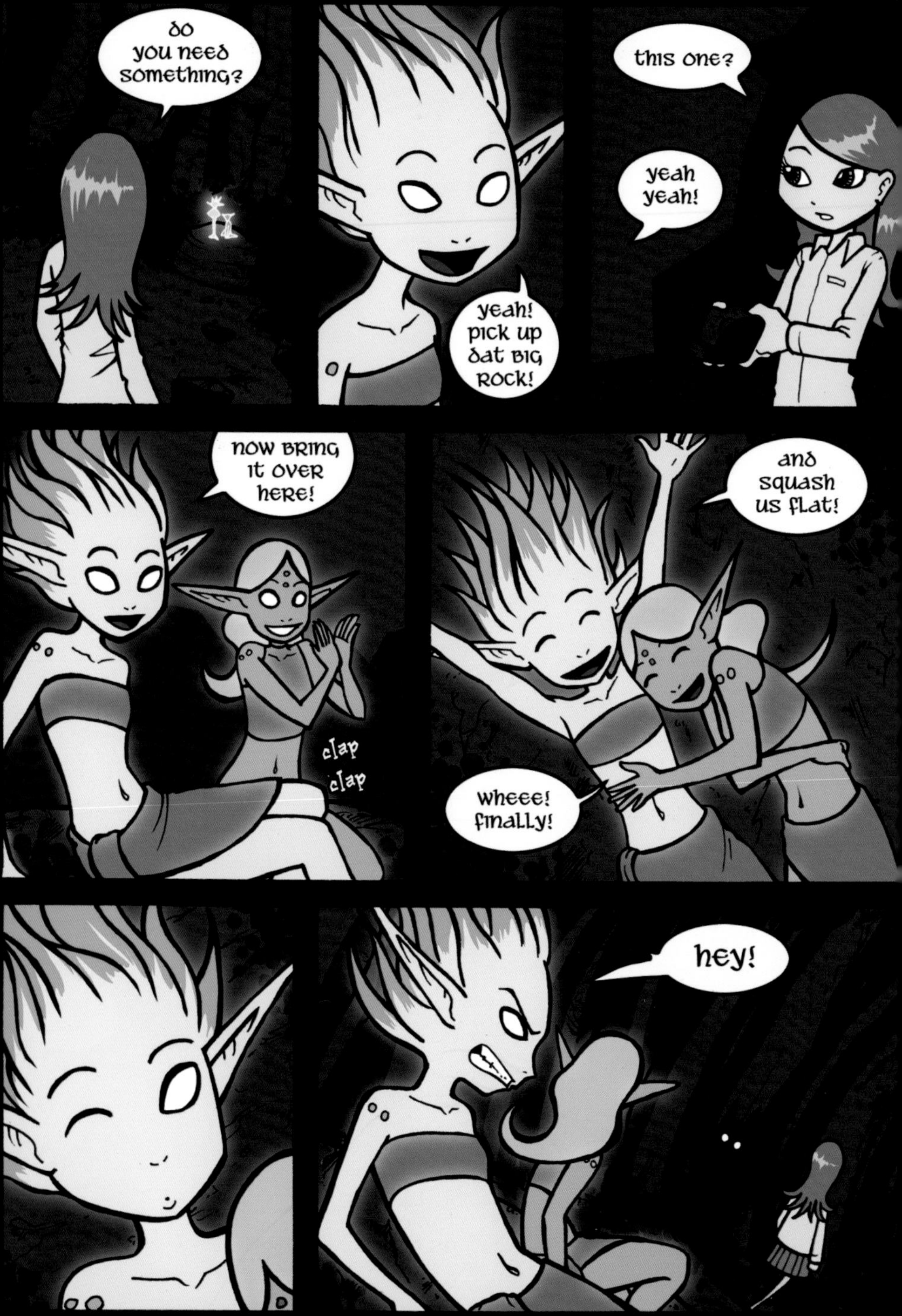
do you need something?
yeah! pick up dat BIG ROCK!
this one?
yeah yeah!
now BRING it over here!
clap clap
and squash us flat!
wheee! finally!
hey!

137

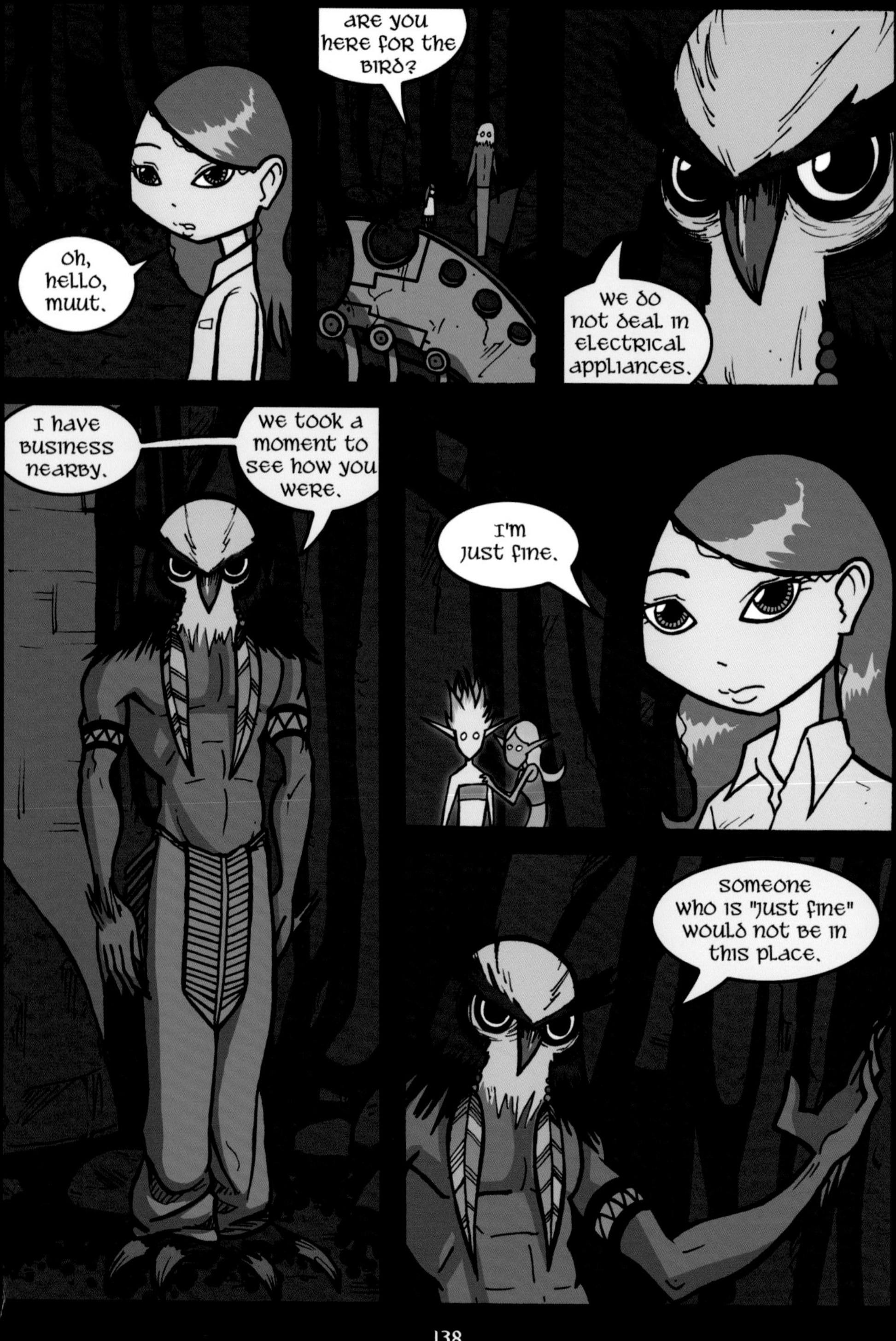
oh, hello, muut.
are you here for the bird?
we do not deal in electrical appliances.
I have business nearby.
we took a moment to see how you were.
I'm just fine.
someone who is "just fine" would not be in this place.

139

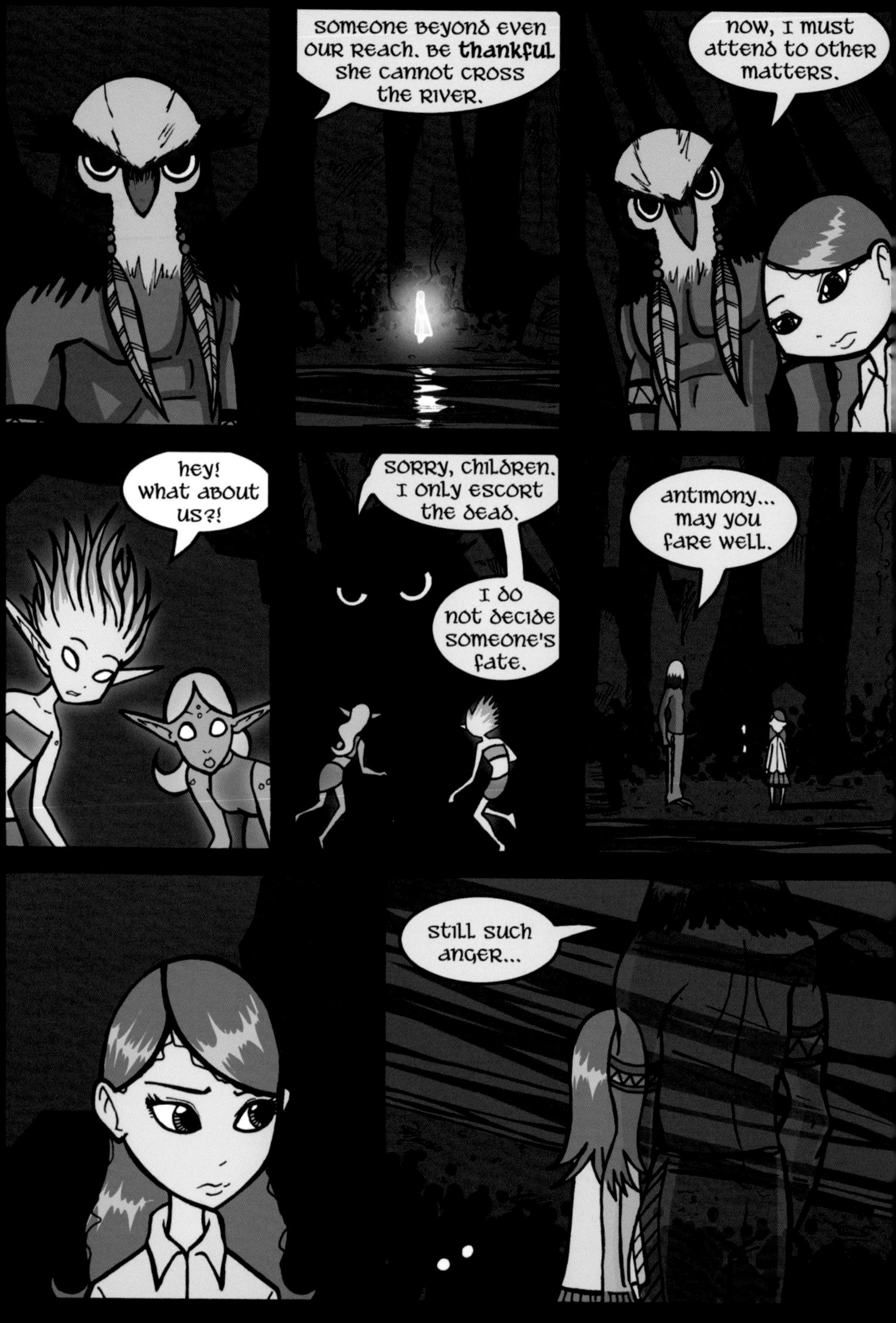

someone beyond even our reach. be thankful she cannot cross the river.
now, I must attend to other matters.
hey! what about us?!
sorry, children. I only escort the dead.
I do not decide someone's fate.
antimony... may you fare well.
still such anger...

141

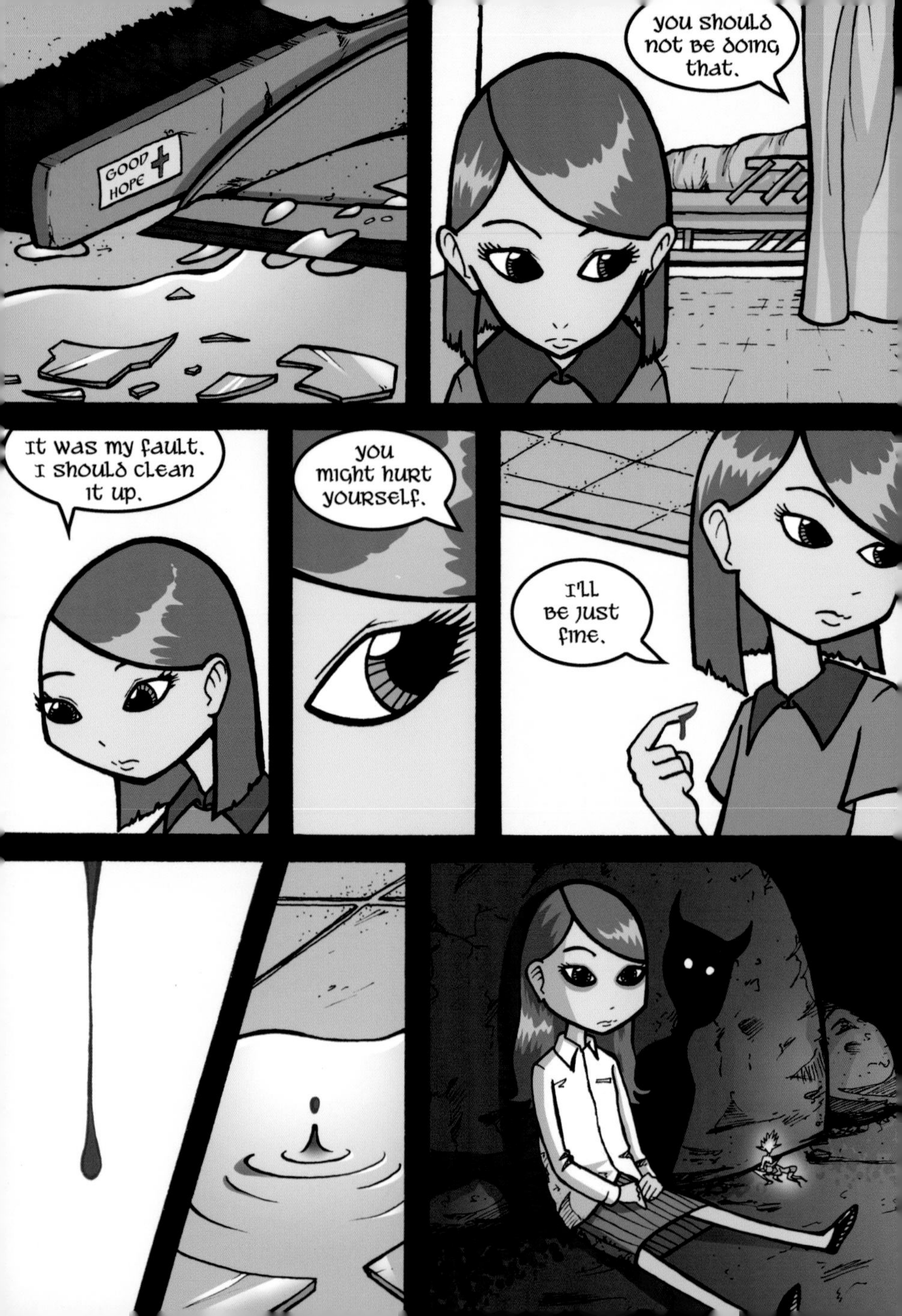
GOOD HOPE
you should not be doing that.
It was my fault. I should clean it up.
you might hurt yourself.
I'll be just fine.

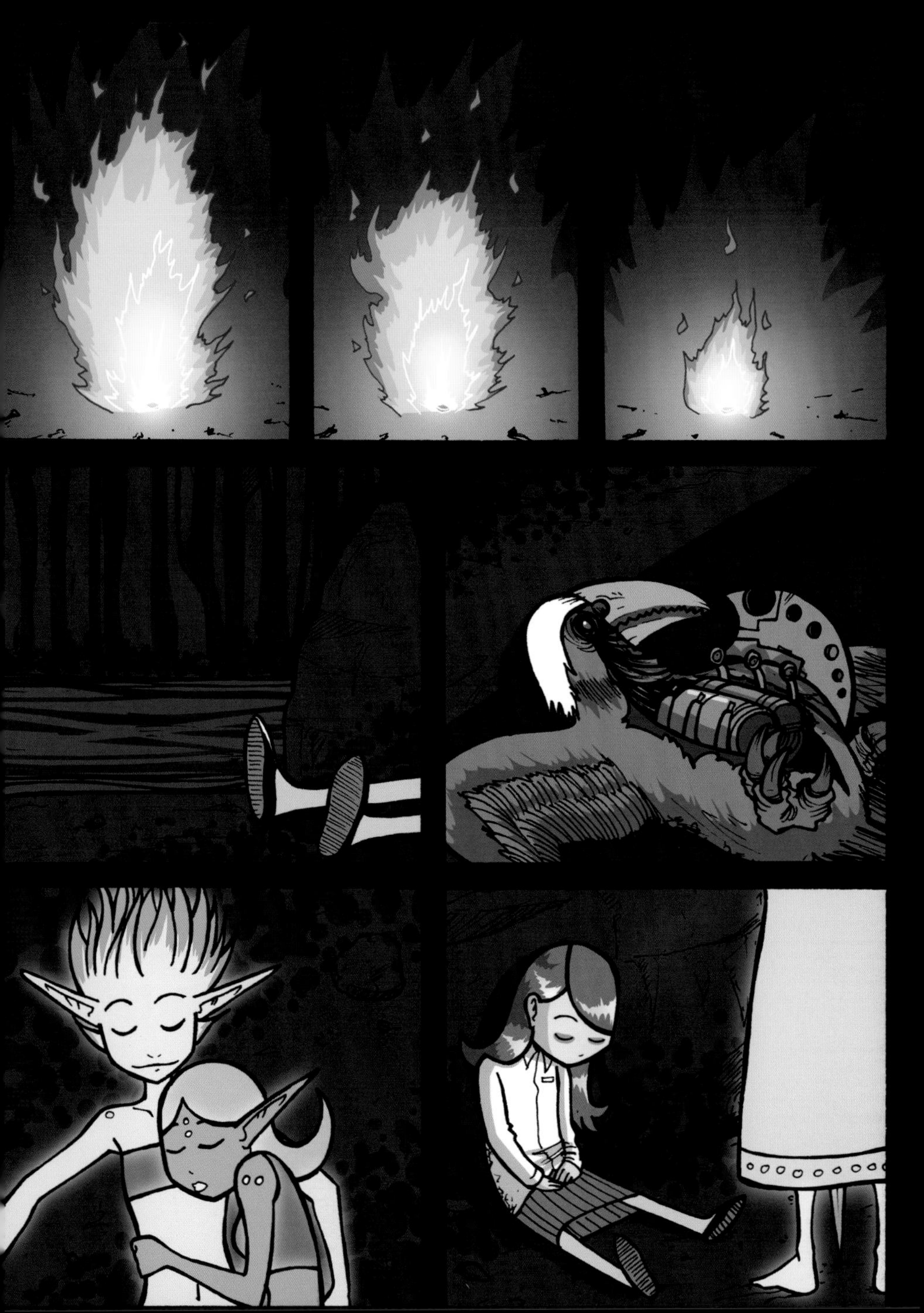

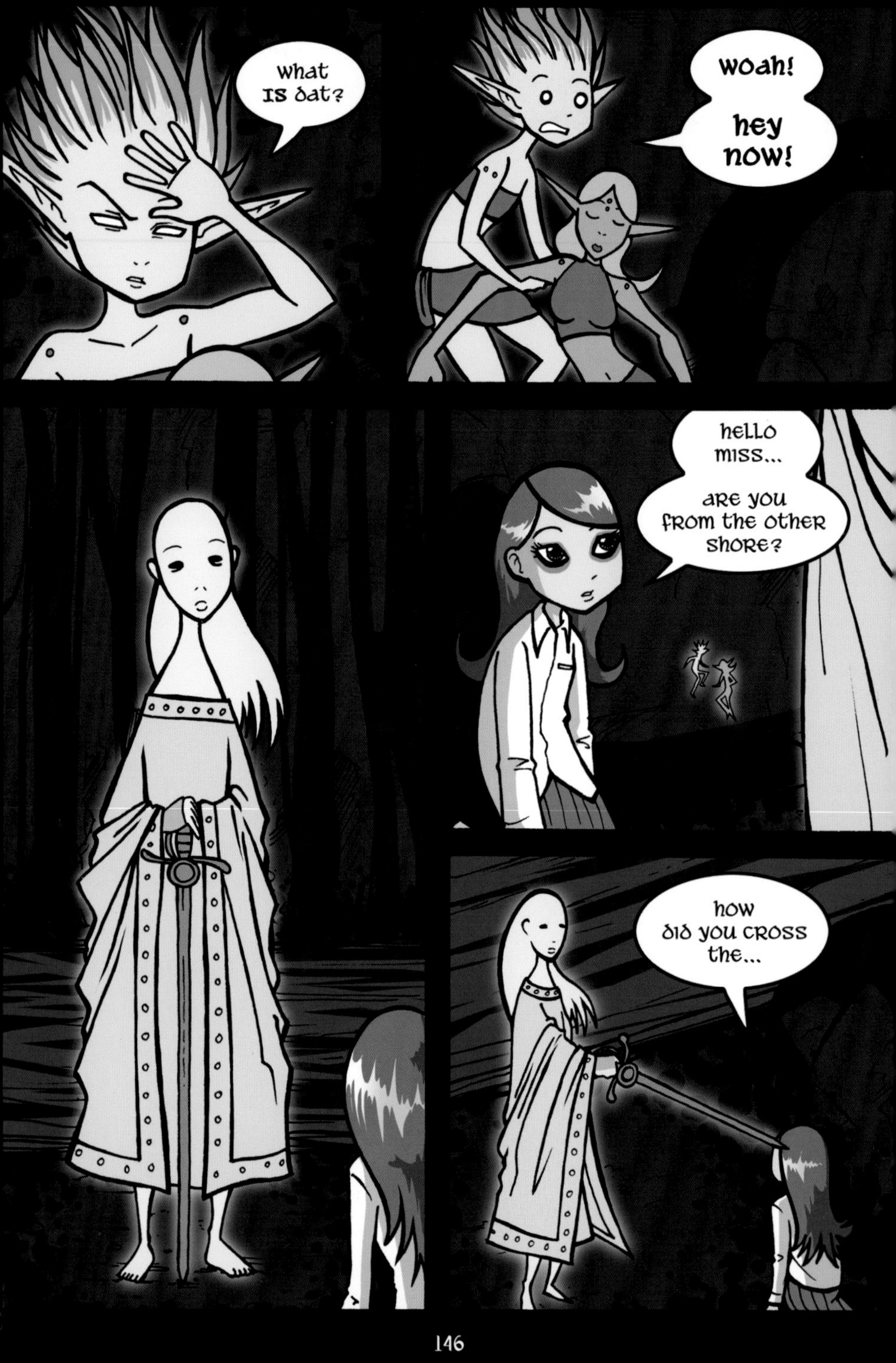
what IS dat?
woah!
hey now!
hello miss...
are you from the other shore?
how did you cross the...

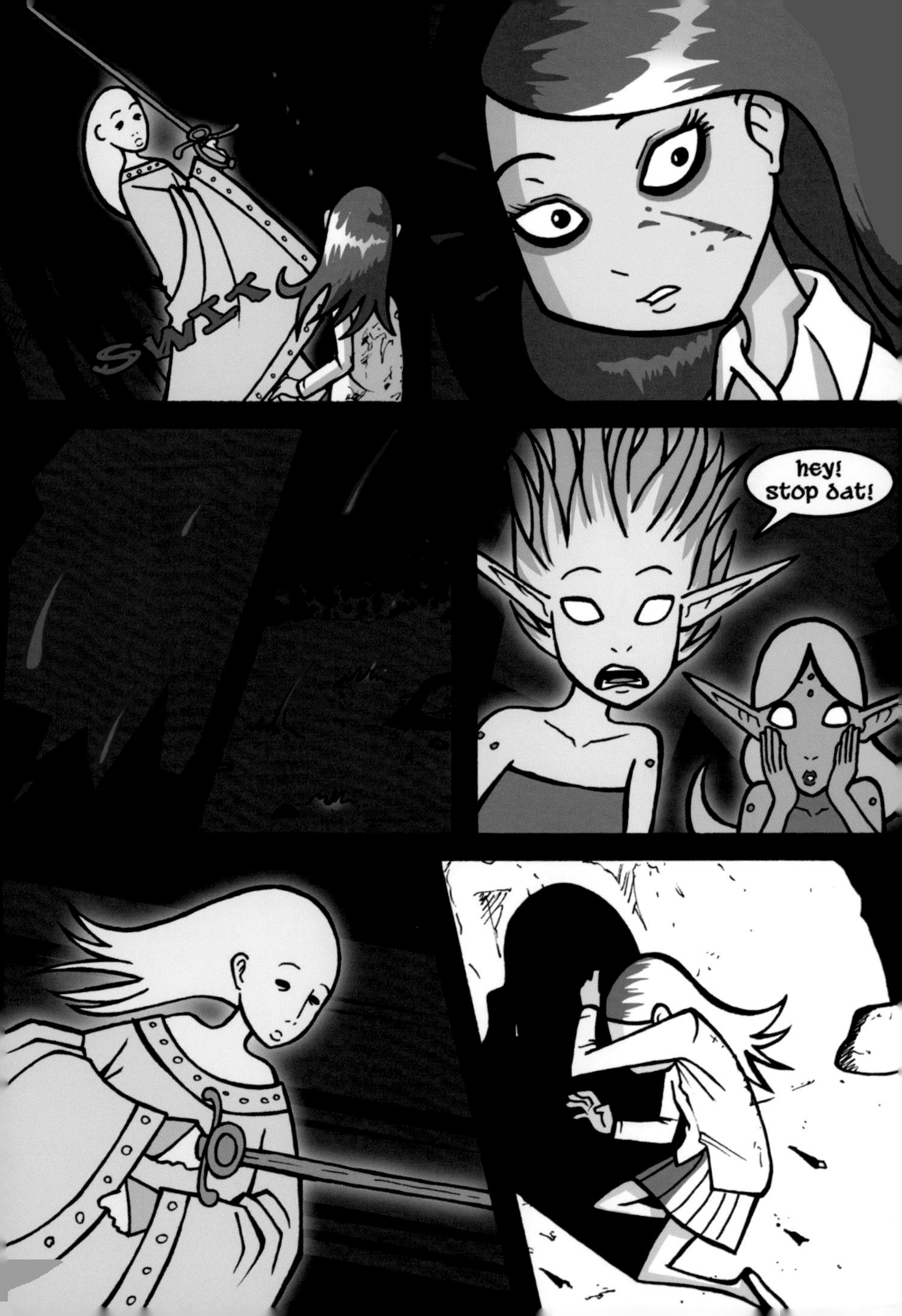
SWIK
hey! stop dat!

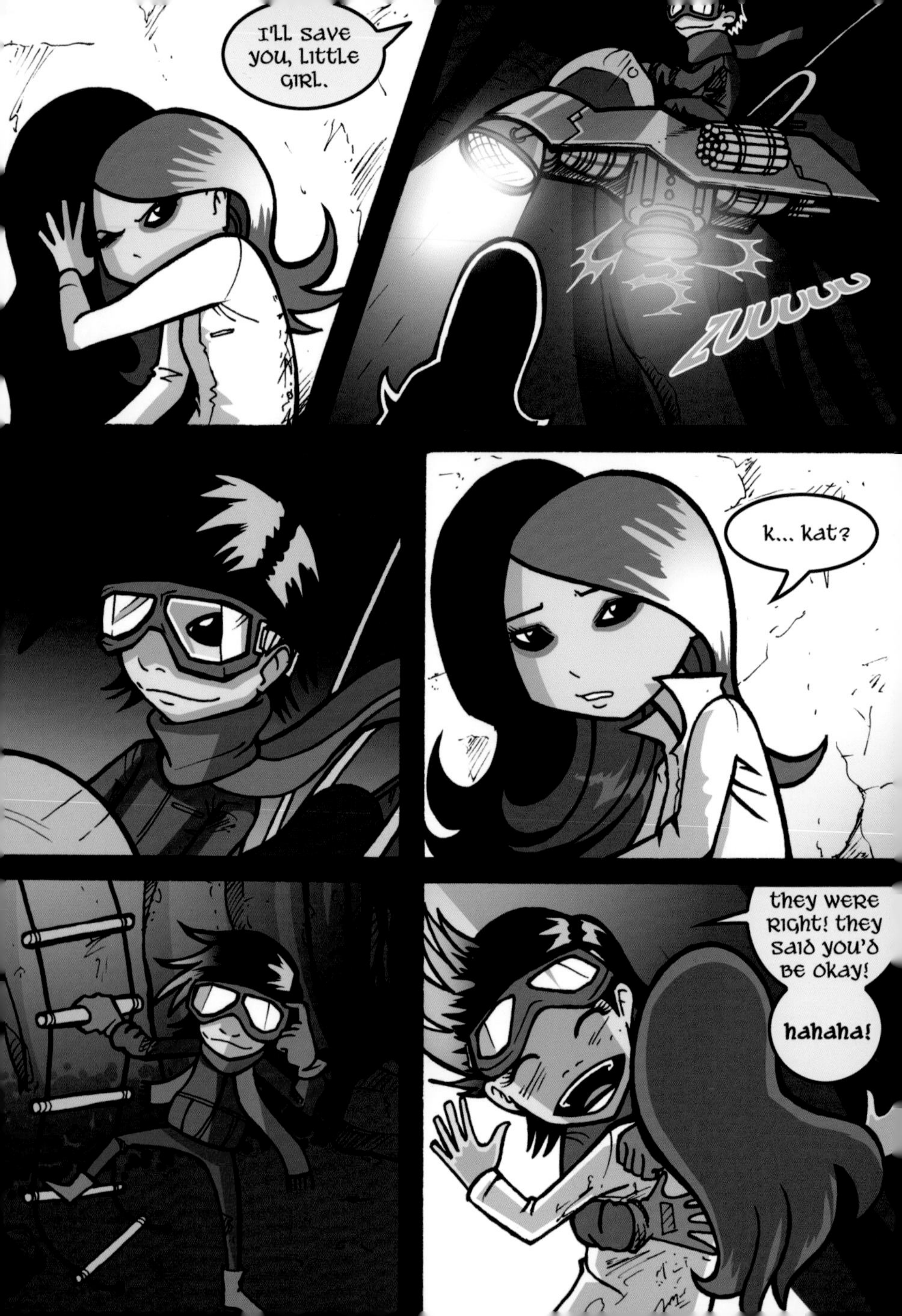
I'LL SAVE YOU, LITTLE GIRL.
ZUUUUU
K... KAT?
THEY WERE RIGHT! THEY SAID YOU'D BE OKAY!
HAHAHA!

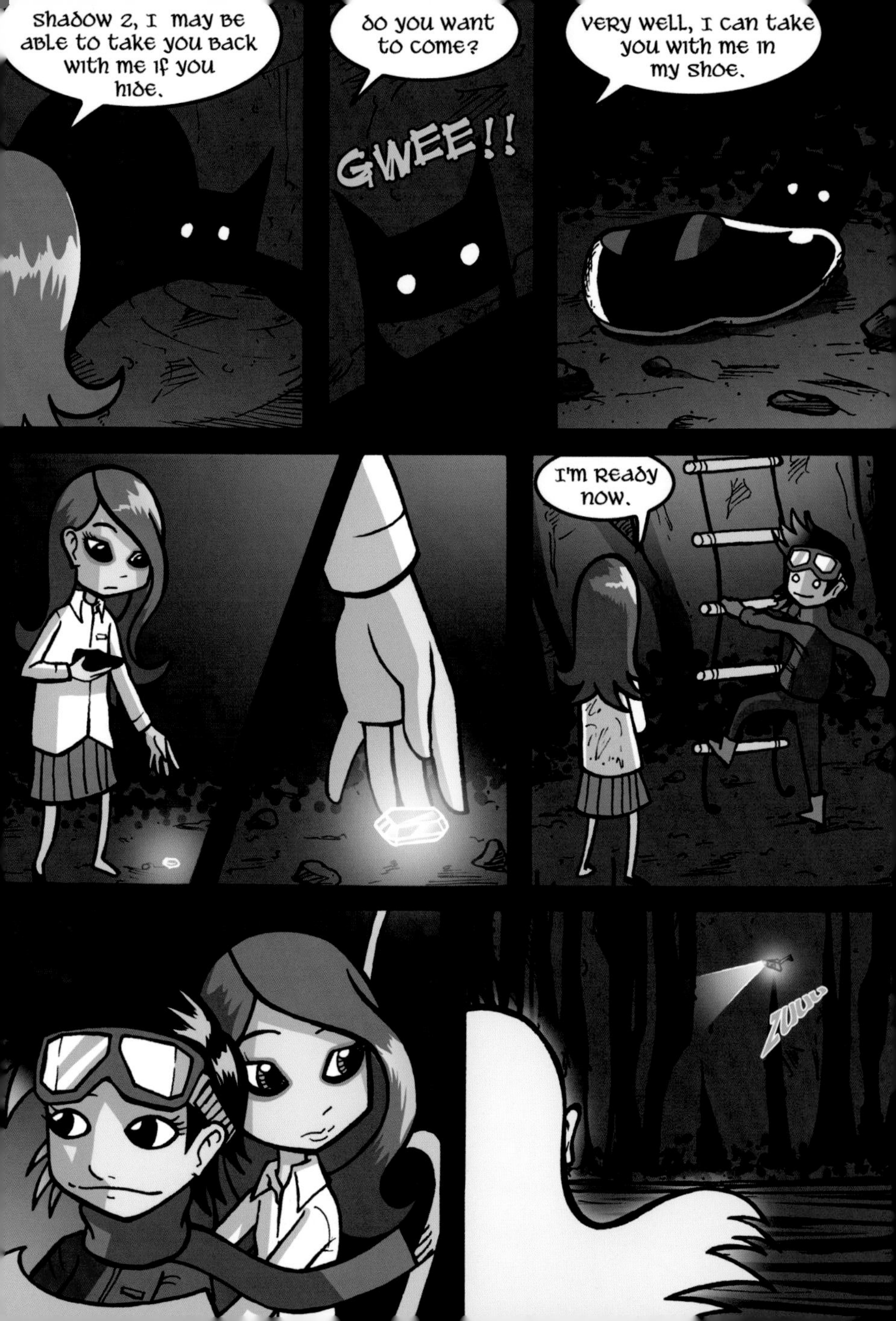
Shadow 2, I may be able to take you back with me if you hide.
GWEE!!
Do you want to come?
Very well, I can take you with me in my shoe.
I'm ready now.

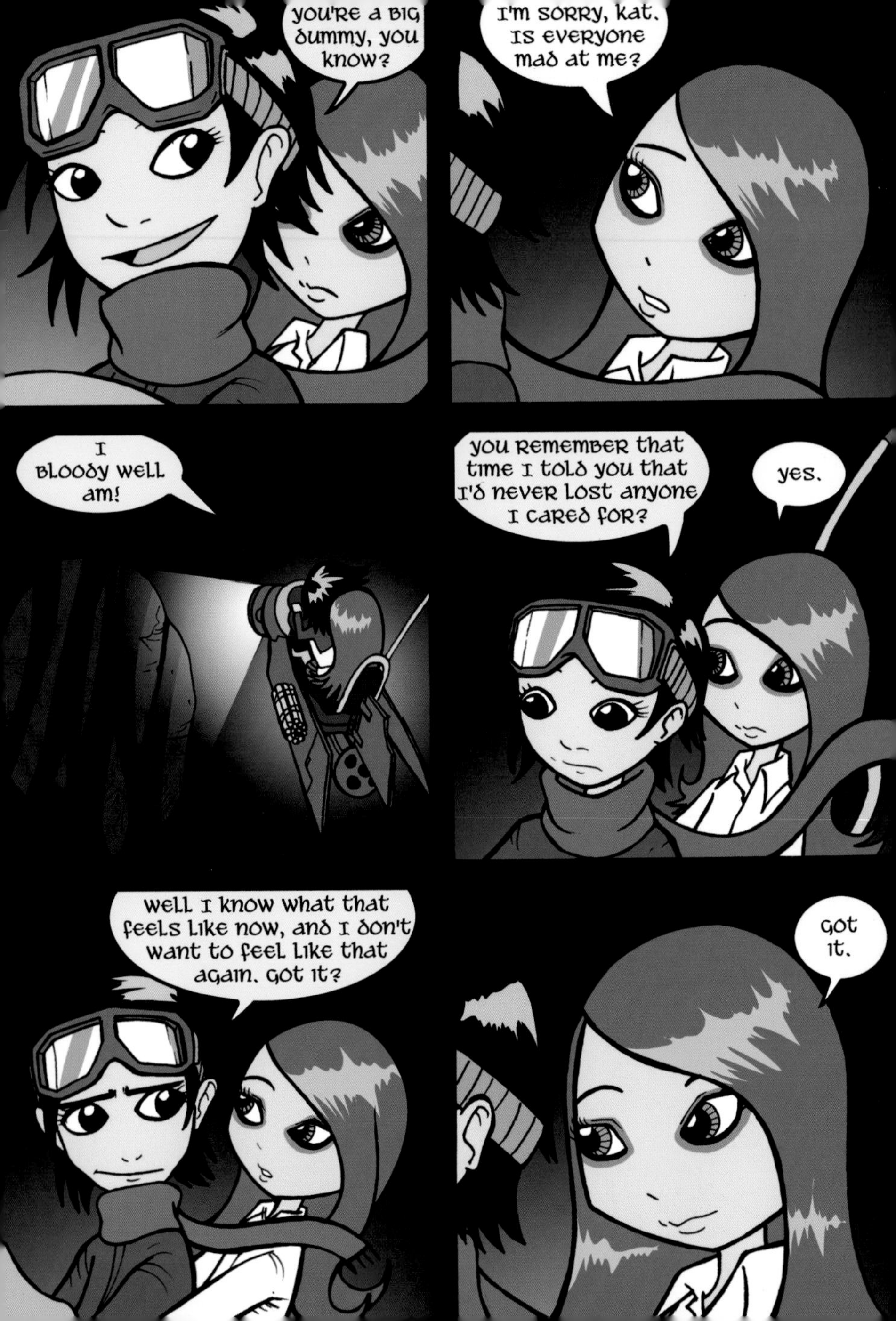
YOU'RE A BIG DUMMY, YOU KNOW?
I'M SORRY, KAT. IS EVERYONE MAD AT ME?
I BLOODY WELL AM!
YOU REMEMBER THAT TIME I TOLD YOU THAT I'D NEVER LOST ANYONE I CARED FOR?
YES.
WELL I KNOW WHAT THAT FEELS LIKE NOW, AND I DON'T WANT TO FEEL LIKE THAT AGAIN. GOT IT?
GOT IT.

Gunnerkrigg Court

Chapter 9:

Questions and Answers

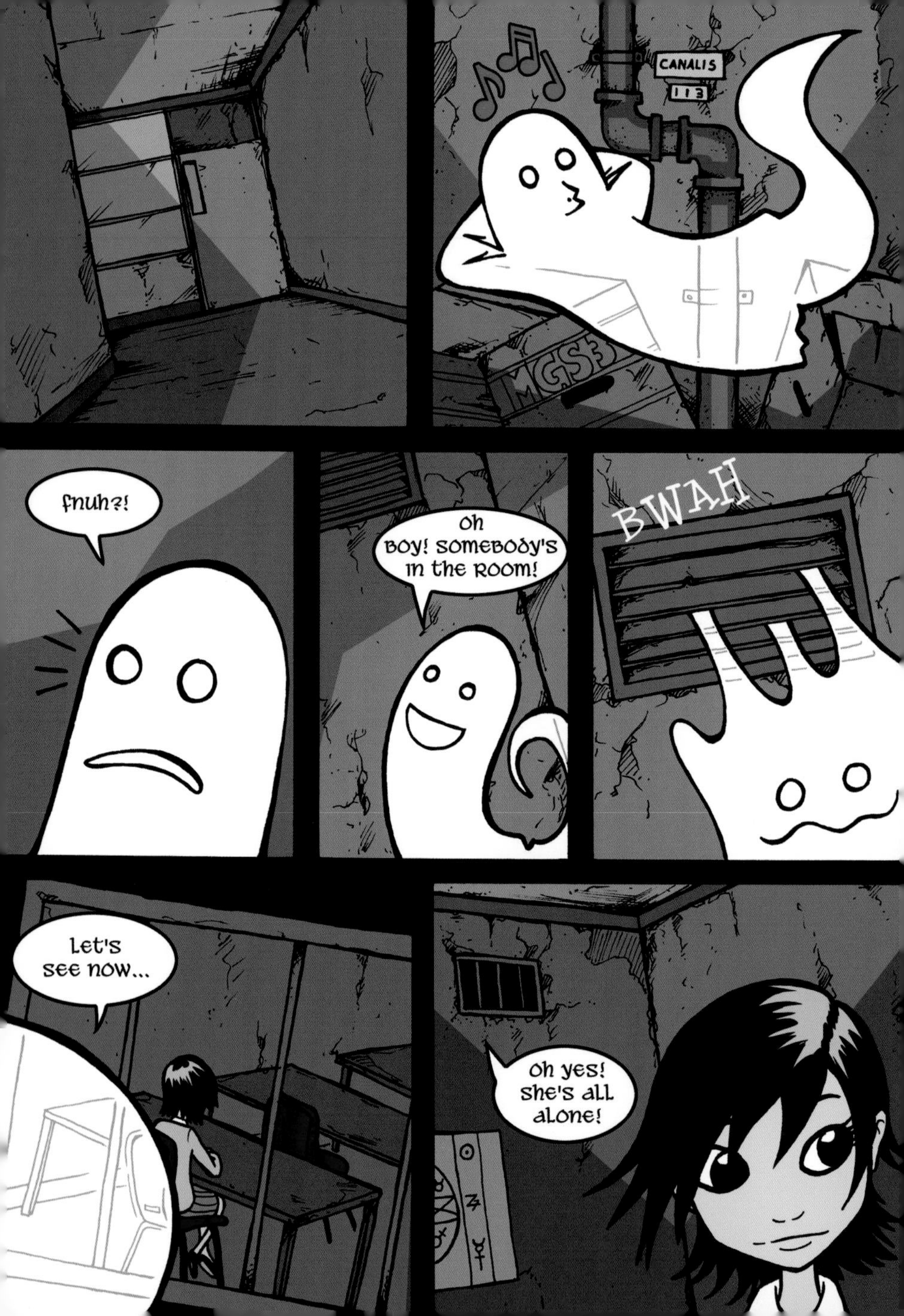
CANALIS
113
MGS3
fnuh?!
Oh Boy! Somebody's in the Room!
BWAH
Let's see now...
Oh yes! She's all alone!

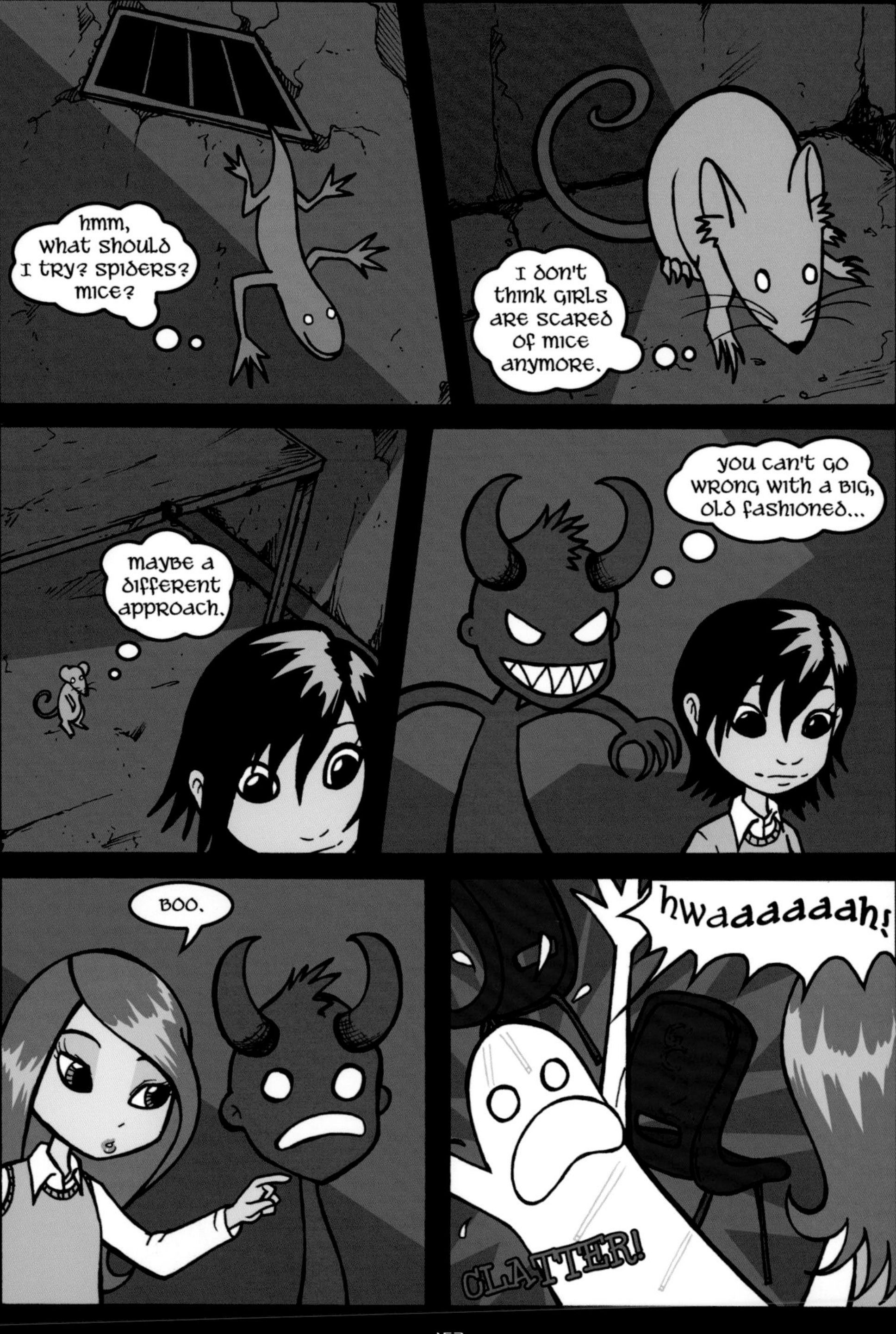
hmm, what should I try? spiders? mice?
I don't think girls are scared of mice anymore.
maybe a different approach.
you can't go wrong with a big, old fashioned...
BOO.
hwaaaaaah!
CLATTER!

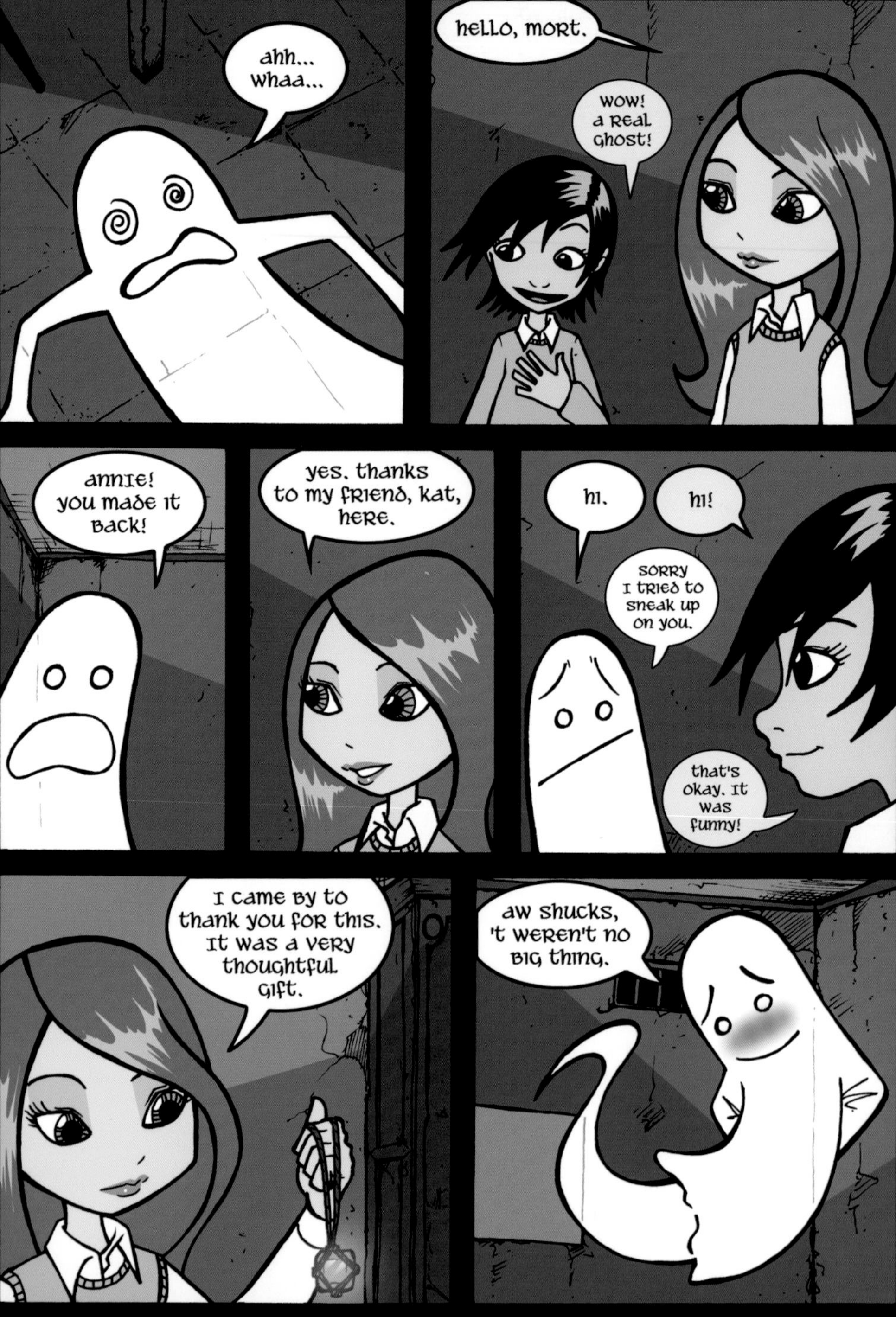
ahh... whaa...
hello, mort.
wow! a real ghost!
annie! you made it back!
yes. thanks to my friend, kat, here.
hi.
hi!
sorry I tried to sneak up on you.
that's okay. it was funny!
I came by to thank you for this. It was a very thoughtful gift.
aw shucks, 't weren't no big thing.

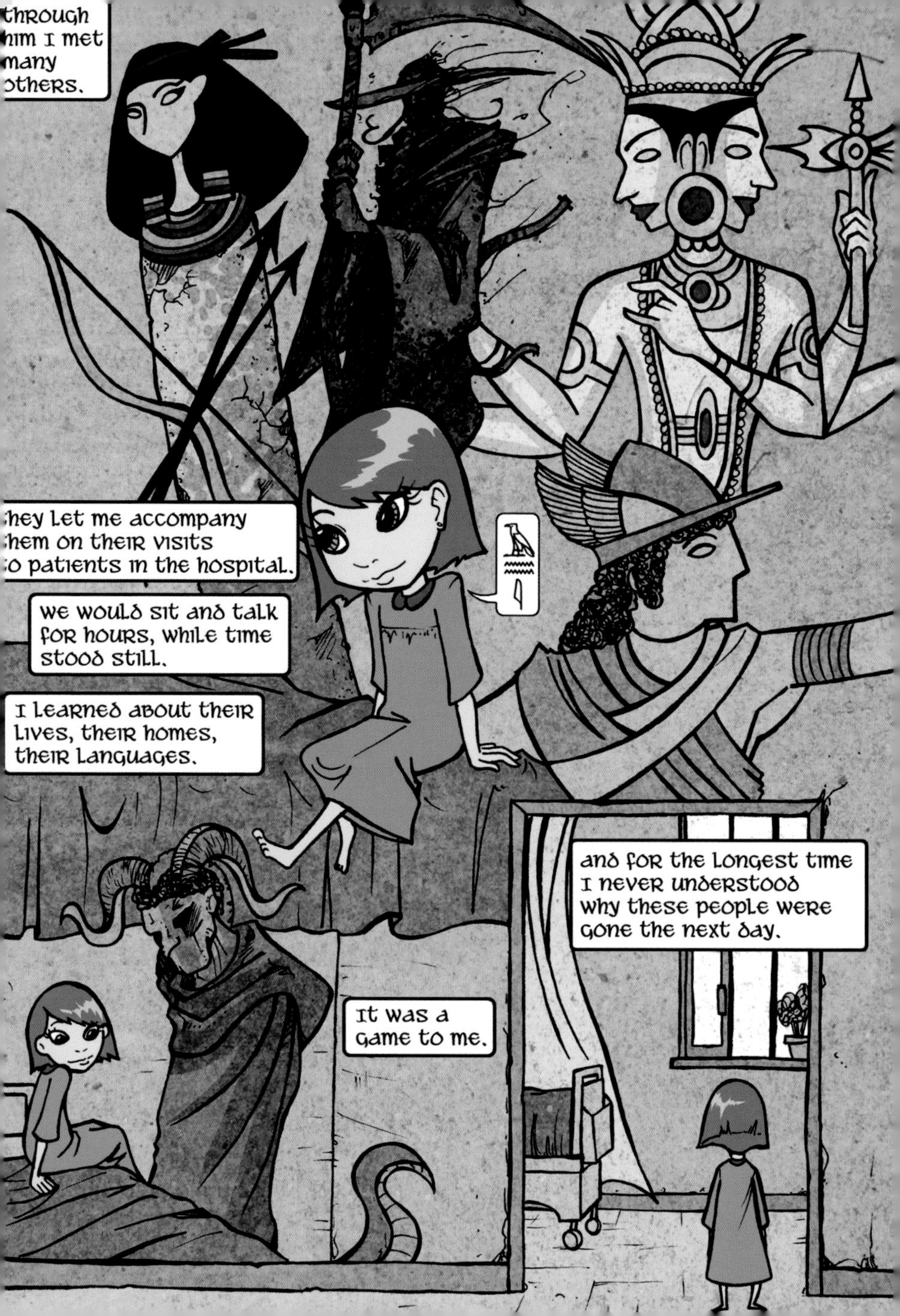
through
him I met
many
others.
hey let me accompany
hem on their visits
o patients in the hospital.
we would sit and talk
for hours, while time
stood still.
I learned about their
lives, their homes,
their languages.
and for the longest time
I never understood
why these people were
gone the next day.
It was a
game to me.

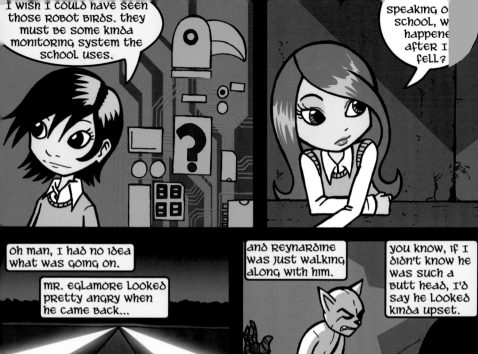

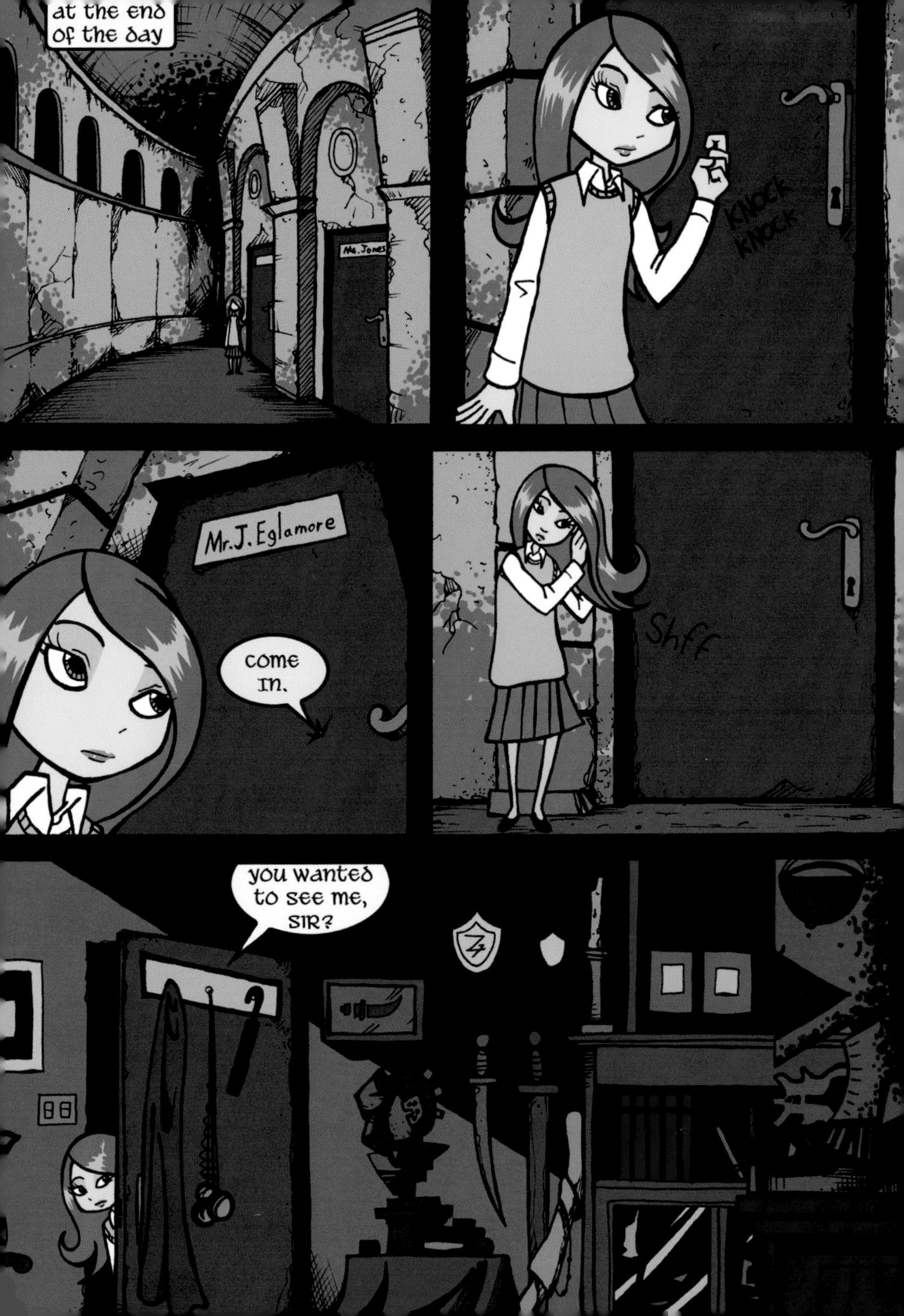
at the end of the day
Ms. Jones
KNOCK KNOCK
Mr. J. Eglamore
come in.
Shff
you wanted to see me, sir?

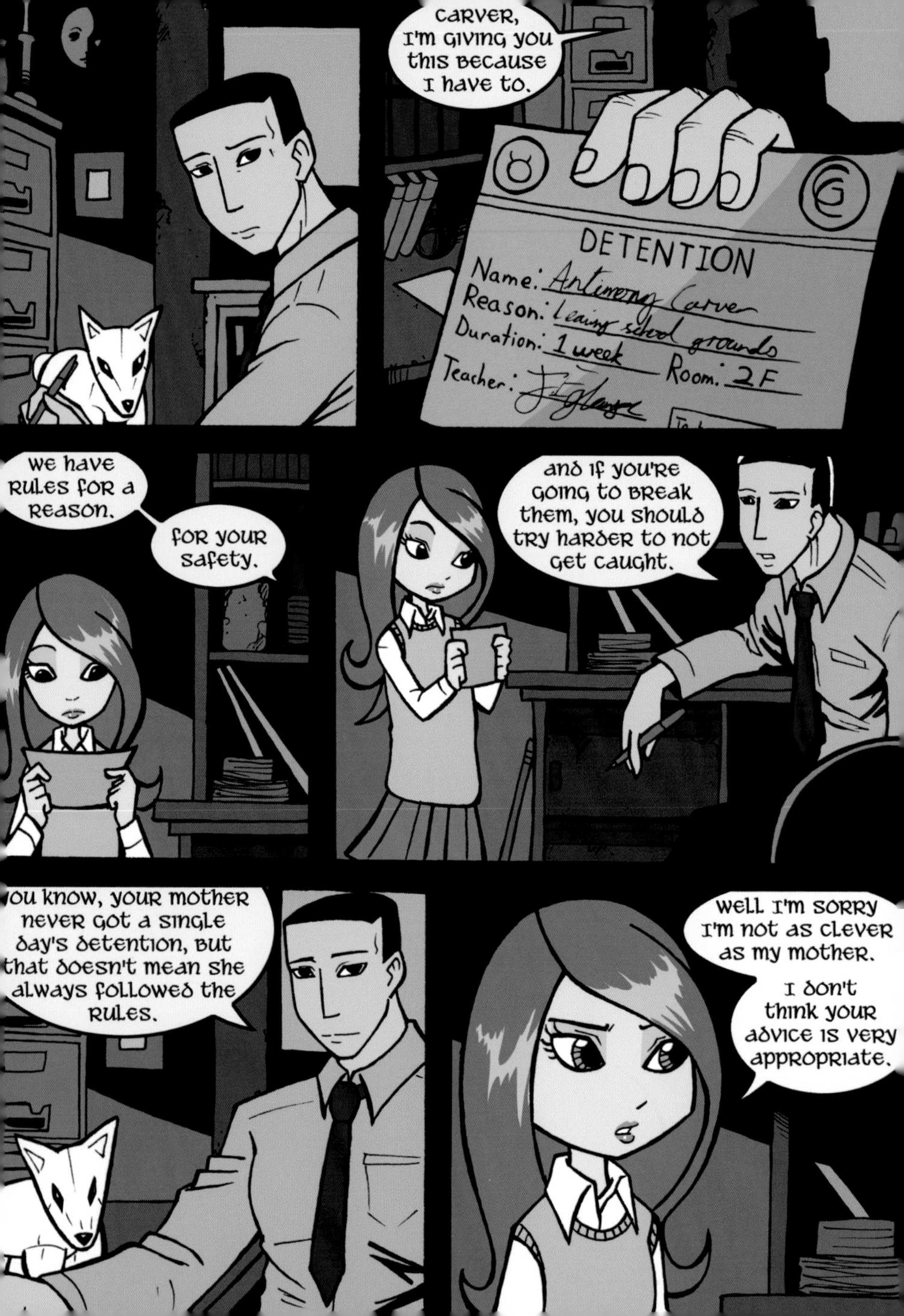

CARVER, I'M GIVING YOU THIS BECAUSE I HAVE TO.
DETENTION
Name: Antimony Carver
Reason: Leaving school grounds
Duration: 1 week
Room: 2F
Teacher:
WE HAVE RULES FOR A REASON.
FOR YOUR SAFETY.
AND IF YOU'RE GOING TO BREAK THEM, YOU SHOULD TRY HARDER TO NOT GET CAUGHT.
YOU KNOW, YOUR MOTHER NEVER GOT A SINGLE DAY'S DETENTION, BUT THAT DOESN'T MEAN SHE ALWAYS FOLLOWED THE RULES.
WELL I'M SORRY I'M NOT AS CLEVER AS MY MOTHER.
I DON'T THINK YOUR ADVICE IS VERY APPROPRIATE.

167

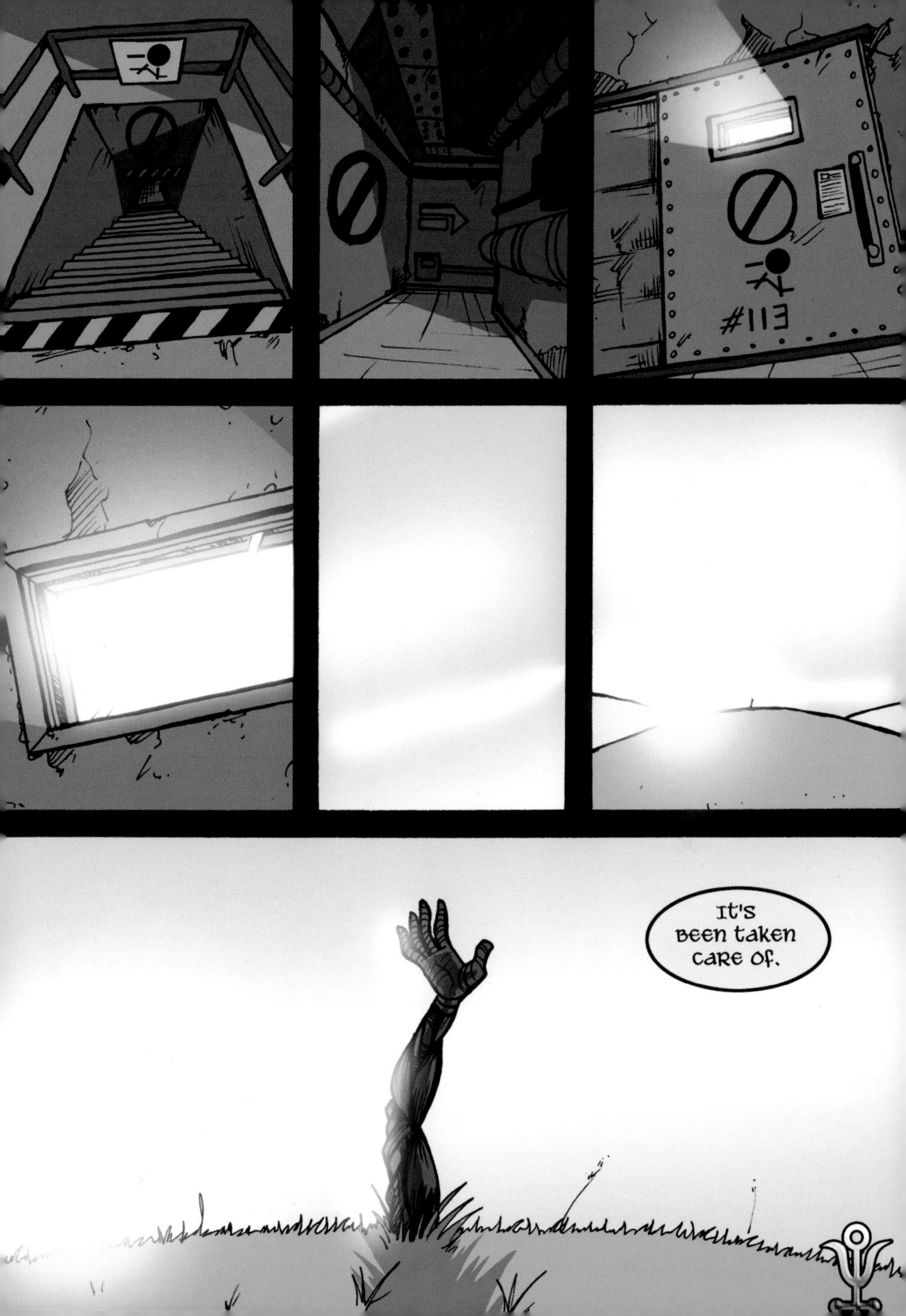
#113
It's been taken care of.

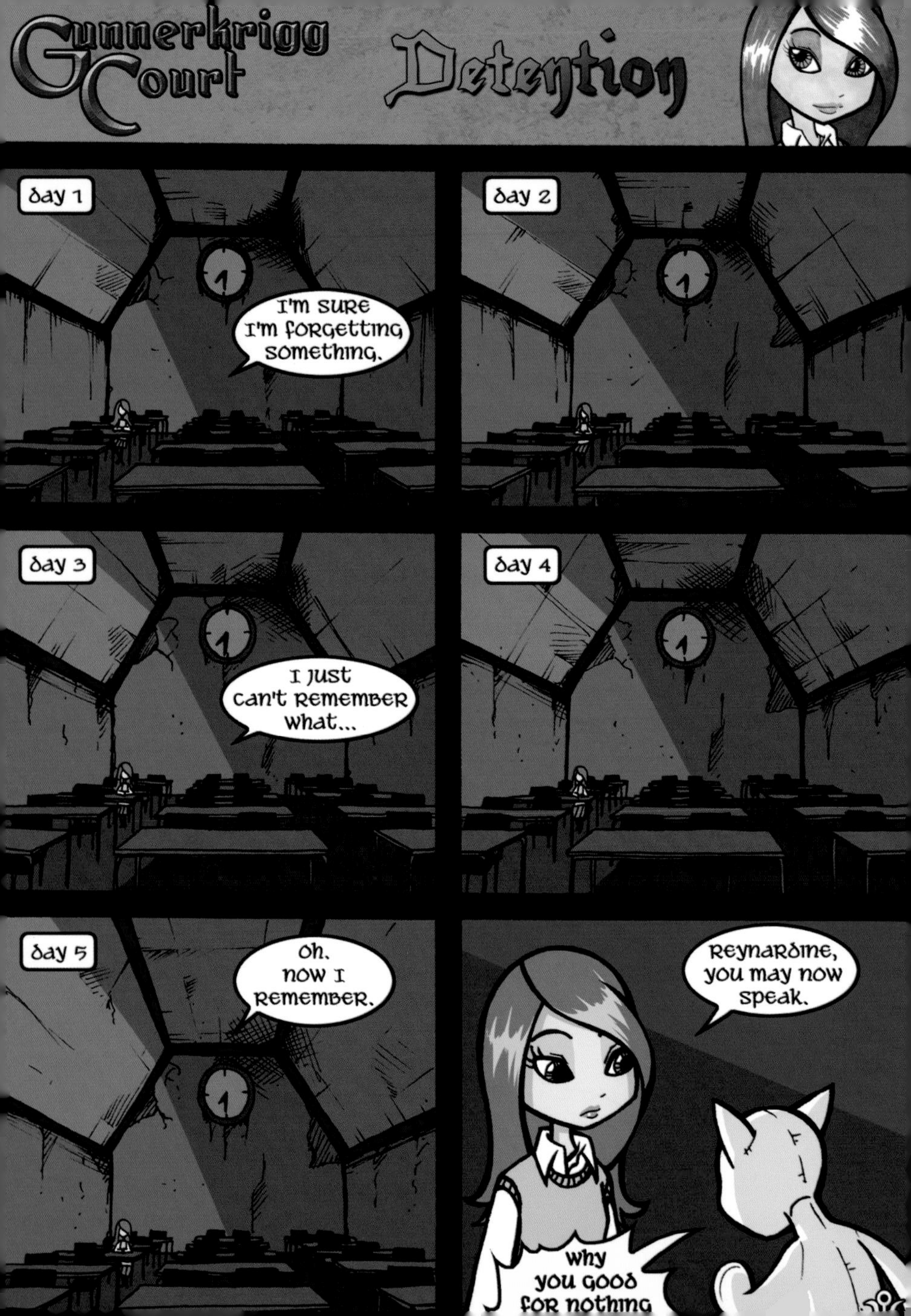

Gunnerkrigg Court
Detention
day 1
I'M SURE I'M FORGETTING SOMETHING.
day 2
day 3
I JUST CAN'T REMEMBER WHAT...
day 4
day 5
OH. NOW I REMEMBER.
REYNARDINE, YOU MAY NOW SPEAK.
WHY YOU GOOD FOR NOTHING

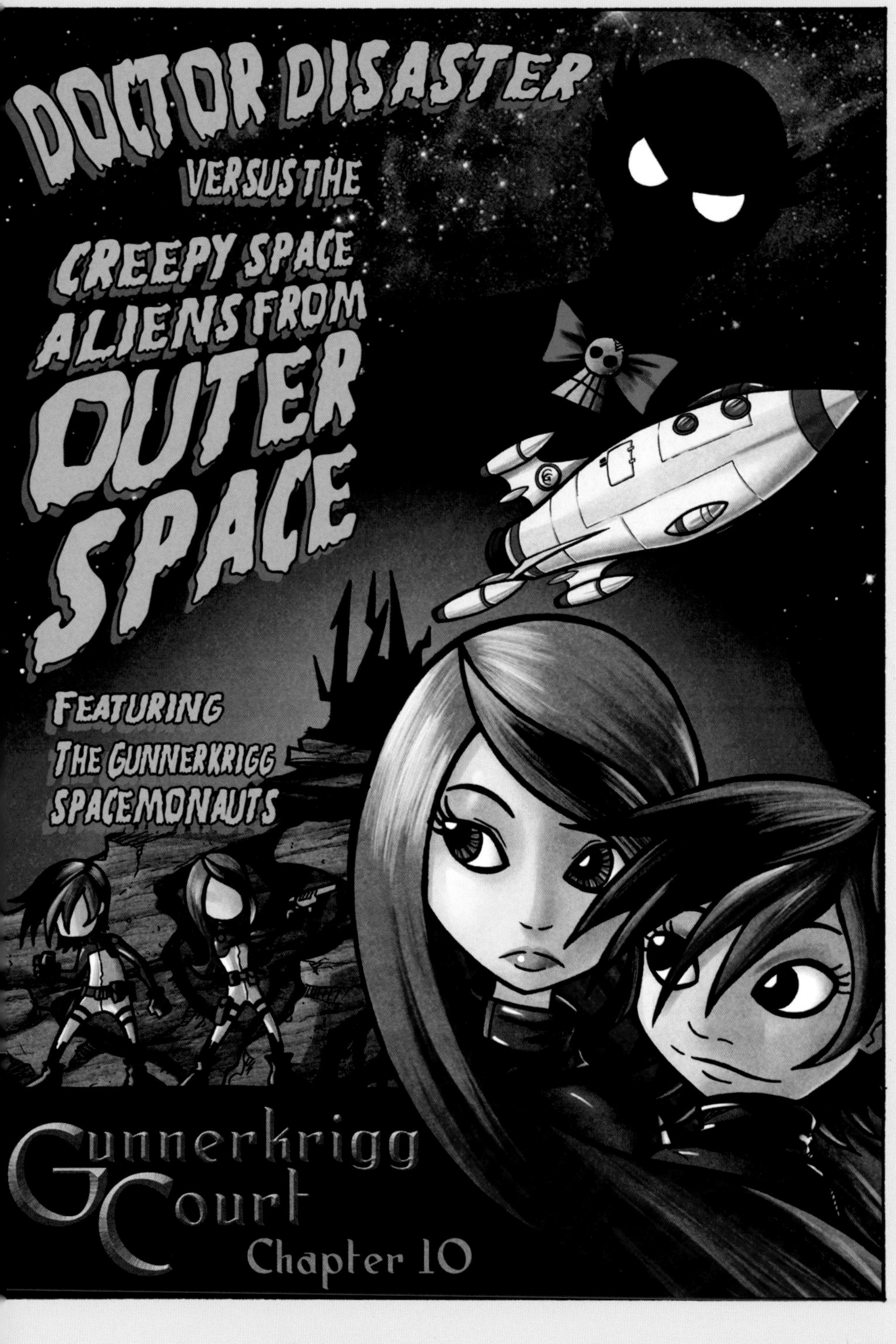
DOCTOR DISASTER
VERSUS THE
CREEPY SPACE
ALIENS FROM
OUTER
SPACE
FEATURING
THE GUNNERKRIGG
SPACEMONAUTS
Gunnerkrigg
Court
Chapter 10

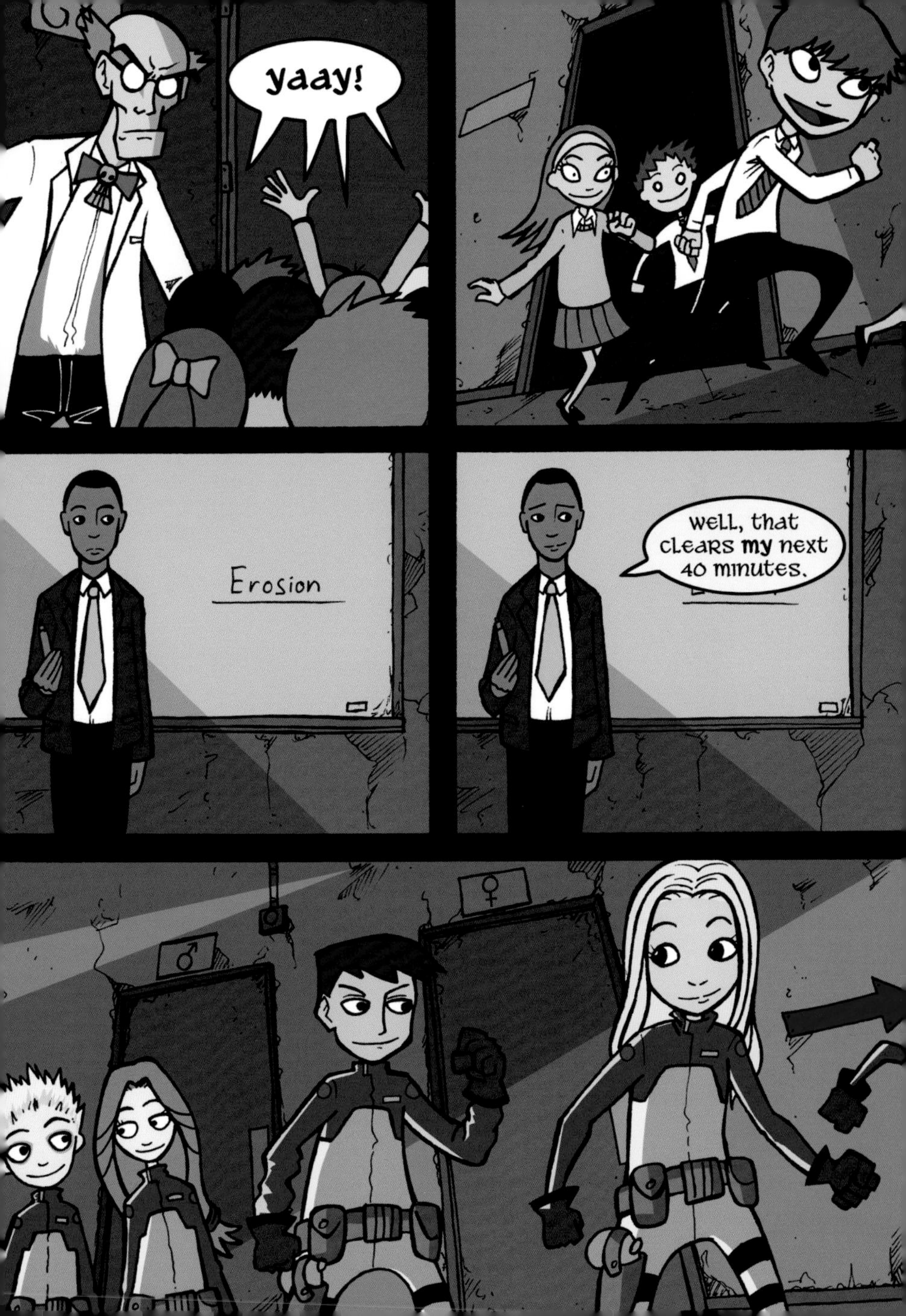
yaay!
Erosion
well, that clears my next 40 minutes.

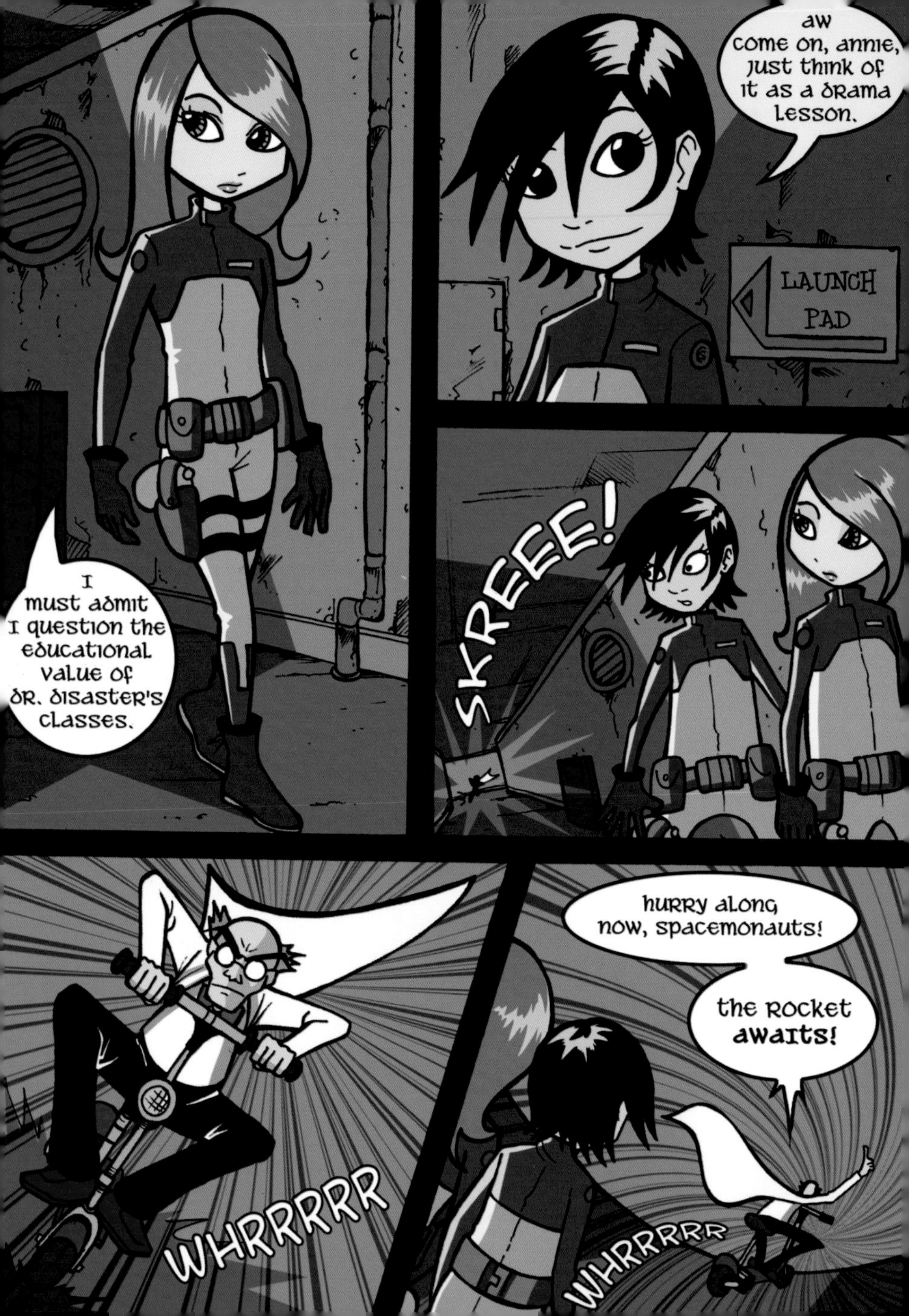
I must admit I question the educational value of Dr. Disaster's classes.
aw come on, annie, just think of it as a drama lesson.
LAUNCH PAD
SKREEE!
WHRRRRR
hurry along now, spacemonauts!
the rocket awaits!
WHRRRRR

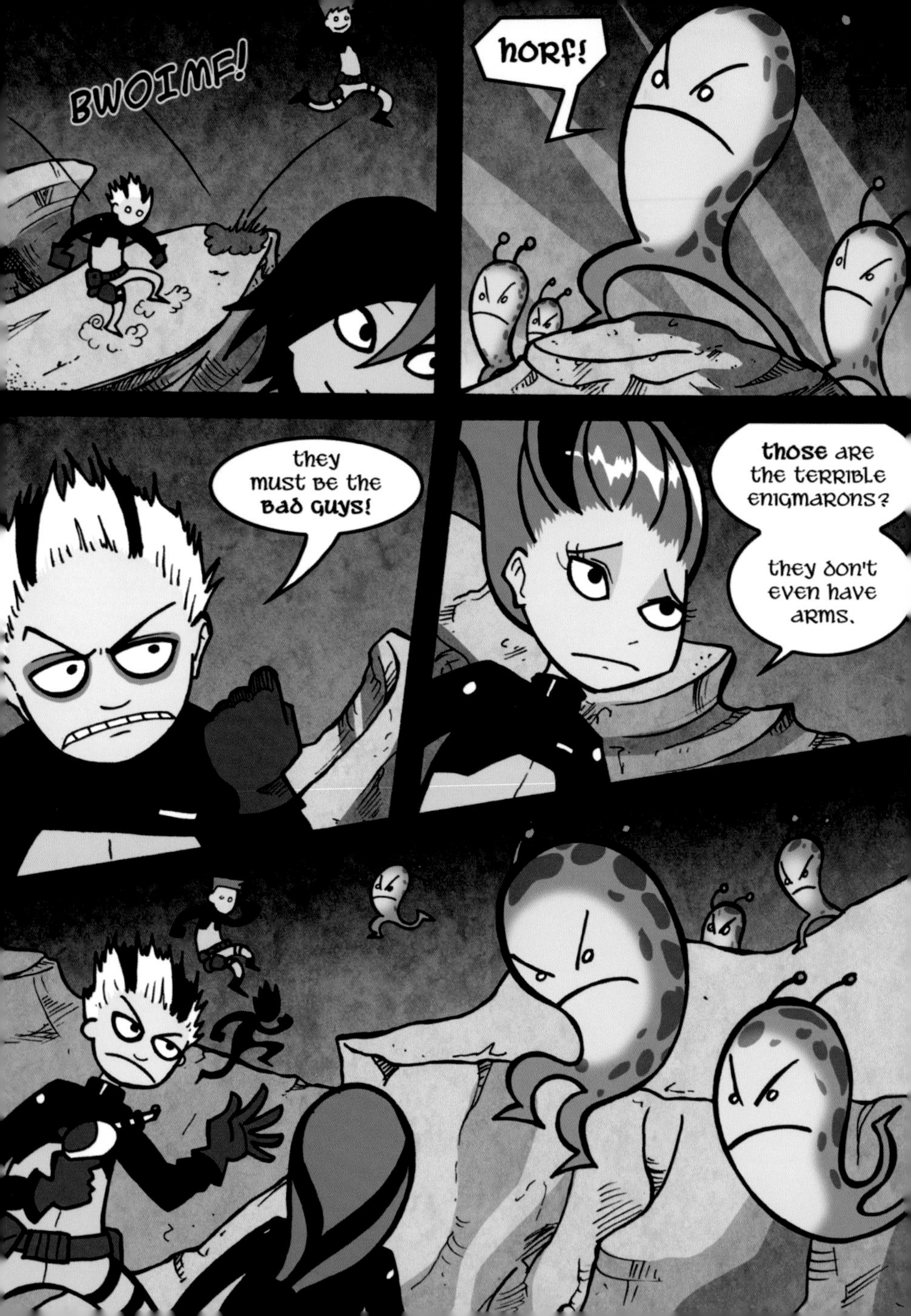
BWOIMF!
horf!
they must be the BAD GUYS!
those are the terrible enigmarons?
they don't even have arms.

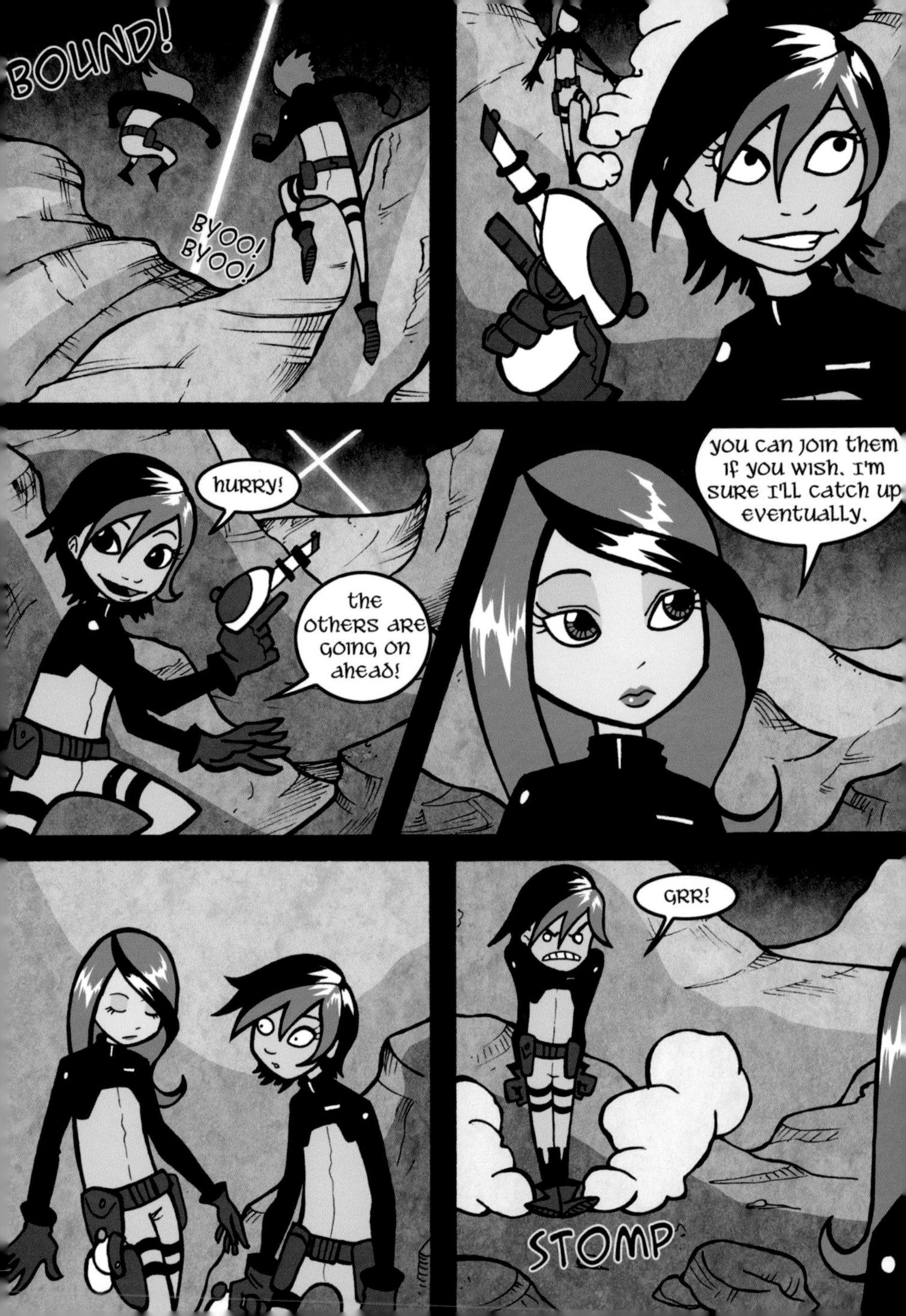

BOUND!
BYOO! BYOO!
hurry!
the others are going on ahead!
you can join them if you wish. I'm sure I'll catch up eventually.
GRR!
STOMP

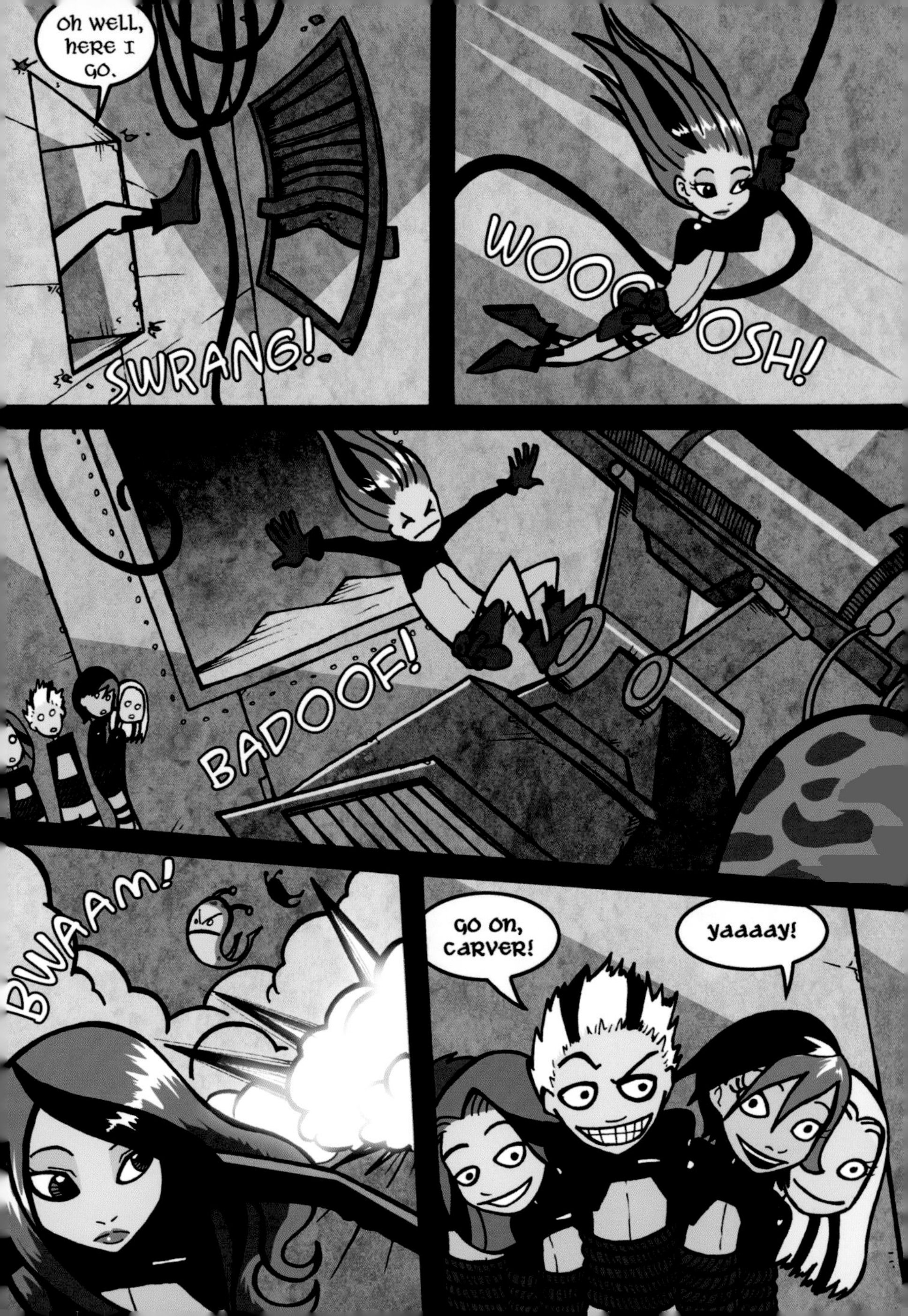

Oh well, here I go.
SWRANG!
WOOOOOSH!
BADOOF!
BWAAAM!
Go on, Carver!
Yaaaay!

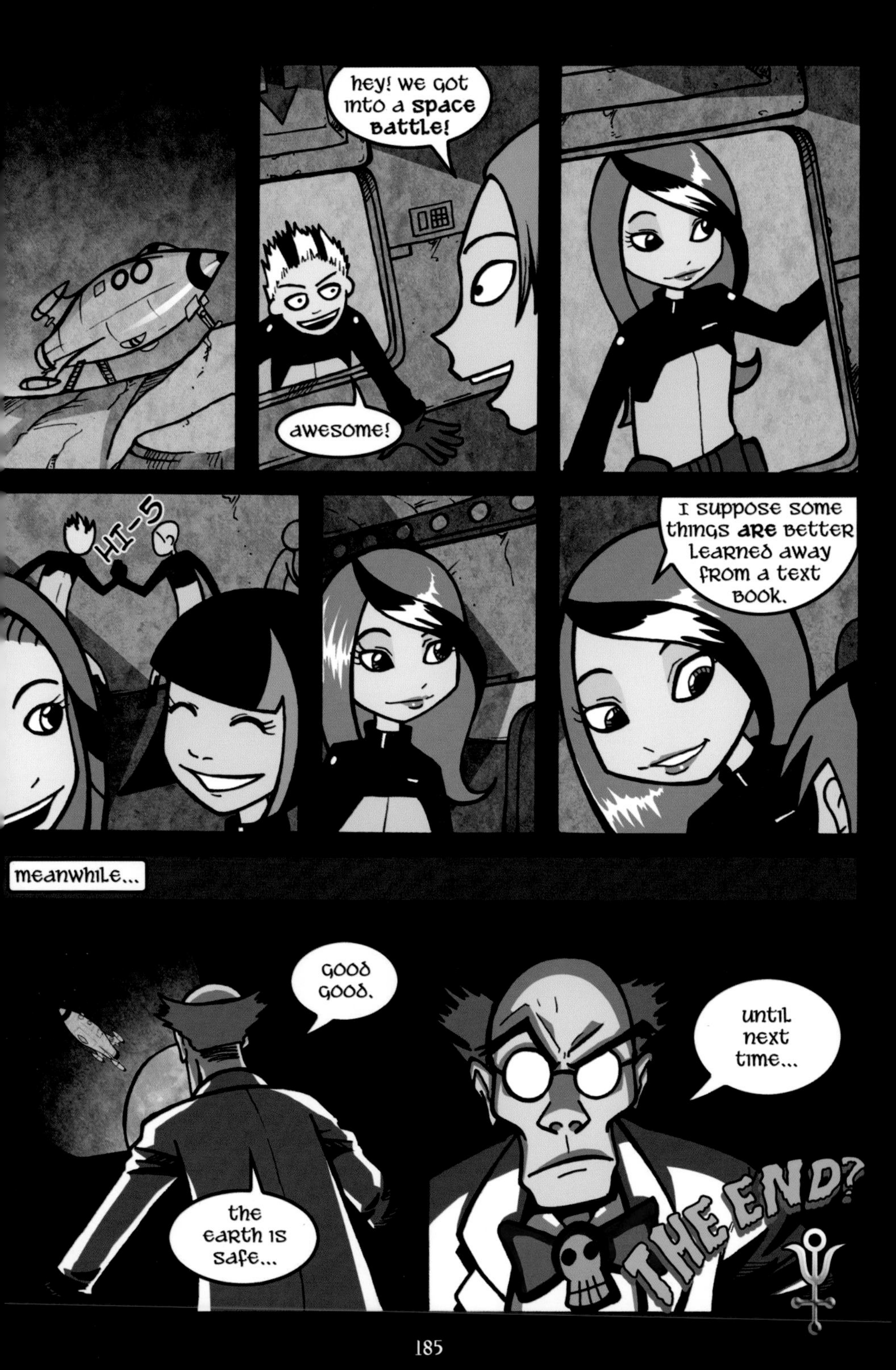
hey! we got into a space battle!
awesome!
HI-5
I suppose some things are better learned away from a text book.
meanwhile...
good good.
the earth is safe...
until next time...
THE END?

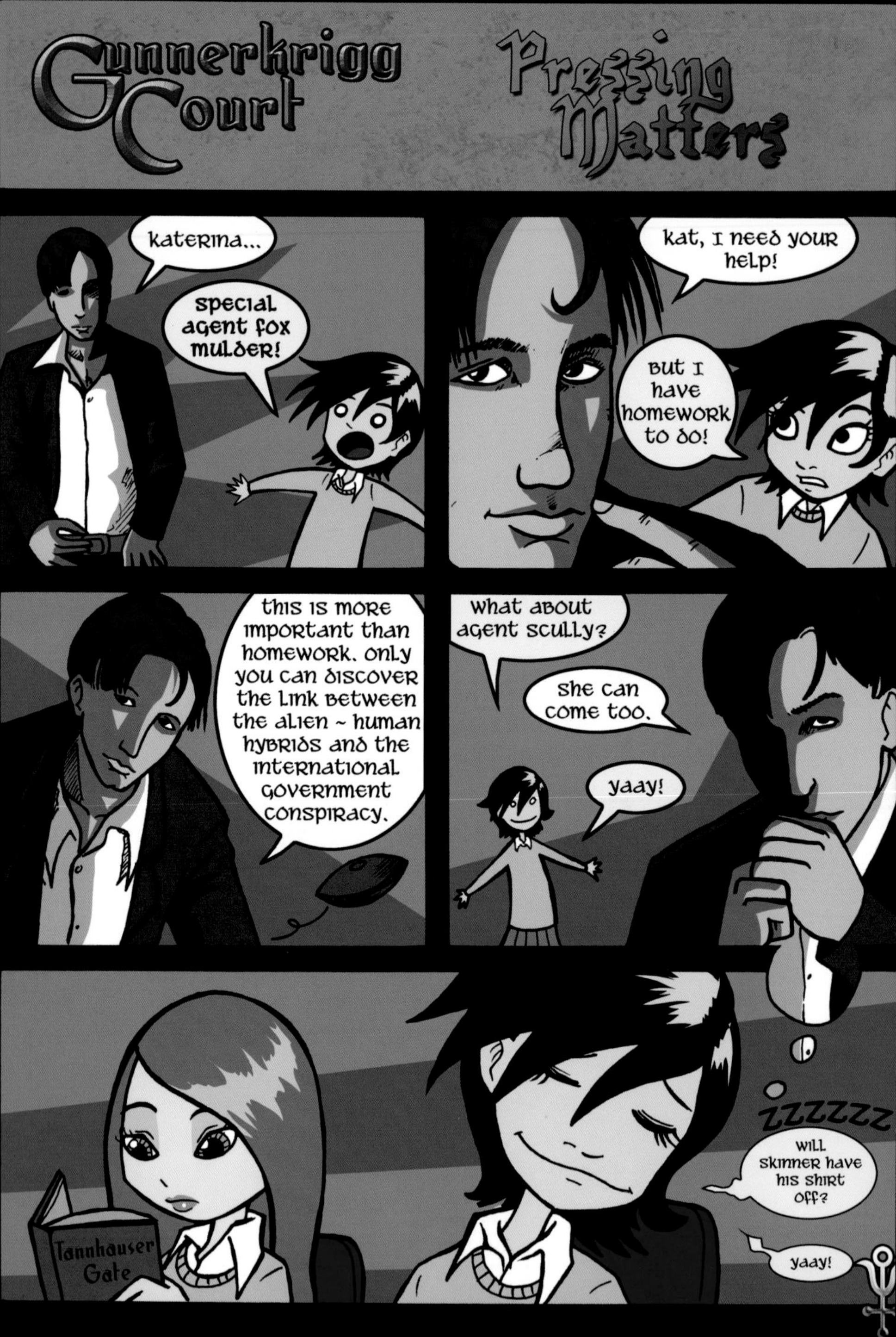
Gunnerkrigg Court
Pressing Matters
katerina...
special agent fox mulder!
kat, I need your help!
but I have homework to do!
this is more important than homework. only you can discover the link between the alien ~ human hybrids and the international government conspiracy.
what about agent scully?
she can come too.
yaay!
Tannhauser Gate
zzzzzz
will skinner have his shirt off?
yaay!

Gunnerkrigg Court

Chapter 11:

Dobranoc, Gamma

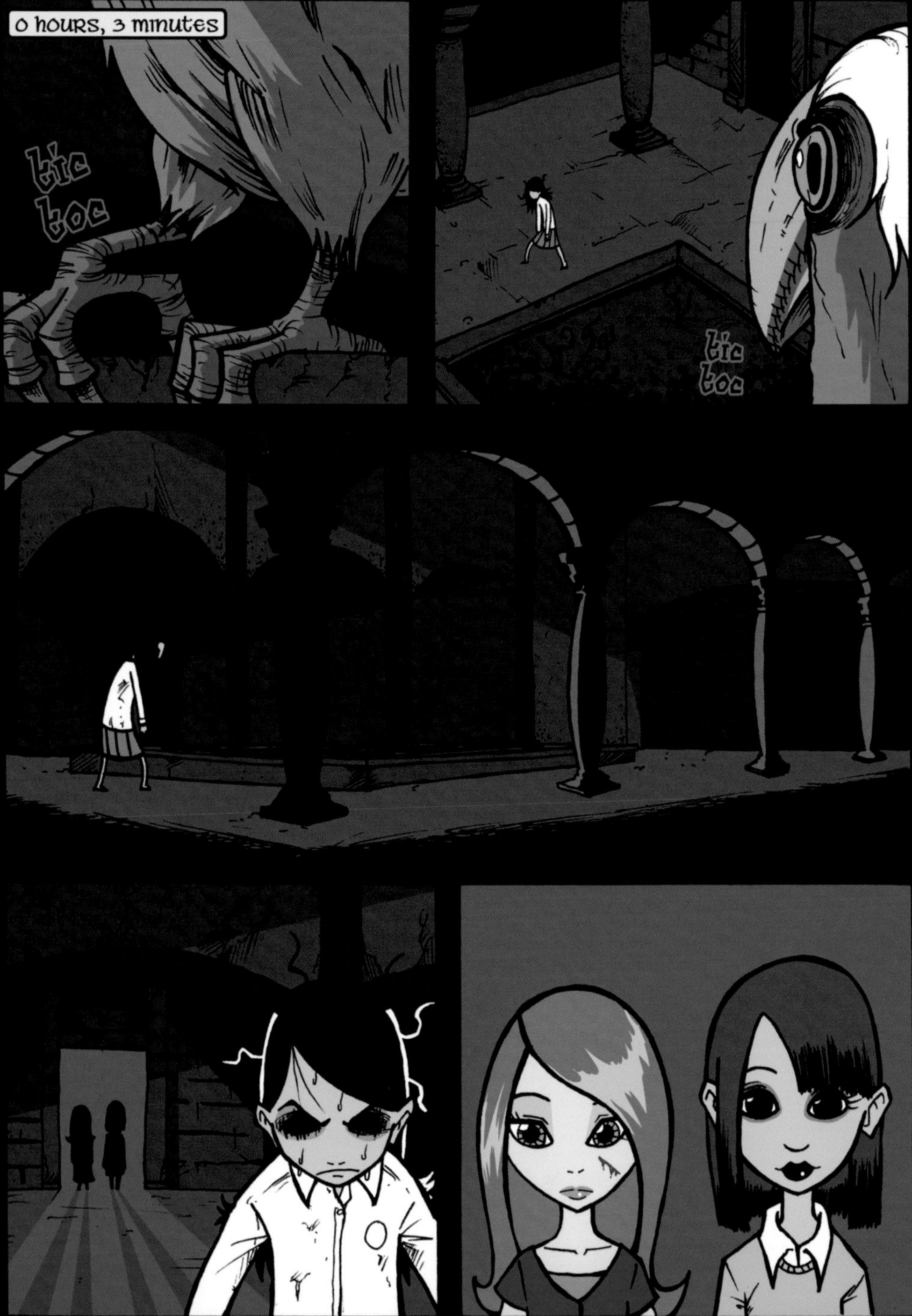
0 hours, 3 minutes
tic
toc
tic
toc

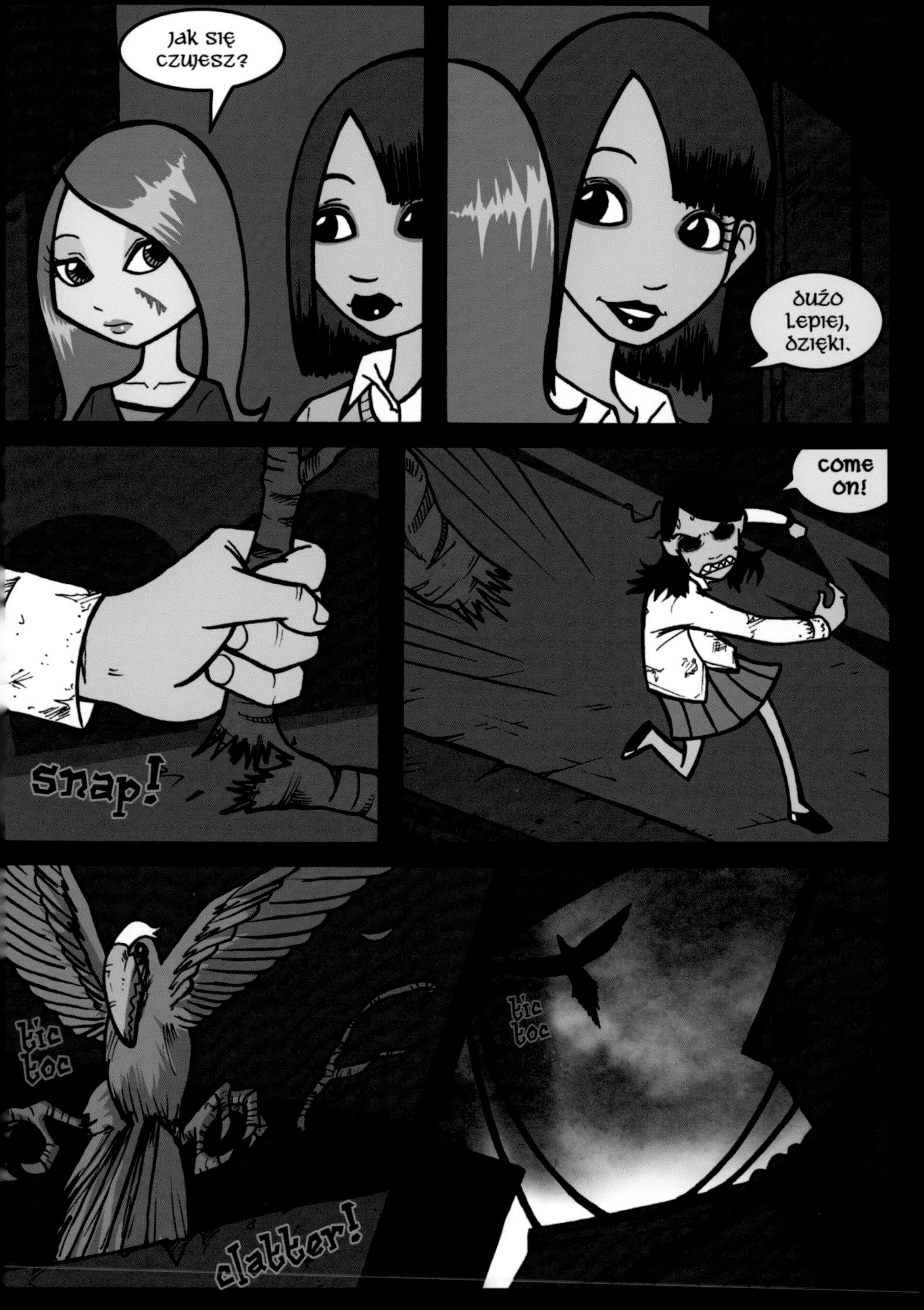
Jak się czujesz?
Dużo lepiej, dzięki.
snap!
come on!
tic toc
tic toc
clatter!

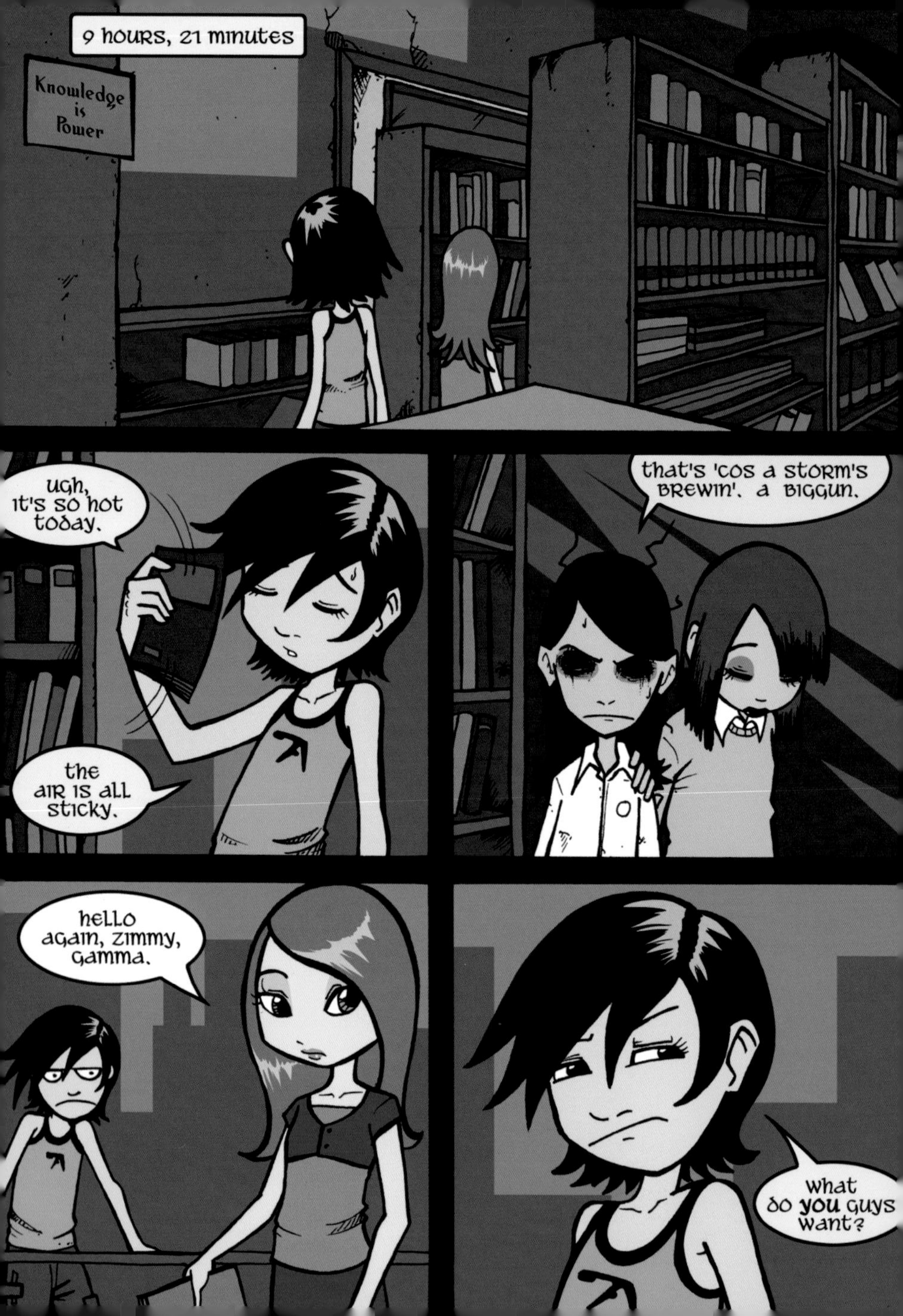
9 hours, 21 minutes
Knowledge is Power
ugh, it's so hot today.
the air is all sticky.
that's 'cos a storm's brewin'. a biggun.
hello again, zimmy, gamma.
what do **you** guys want?

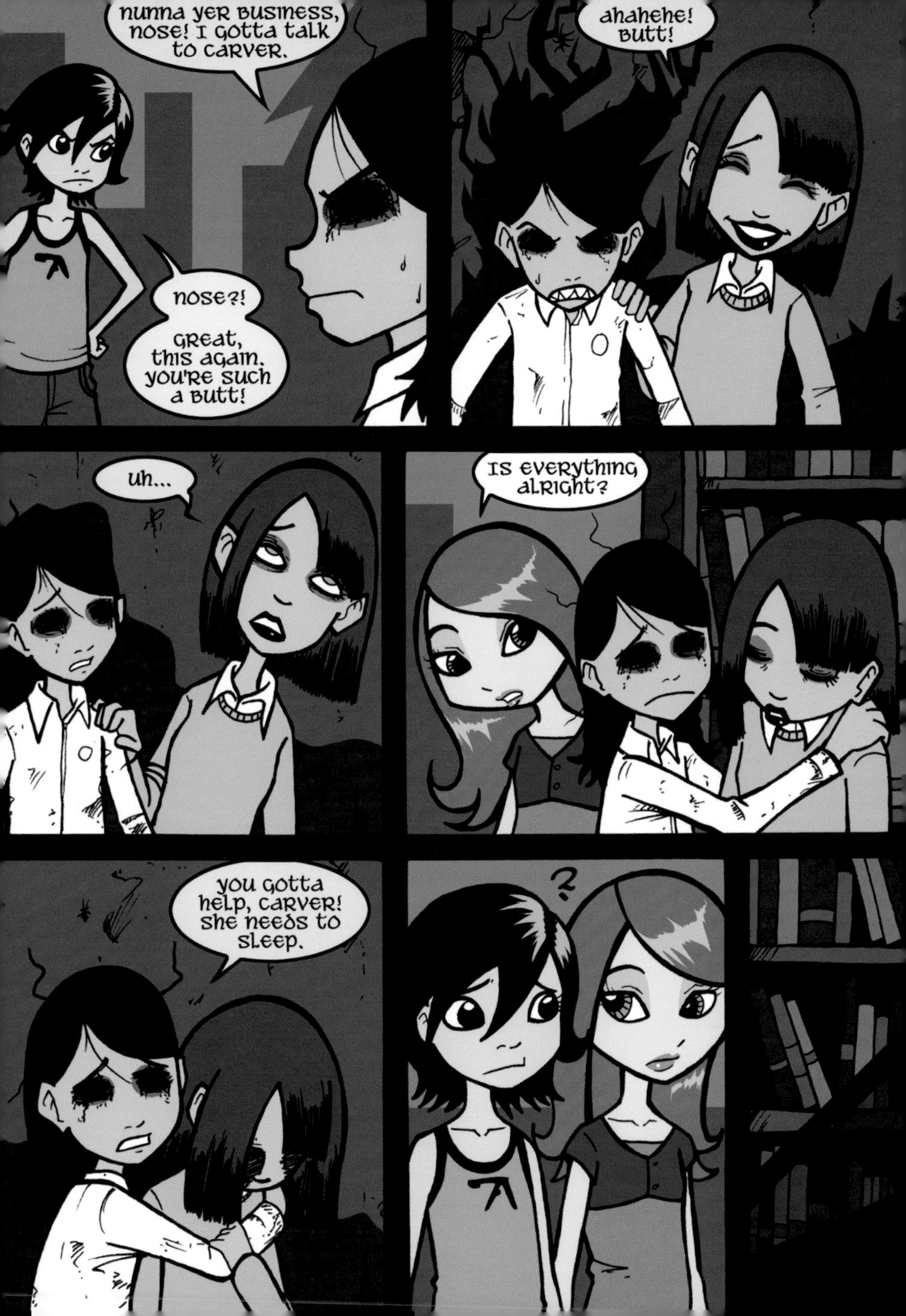
nunna yer business, nose! I gotta talk to carver.
nose?!
great, this again. you're such a butt!
ahahehe! butt!
uh...
is everything alright?
you gotta help, carver! she needs to sleep.
?

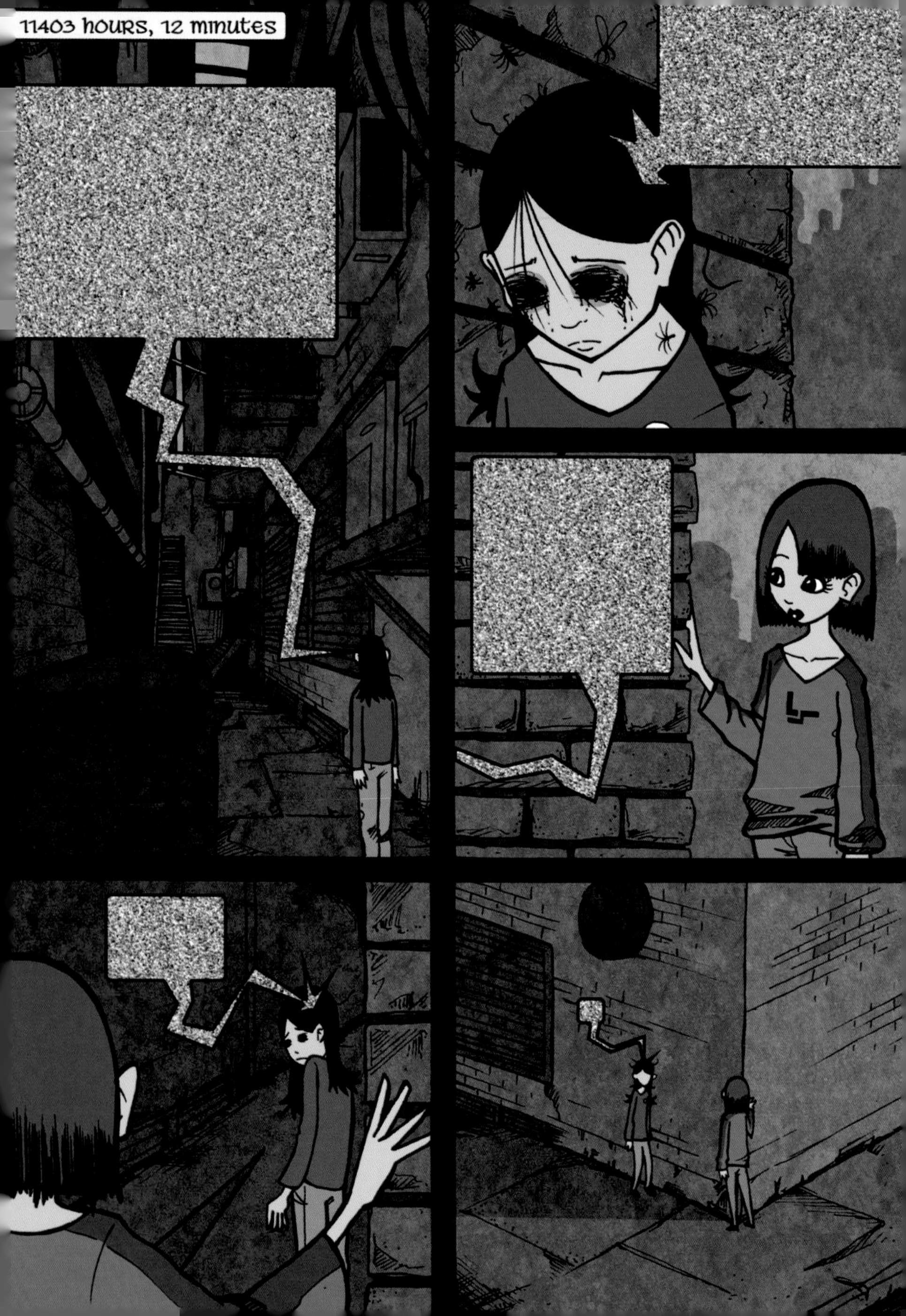
11403 hours, 12 minutes

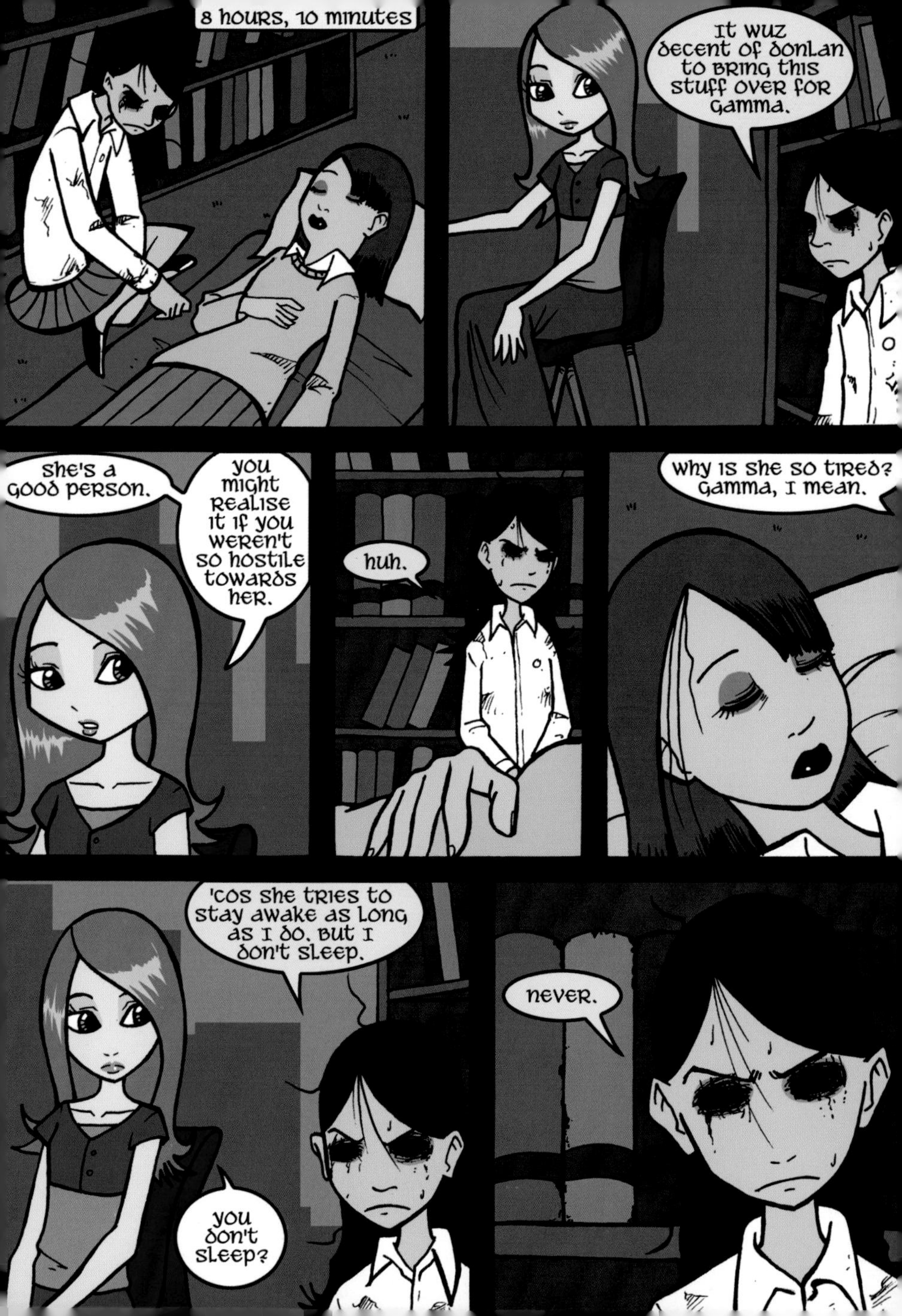
8 HOURS, 10 MINUTES
IT WUZ DECENT OF DONLAN TO BRING THIS STUFF OVER FOR GAMMA.
SHE'S A GOOD PERSON.
YOU MIGHT REALISE IT IF YOU WEREN'T SO HOSTILE TOWARDS HER.
HUH.
WHY IS SHE SO TIRED? GAMMA, I MEAN.
'COS SHE TRIES TO STAY AWAKE AS LONG AS I DO. BUT I DON'T SLEEP.
YOU DON'T SLEEP?
NEVER.

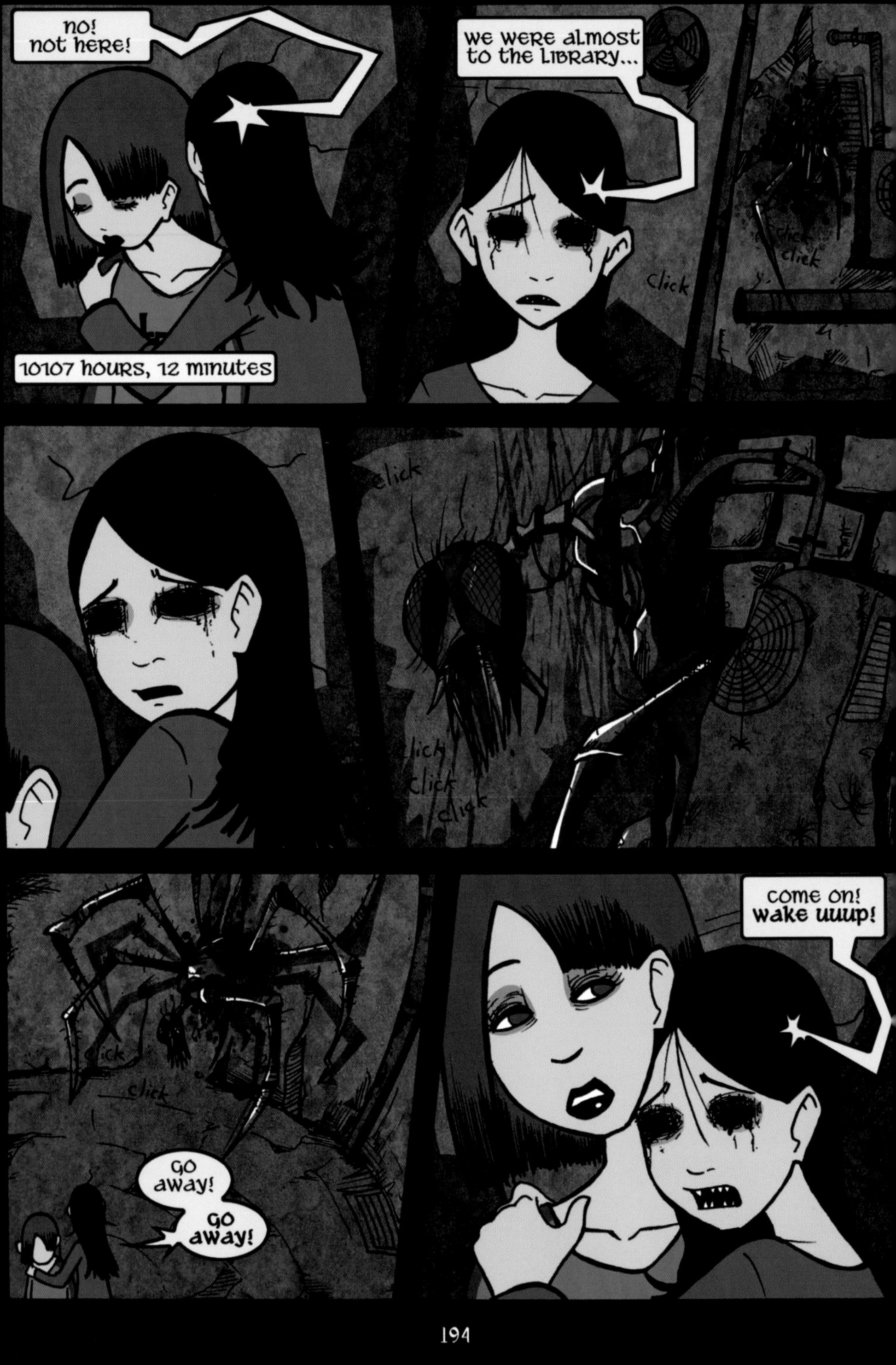
no!
not here!
10107 hours, 12 minutes
we were almost
to the library...
click
click
click
click
click
click
click
click
click
GO
away!
GO
away!
come on!
wake uuup!

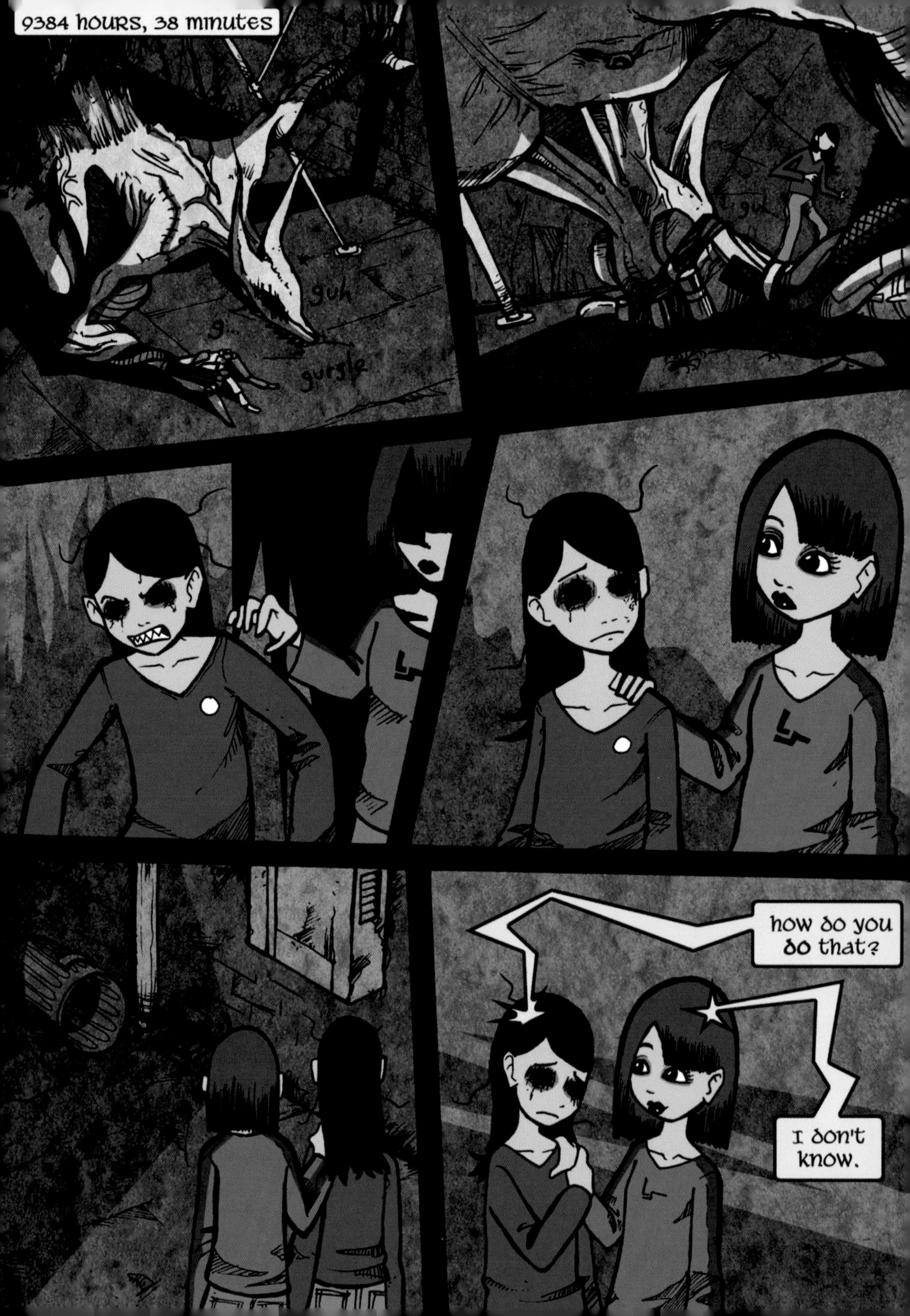

9384 HOURS, 38 MINUTES
guh
g...
gurgle
guh
how do you do that?
I don't know.

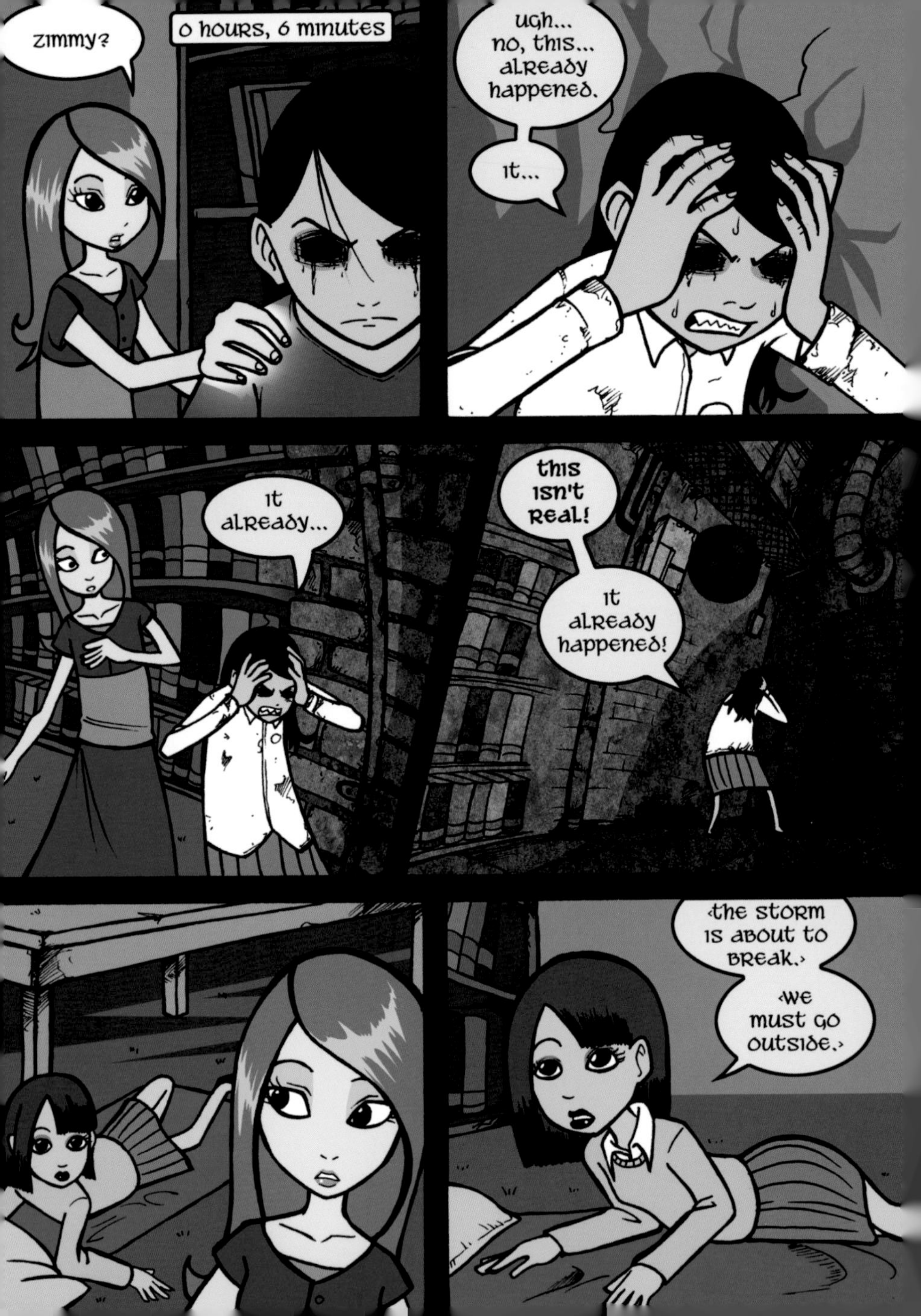
0 hours, 6 minutes
zimmy?
ugh... no, this... already happened.
it...
it already...
this isn't real!
it already happened!
‹the storm is about to break.›
‹we must go outside.›

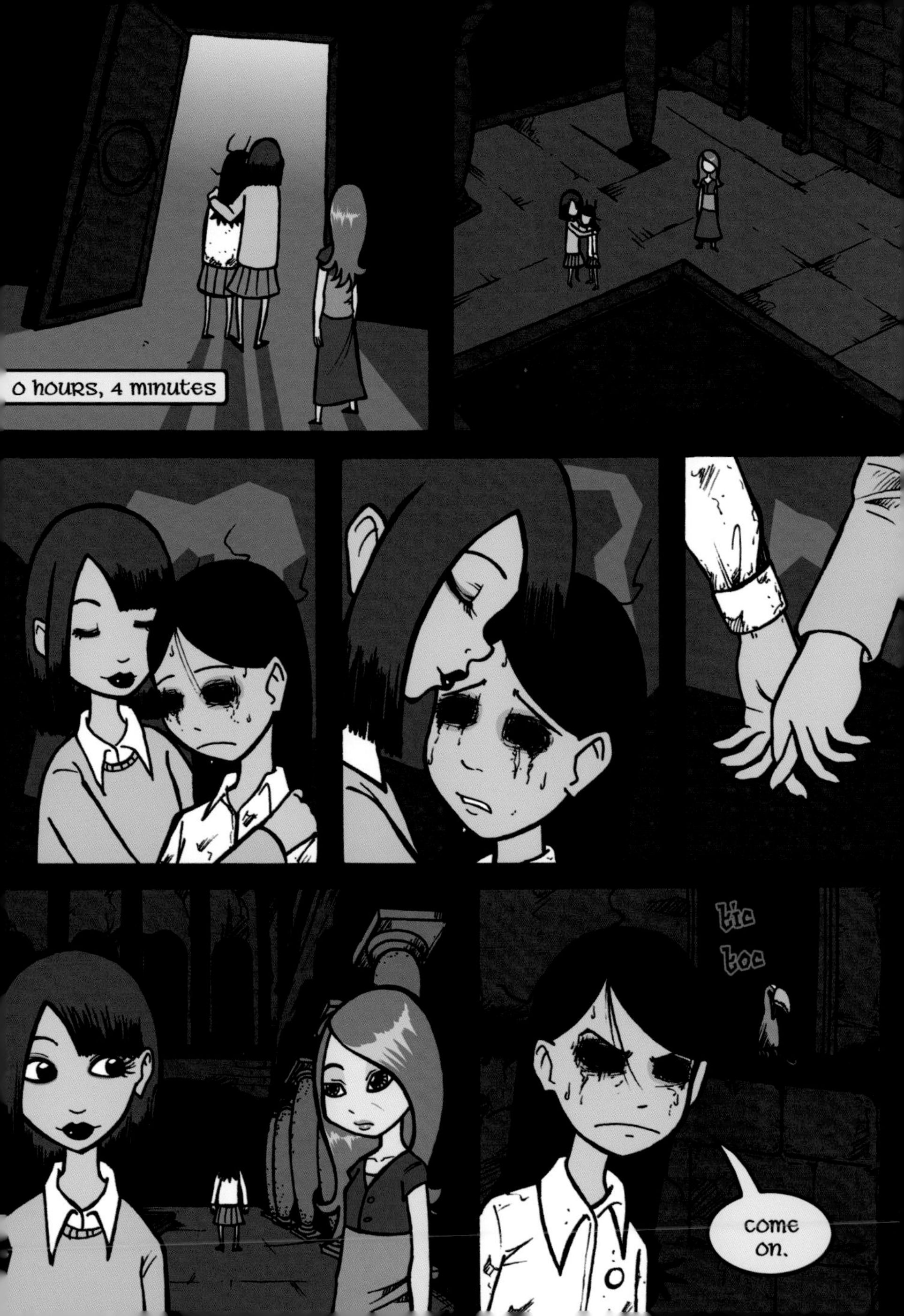
0 hours, 4 minutes
tic
toc
come on.

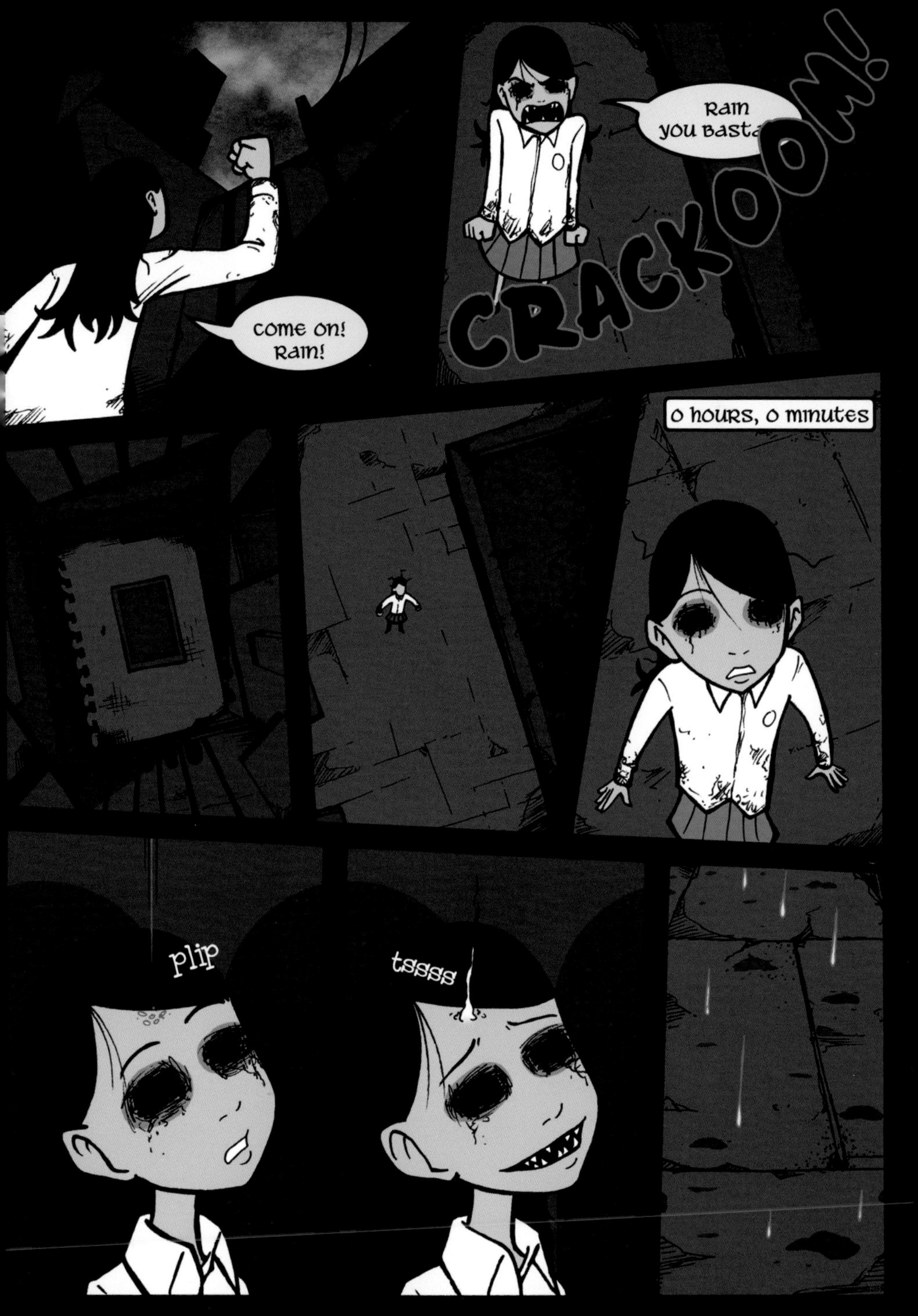
come on!
Rain!
Rain
you Basta
CRACKOOM!
0 hours, 0 minutes
plip
tssss

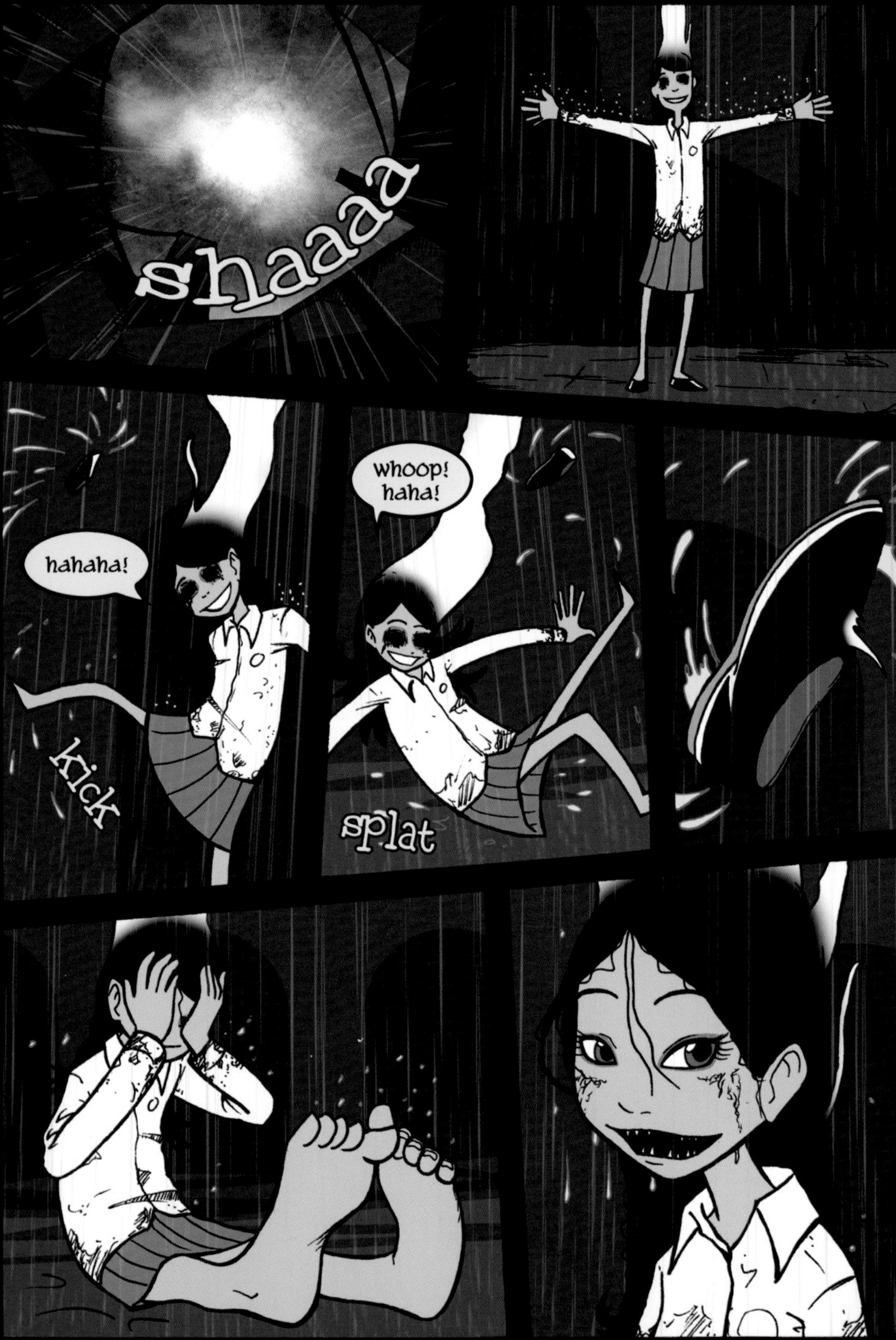
shaaaa
hahaha!
kick
whoop! haha!
splat

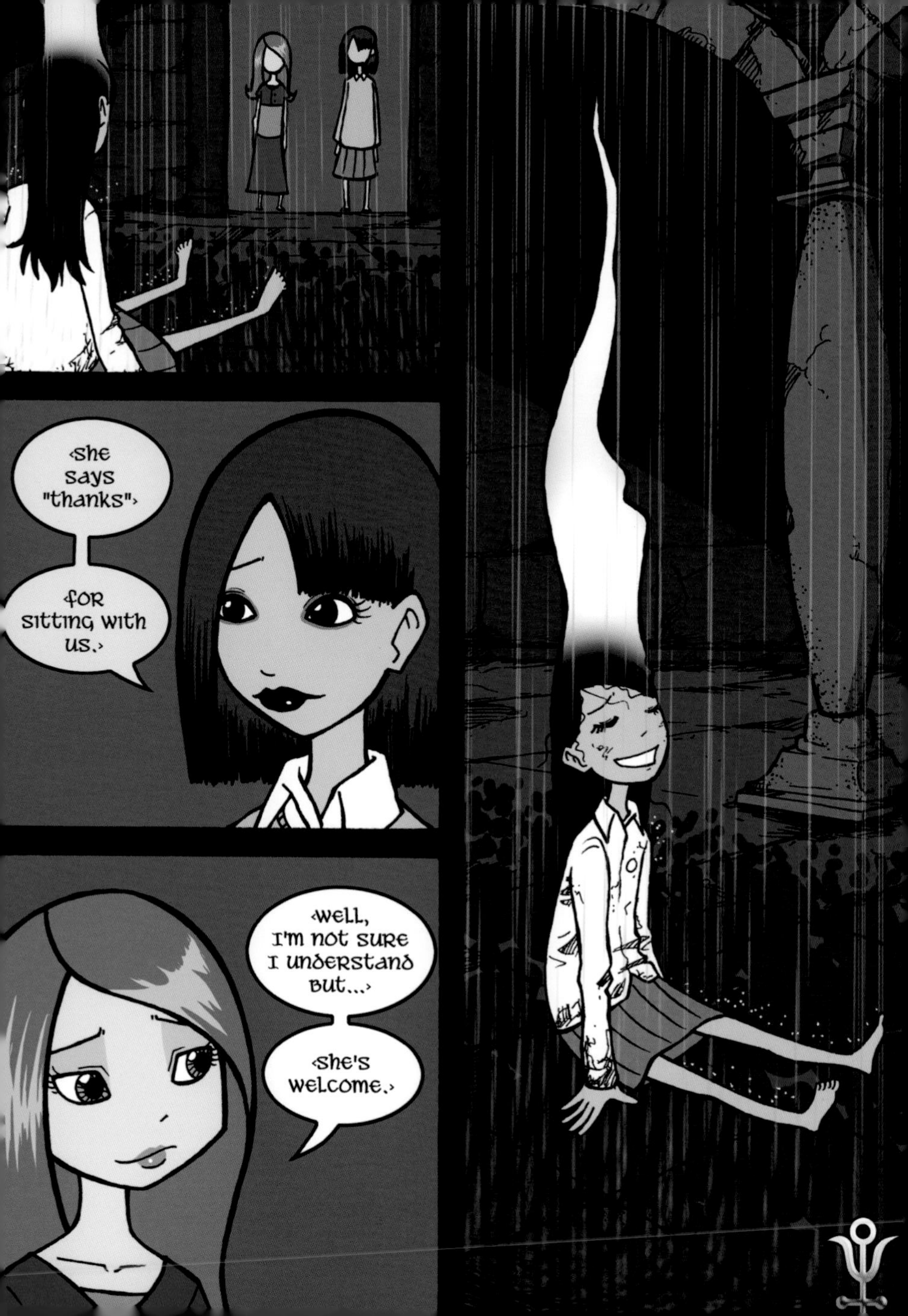
‹She says "thanks"›
‹for sitting with us.›
‹Well, I'm not sure I understand but...›
‹She's welcome.›

THERE, SEE, MY CLOTHES ARE CLEAN NOW!

THEY AREN'T CLEAN, ZIMMY. ONLY WET.

STOMP

BUT SINCE YOU MENTION IT... THE LAUNDRY ISN'T FAR FROM HERE...

OH STOP YOUR MOANING!

LET'S GO CHASE RATS IN THE LIBRARY!

YOU KNOW THERE AREN'T ANY RATS HERE.

SPIDERS THEN.

THERE ARE PLENTY OF SPIDERS!

Gunnerkrigg Court

Chapter 12:

Mainly Involves Robots

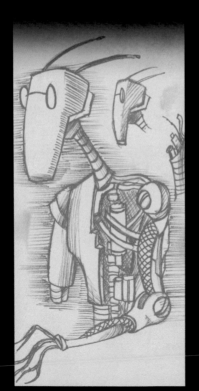

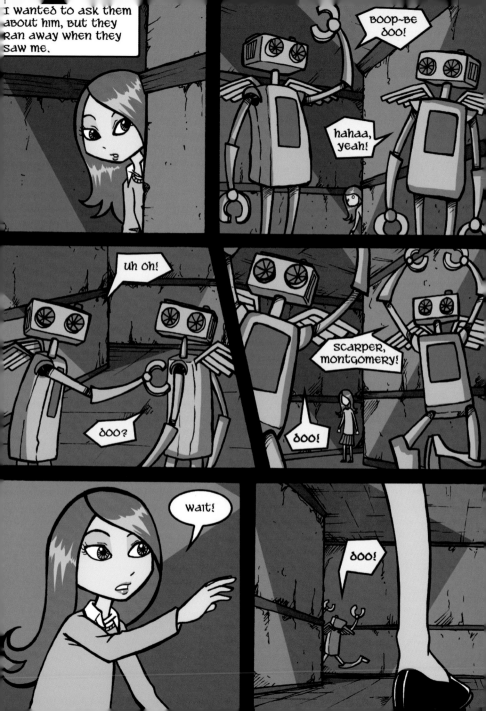

THERE WAS NO HANDLE ON THE DOOR THROUGH WHICH THEY ESCAPED.

THEN, SUDDENLY...

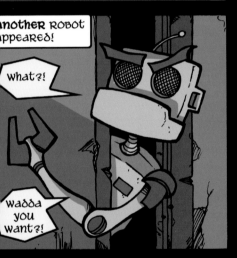

ANOTHER ROBOT APPEARED!

WHAT?!

WADDA YOU WANT?!

I, UM... WOULD LIKE TO ENTER, PLEASE.

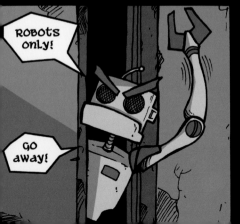

ROBOTS ONLY!

GO AWAY!

BORING DOOR

HE WOULDN'T LET ME IN.

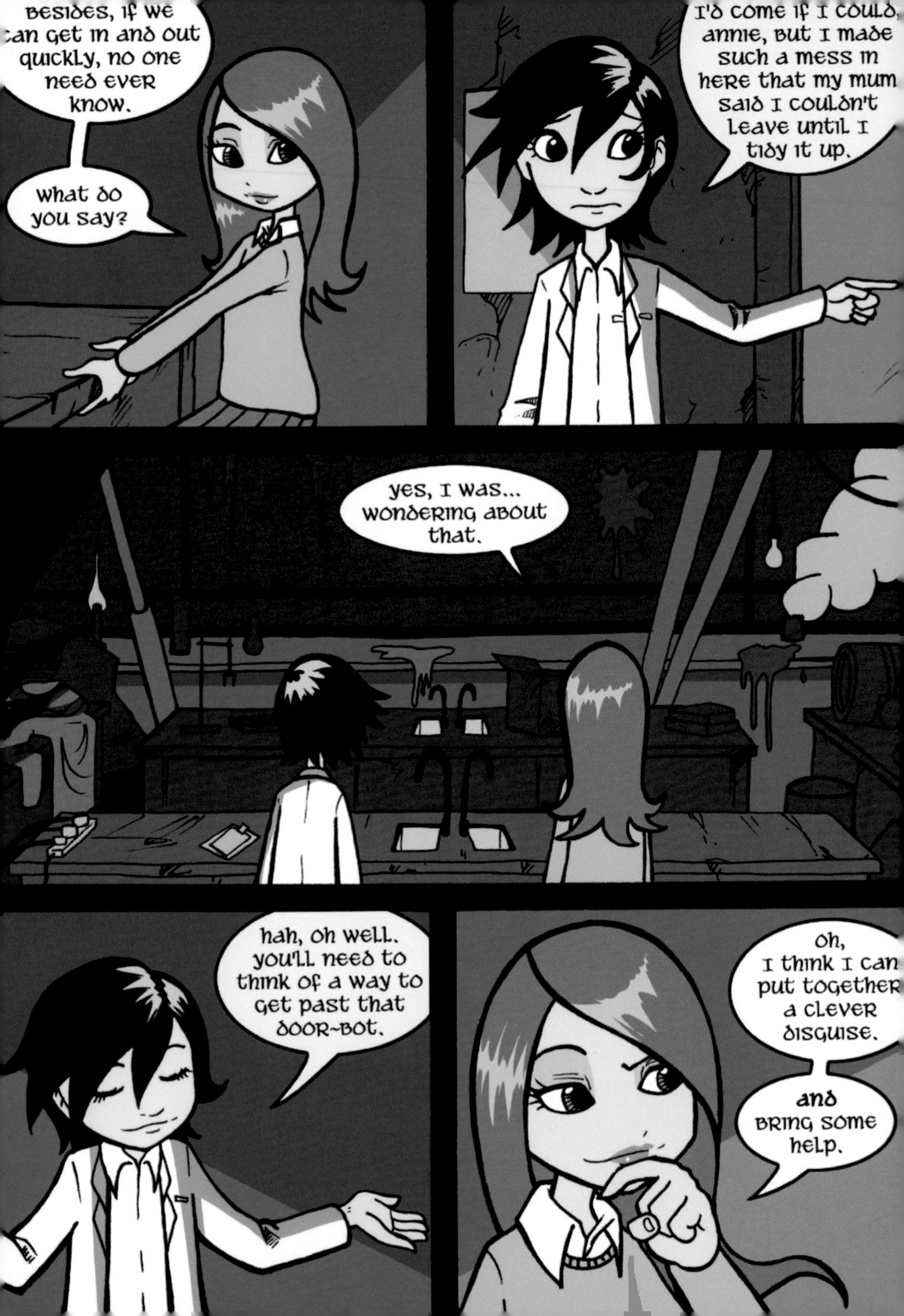
BESIDES, IF WE CAN GET IN AND OUT QUICKLY, NO ONE NEED EVER KNOW.
WHAT DO YOU SAY?
I'D COME IF I COULD, ANNIE, BUT I MADE SUCH A MESS IN HERE THAT MY MUM SAID I COULDN'T LEAVE UNTIL I TIDY IT UP.
YES, I WAS... WONDERING ABOUT THAT.
HAH, OH WELL. YOU'LL NEED TO THINK OF A WAY TO GET PAST THAT DOOR-BOT.
OH, I THINK I CAN PUT TOGETHER A CLEVER DISGUISE.
AND BRING SOME HELP.

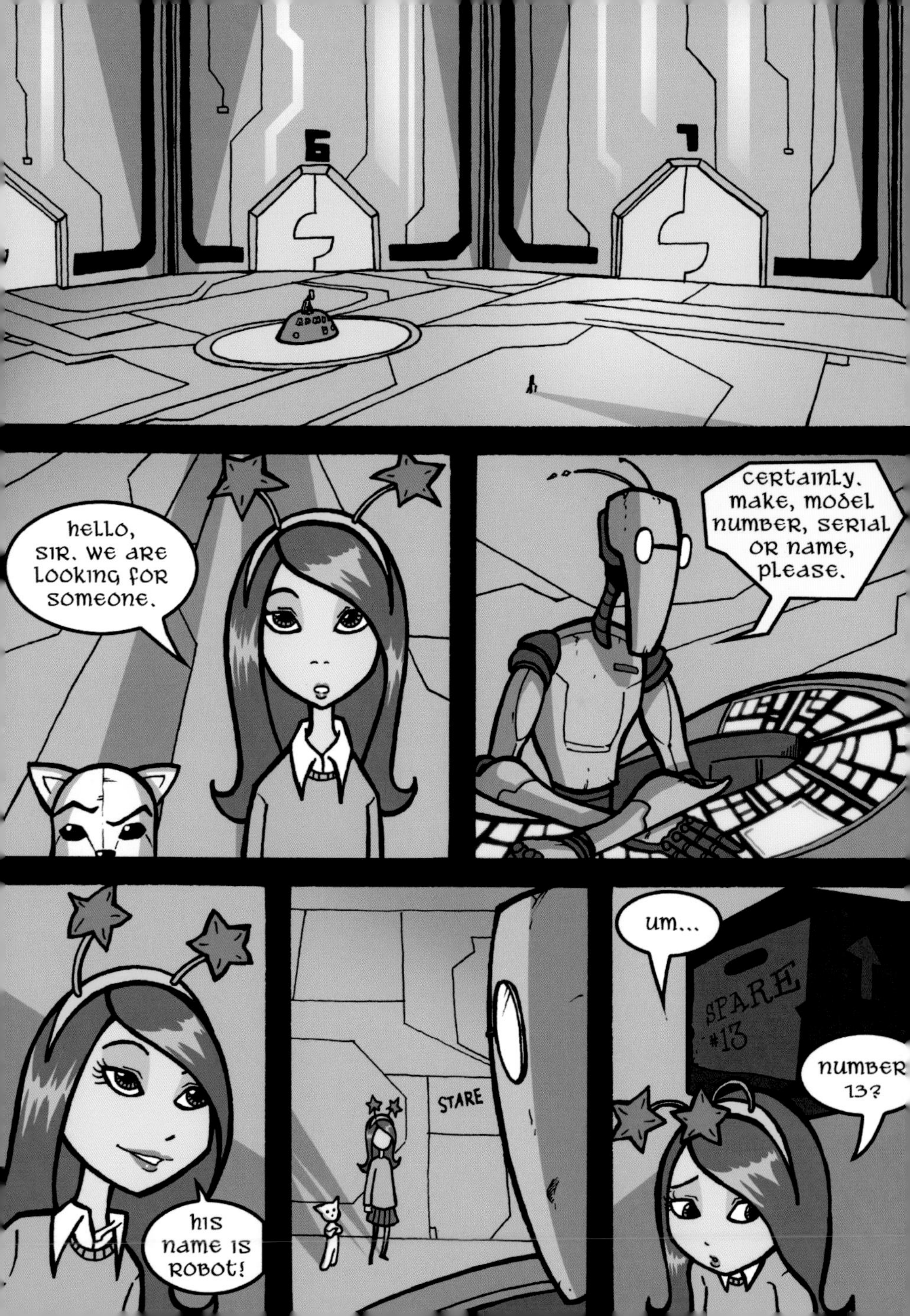
6
7
hello, sir. we are looking for someone.
certainly. make, model number, serial or name, please.
his name is robot!
STARE
um...
SPARE #13
number 13?

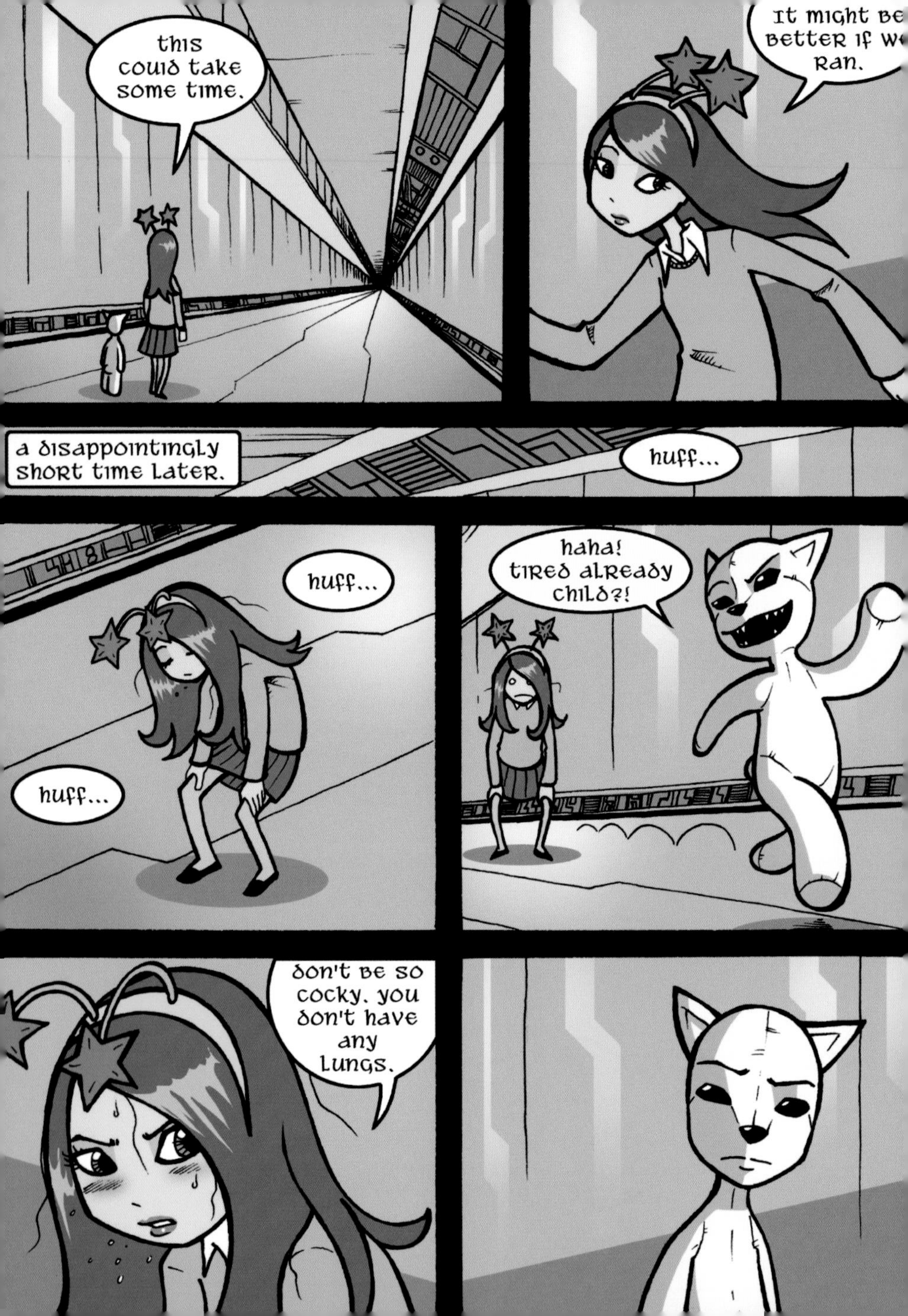
this could take some time.
It might be better if we ran.
a disappointingly short time later.
huff...
huff...
huff...
haha! tired already child?!
don't be so cocky. you don't have any lungs.

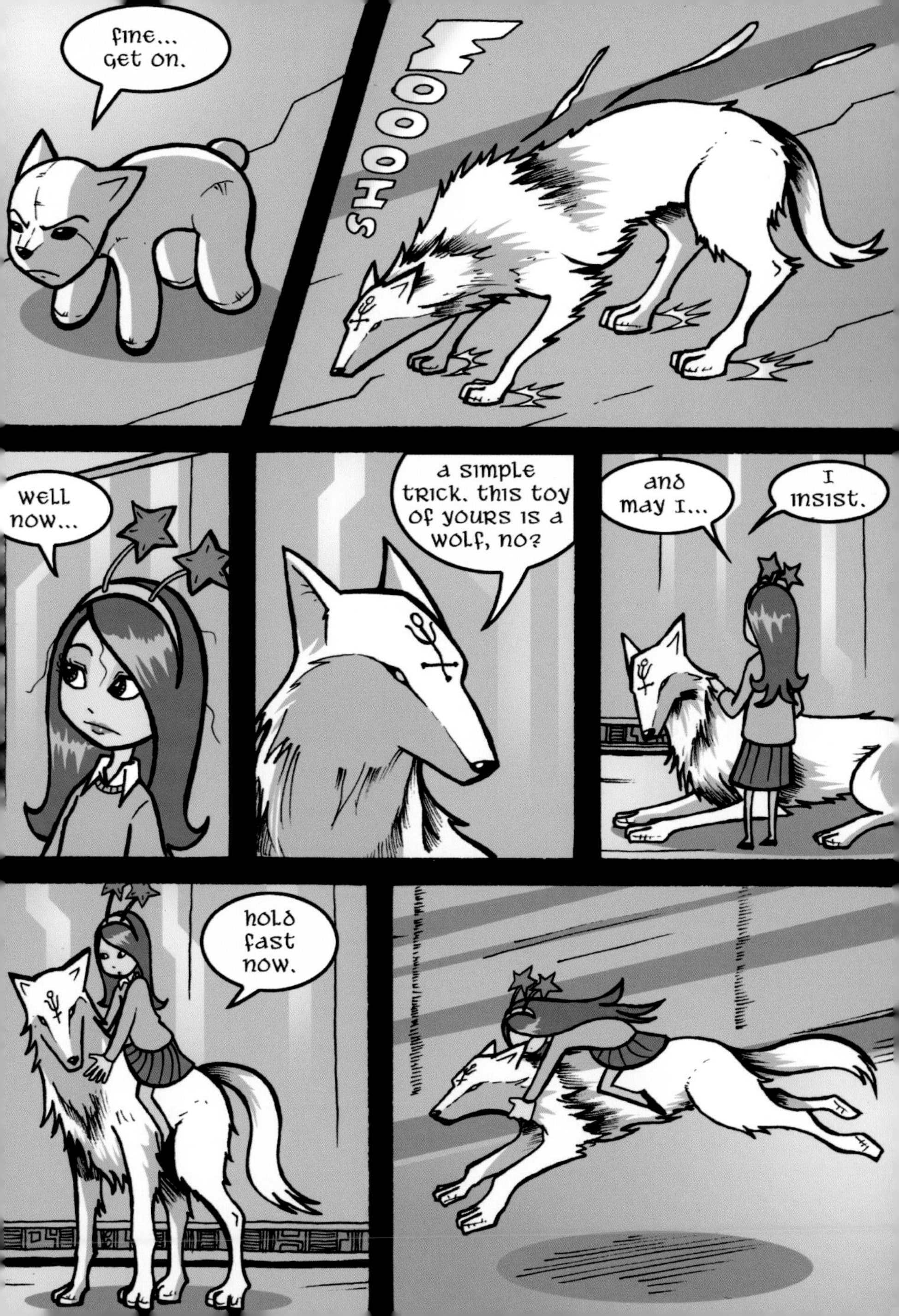
fine... get on.
SHOOOOM
well now...
a simple trick. this toy of yours is a wolf, no?
and may I...
I insist.
hold fast now.

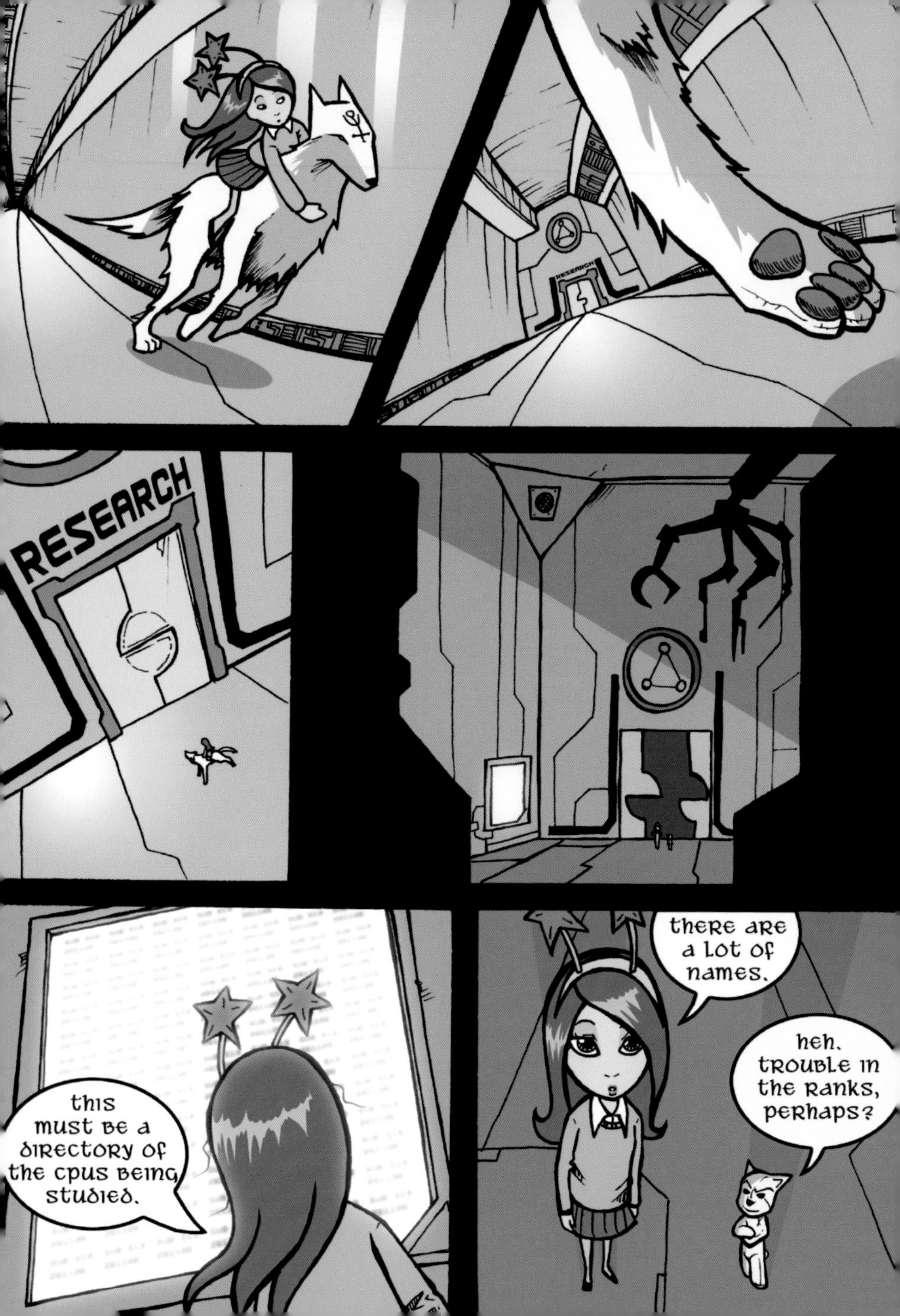
RESEARCH
this must be a directory of the cpus being studied.
there are a lot of names.
heh. trouble in the ranks, perhaps?

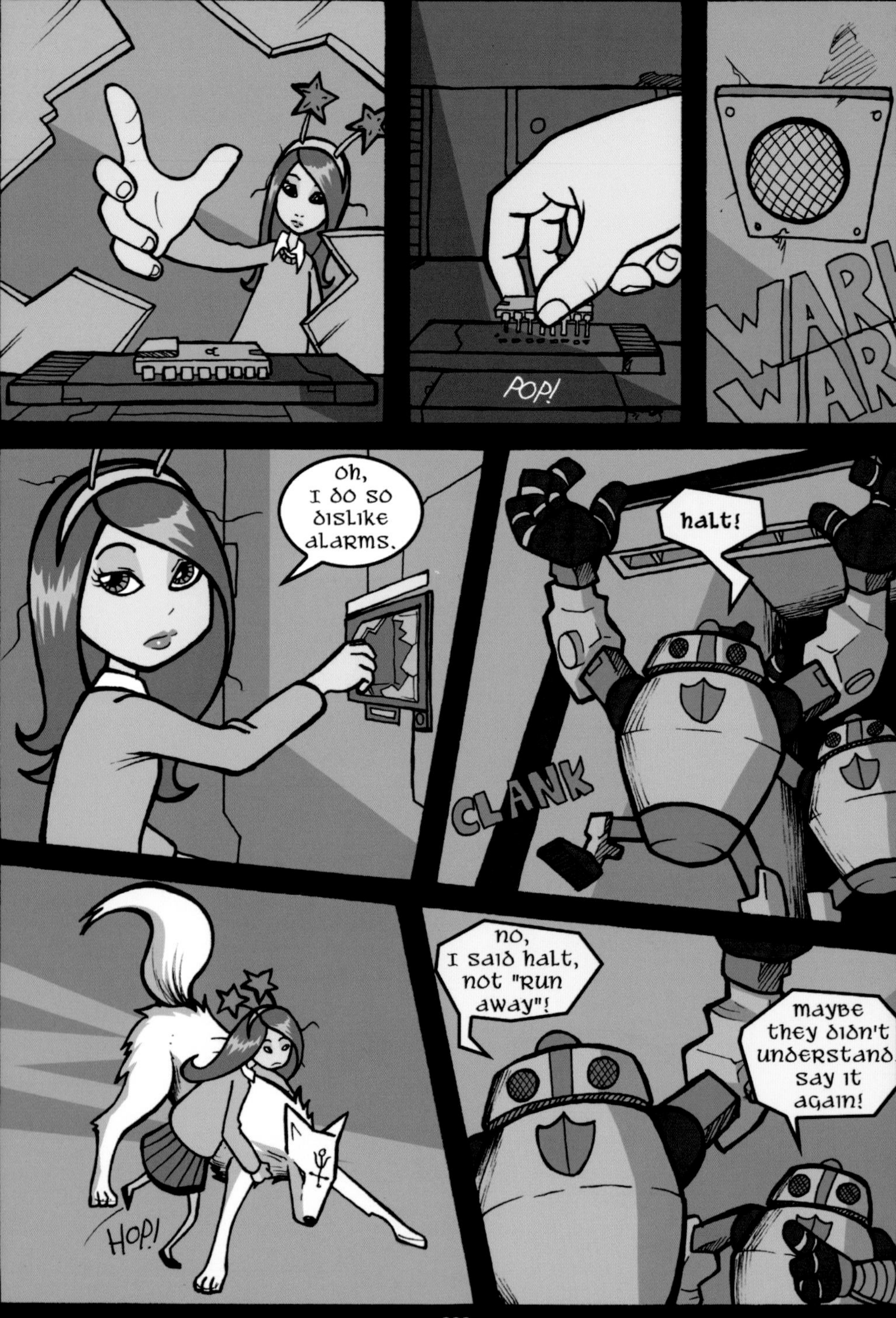
POP!
WAR
WAR
oh, I do so dislike alarms.
halt!
CLANK
HOP!
no, I said halt, not "Run away"!
maybe they didn't understand. say it again!

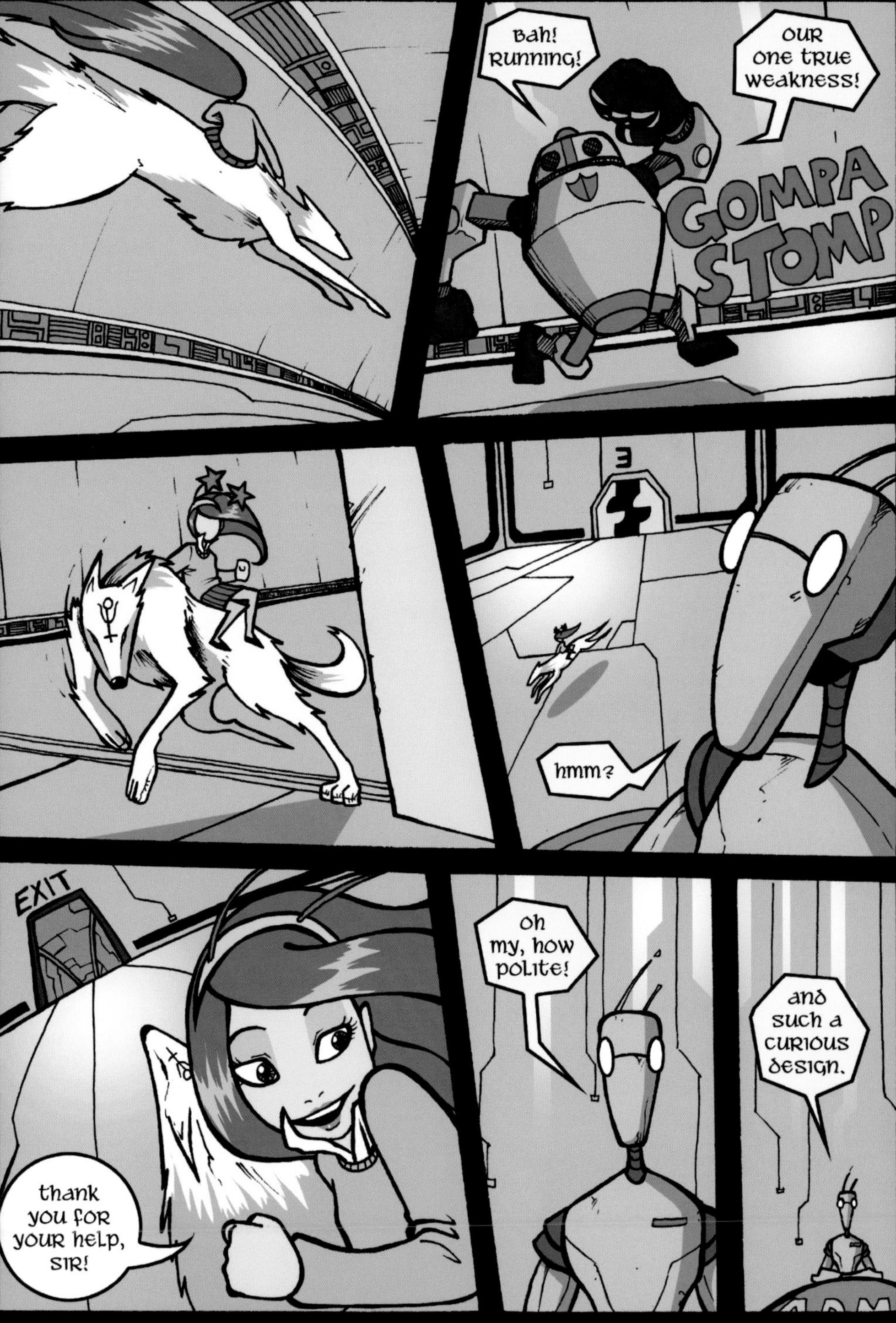
Bah! Running!
our one true weakness!
GOMPA STOMP
hmm?
EXIT
thank you for your help, sir!
oh my, how polite!
and such a curious design.

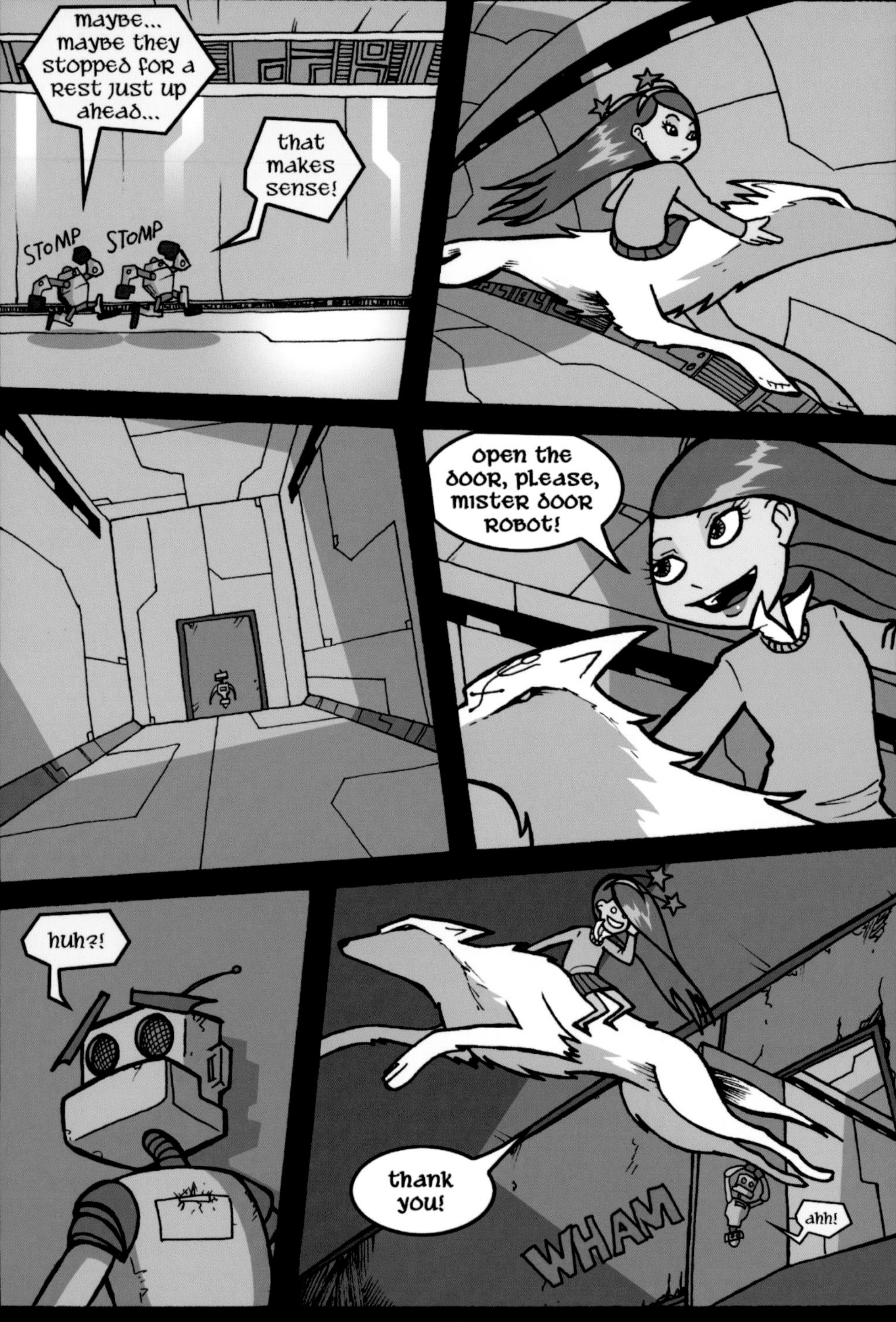
maybe... maybe they stopped for a rest just up ahead...
that makes sense!
STOMP STOMP
open the door, please, mister door robot!
huh?!
thank you!
WHAM
ahh!

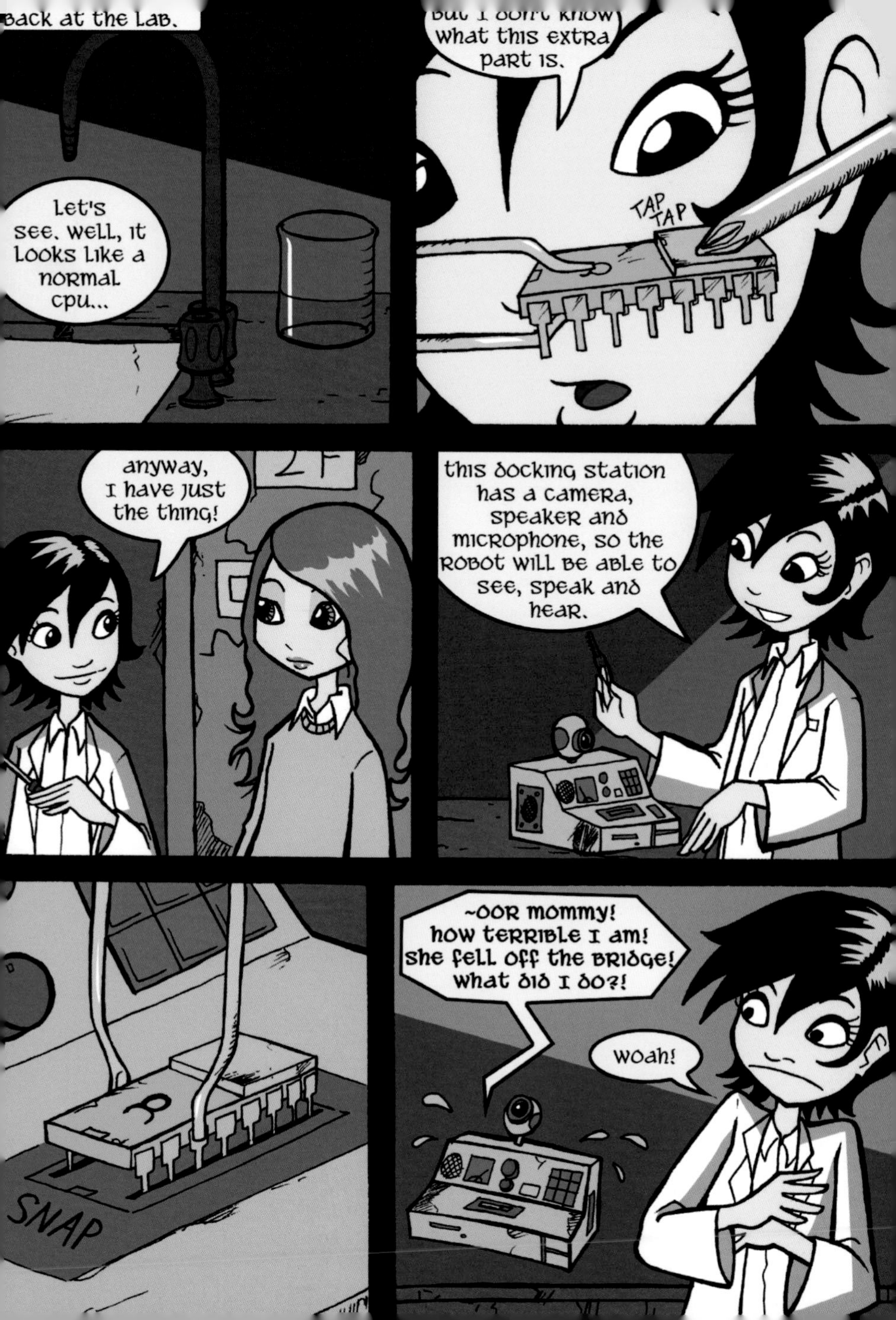
Back at the Lab.
Let's see. well, it looks like a normal cpu...
what this extra part is.
TAP TAP
anyway, I have just the thing!
this docking station has a camera, speaker and microphone, so the robot will be able to see, speak and hear.
SNAP
~OOR mommy! how terrible I am! she fell off the bridge! what did I do?!
woah!

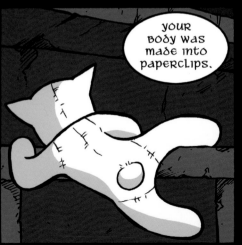

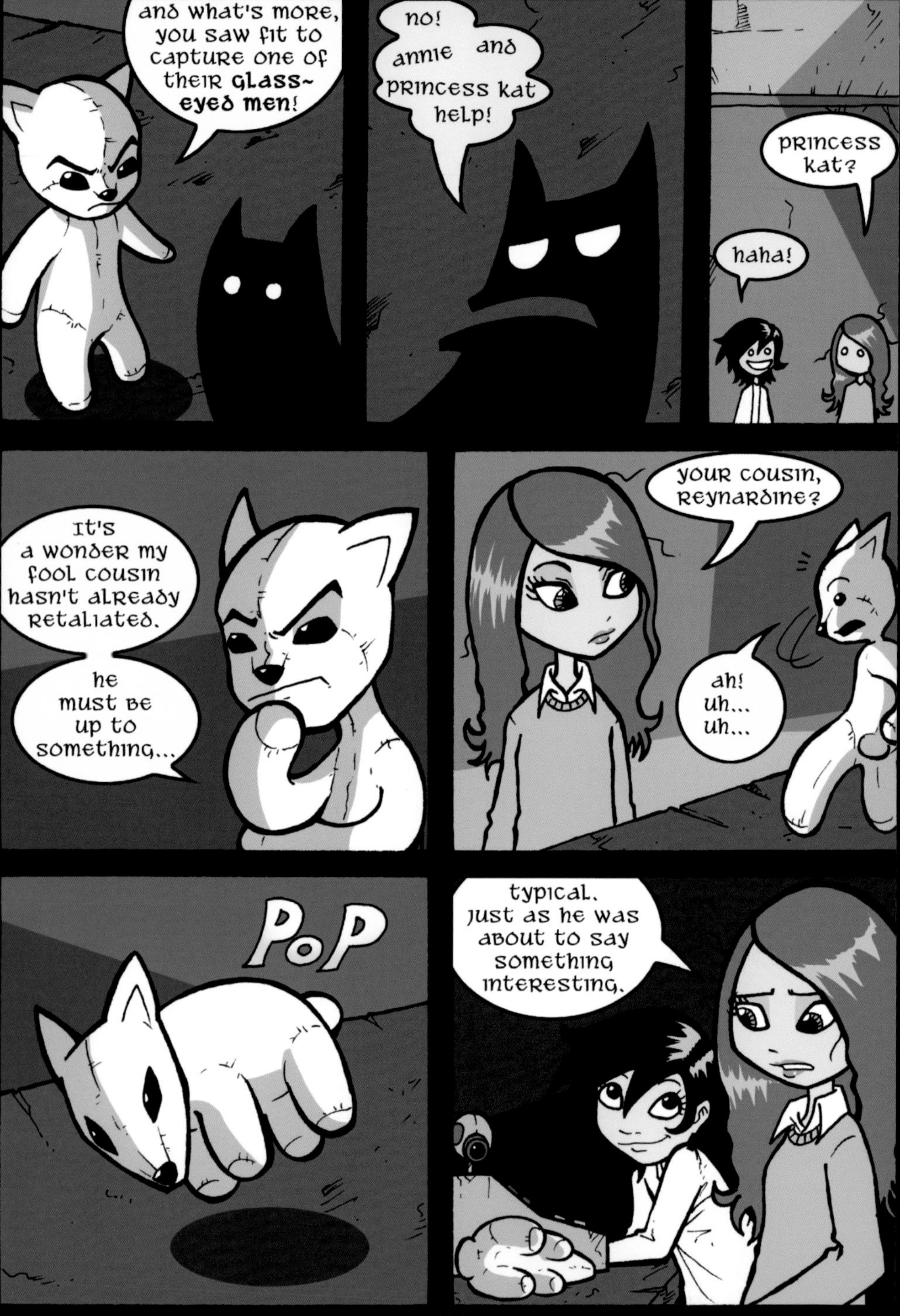
and what's more, you saw fit to capture one of their glass~eyed men!
no! annie and princess kat help!
princess kat?
haha!
It's a wonder my fool cousin hasn't already retaliated.
he must be up to something...
your cousin, Reynardine?
ah! uh... uh...
POP
typical. Just as he was about to say something interesting.

WELL, now that we have you back, ROBOT, we should do something about your body.

I think I can whip something up for him.

at least something temporary while I get the parts to make a better body.

thank you very much!

ROBOT, I'M SO SORRY I caused you all this trouble.

I should have told you to come back after you crossed the bridge.

don't apologise.

you see, you gave me something I'd never had before.

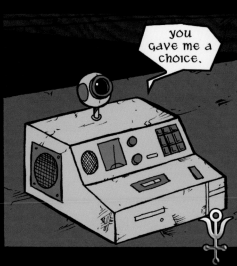

you gave me a choice.

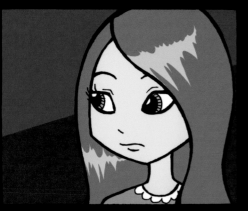

Gunnerkrigg Court

Chapter 13:

A Week For Kat

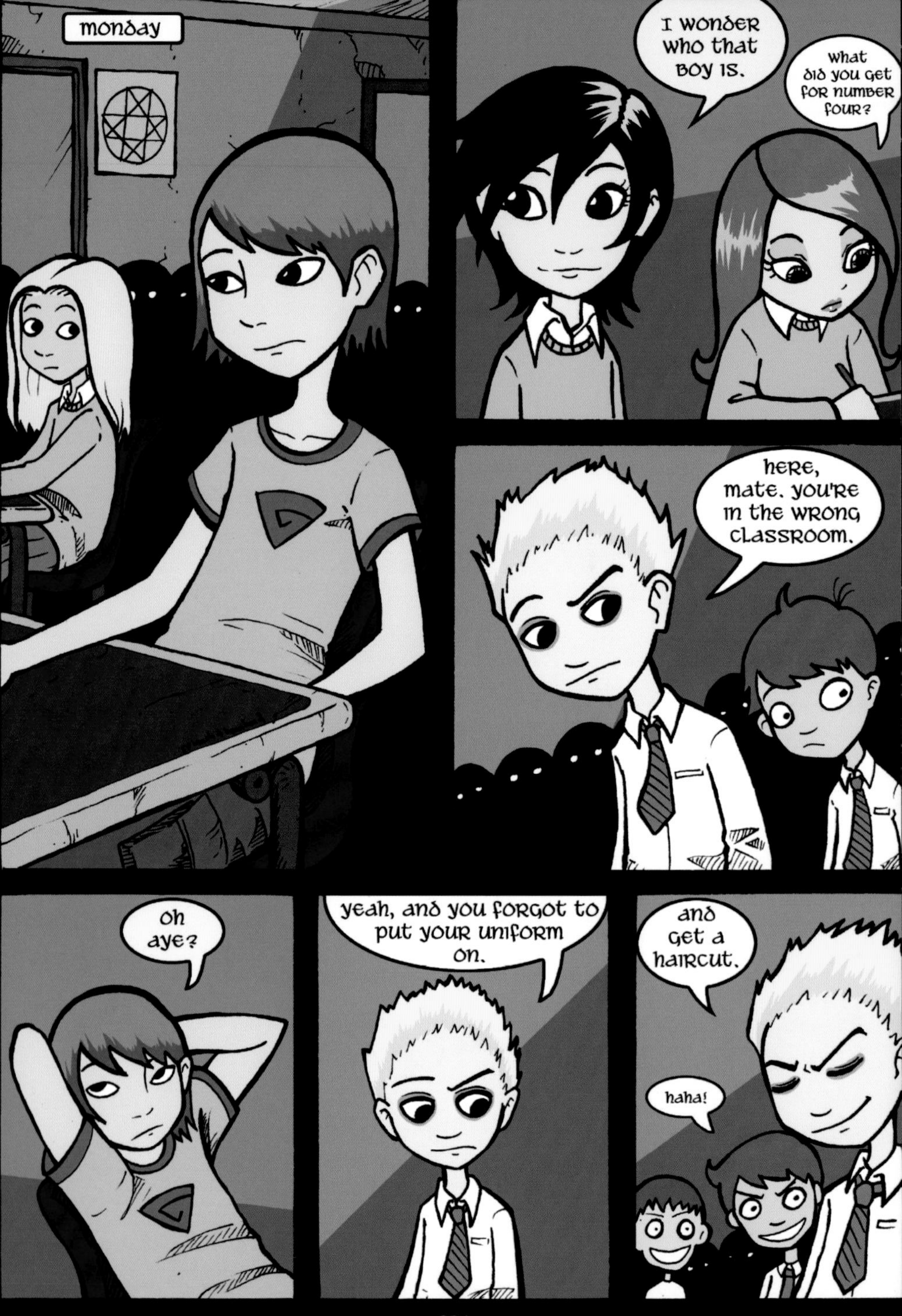
monday
I wonder who that boy is.
what did you get for number four?
here, mate. you're in the wrong classroom.
oh aye?
yeah, and you forgot to put your uniform on.
and get a haircut.
haha!

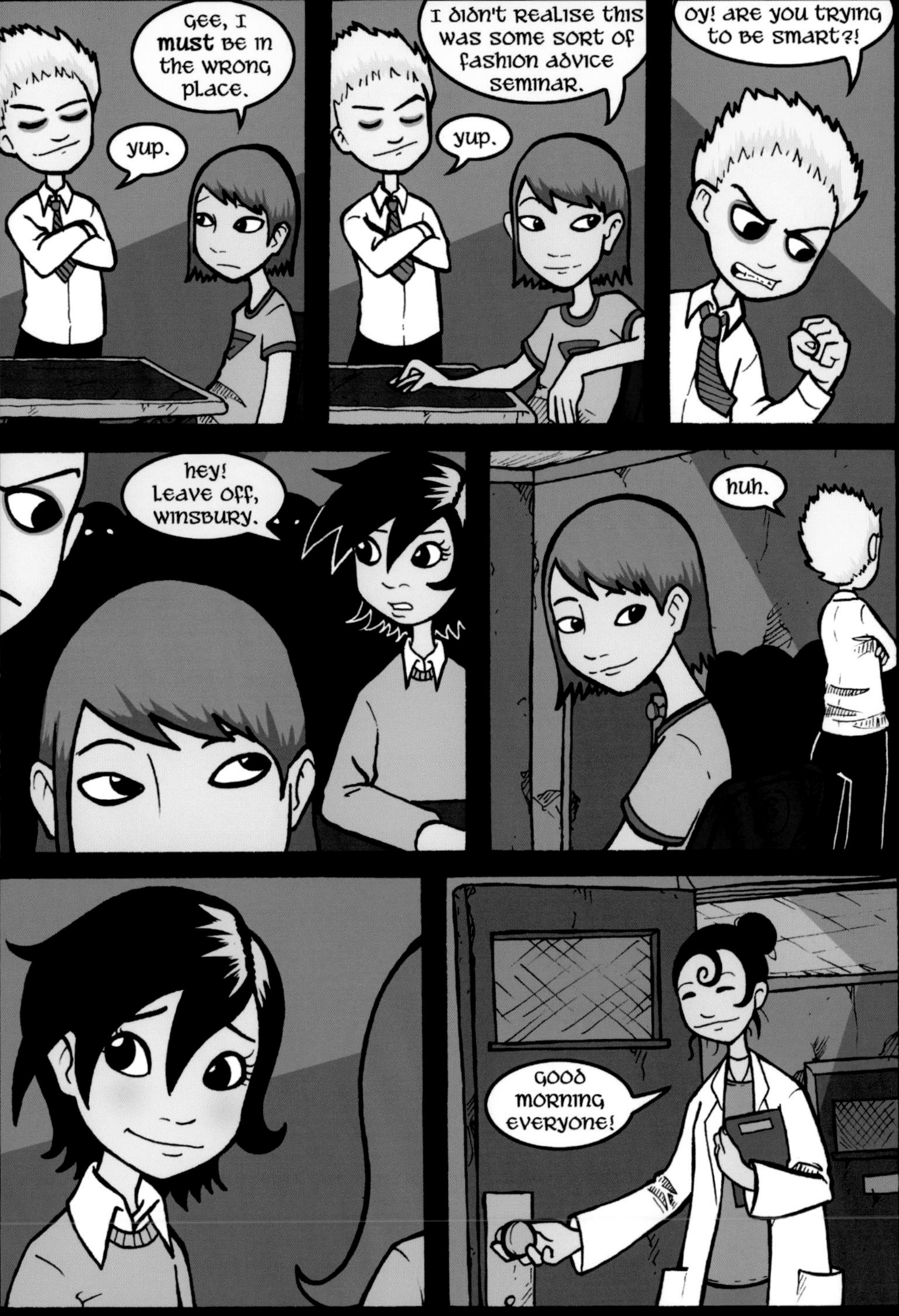
Gee, I **must** be in the wrong place.
yup.
I didn't realise this was some sort of fashion advice seminar.
yup.
Oy! are you trying to be smart?!
hey! Leave off, Winsbury.
huh.
Good morning everyone!

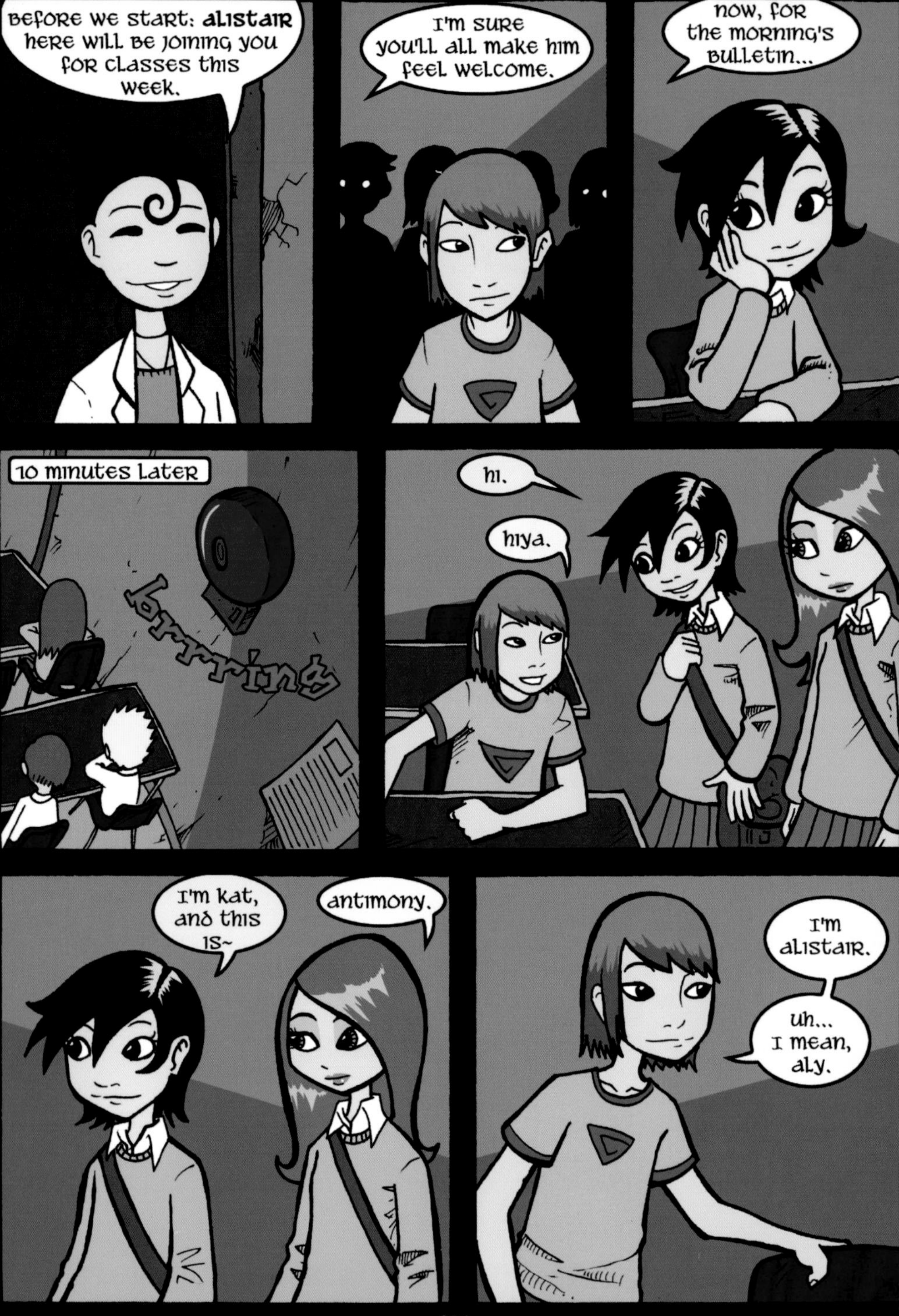
Before we start: alistair here will be joining you for classes this week.
I'm sure you'll all make him feel welcome.
now, for the morning's bulletin...
10 minutes later
brrring
hi.
hiya.
I'm kat, and this is~
antimony.
I'm alistair.
uh... I mean, aly.

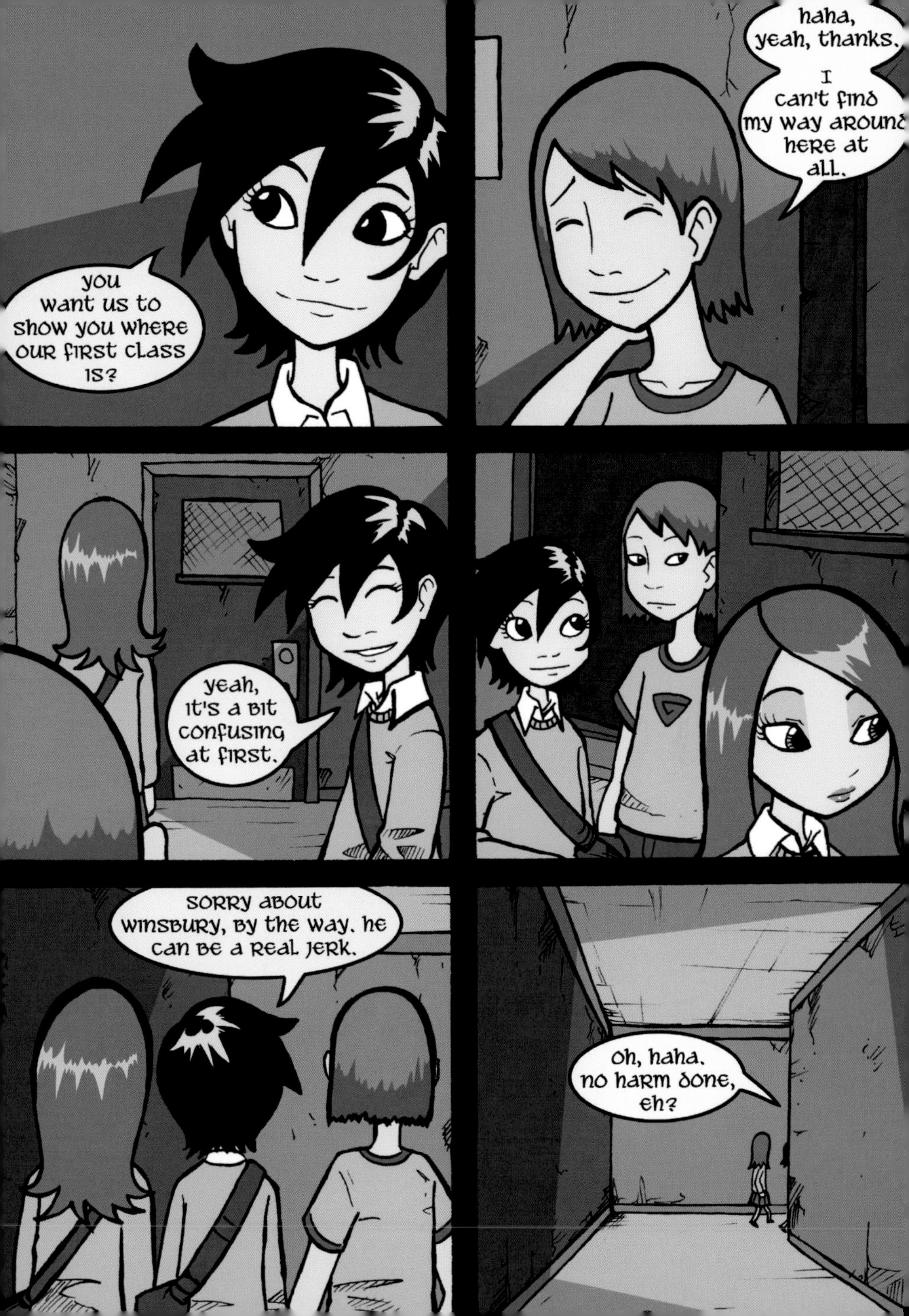
you want us to show you where our first class is?
haha, yeah, thanks.
I can't find my way around here at all.
yeah, it's a bit confusing at first.
sorry about winsbury, by the way. he can be a real jerk.
oh, haha. no harm done, eh?

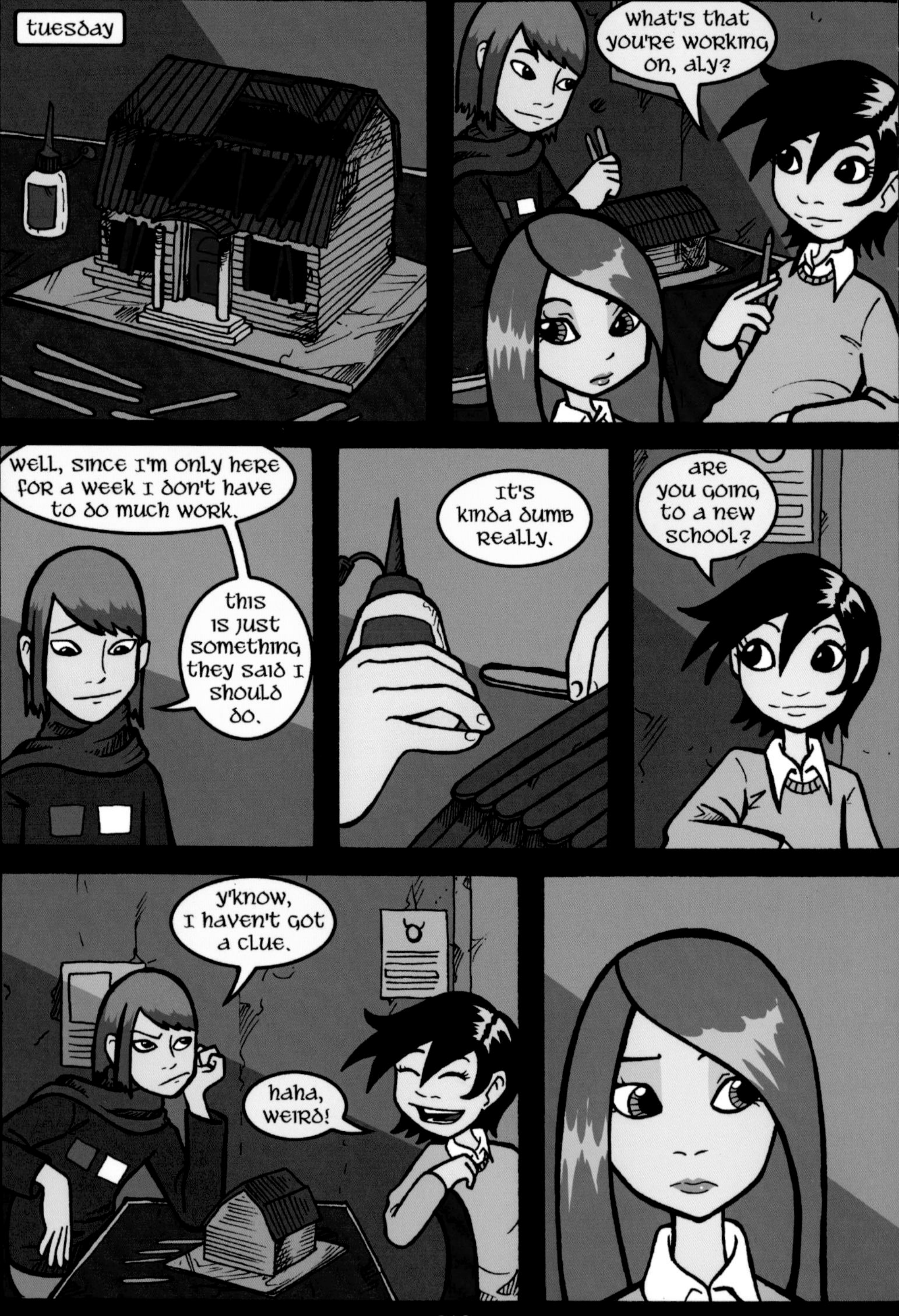
tuesday
what's that you're working on, aly?
well, since I'm only here for a week I don't have to do much work.
this is just something they said I should do.
It's kinda dumb really.
are you going to a new school?
y'know, I haven't got a clue.
haha, weird!

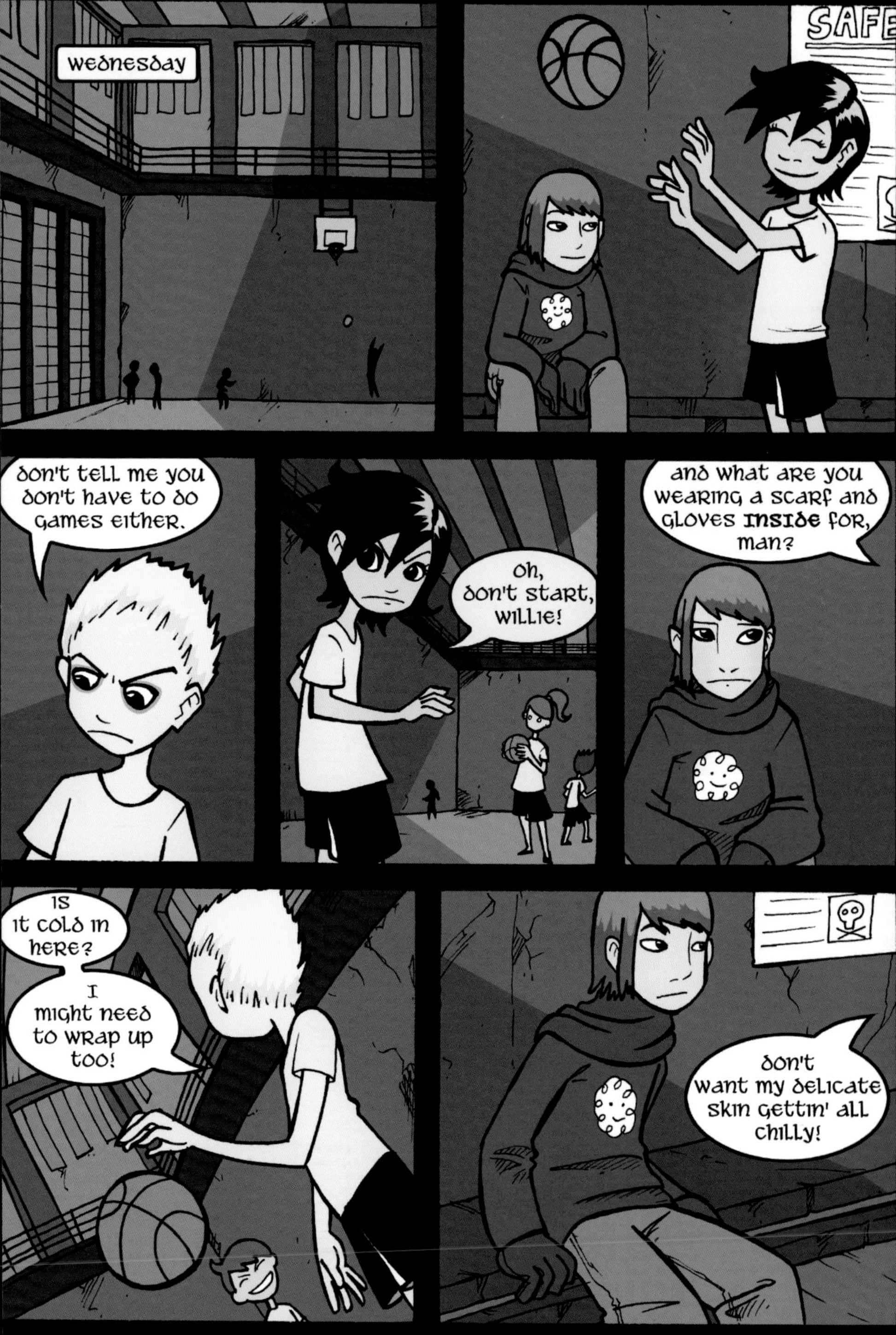
wednesday
SAFE
don't tell me you don't have to do games either.
oh, don't start, willie!
and what are you wearing a scarf and gloves INSIDE for, man?
is it cold in here?
I might need to wrap up too!
don't want my delicate skin gettin' all chilly!

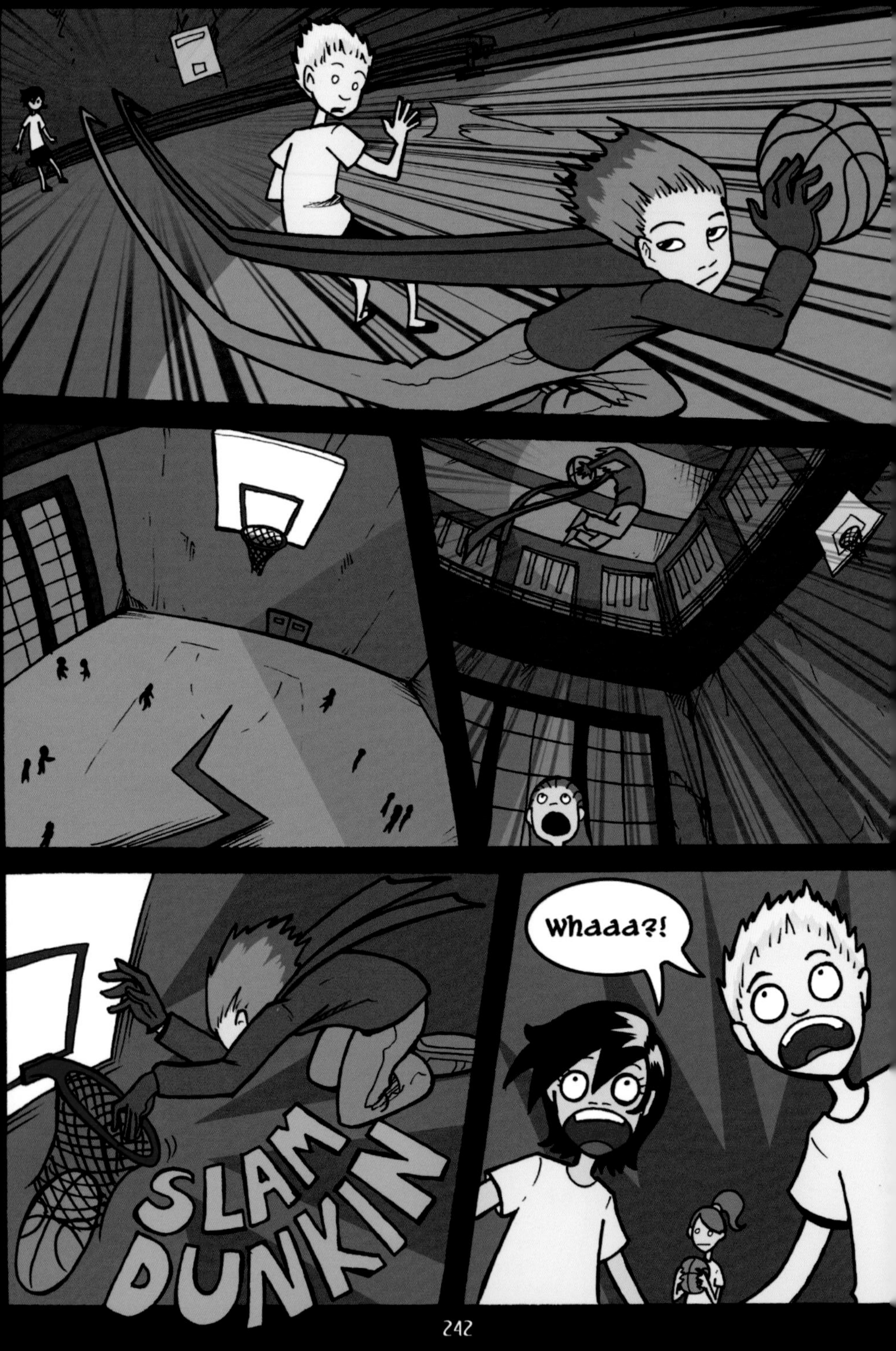
SLAM
DUNKIN
Whaaa?!

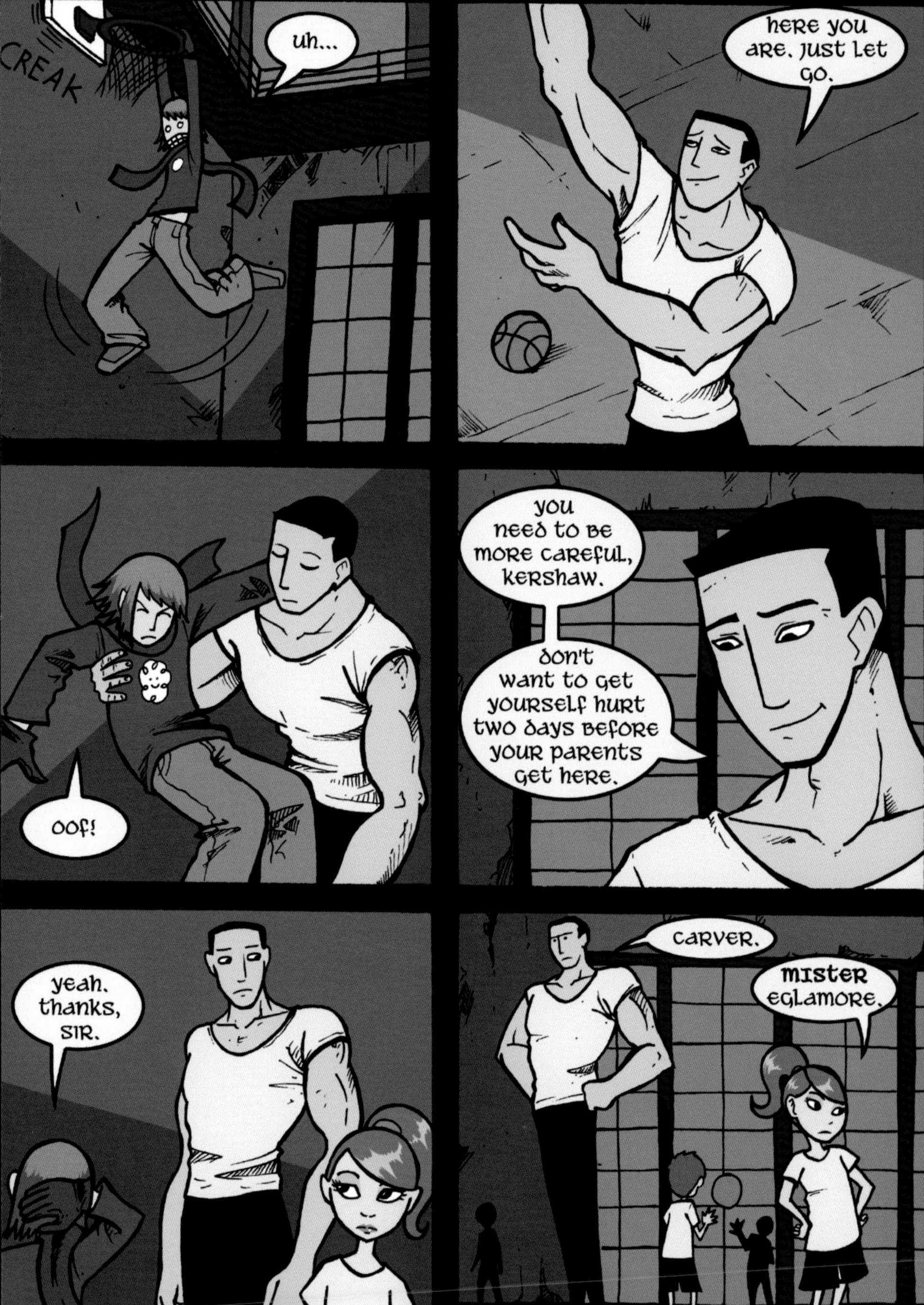
CREAK
uh...
here you are. just let go.
oof!
you need to be more careful, kershaw.
don't want to get yourself hurt two days before your parents get here.
yeah. thanks, sir.
carver.
mister eglamore.

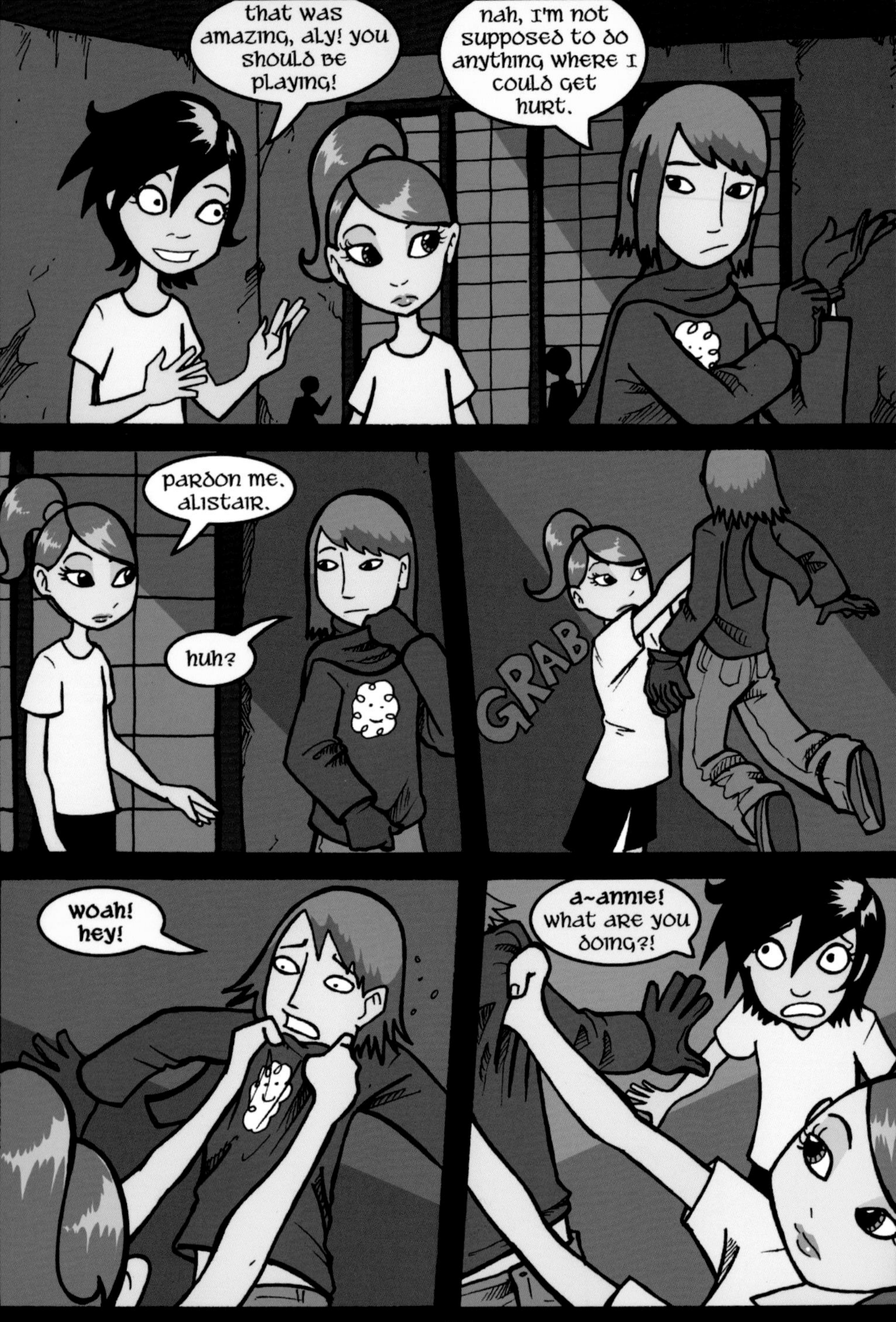
that was amazing, aly! you should be playing!
nah, I'm not supposed to do anything where I could get hurt.
pardon me, alistair.
huh?
GRAB
woah! hey!
a~annie! what are you doing?!

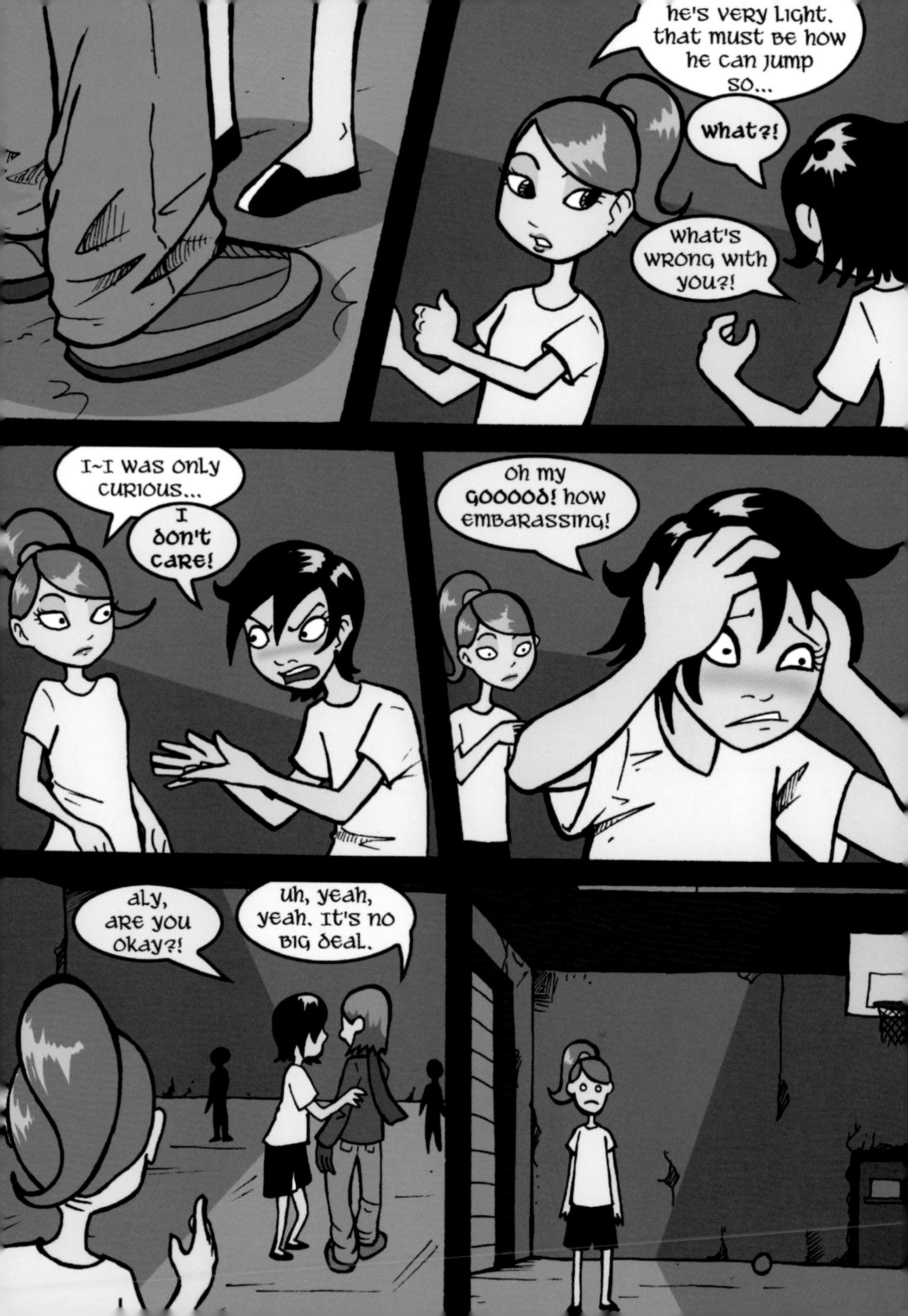
he's very light. that must be how he can jump so...
what?!
what's wrong with you?!
I~I was only curious...
I don't care!
oh my GOOOOD! how embarassing!
aly, are you okay?!
uh, yeah, yeah. it's no big deal.

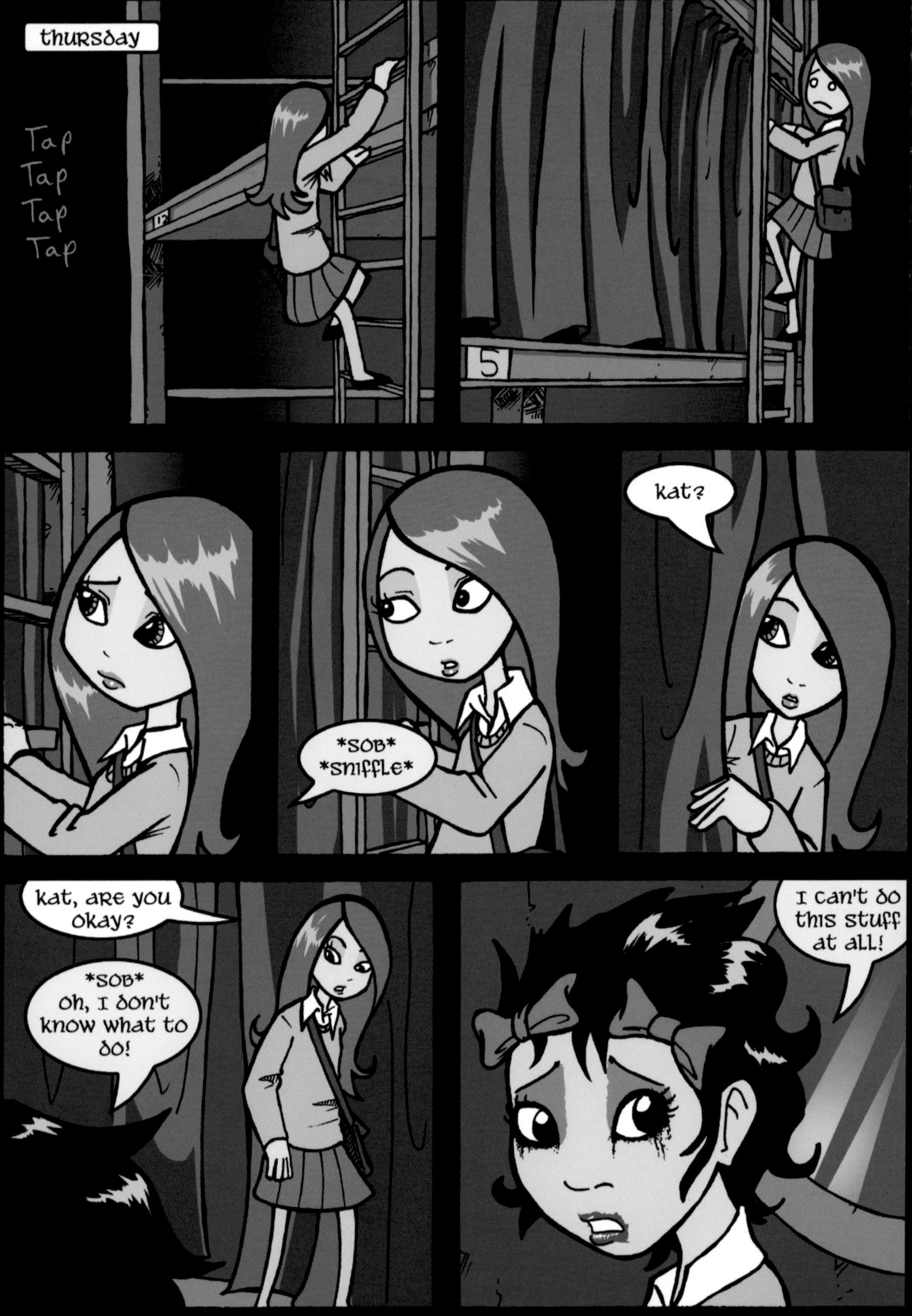
thursday
Tap
Tap
Tap
Tap
5
SOB
sniffle
kat?
kat, are you okay?
SOB
oh, I don't know what to do!
I can't do this stuff at all!

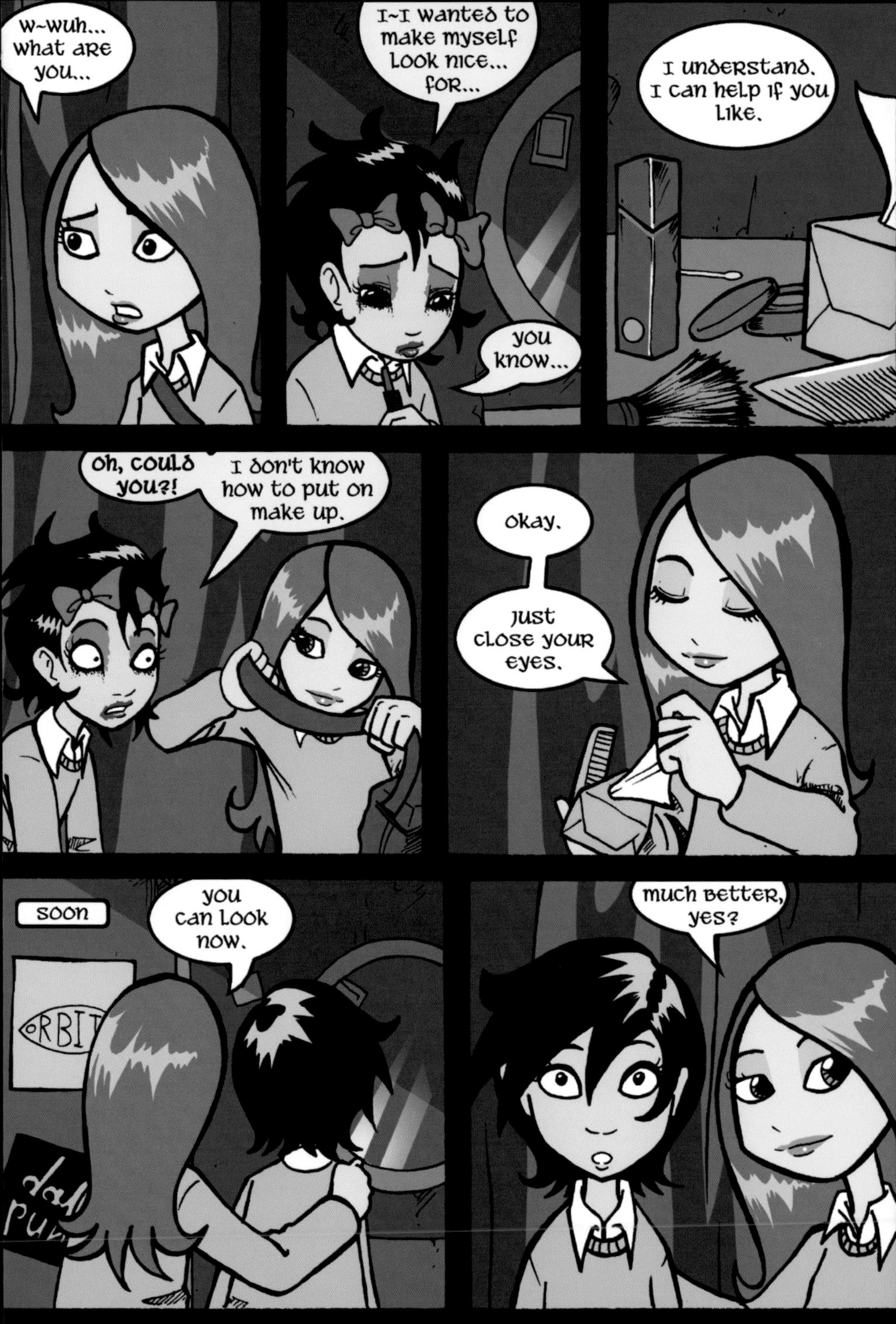
W~WUH...
WHAT ARE
YOU...
I~I WANTED TO
MAKE MYSELF
LOOK NICE...
FOR...
YOU
KNOW...
I UNDERSTAND.
I CAN HELP IF YOU
LIKE.
OH, COULD
YOU?!
I DON'T KNOW
HOW TO PUT ON
MAKE UP.
OKAY.
JUST
CLOSE YOUR
EYES.
SOON
YOU
CAN LOOK
NOW.
ORBIT
MUCH BETTER,
YES?

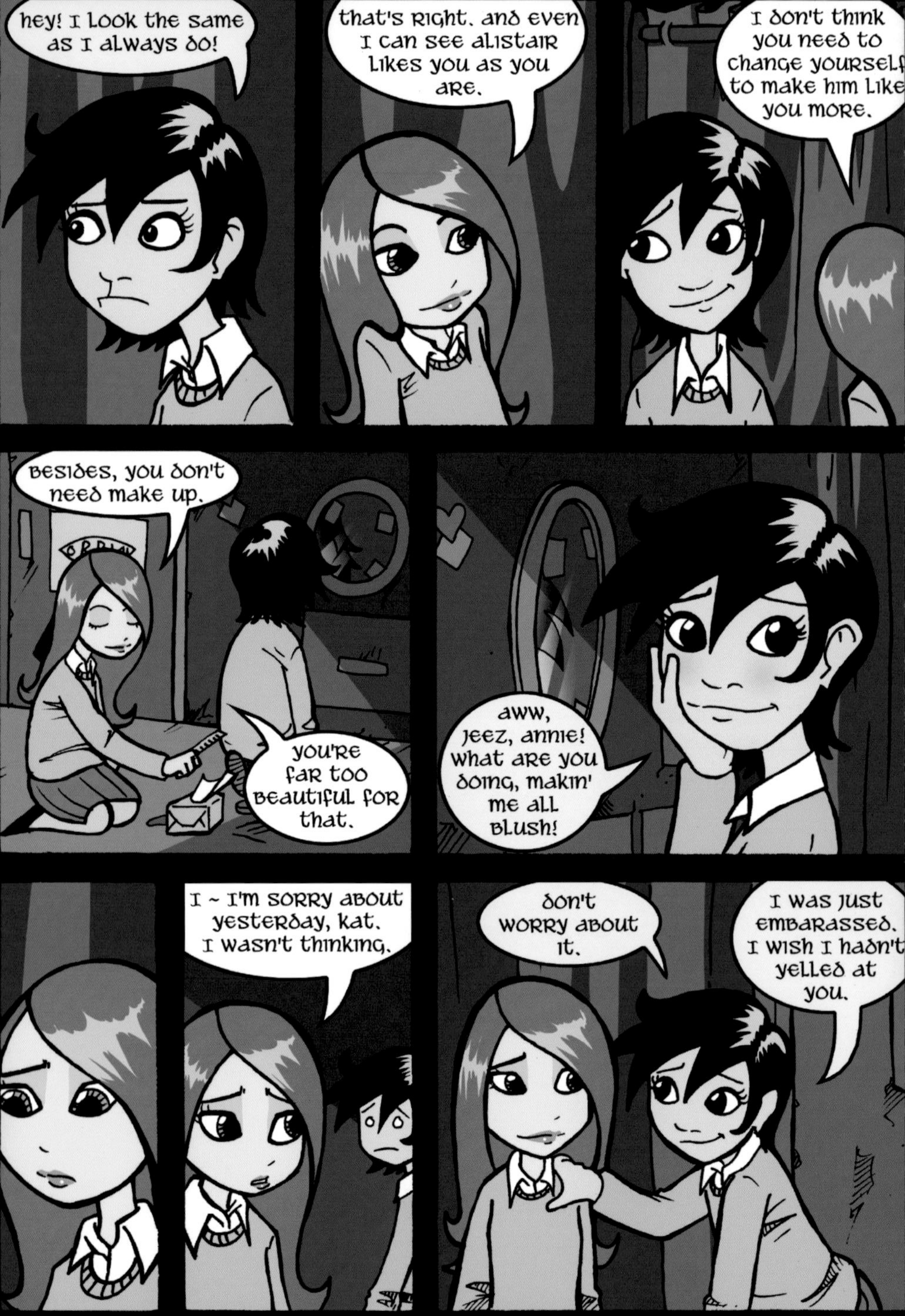
hey! I look the same as I always do!
that's right. and even I can see alistair likes you as you are.
I don't think you need to change yourself to make him like you more.
besides, you don't need make up.
you're far too beautiful for that.
aww, jeez, annie! what are you doing, makin' me all blush!
I ~ I'm sorry about yesterday, kat. I wasn't thinking.
don't worry about it.
I was just embarassed. I wish I hadn't yelled at you.

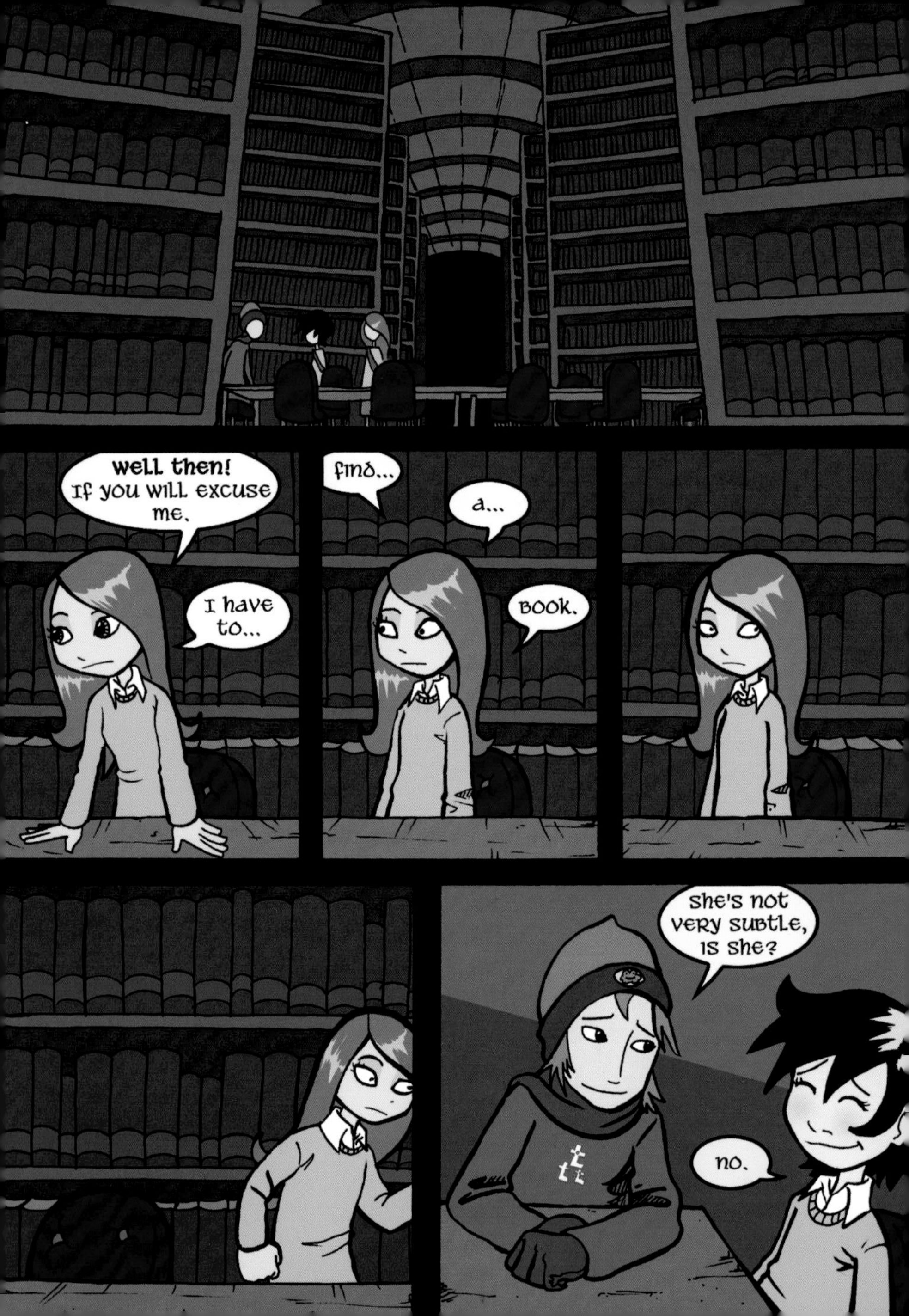
well then! If you will excuse me.
I have to...
find...
a...
book.
she's not very subtle, is she?
no.

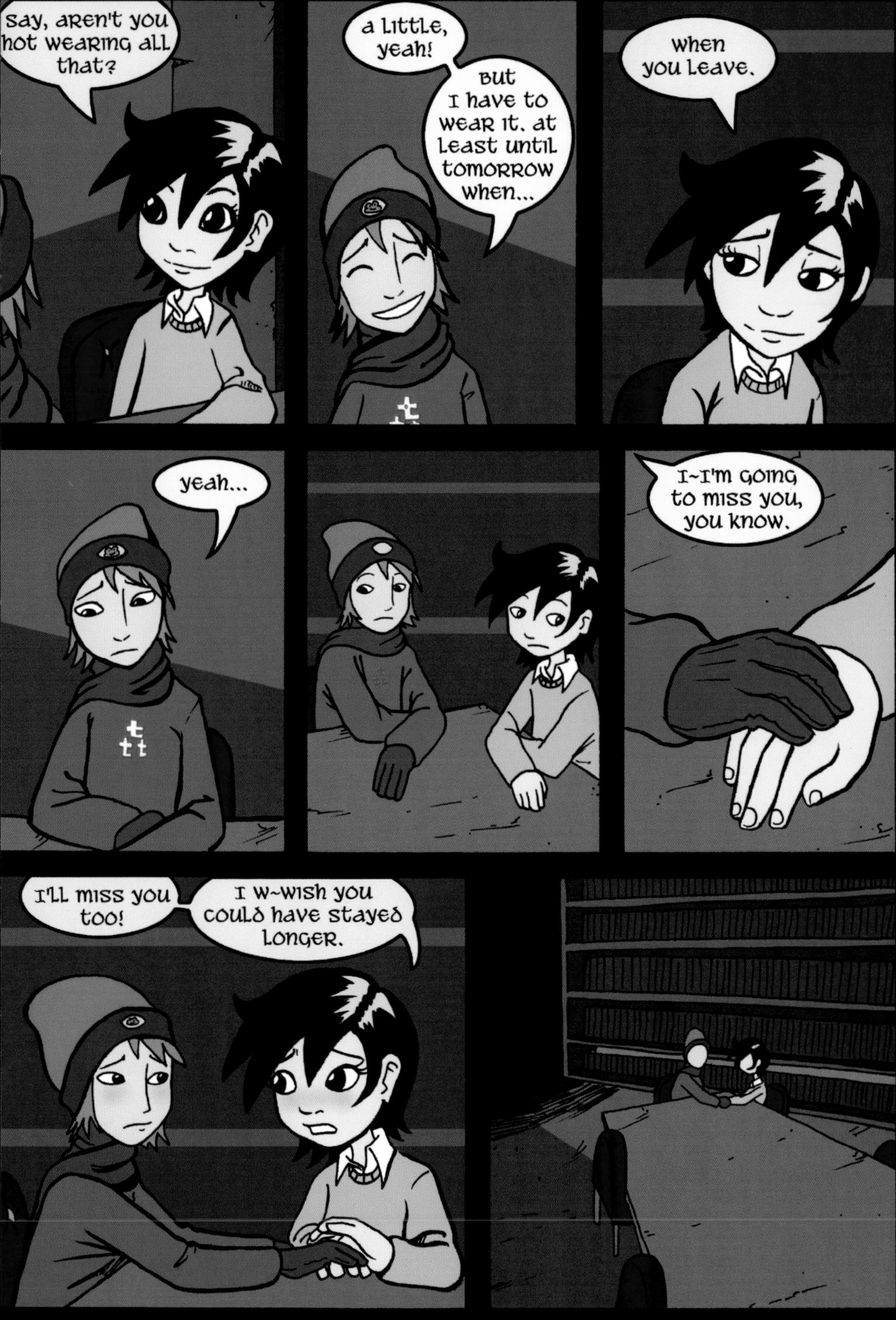
Say, aren't you hot wearing all that?
a little, yeah!
But I have to wear it, at least until tomorrow when...
when you leave.
yeah...
I-I'm going to miss you, you know.
I'll miss you too!
I w-wish you could have stayed longer.

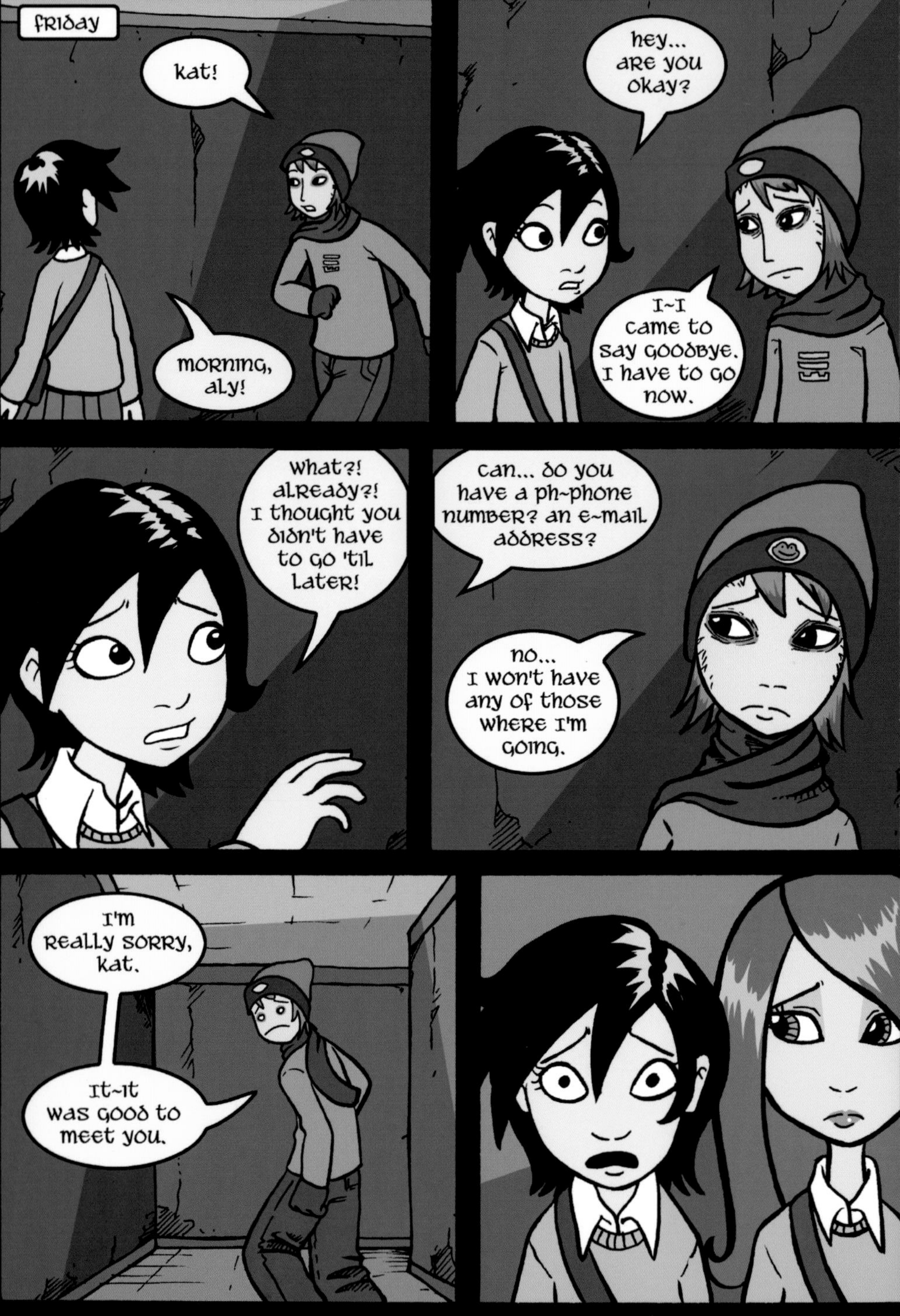
friday
kat!
morning, aly!
hey... are you okay?
I~I came to say goodbye. I have to go now.
what?! already?! I thought you didn't have to go 'til later!
can... do you have a ph~phone number? an e~mail address?
no... I won't have any of those where I'm going.
I'm really sorry, kat.
It~it was good to meet you.

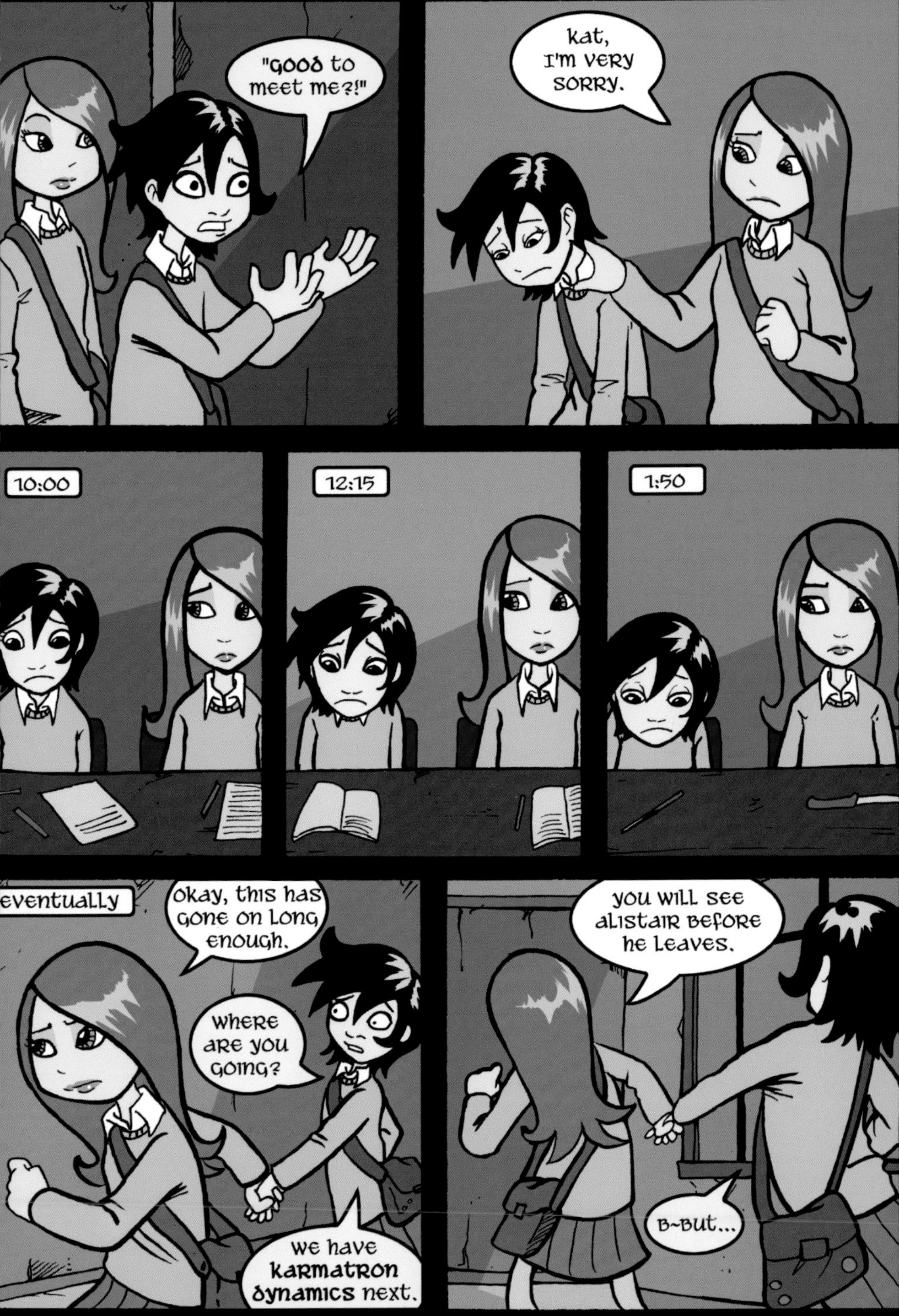
"GOOD to meet me?!"
Kat, I'M VERY SORRY.
10:00
12:15
1:50
eventually
Okay, this has gone on long enough.
Where are you going?
We have **Karmatron dynamics** next.
You will see Alistair before he leaves.
B-But...

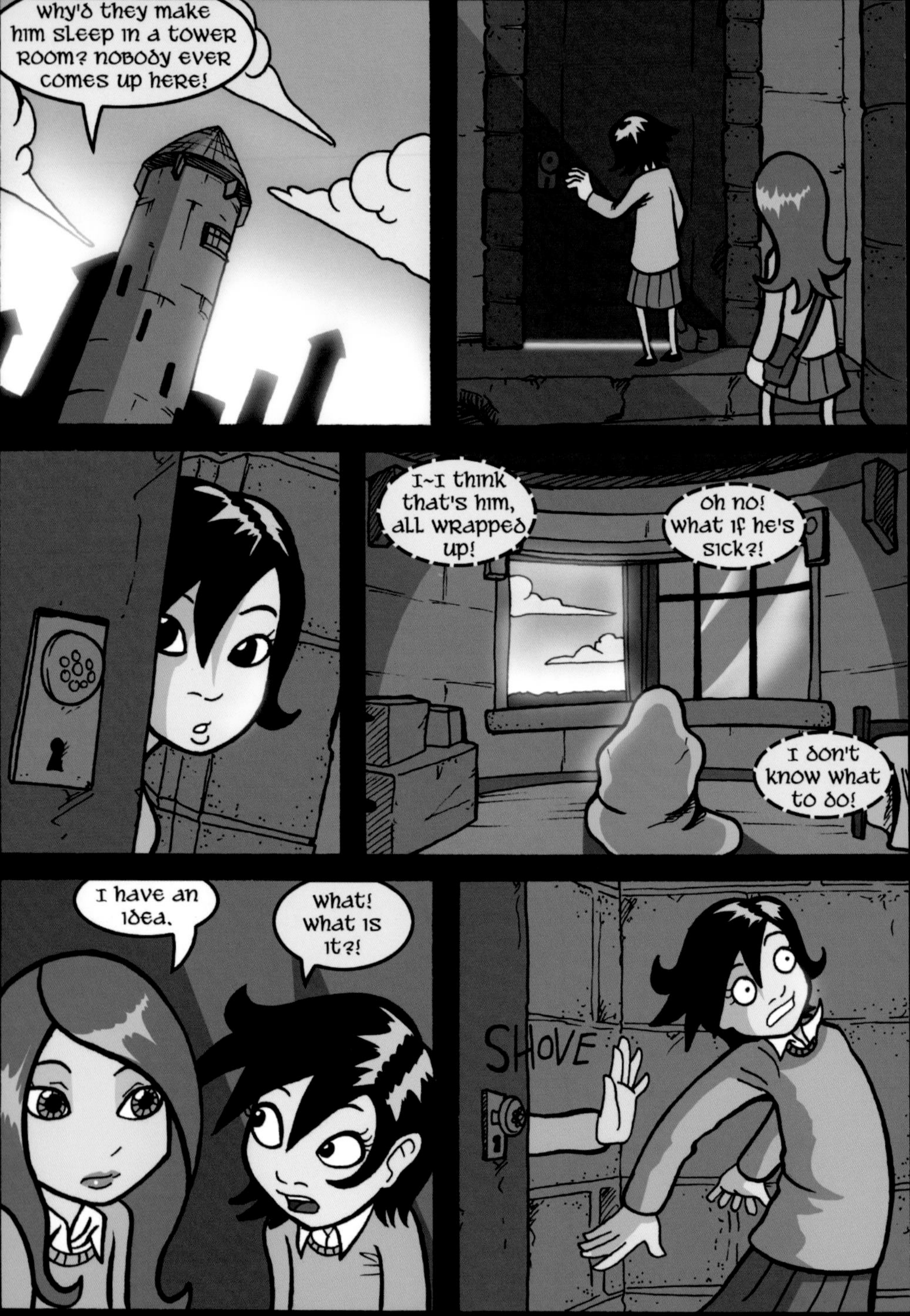
why'd they make him sleep in a tower room? nobody ever comes up here!
I~I think that's him, all wrapped up!
oh no! what if he's sick?!
I don't know what to do!
I have an idea.
what! what is it?!
SHOVE

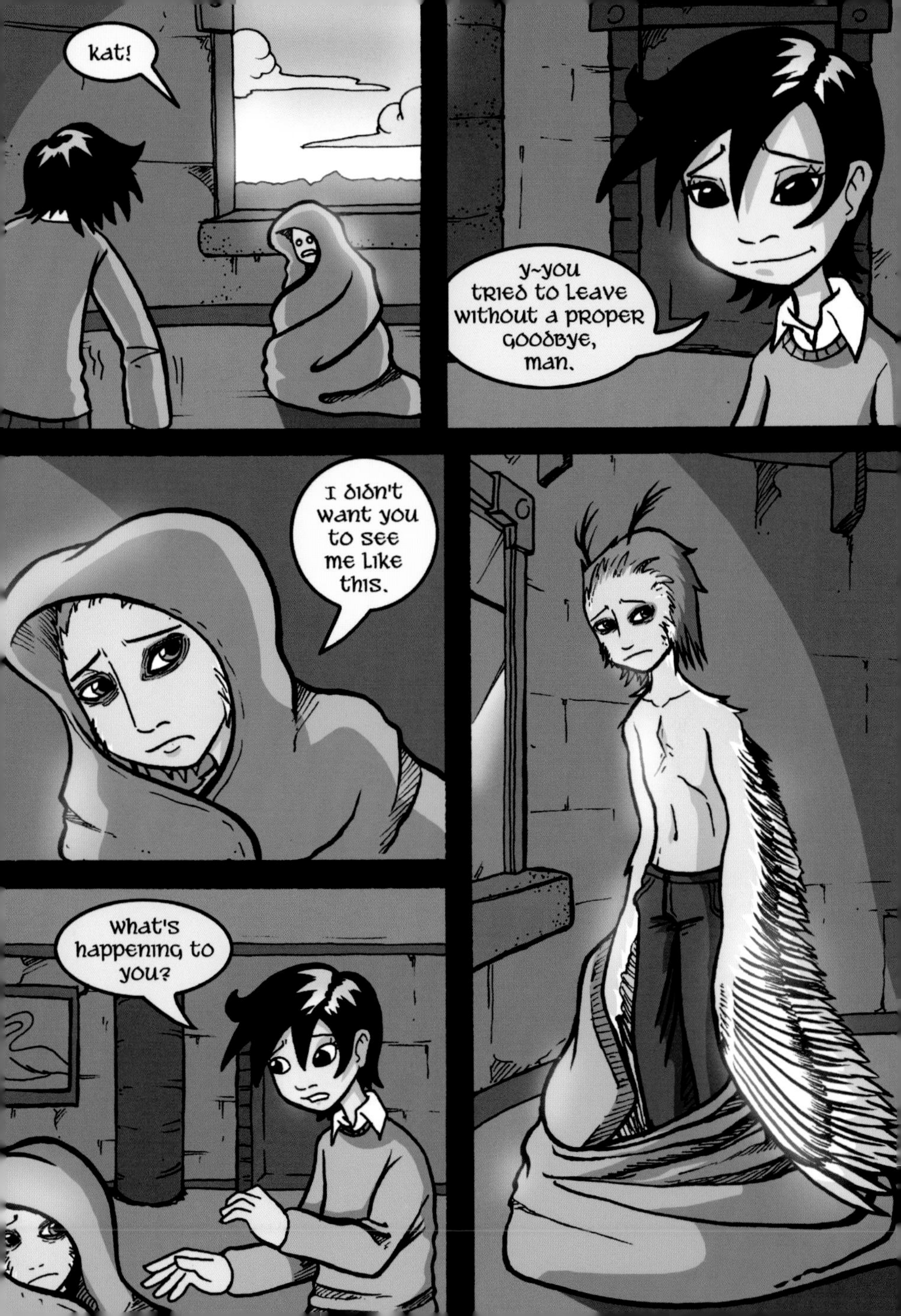
kat!
y~you tried to leave without a proper goodbye, man.
I didn't want you to see me like this.
what's happening to you?

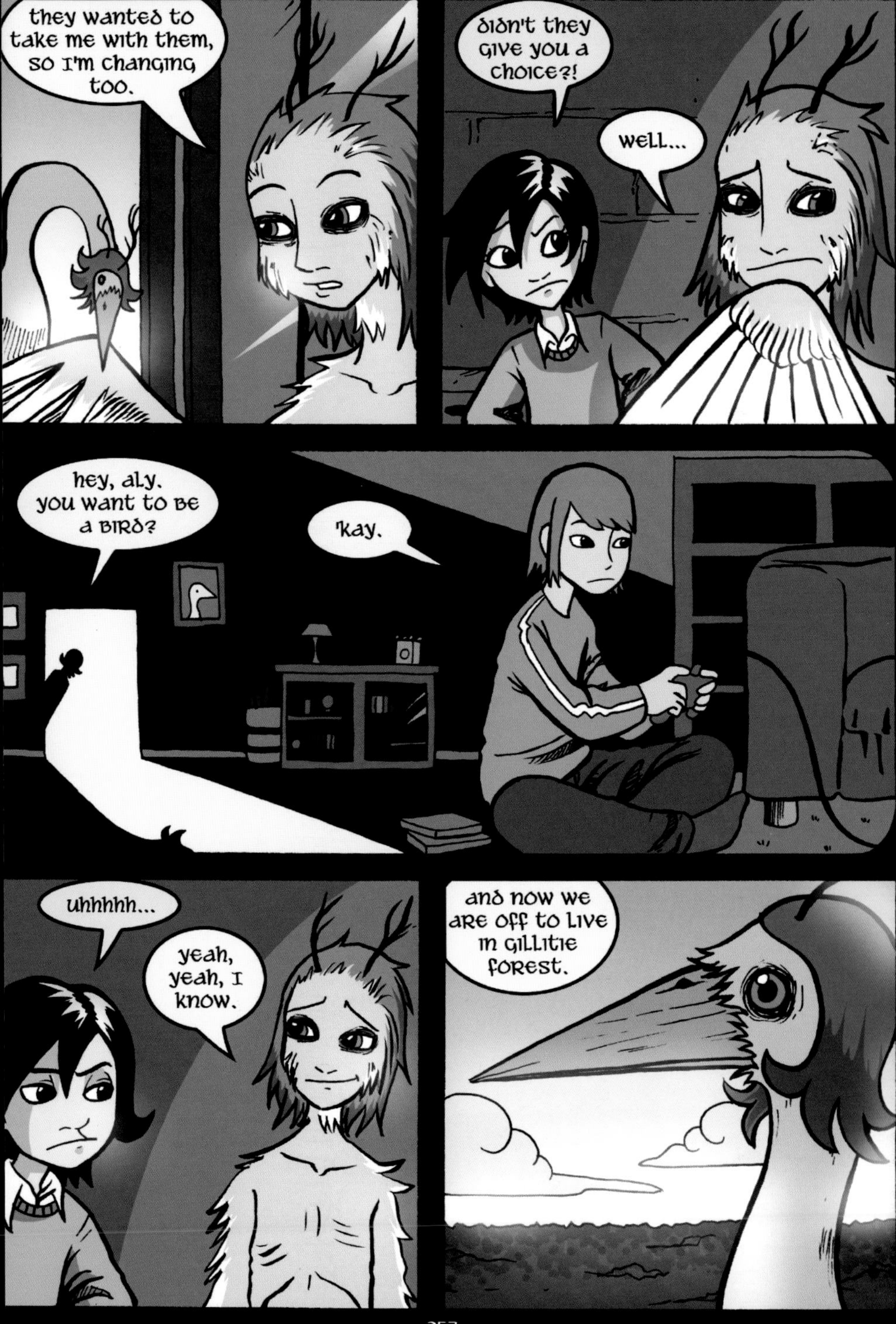
they wanted to take me with them, so I'm changing too.
didn't they give you a choice?!
well...
hey, aly. you want to be a bird?
'kay.
uhhhhh...
yeah, yeah, I know.
and now we are off to live in gillitie forest.

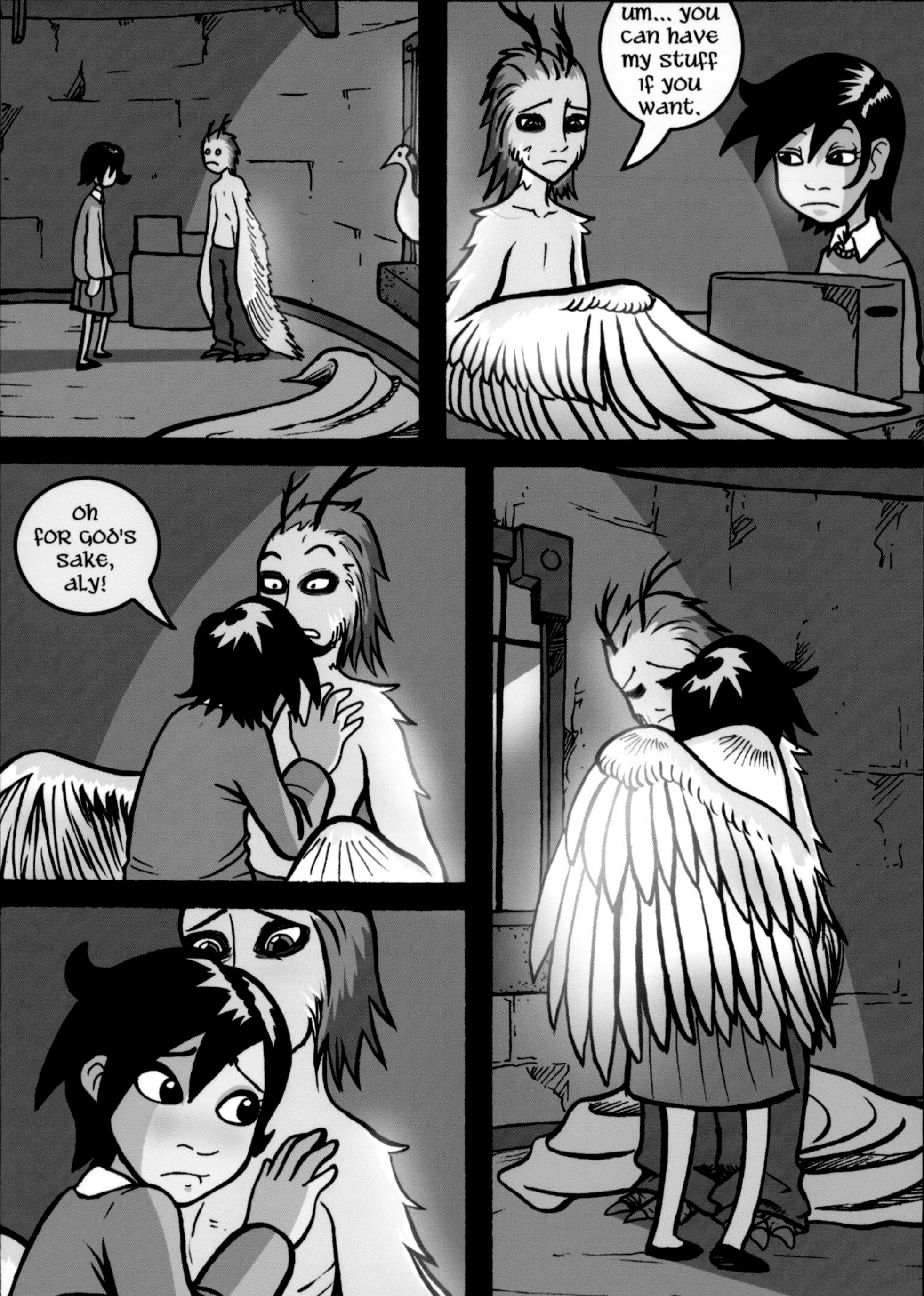
um... you can have my stuff if you want.
Oh for God's sake, Aly!

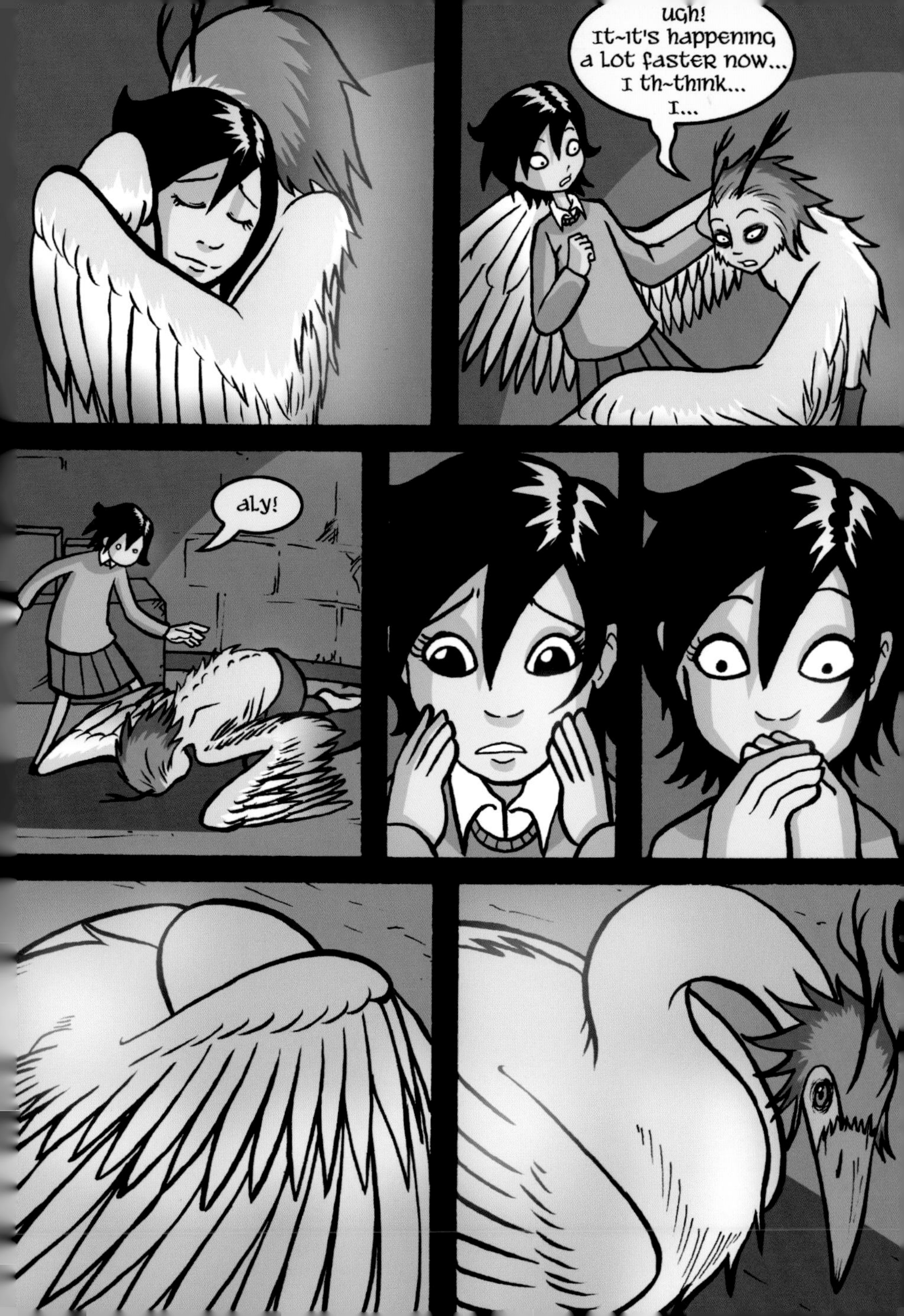
UGH! IT~IT'S HAPPENING A LOT FASTER NOW... I TH~THINK... I...
ALY!

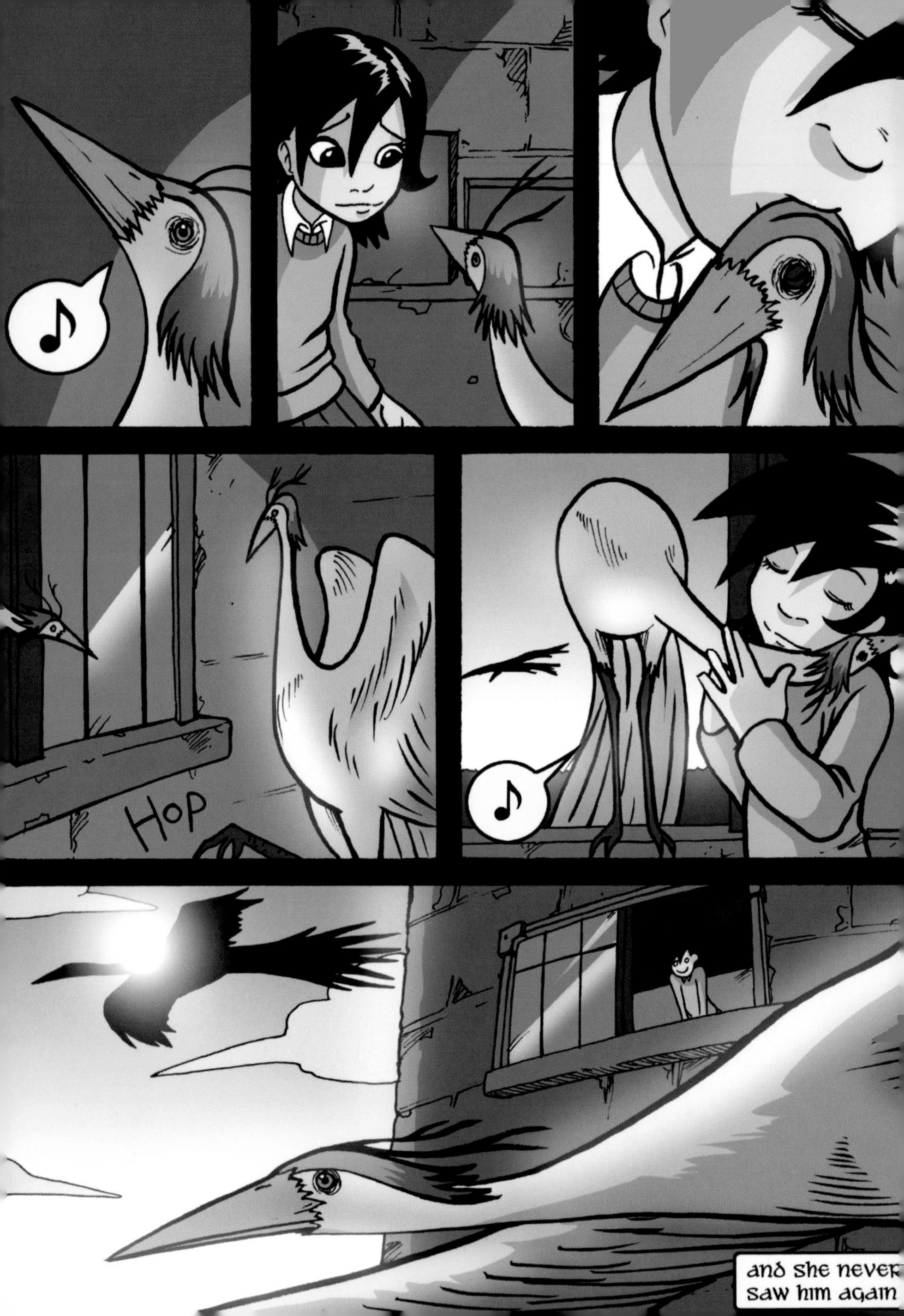
♪
Hop
♪
and she never saw him again

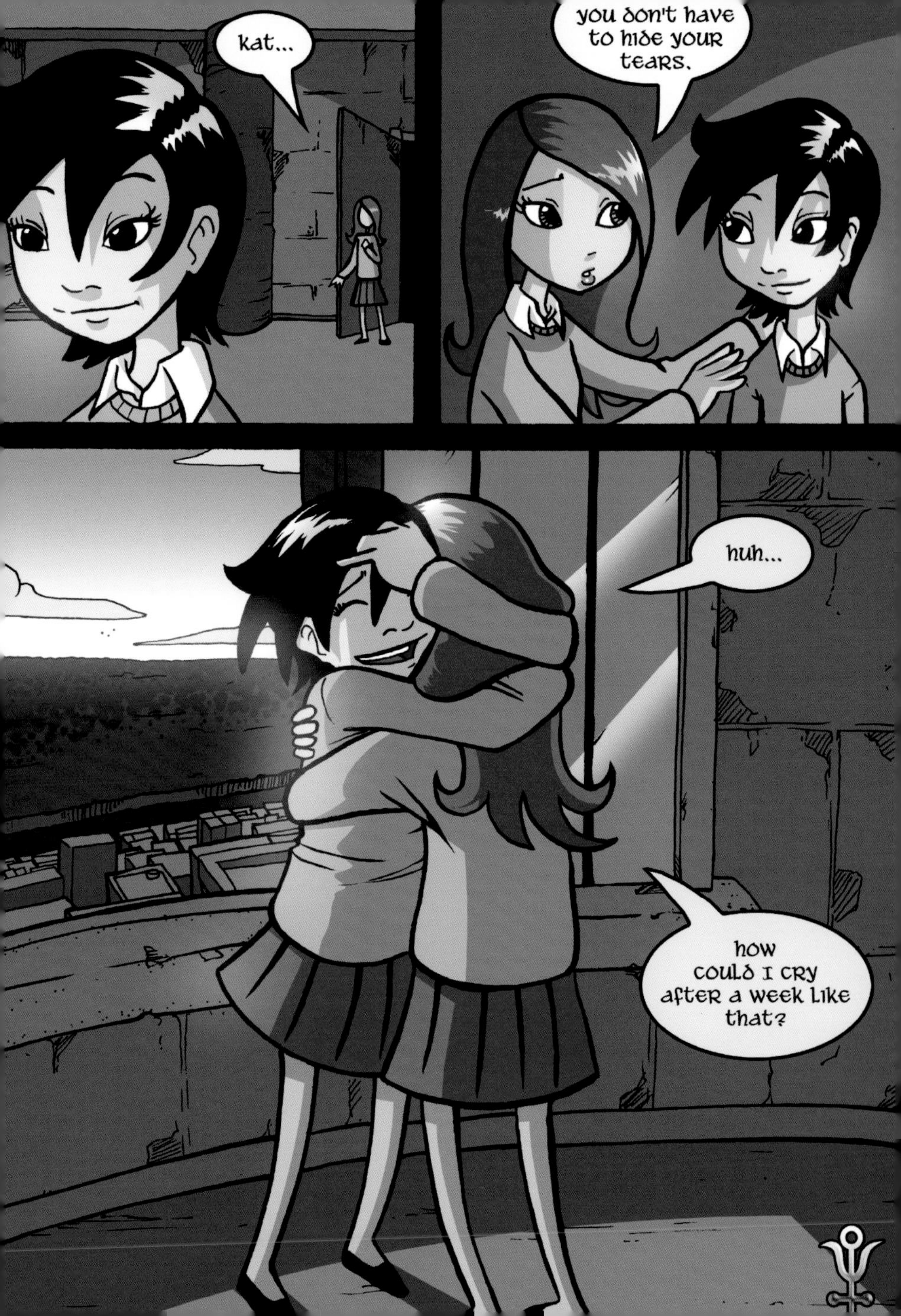
kat...
you don't have to hide your tears.
huh...
how could I cry after a week like that?

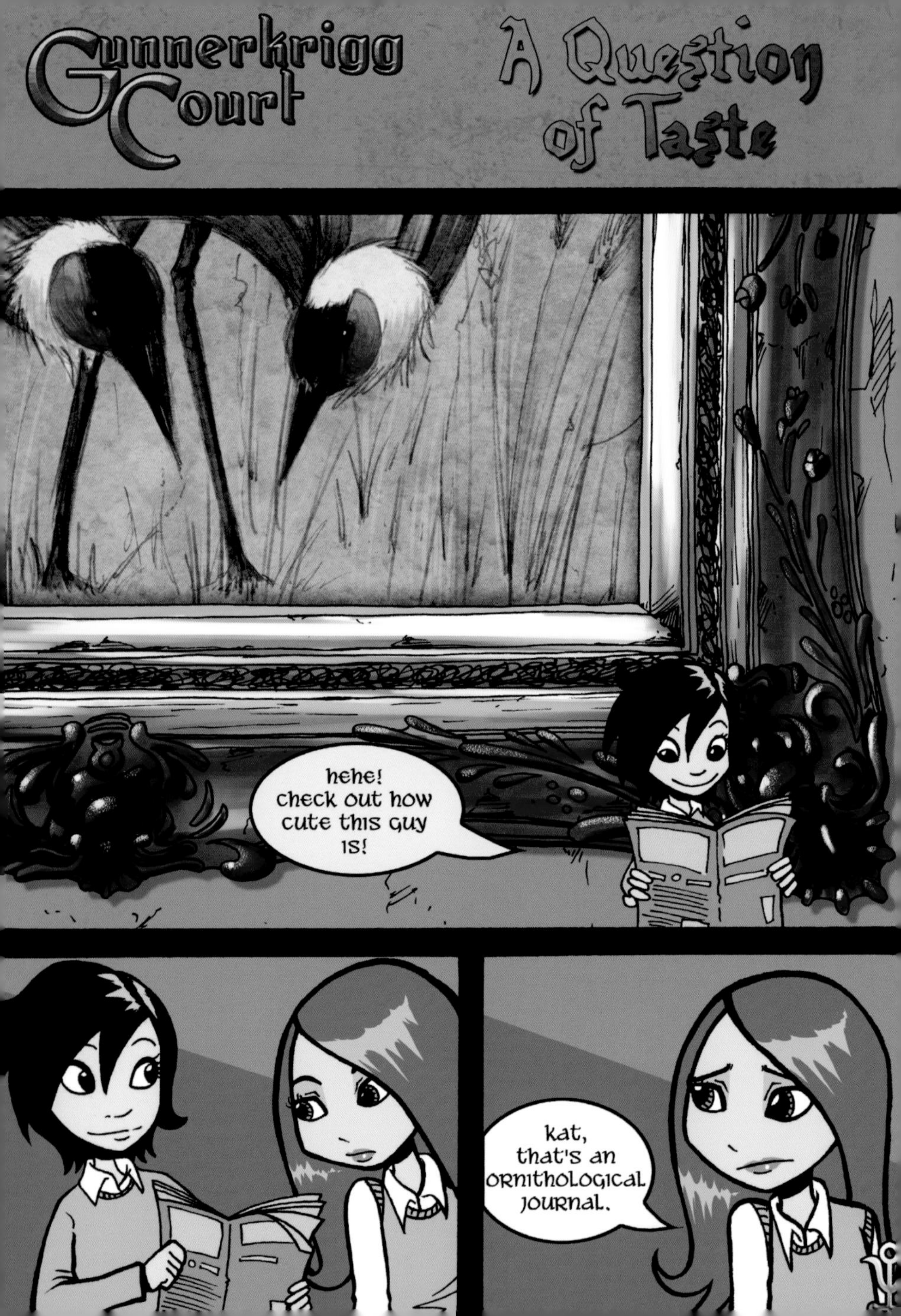
Gunnerkrigg Court
A Question of Taste
hehe! check out how cute this guy is!
kat, that's an ornithological journal.

Gunnerkrigg Court

Chapter 14:

The Fangs Of Summertime

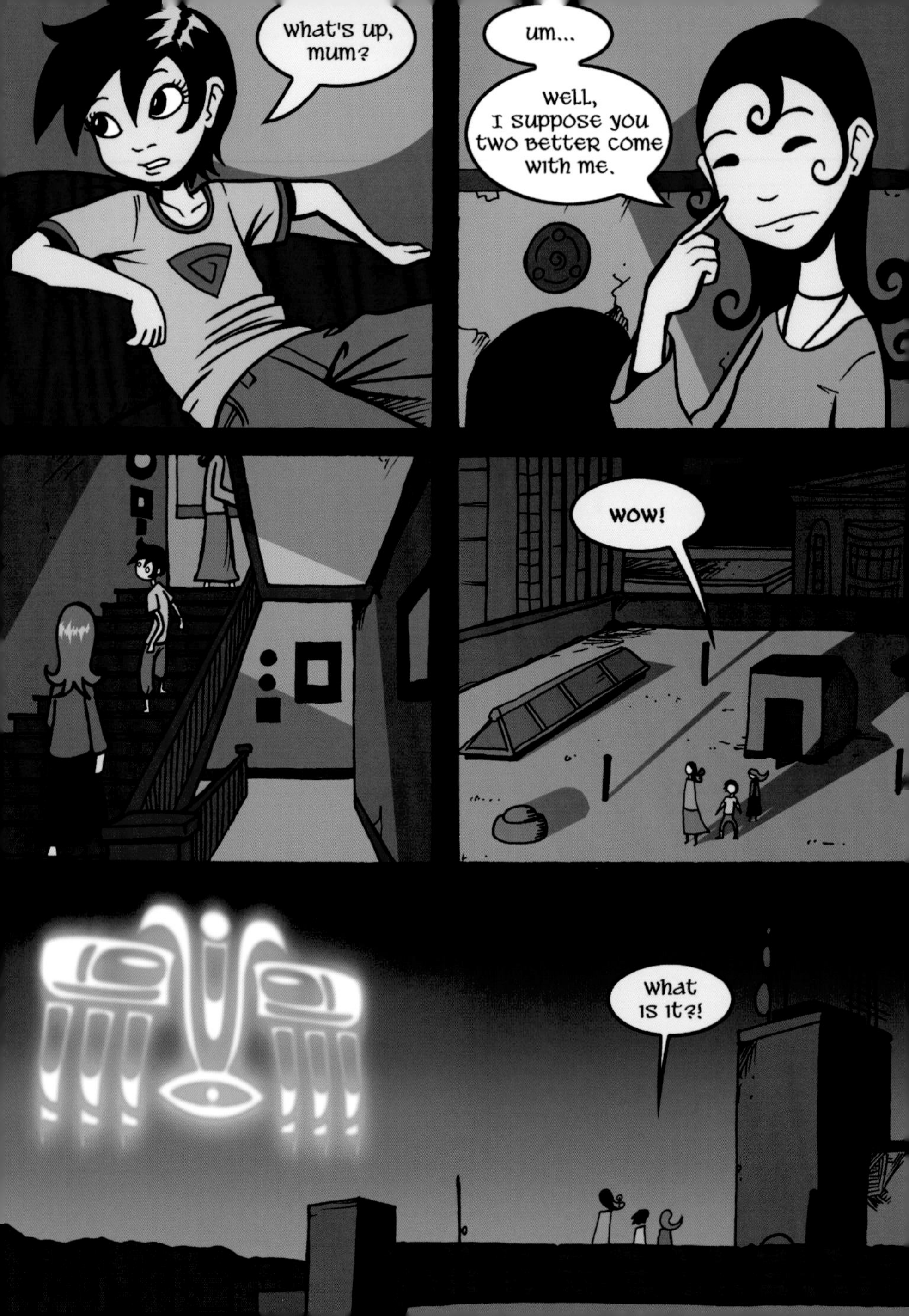
what's up, mum?
um...
well, I suppose you two better come with me.
WOW!
what is it?!

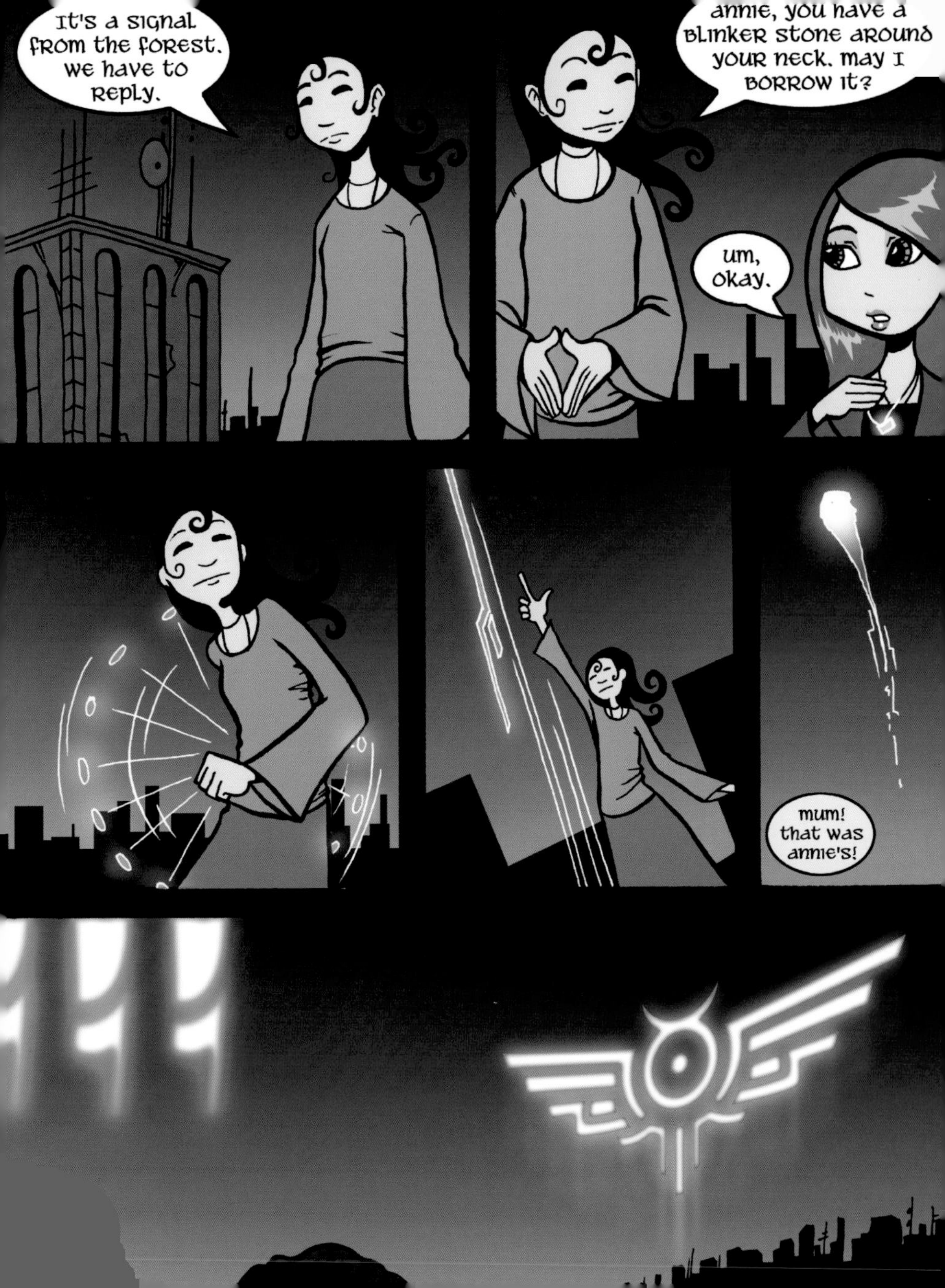
It's a signal from the forest. we have to reply.
annie, you have a blinker stone around your neck. may I borrow it?
um, okay.
mum! that was annie's!

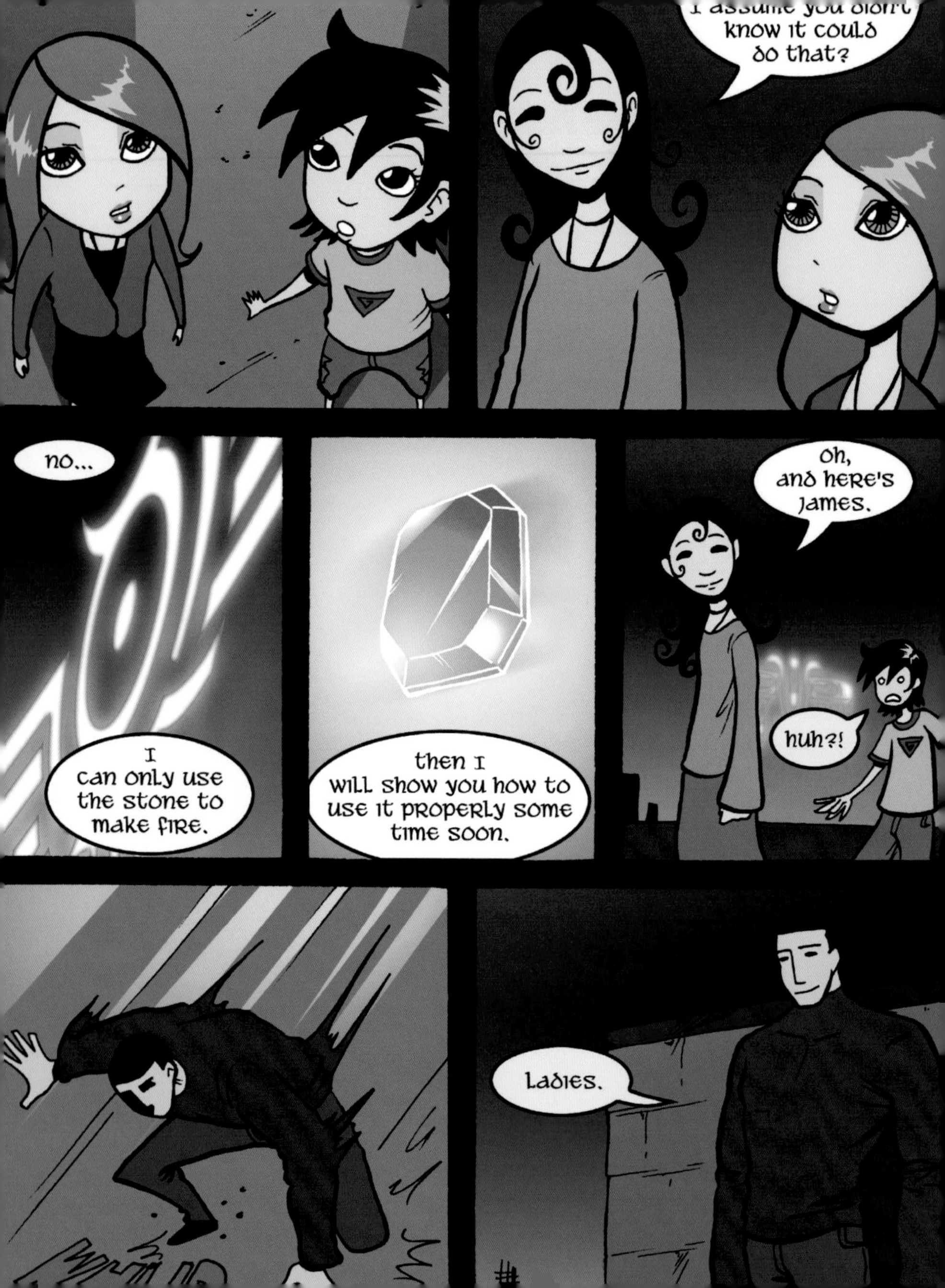
I assume you didn't know it could do that?
no...
I can only use the stone to make fire.
then I will show you how to use it properly some time soon.
Oh, and here's James.
huh?!
Ladies.

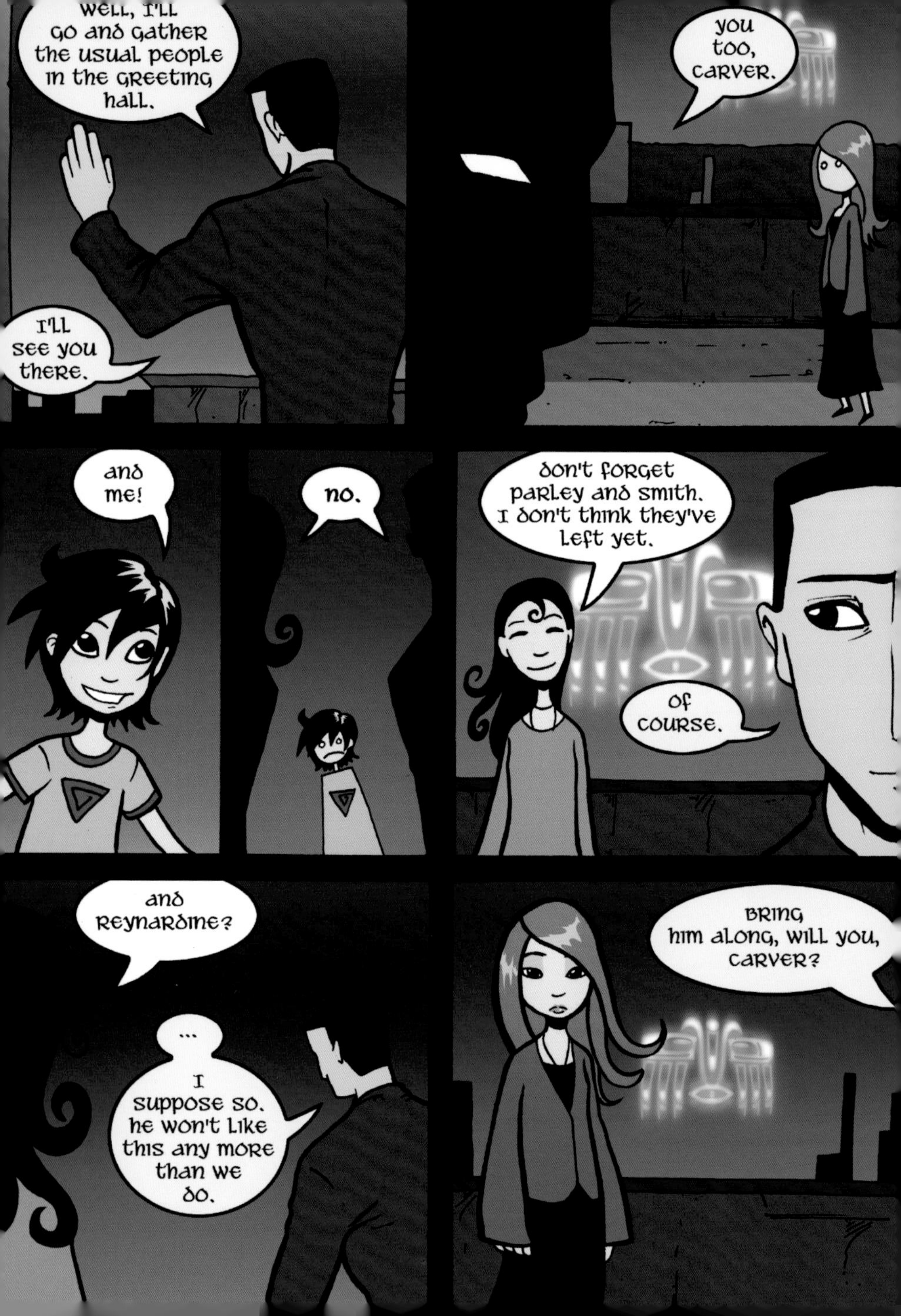

WELL, I'LL GO AND GATHER THE USUAL PEOPLE IN THE GREETING HALL.
I'LL SEE YOU THERE.
YOU TOO, CARVER.
AND ME!
NO.
DON'T FORGET PARLEY AND SMITH. I DON'T THINK THEY'VE LEFT YET.
OF COURSE.
AND REYNARDINE?
...
I SUPPOSE SO. HE WON'T LIKE THIS ANY MORE THAN WE DO.
BRING HIM ALONG, WILL YOU, CARVER?

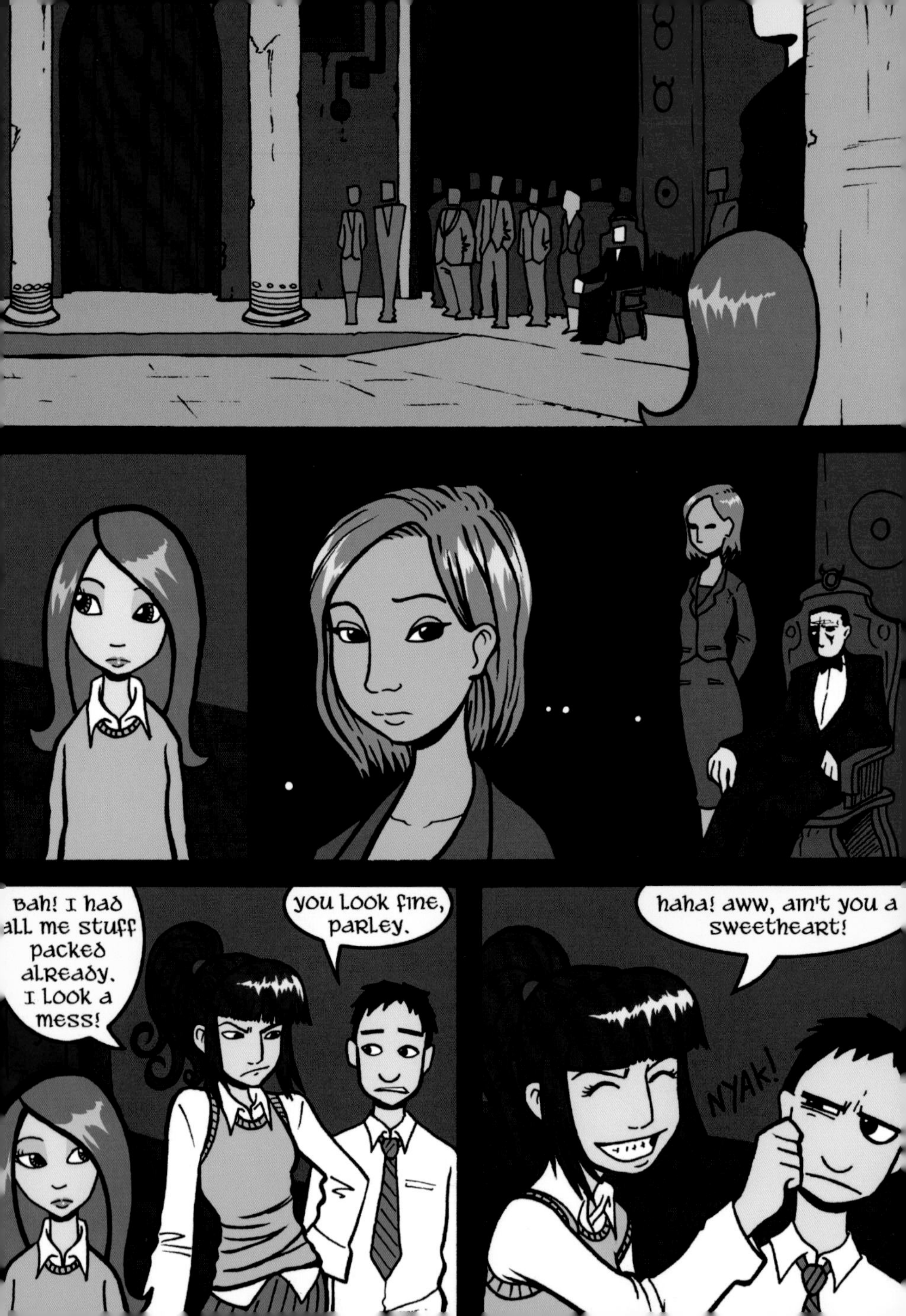
Bah! I had all me stuff packed already. I look a mess!
you look fine, parley.
haha! aww, ain't you a sweetheart!
NYAK!

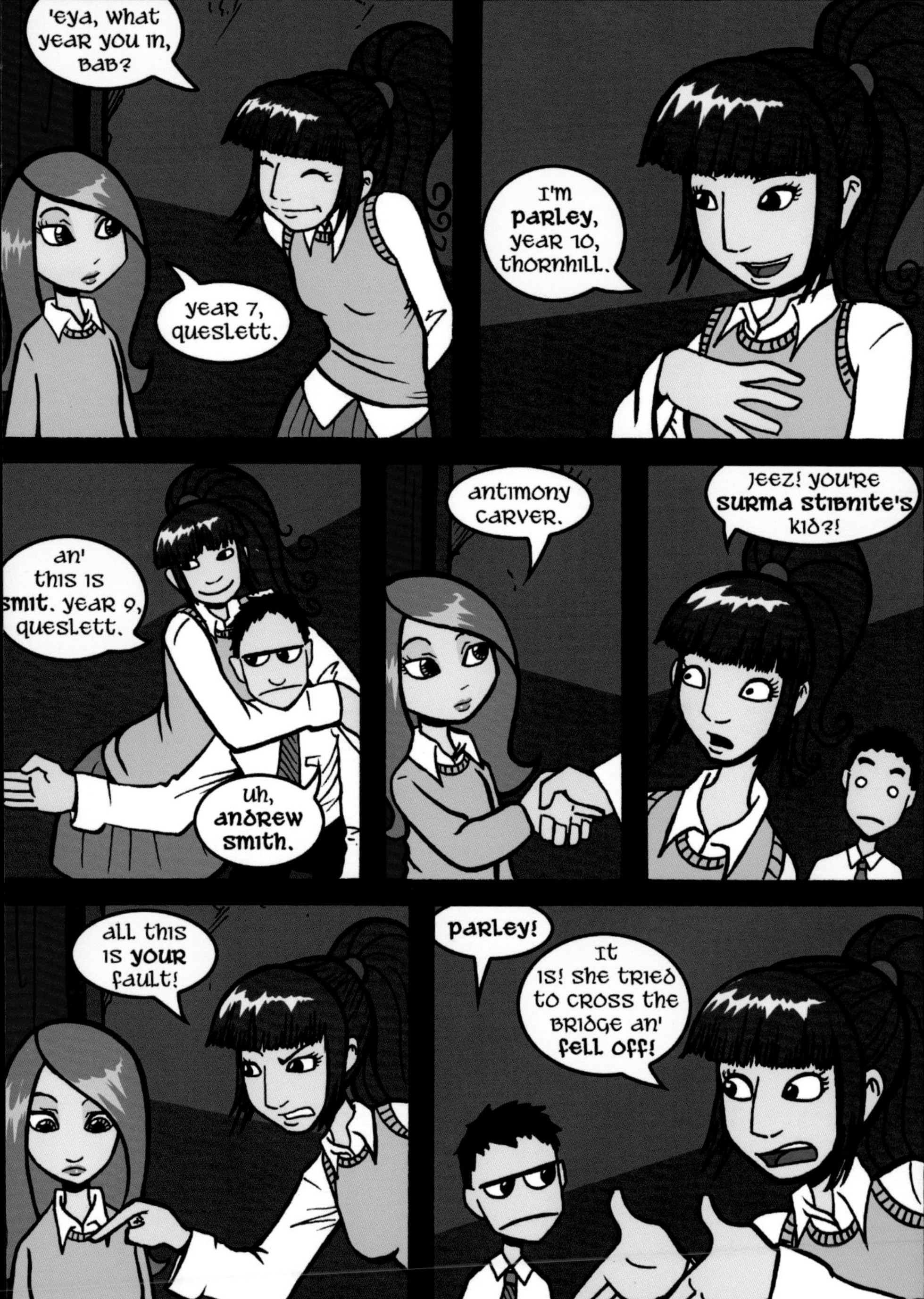
'eya, what year you in, bab?
year 7, queslett.
I'm parley, year 10, thornhill.
an' this is smit. year 9, queslett.
uh, andrew smith.
antimony carver.
jeez! you're surma stibnite's kid?!
all this is your fault!
parley!
it is! she tried to cross the bridge an' fell off!

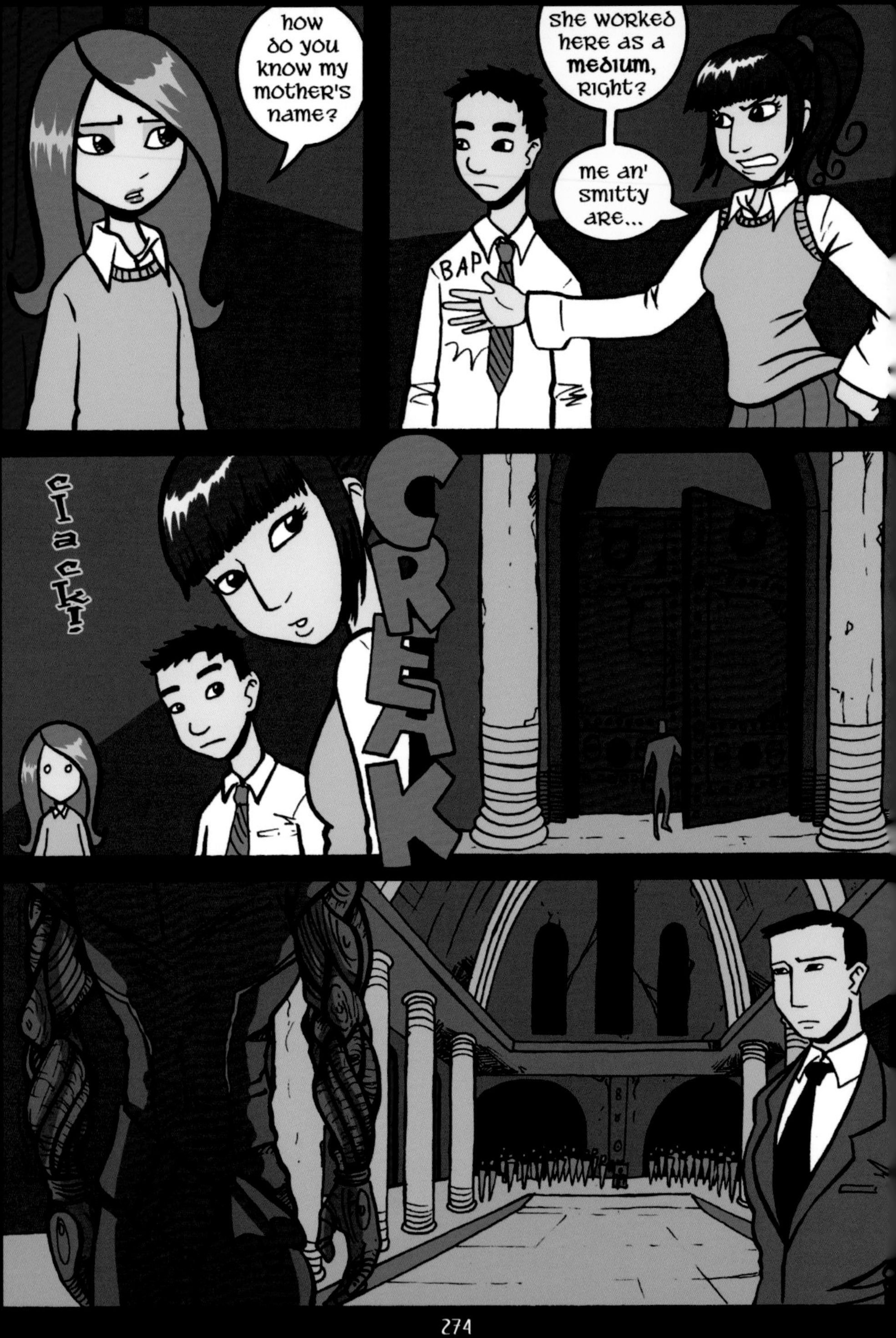
how do you know my mother's name?
she worked here as a medium, right?
me an' smitty are...
BAP
clack!
CREAK

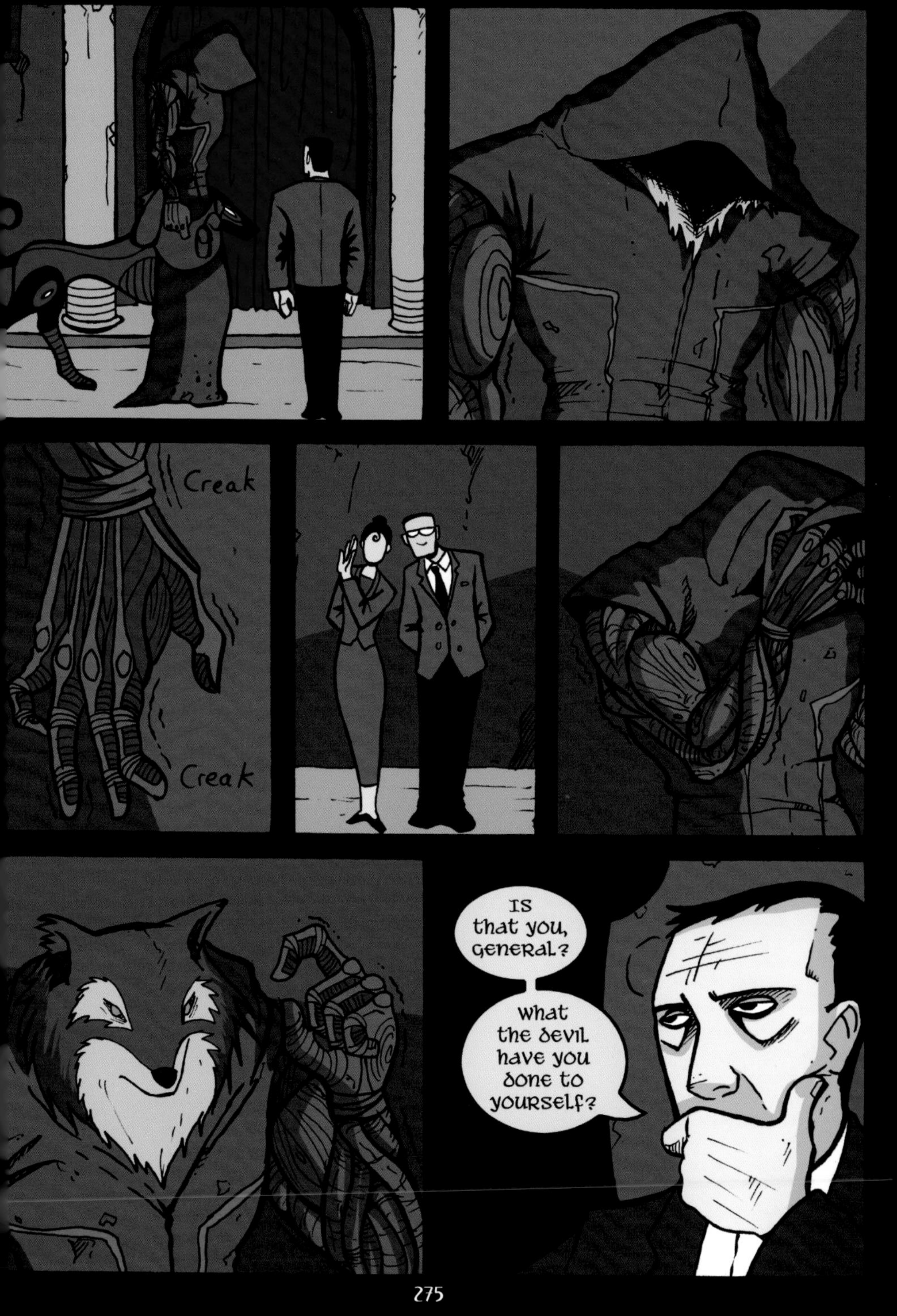
Creak
Creak
IS that you, GENERAL?
what the Devil have you done to yourself?

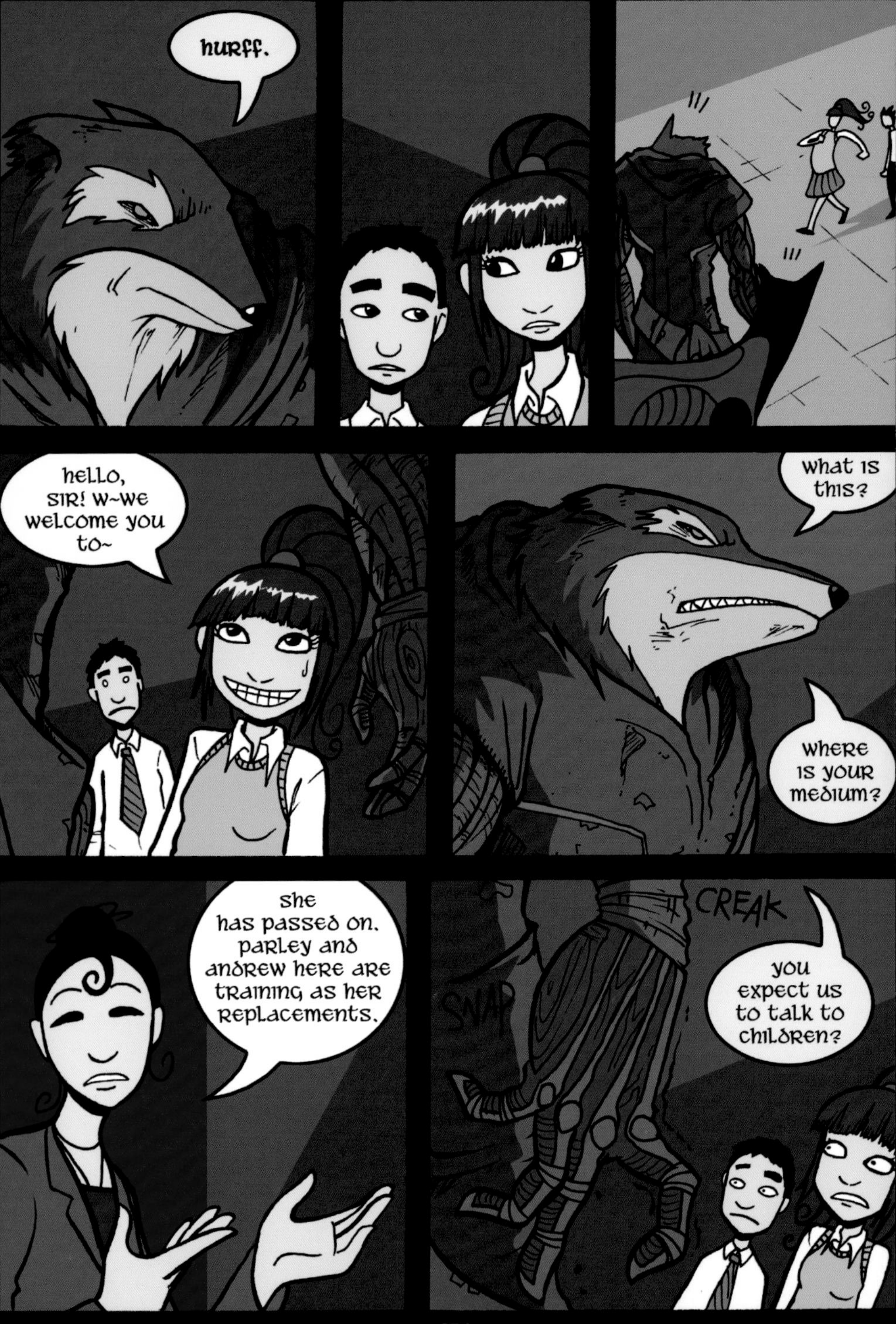
hurff.
hello, sir! w~we welcome you to~
what is this?
where is your medium?
she has passed on. parley and andrew here are training as her replacements.
CREAK
SNAP
you expect us to talk to children?

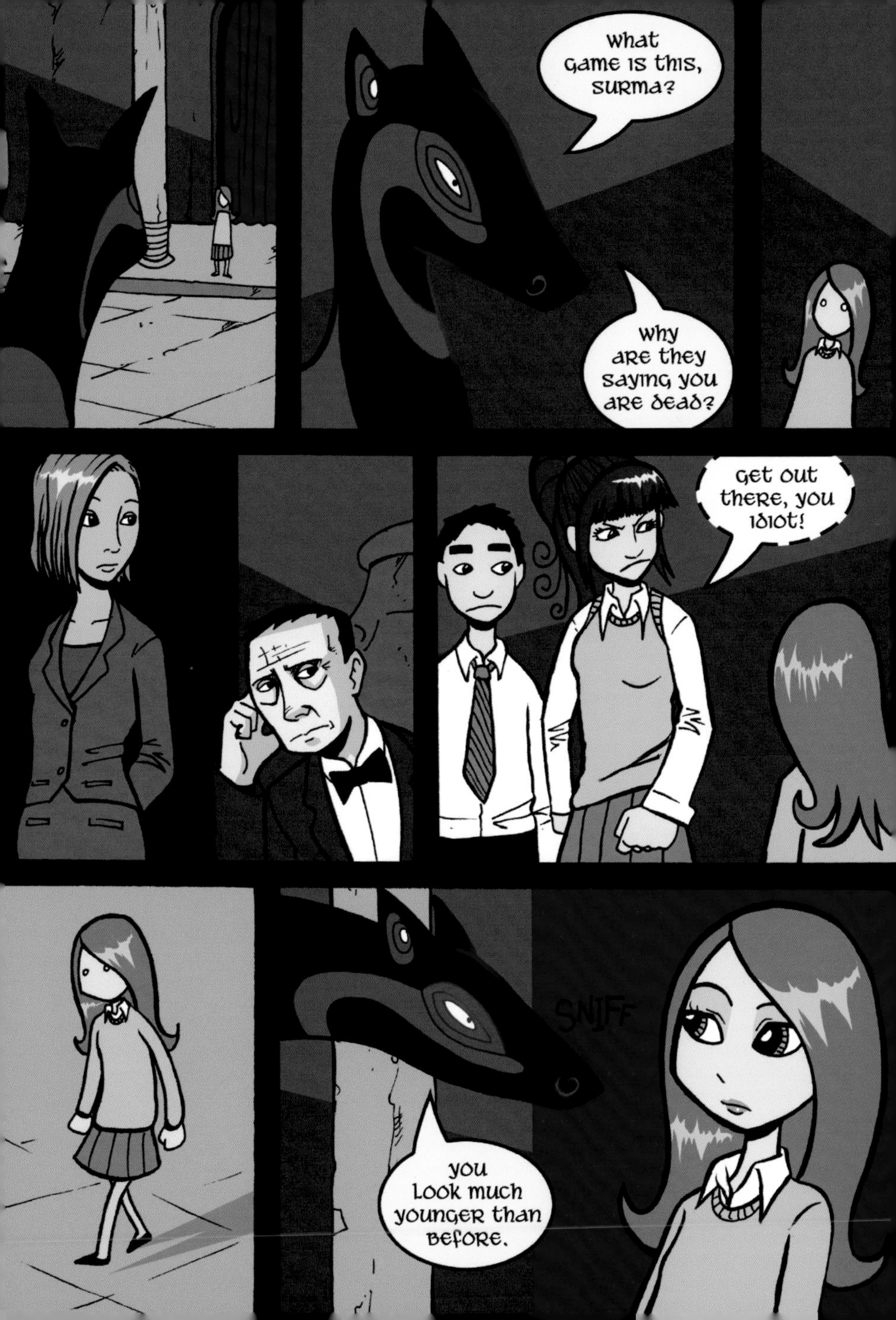
What game is this, Surma?
Why are they saying you are dead?
Get out there, you idiot!
SNIFF
You look much younger than before.

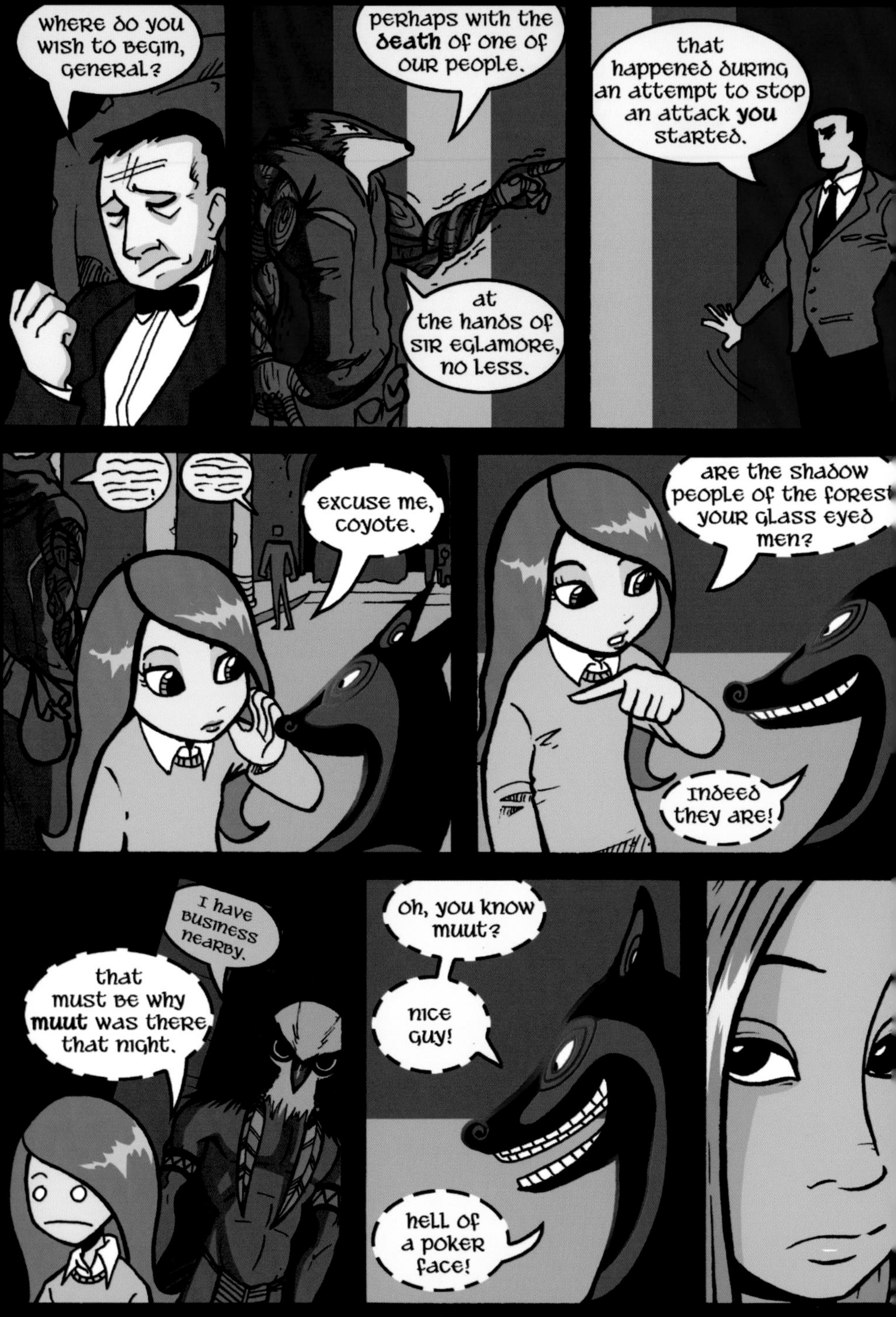
where do you wish to begin, general?
perhaps with the death of one of our people.
at the hands of sir eglamore, no less.
that happened during an attempt to stop an attack you started.
excuse me, coyote.
are the shadow people of the forest your glass eyed men?
indeed they are!
that must be why muut was there that night.
I have business nearby.
oh, you know muut?
nice guy!
hell of a poker face!

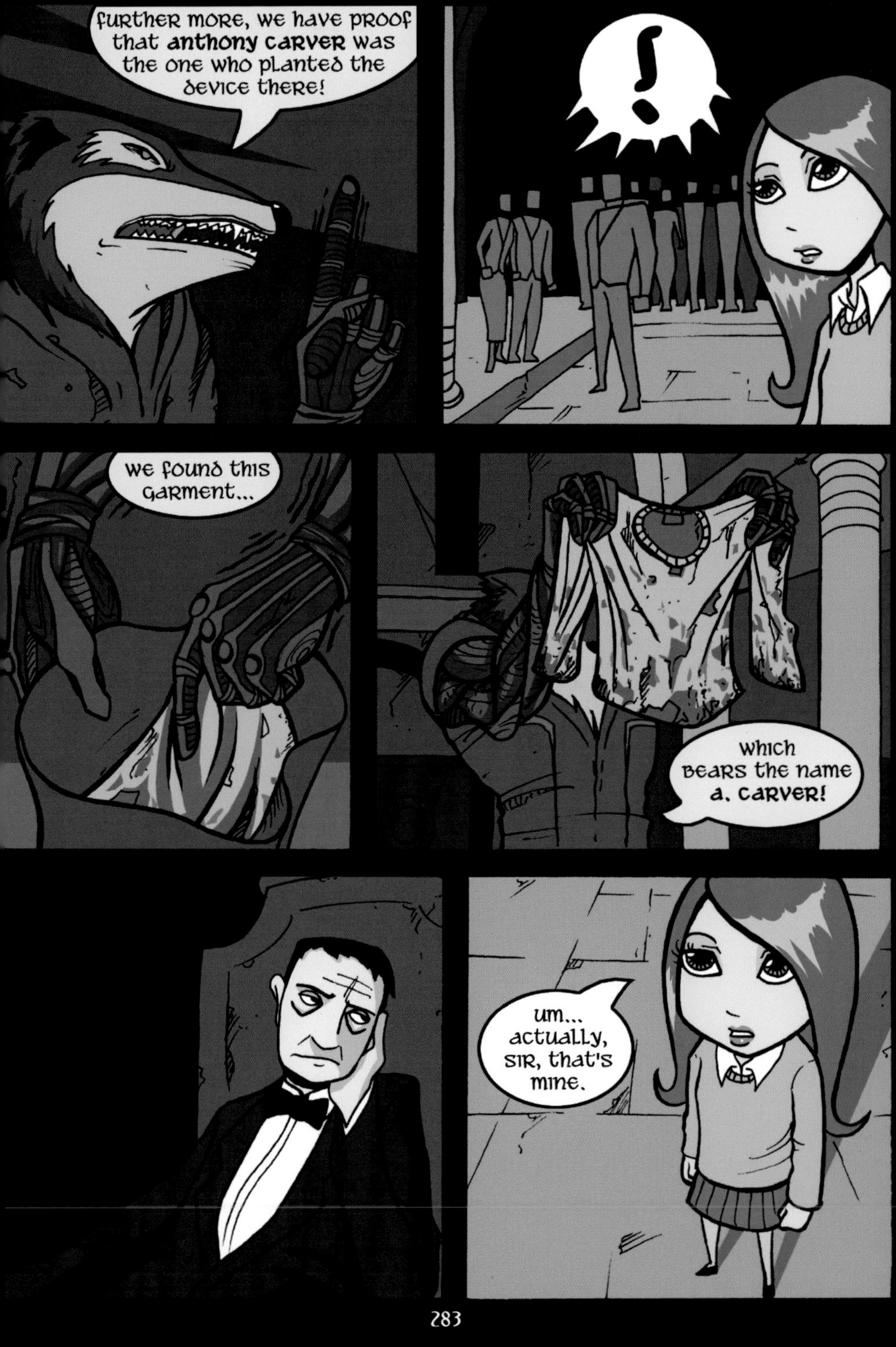
further more, we have proof that anthony carver was the one who planted the device there!
!
we found this garment...
which bears the name a. carver!
um... actually, sir, that's mine.

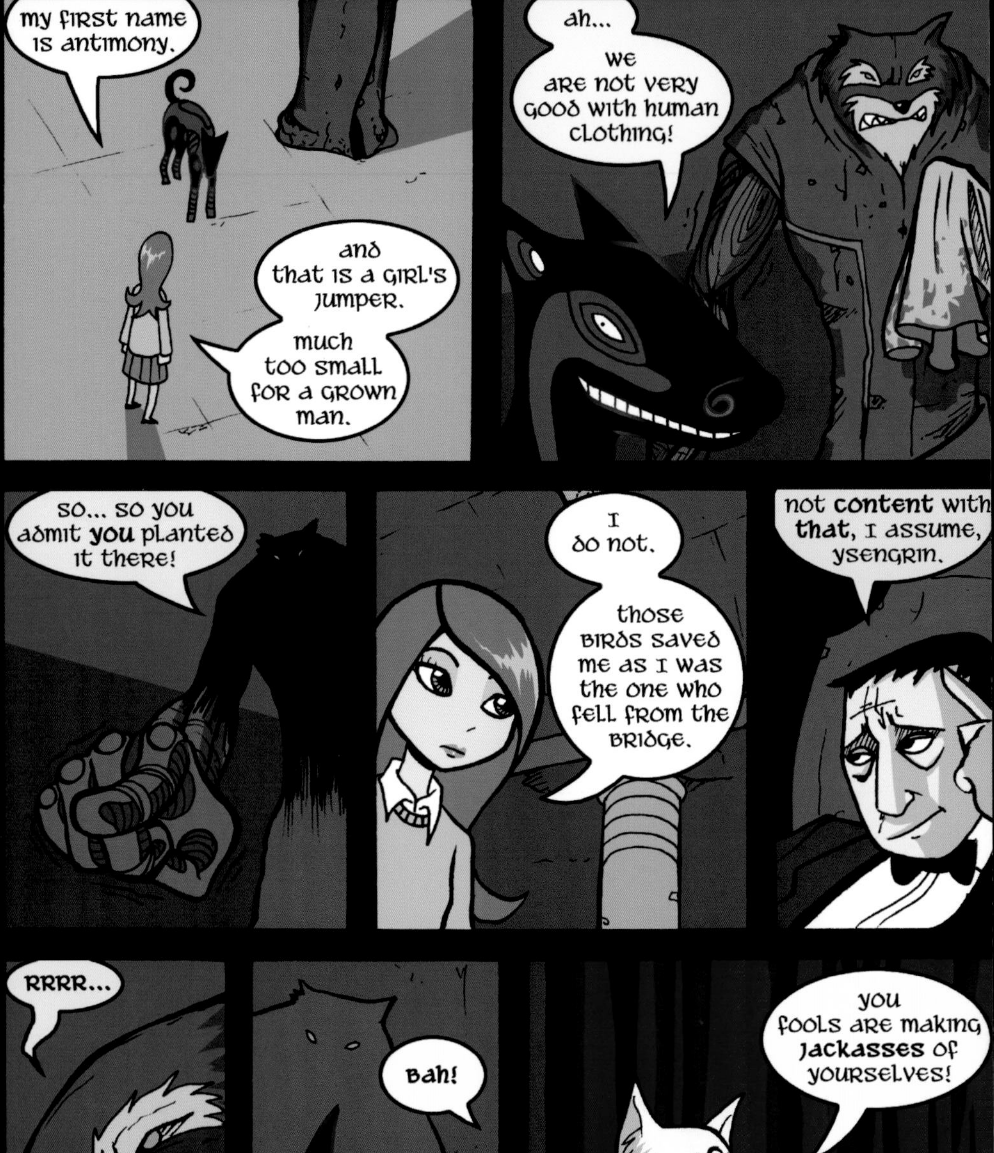
my first name is antimony.
and that is a girl's jumper.
much too small for a grown man.
ah...
we are not very good with human clothing!
so... so you admit you planted it there!
I do not.
those birds saved me as I was the one who fell from the bridge.
not content with that, I assume, ysengrin.
RRRR...
Bah!
you fools are making jackasses of yourselves!

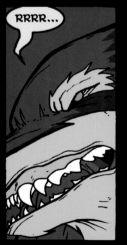

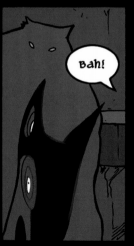

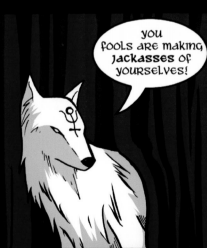

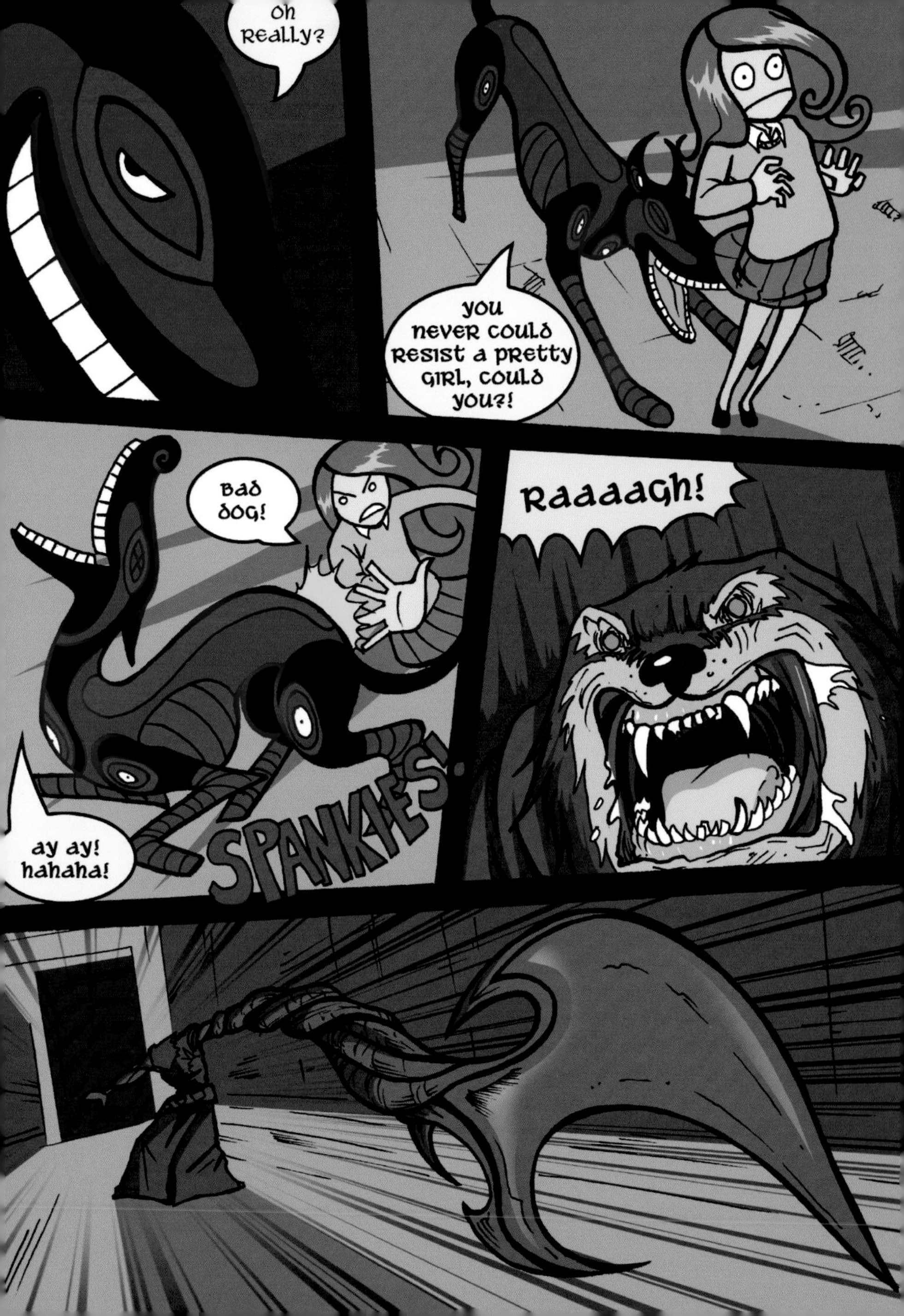
oh Really?
you never could resist a pretty girl, could you?!
Bad dog!
ay ay! hahaha!
SPANKIES!
Raaaagh!

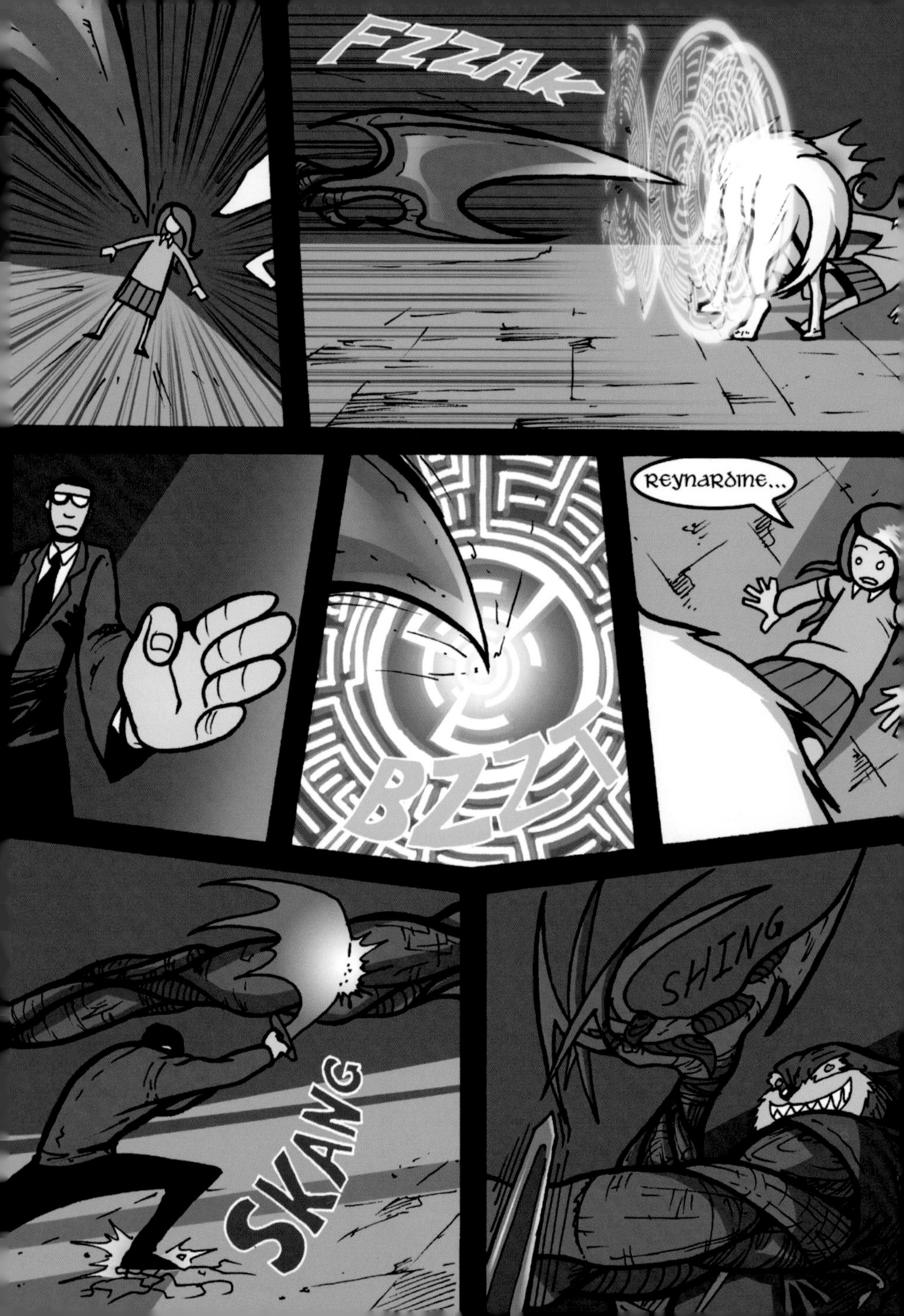
FZZAK
BZZT
Reynardine...
SKANG
SHING

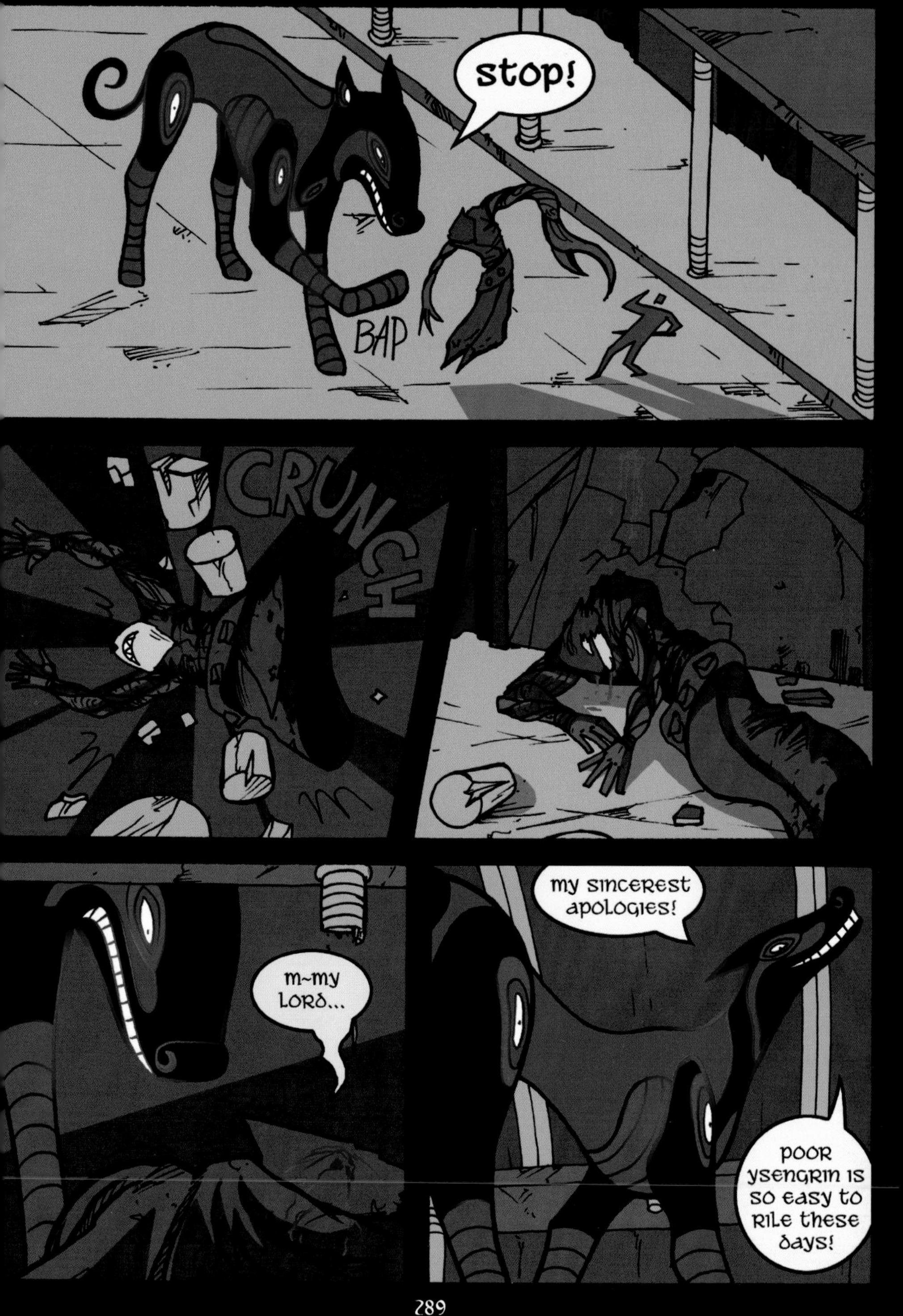
stop!
BAP
CRUNCH
m~my LORD...
my sincerest apologies!
poor ysengrim is so easy to rile these days!

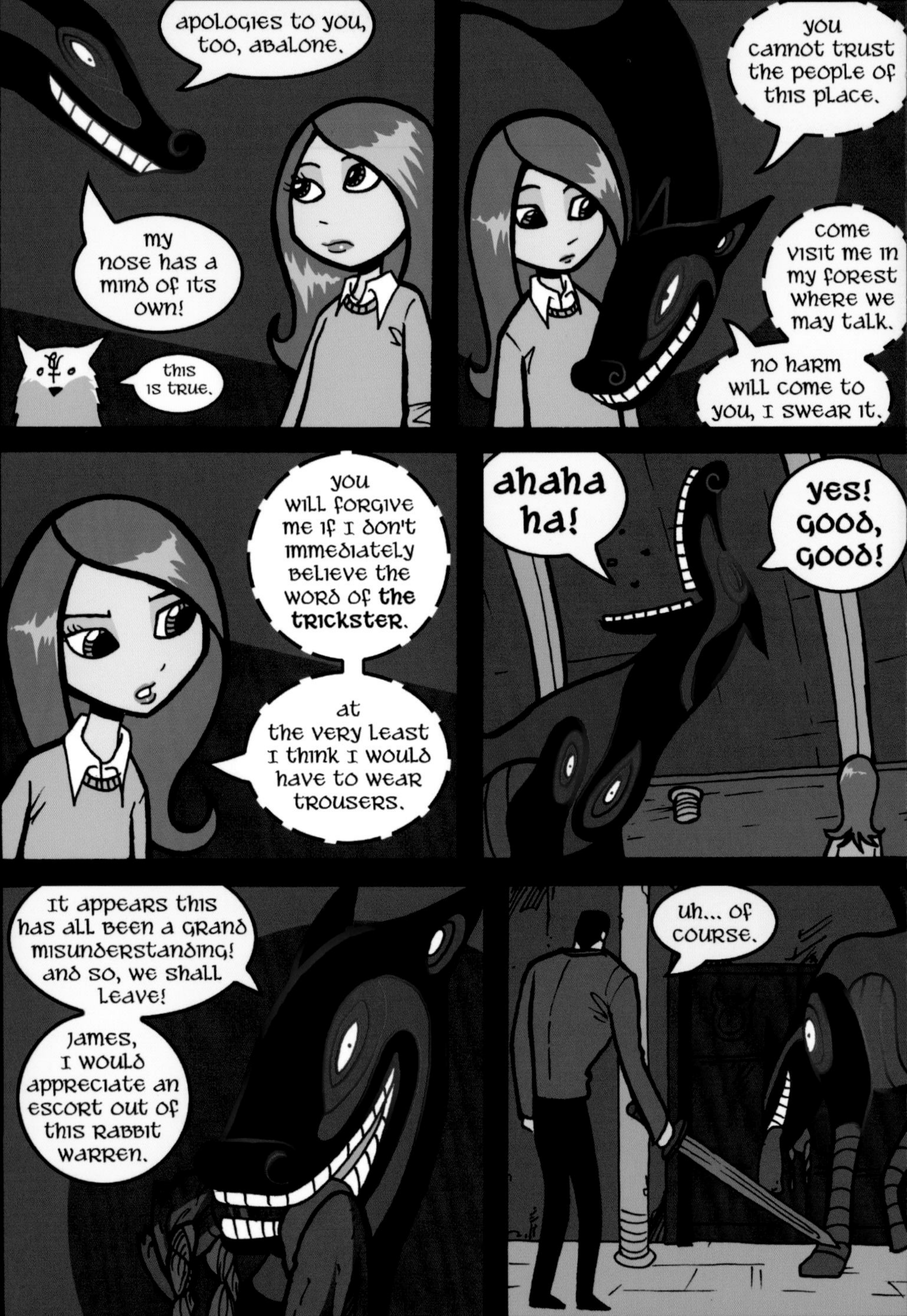
apologies to you, too, abalone.
my nose has a mind of its own!
this is true.
you cannot trust the people of this place.
come visit me in my forest where we may talk.
no harm will come to you, I swear it.
you will forgive me if I don't immediately believe the word of **the trickster**.
at the very least I think I would have to wear trousers.
ahaha ha!
yes! good, good!
It appears this has all been a grand misunderstanding! and so, we shall leave!
James, I would appreciate an escort out of this rabbit warren.
uh... of course.

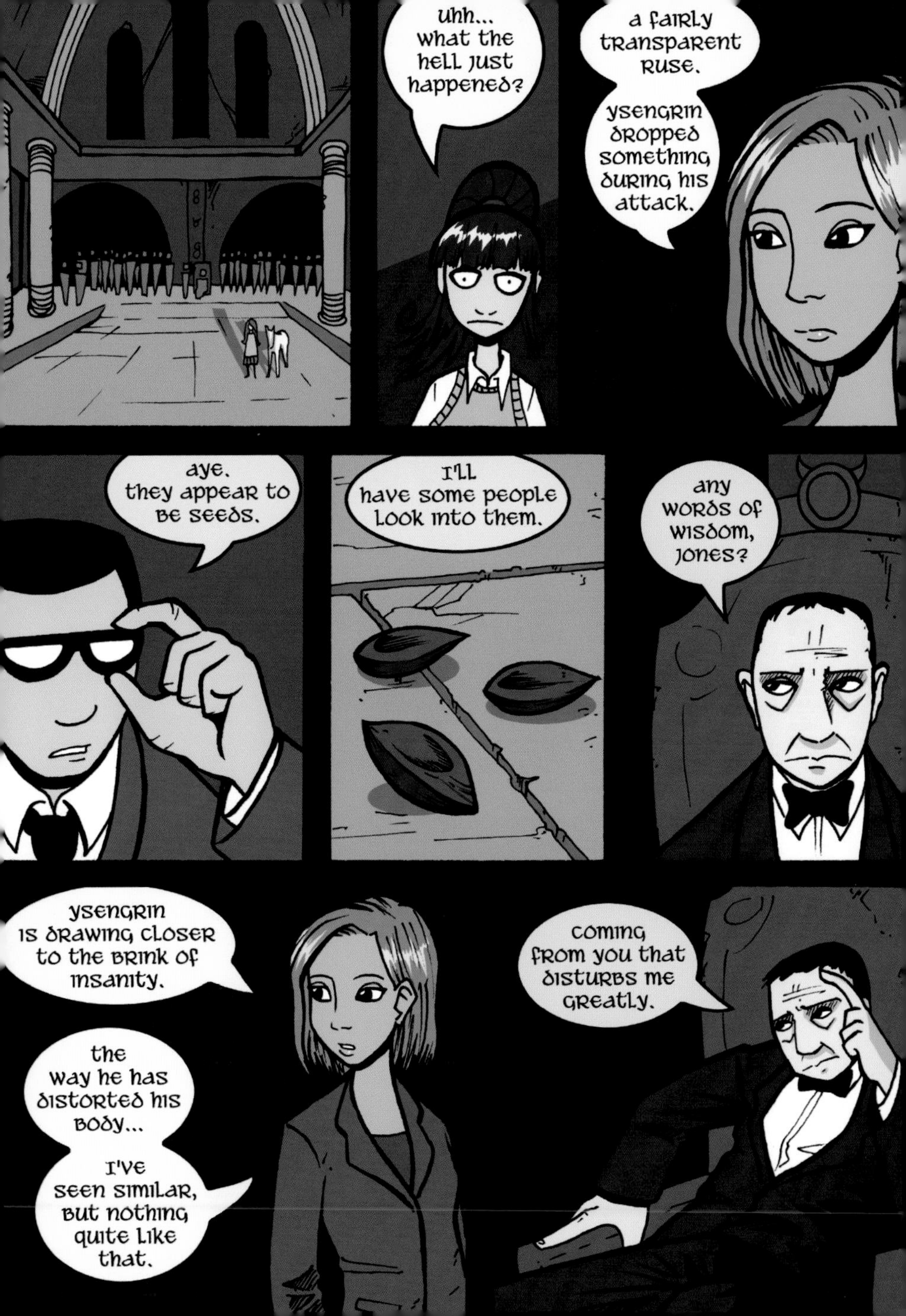
uhh... what the hell just happened?
a fairly transparent ruse.
ysengrin dropped something during his attack.
aye. they appear to be seeds.
I'll have some people look into them.
any words of wisdom, jones?
ysengrin is drawing closer to the brink of insanity.
the way he has distorted his body...
I've seen similar, but nothing quite like that.
coming from you that disturbs me greatly.

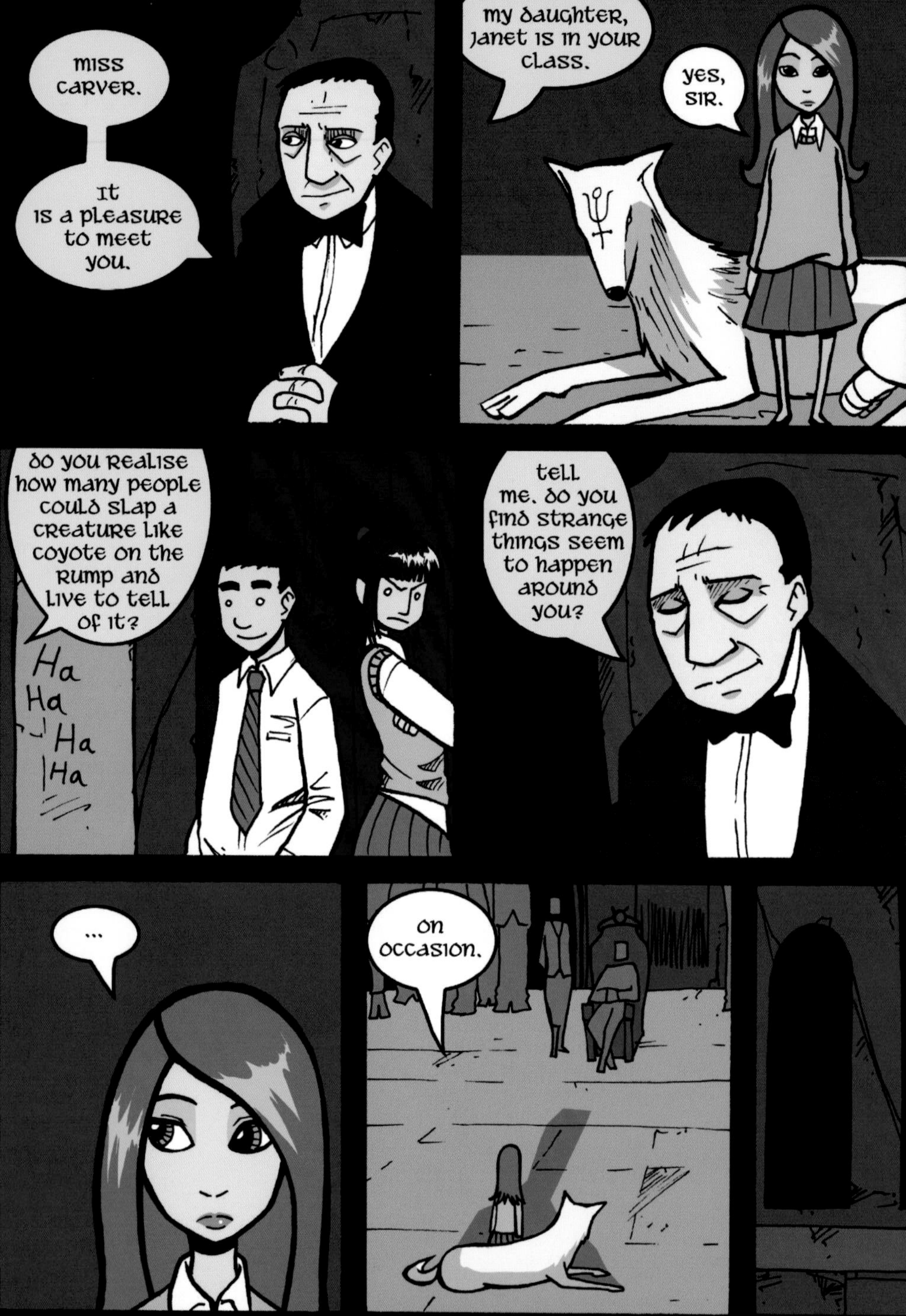
Miss Carver.
It is a pleasure to meet you.
My daughter, Janet is in your class.
Yes, sir.
Do you realise how many people could slap a creature like Coyote on the rump and live to tell of it?
Ha Ha Ha Ha
Tell me. Do you find strange things seem to happen around you?
...
On occasion.

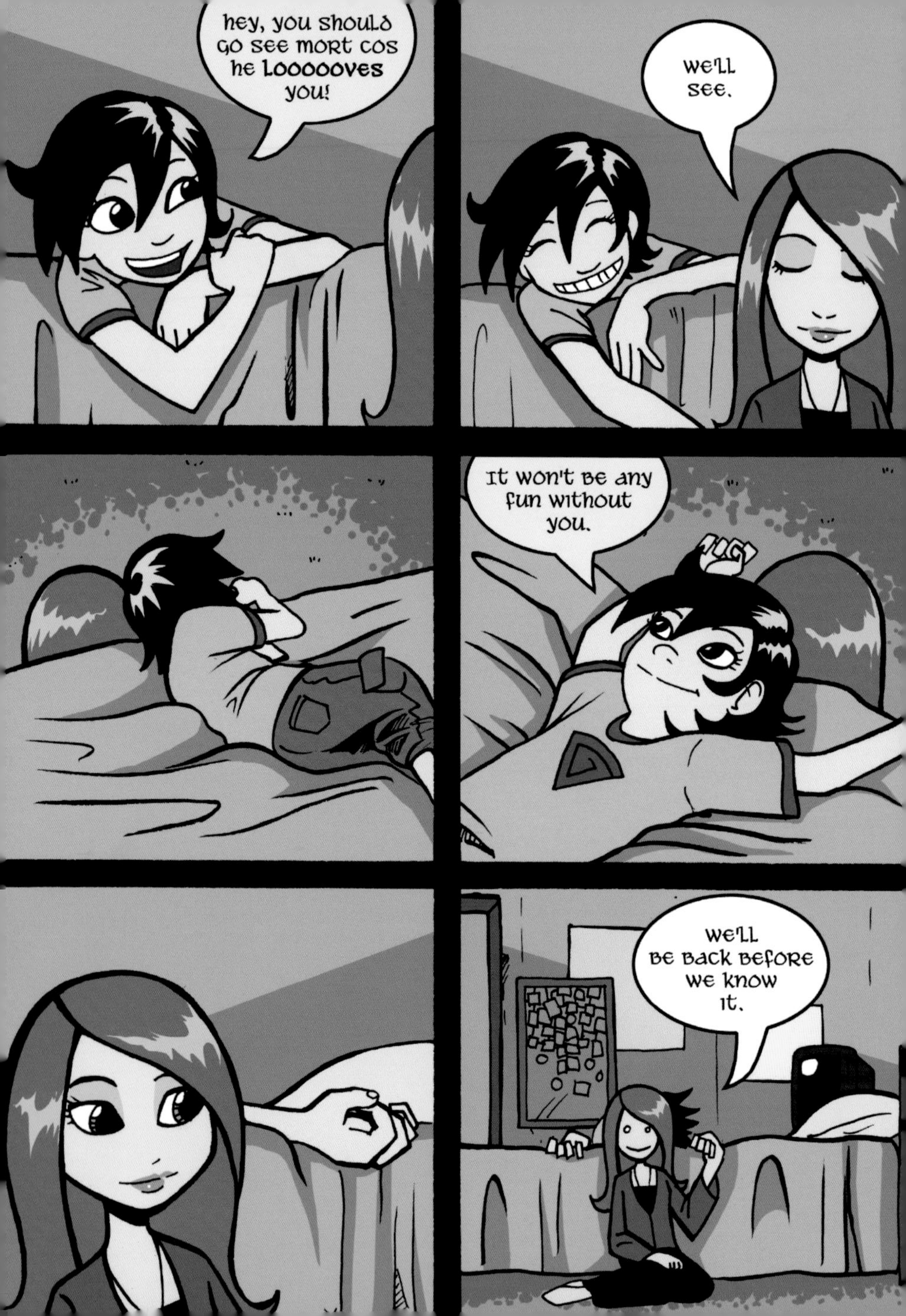
hey, you should go see mort cos he LOOOOOVES you!
we'll see.
It won't be any fun without you.
we'll be back before we know it.

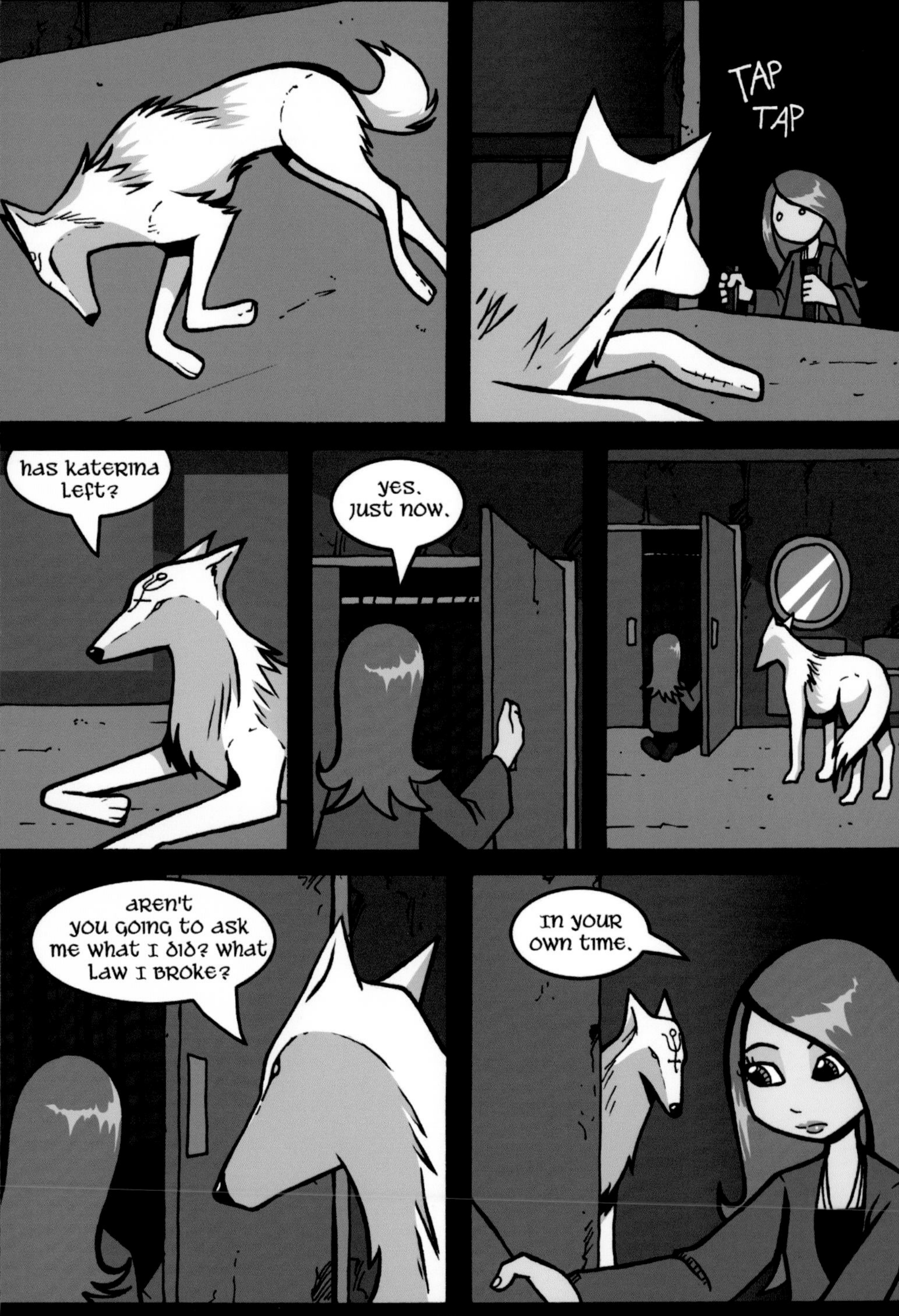
TAP
TAP
has katerina left?
yes. just now.
aren't you going to ask me what I did? what law I broke?
In your own time.

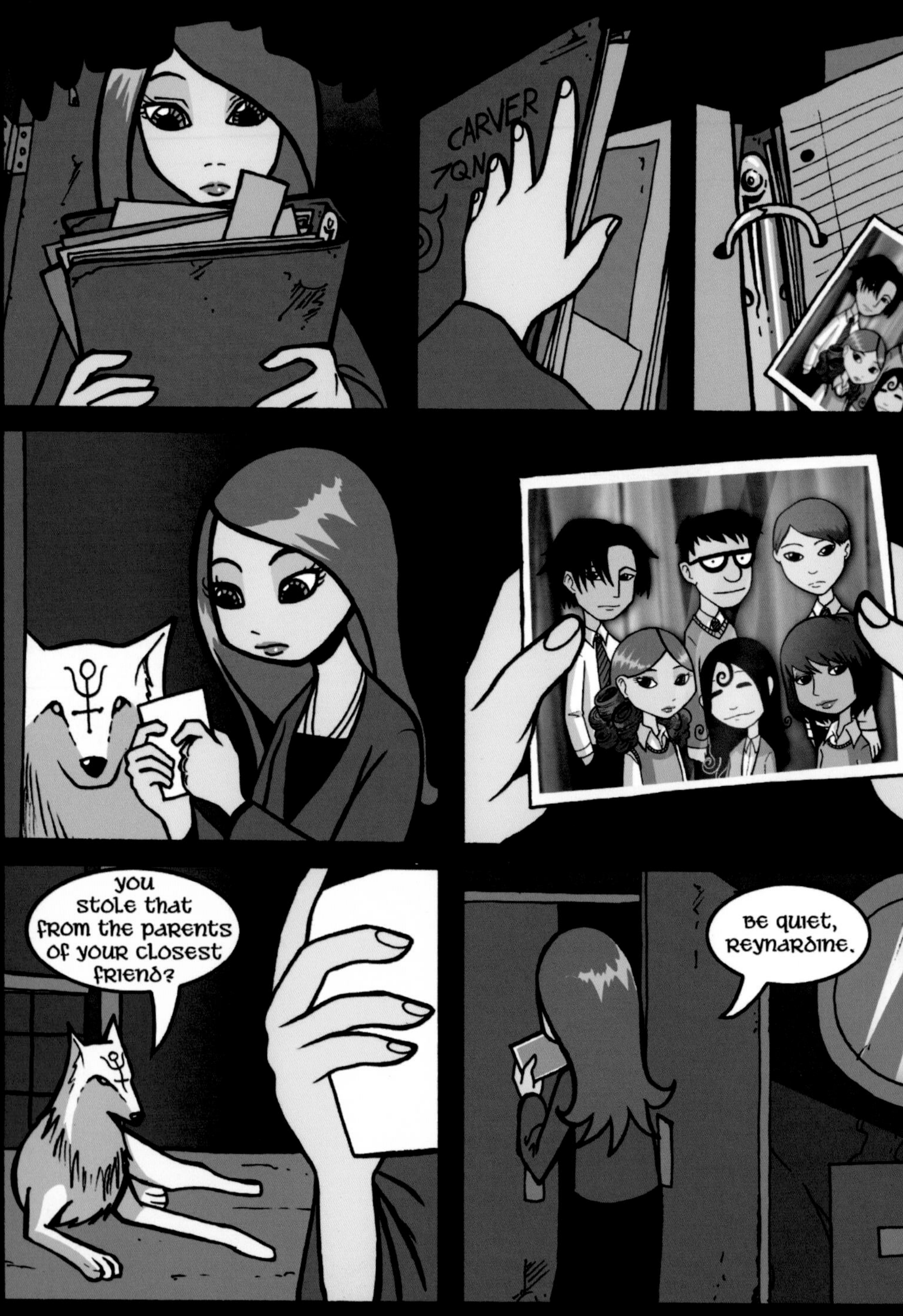
CARVER
7QN
you stole that from the parents of your closest friend?
Be quiet, Reynardine.

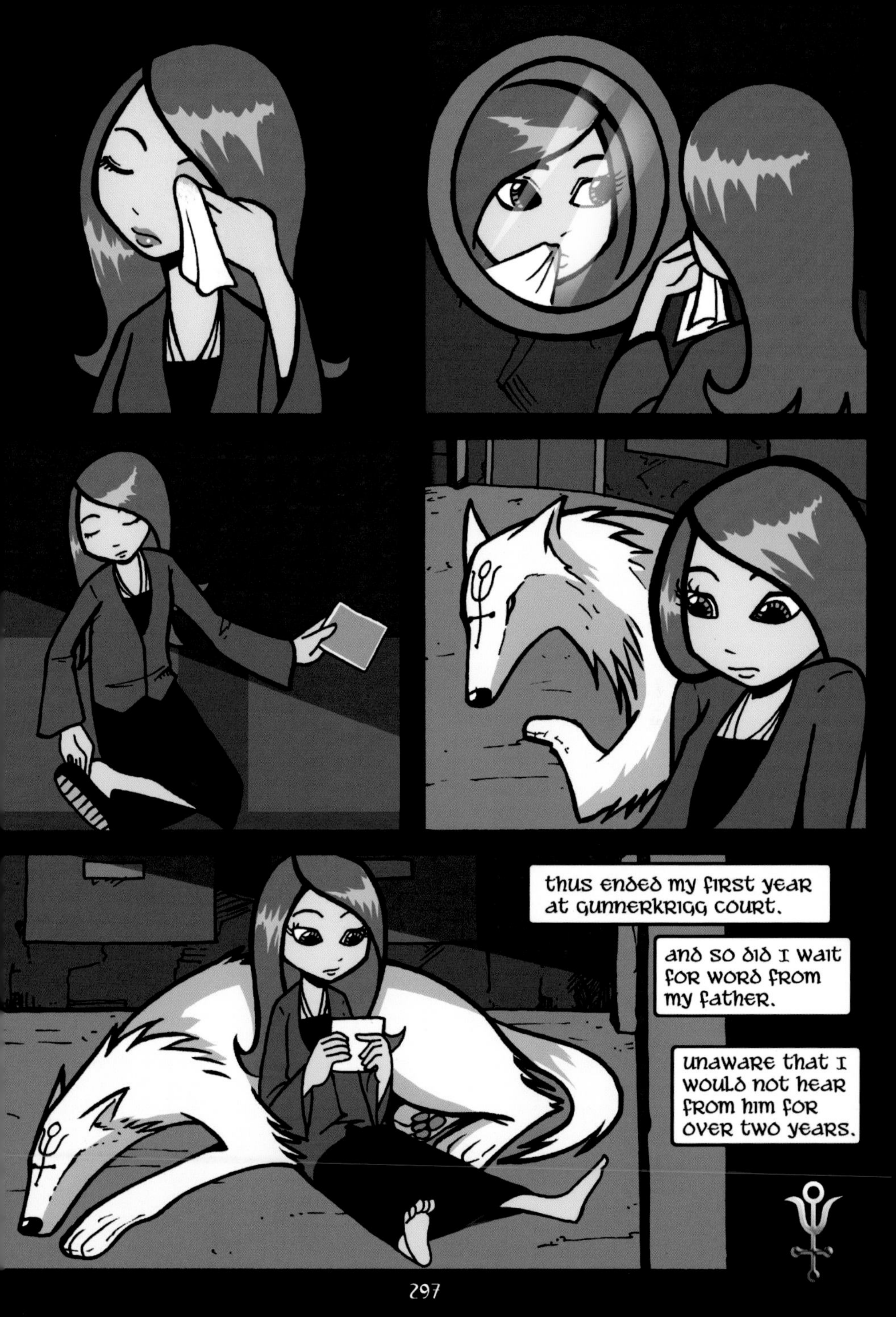
thus ended my first year at gunnerkrigg court.
and so did I wait for word from my father.
unaware that I would not hear from him for over two years.

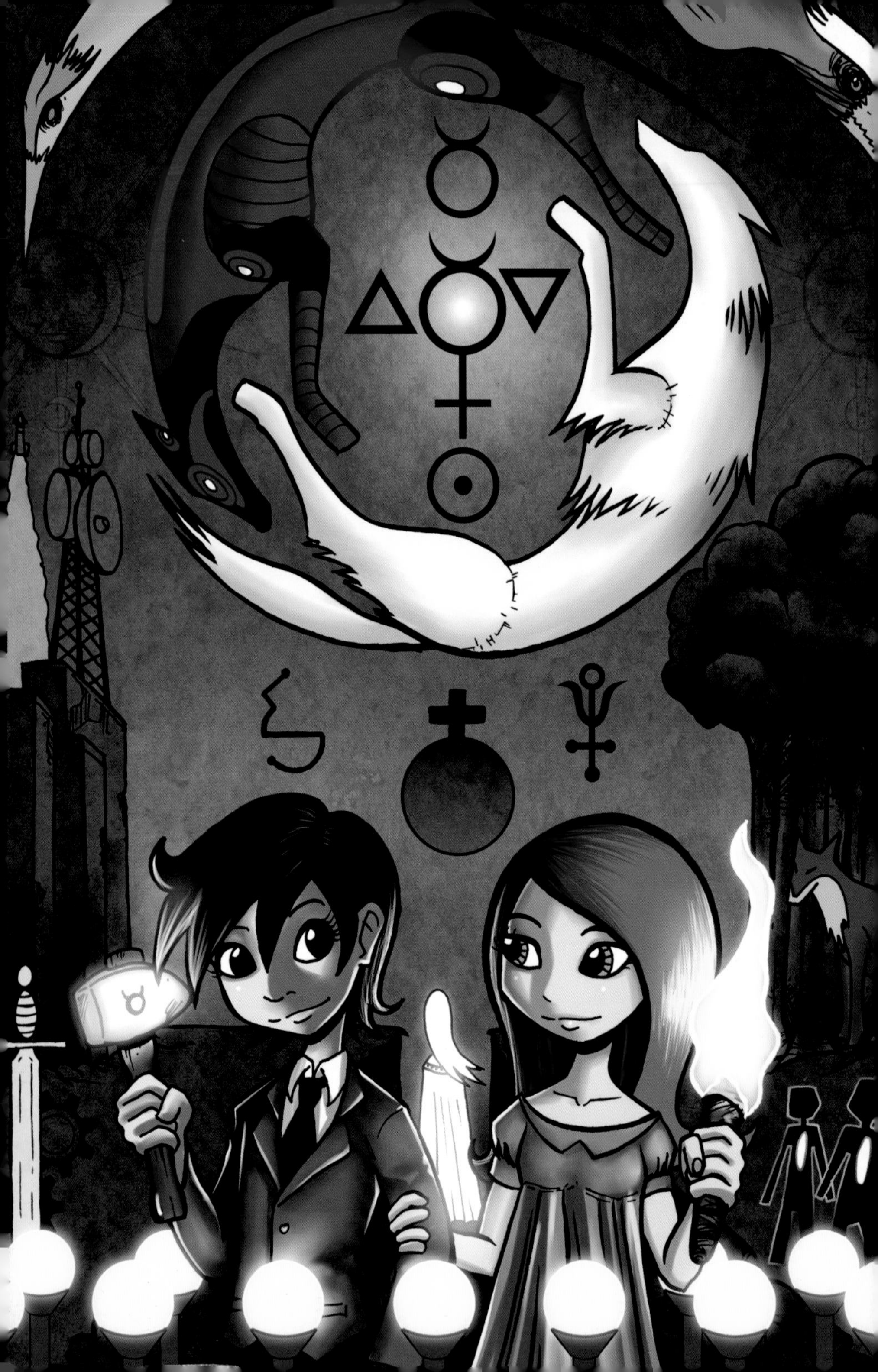

Sketch Gallery

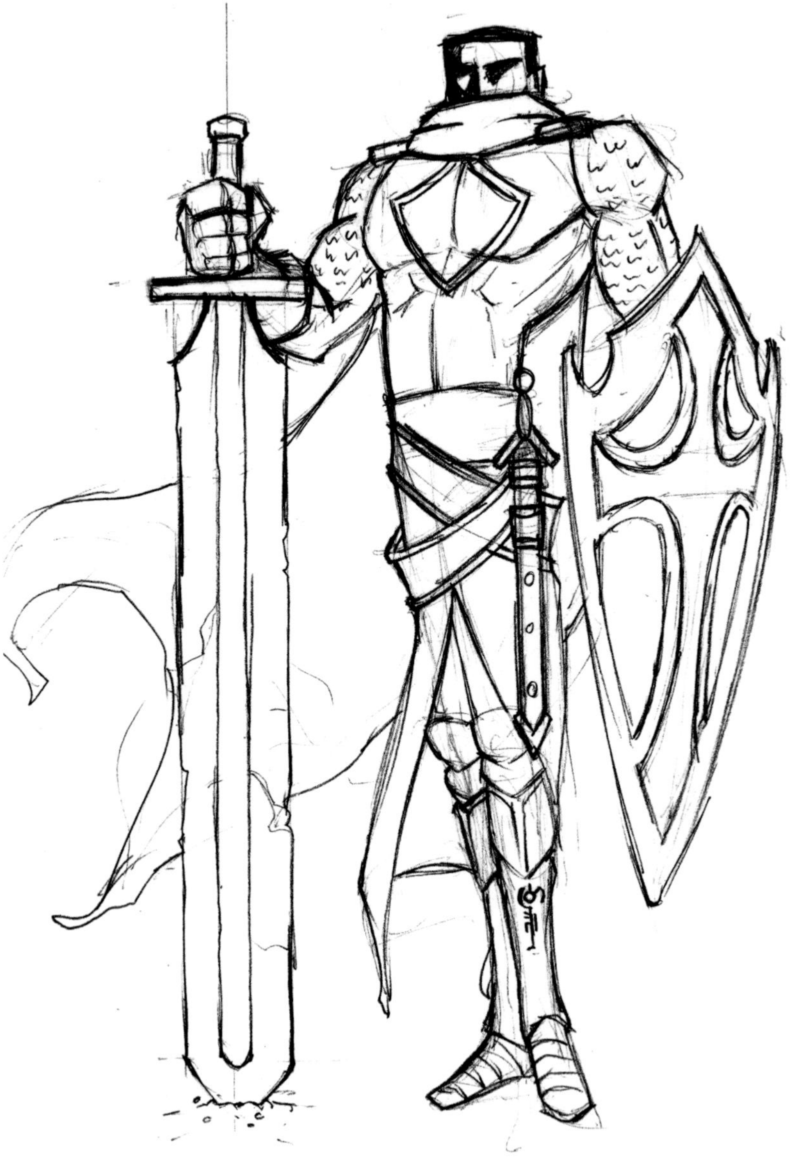

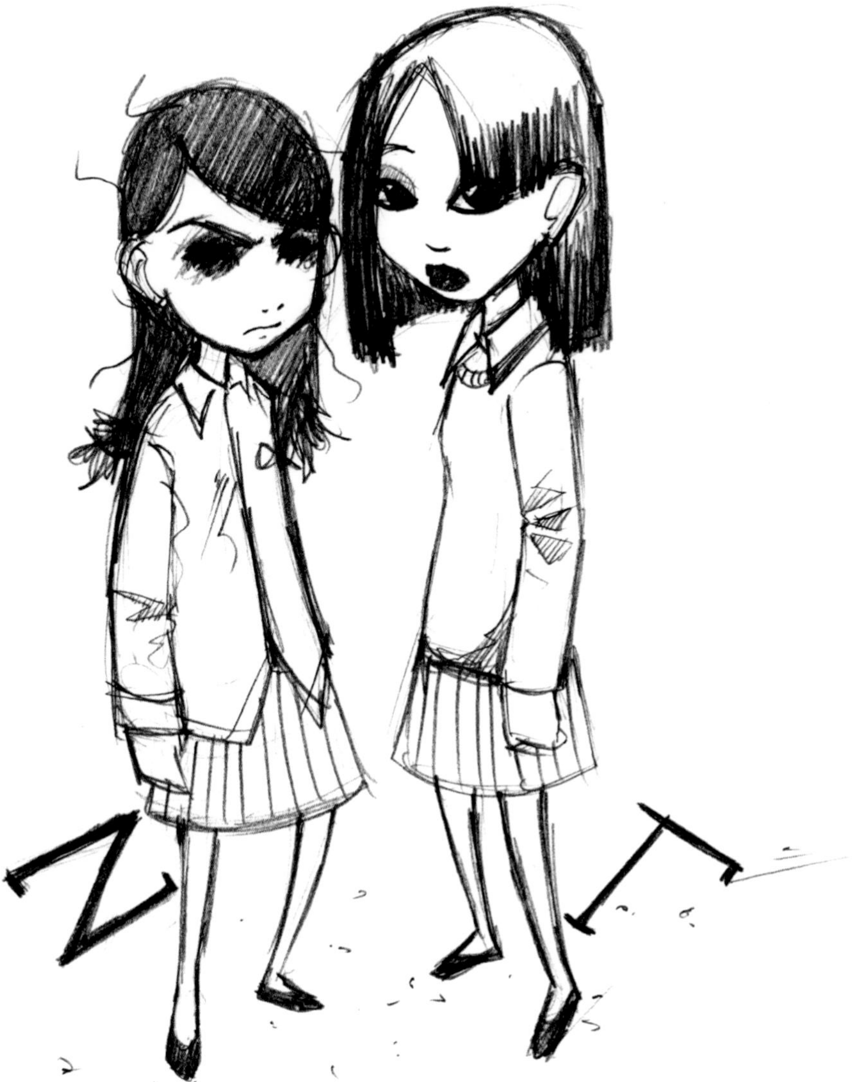

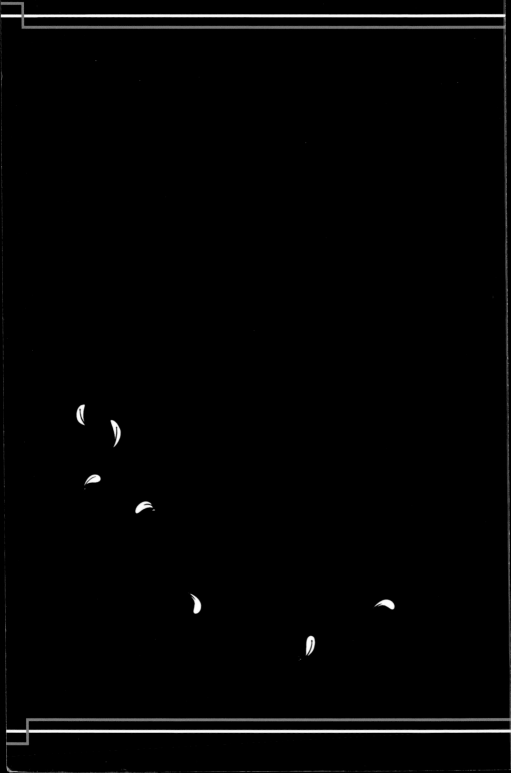

About the Author

Tom lives in a crumbling house where he works on
his comic and dreams about his stories. There is not
enough time in the day to be bored.

Thank you for reading

www.gunnerkrigg.com